MYTHS & VOICES

MYTHS & VOICES

CONTEMPORARY CANADIAN FICTION

EDITED BY DAVID LAMPE

WHITE PINE PRESS

Acknowledgements:
"Two Fishermen" by Morley Callaghan from *Stories* (1959) by permission of Barry Callaghan, Literary Executor.

"Waking in Eden" by Seán Virgo from *Waking in Eden* (1990) by permission of Exile Editions.

"Horror Comics," "The Victory Burlesk," and "Murder in the Dark" by Margaret Atwood from *Murder in the Dark* (1983) by permission of Coach House.

"When Things Get Worst" by Barry Callaghan from *Saturday Night* (1989). Revised text by permission of the author.

"The Salem Letters" by Diane Keating from *The Crying Out* (1988) by permission of Exile Editions.

"The Heart Must From Its Breaking" by Leon Rooke from *Exile* (1988) by permission of Barry Callaghan.

Acknowledgements continue on page 419

Publication of this book was made possible,
in part, by grants from
the National Endowment for the Arts
and the New York State Council on the Arts.

Book design by Watershed Design.

Cover painting by Susan Barnes.

Printed in the United States of America.

9 8 7 6 5 4 3 2 1

ISBN 1-877727-28-8

WHITE PINE PRESS
10 Village Square
Fredonia, New York 14063

CONTENTS

Preface - David Lampe / 11
Morley Callaghan - *Two Fishermen* / 21
Seán Virgo - *Waking in Eden* / 32
Margaret Atwood - *Victory Burlesk* / 59
               Making Poison / 61
               Murder in the Dark / 63
Barry Callaghan - *When Things Get Worst* / 66
Diane Keating - *The Salem Letters* / 89
Leon Rooke - *The Heart Must From Its Breaking* / 125
Eric McCormack - *Knox Abroad* / 145
Jacques Ferron - *The Chronicle of Anse Saint-Roch* / 162
Guy Vanderhaeghe - *What I Learned from Caesar* / 176
Brian Brett - *Tanganyika* / 189
Alistair MacLeod - *As Birds Bring Forth the Sun* / 197
Michel Tremblay - *Circe* / 207
Carole Shields - *Today is the Day* / 210
Alexandre Amprimoz - *Saint Augustine* / 216
Hubert Aquin - *Back on April Eleventh* / 218
Victor-Lévy Beaulieu - *Cut One* / 231
Marie-Claire Blais - *Deaf to the City* / 248
Austin Clarke - *Sometimes, a Motherless Child* / 276
Mavis Gallant - *The Wedding Ring* / 319
Joe Rosenblatt - *Horse Meat* / 324
Patrick Lane - *Marylou Had Her Teeth Out* / 331
Anne Dandurand - *The Inside Killer* / 343
Bill Gaston - *The Forest Path to Malcolm's* / 352
Gloria Sawai - *The Day I Sat With Jesus* / 369
Alice Munro - *Meneseteung* / 386
Biographical Notes / 412

To Ruth,
who endured, enabled,
and sometimes, I hope,
enjoyed.

When the Breton explorer Jacques Cartier arrived at the mouth of the Saint Lawrence River and looked out at the shore around him, he is said to have remarked, "This is the land God gave to Cain." Stone, dark trees, and water. He also speculated that he had come to Arcadia—a cold and clear blue sky covered this new world. Fierce subjects these, Arcadia and Cain, but that was a long time ago. And Cain grew up in Arcadia, which the French called Quebec. The Portugese called it *Ca Nada*, Nowhere. What is it like to grow up in Cain's Country believing it's Arcadia, calling it CANADA?

MYTHS & VOICES

PREFACE

"If he [the explorer] is wise, he will adopt a subtler strategy. He will attack his subject in unexpected places; he will fall upon the flank, or the rear; he will shoot a sudden revealing searchlight into obscure recesses, hitherto undivined. He will row out over that great ocean of material, and lower down into it, here and there, a little bucket, which will bring to the light of day some characteristic specimen, from those far depths, to be examined with a careful curiosity."

—Lytton Strachey
Eminent Victorians (1918)

These twenty-seven stories, my "little bucket" from the range of modern Canadian short fiction, may answer some questions regarding the myth of Cain and the voices of his descendants in the Arcadia that is modern Canada. But in doing so, they will probably raise many more than are answered—at least that has been my hope in putting this book together. These stories from the largest country in the world are drawn from the Maritimes, Quebec, Ontario, Saskatchewan, and British Columbia. They are stories by both men and women, by French- and English-speaking writers. Yet the criteria for this collection has not been geography, sociology, or even political correctness. Instead I have chosen stories that seemed fresh and forceful, stories that I enjoyed reading. By "fresh" I mean that I have tried to avoid the incest of anthologies. By "forceful" I mean stories in which the energy of narrative (the plot, point of view, characters, or language) pushes the reader beyond static satisfaction with "the single perfect sentence."

i

> "the first garden was the flesh
>   the second mind
>   there never was a wilderness."
>   —D. G. Jones
>   "Dilemmas" (1977)

This collection begins, as any consideration of Modern Canadian fiction must, with Morley Callaghan. In "Two Fishermen" Canada's first modernist follows an ambitious, awkward young reporter as he covers the hanging of Thomas Delaney who "had killed old Matthew Rhinehart whom he had caught molesting his wife when she had been berry-picking in the hills behind the town." Local sympathy for Delaney runs high. And the ritual of a public execution, that social violence that is itself a response to Cain's primal act, is presented by Morley Callaghan so that issues of community and betrayal, violence and decorum, shame and face are all examined in this understated masterpiece.

Descendants of Cain, after all, were the founders of cities, and most Canadians today live in urban rather than rural society. That does not mean that there is not an operative mythology of the bush and stockade, of *Wacousta* and *Survival* or *Surfacing*. It does mean that this anthology is interested in another myth and records other voices. The second story is Seán Virgo's "Waking in Eden," which reminds us that "all stories are ritual," invokes a mythic explanation of communication, of the dream of "conjunctions and love" and then recreates that pattern in a modern narrative. Like the porcelain in the story, Virgo's story is itself "a human miracle" that like porcelain allows us to "see through the skin" to witness the primal nature of mind and desire. Another kind of fallen urban world is the subject of Margaret Atwood's sketches from *Murder in the* Dark. In distilled form they outline the alternately acid and adolescent Eden shown in her *Cat's Eye* (1988).

The next three stories continue this imaginative and inventive range of "Canadian Gothic." Barry Callaghan's "When Things Get Worst" (the opening section of a Becketesque novel in progress) takes its title from John Berryman and delights in mixing the high world of literature and allusion with the low world of semi-literate violence and few illusions. The dark vision of this story is presented with grim comic exuberance and wild inventive energy. Diane Keating sets her "Salem Letters" (another section from a novel in progress) in the grim world of Puritan Massachusetts during Salem's infamous 17th century witch trials to explore the intense human drama of extreme situations and conflicts. Transplanted North American Leon Rooke begins his powerful "The Heart Must From Its Breaking" with his characters giggling as they consider an "empty heaven" and then proceeds to consider the actual disappearance of several children.The bizarre sequence of events is imaginatively vindicated by the mundane and believable voices narrating the story, thus creating a world where presence is absence and absence is presence.

ii

"For myth is the beginning of literature, and also at its end."
—Jorge Luis Borges (1955)

If a myth is a story set in the past which explains the present and allows for a future, then certainly a number of these stories are understandable in those terms. Both Eric McCormack's "Knox Abroad" and Jacques Ferron's "Chronicle of Anse Saint-Roche" reach into the past with imaginative and explanatory results. McCormack would seem to share Alan Jackson's assessment:

> O Knox he was a bad man
> He split the Scottish mind
> The one half he made cruel
> And the other half unkind.

McCormack's Knox shows both of these sides in his assessment of the natives and land. "*I canna dae wi'it*," he avers, and thus ironically names the place. Ferron's equally ironic history is of a place originally christened "Valley of Mercy" and later renamed by fishermen from Saint-Roch-des-Aulnaies. His chronicle, which "records facts that may appear unseemly," is, he warns us, like life itself: "What counts is that in the end events all fall into place."

For the narrator of Guy Vanderhaeghe's "What I Learned from Caesar," myth takes on a personal dimension, a means of finding Eden in another place: "The oldest story is the story of flight, the search for greener pastures." In this case that idyllic world is established by misreading Caesar's *Gallic Wars*, "Of all people the Belgae are the most courageous." Brian Brett's "Tanganyika" also looks toward another setting, in this case Africa, at the start of his remarkable fantasy: "After Jim Luster died, he went to Tanganyika." Alistair MacLeod's "As Birds Bring Forth the Sun" is also concerned with death, which in this case takes the form of "*cú mòr glas a bhais*, the big grey dog of death" that haunts males in his family:

> We are aware that there are men who believe the earth is flat and that birds bring forth the sun . . . . We would shut our eyes and plug our ears, even as we know such actions to be of no avail. Open still and fearful to the grey hair rising on our necks if and when we hear the scrabble of the paws and the scratching at the door.

Two other stories use voice as a narrative strategy to relocate myth. Michel Tremblay's "Circe" gives us the ancient story retold by a sailor in *contes* form, while Carole Shields' "Today is the Day" portrays what would seem to be ritual tribal action, a primitive initiation and impending sacrifice in a modern society where either the myth or the society have lost all sense of meaning. Alexandre Amprimoz's mad scholar in "Saint Augustine" names his pet rattlesnake after the saint. As the story ends "*The City of God* drops from his hands. Saint Augustine bangs one of its eight heads against the glass, the terrarium begins to break . . ."

iii

"Shall nothing be restrained from them
which they have imagined to do?"
—Saint Augustine
The City of God XVI.6

If one group of stories treats myths, another group celebrates the range of voice and experience accessible through fiction. Canada's bilingual tradition is unique in North America and may account, in part, for this range and diversity, for indeed, short fiction has a very different tradition in French Canada. Some resonances of that difference emerge in Hubert Aquin's haunting "Back on April Eleventh," a suicide note that takes on the qualities of a voice describing through written form its own end:

I can scarcely see the falling snow, but what I do see is like blots of ink. My love, I'm shivering with cold. The snow is falling somehow within me, my last snowfall. In a few seconds I'll no longer exist, I will be no more. And I'm so sorry I won't be at the dock on April eleventh.

The section "Cut One" from Victor-Lévy Beaulieu's

novel, A *Quebecois Dream*, catches the mad exuberance, vileness, violence, and disorientation of Joseph-David-Barthélémy Dupuis. The amazing narrative circle of Marie-Claire Blais' "Deaf to the City" begins with Hôtel des Voyageurs and then moves unobtrusively but incisively through the experience and consciousness of eight characters (or voices) to finally return us to that shabby hotel aware of the complexity of something as evanescent as a "white lilac branch," an innocent indicator of spring or the ghostly reminder of the death camp at Mauthausen.

Austin Clarke's "Sometimes, a Motherless Child" is as up to date as the title of the collection it is taken from, *In This City* (1992), presenting the conflict of black youth and police in Toronto modulated here through the voices of those young men and the mother who realizes she has lost her child. Mavis Gallant's narrator in "The Wedding Ring" reaches into the past for a wistful childhood experience now recalled with adult insight into the divorce of her parents.

Joe Rosenblatt's visceral first person narrative, "Horse Meat," reminds us of brutality easily ignored and makes brutally clear the sentimental hypocrisy that rewards equine loyalty with the glue factory. Patrick Lane's first person observer in "Marylou Had Her Teeth Out" makes us painfully aware of the stubborn brutality of poverty and ignorance which continues to cause the kind of human suffering that an enlightened society too often attempts to ignore.

The power of Anne Dandurand's story "The Inside Killer" depends on the calm, convincing nature of the voice in which it is told. Bill Gaston's "The Forest Path to Malcolm's" adds a surprising new note to the already legendary history of Malcolm Lowry's famous sojourn in Vancouver, while Gloria Sawai's brilliantly comic "The Day I Sat With Jesus" puts a suburban twist on the idea of divine visitation, which becomes a simple chat over coffee.

Alice Munro's narrator in "Meneseteung" seems initially certain about the quite decorous Almeda Joynt Roth, her early poems, and her provincial town, only to end with less certainty and much greater sympathy:

> I may have got it wrong. I don't know if she ever took laudanum. Many ladies did. I don't know if she ever made grape jelly.

iv

My own enjoyment in reading Canadian short stories over the past years was encouraged by a Canadian Faculty Enrichment Grant and has been given piquancy by my wife Ruth, who has often endured car trips to Toronto or has allowed me to make those trips myself. It is probably because she shelters me from so many of the issues of the practical world that I have been able to proceed in those of the imagination. I have been fortunate in my marriage and in my friends.

It is my hope that as an "alien" though sympathetic reader, I have found some compelling stories that will move other North American readers to begin their own exploration of this most powerful and varied form of Canadian art—the wild myths and strangely modulated voices from "the land God gave to Cain," stories as fresh, vital, and elemental as that land itself.

—David Lampe
Buffalo, NY
July 1993

MYTHS & VOICES

Two Fishermen

·

Morley Callahan

The only reporter on the town paper, the *Examiner*, was Michael Foster, a tall, long-legged, eager young fellow, who wanted to go to the city some day and work on an important newspaper.

The morning he went into Bagley's Hotel, he wasn't at all sure of himself. He went over to the desk and whispered to the proprietor, Ted Bagley, 'Did he come here, Mr. Bagley?'

Bagley said slowly, 'Two men came here from this morning's train. They're registered.' He put his spatulate forefinger on the open book and said, 'Two men. One of them's a drummer. This one here, T. Woodley. I know because he was through this way last year and just a minute ago he walked across the road to Molson's hardware store. The other one . . . here's his name, K. Smith.'

'Who's K. Smith?' Michael asked.

'I don't know. A mild, harmless-looking little guy.'

'Did he look like the hangman, Mr. Bagley?'

'I couldn't say that, seeing as I never saw one. He was awfully polite and asked where he could get a boat so he could go fishing on the lake this evening, so I said likely down at Smollet's place by the power-house.'

'Well, thanks. I guess if he was the hangman, he'd go over to the jail first,' Michael said.

He went along the street, past the Baptist church to the old jail with the high brick fence around it. Two tall maple trees, with branches drooping low over the sidewalk, shaded one of the walls from the morning sunlight. Last night, behind those walls, three carpenters, working by lamplight, had nailed the timbers for the scaffold. In the morning, young Thomas Delaney, who had grown up in the town, was being hanged: he had killed old Mathew Rhinehart whom he had caught molesting his wife when she had been berry-picking in the hills behind the town. There had been a struggle and Thomas Delaney had taken a bad beating before he had killed Rhinehart. Last night a crowd had gathered on the sidewalk by the lamp-post, and while moths and smaller insects swarmed around the high blue carbon light, the crowd had thrown sticks and bottles and small stones at the out-of-town workmen in the jail yard. Billy Hilton, the town constable, had stood under the light with his head down, pretending not to notice anything. Thomas Delaney was only three years older than Michael Foster.

Michael went straight to the jail office, where Henry Steadman, the sheriff, a squat, heavy man, was sitting on the desk idly wetting his long moustache with his tongue. 'Hello, Michael, what do you want?' he asked.

'Hello, Mr. Steadman, the *Examiner* would like to know if the hangman arrived yet.'

'Why ask me?'

'I thought he'd come here to test the gallows. Won't he?'

'My, you're a smart young fellow, Michael, thinking

of that.'

'Is he in there now, Mr. Steadman?'

'Don't ask me. I'm saying nothing. Say. Michael, do you think there's going to be trouble? You ought to know. Does anybody seem sore at me? I can't do nothing. You can see that.'

'I don't think anybody blames you, Mr. Steadman. Look here, can't I see the hangman? Is his name K. Smith?'

'What does it matter to you, Michael? Be a sport, go on away and don't bother us any more.'

'All right, Mr. Steadman,' Michael said very competently, 'just leave it to me.'

Early that evening, when the sun was setting, Michael Foster walked south of the town on the dusty road leading to the power-house and Smollet's fishing pier. He knew that if Mr. K. Smith wanted to get a boat he would go down to the pier. Fine powdered road dust whitened Michael's shoes. Ahead of him he saw the power-plant, square and low, and the smooth lake water. Behind him the sun was hanging over the blue hills beyond the town and shining brilliantly on square patches of farm land. The air around the powerhouse smelt of steam.

Out on the jutting, tumbledown pier of rock and logs, Michael saw a little fellow without a hat, sitting down with his knees hunched up to his chin, a very small man with little gray baby curls on the back of his neck, who stared steadily far out over the water. In his hand he was holding a stick with a heavy fishing-line twined around it and a gleaming copper spoon bait, the hooks brightened with bits of feathers such as they used in the neighbourhood when trolling for lake trout. Apprehensively Michael walked out over the rocks toward the stranger and called, 'Were you thinking of going fishing, mister?' Standing up, the man smiled. He had a large head, tapering down to a small chin, a birdlike neck and a very wistful smile. Puckering his mouth up, he said shyly to Michael, 'Did you intend to go fishing?'

'That's what I came down here for. I was going to get a boat back at the boat-house there. How would you like it if we went together?'

'I'd like it first rate,' the shy little man said eagerly. 'We could take turns rowing. Does that appeal to you?'

'Fine. Fine. You wait here and I'll go back to Smollet's place and ask for a row-boat, and I'll row around here and get you.'

'Thanks. Thanks very much,' the mild little man said as he began to untie his line. He seemed very enthusiastic.

When Michael brought the boat around to the end of the old pier and invited the stranger to make himself comfortable so he could handle the line, the stranger protested comically that he ought to be allowed to row.

Pulling strongly at the oars, Michael was soon out in the deep water and the little man was letting his line out slowly. In one furtive glance, he had noticed that the man's hair, gray at the temples, was inclined to curl to his ears. The line was out full length. It was twisted around the little man's forefinger, which he let drag in the water. And then Michael looked at him and smiled because he thought he seemed so meek and quizzical. 'He's a nice little guy,' Michael assured himself and he said, 'I work on the town paper, the *Examiner*.'

'Is it a good paper? Do you like the work?'

'Yes. But it's nothing like a first-class city paper and I don't expect to be working on it long. I want to get a reporter's job on a city paper. My name's Michael Foster.'

'Mine's Smith. Just call me Smitty.'

'I was wondering if you'd been over to the jail yet.'

Up to this time the little man had been smiling with the charming ease of a small boy who finds himself free, but now he became furtive and disappointed. Hesitating, he said, 'Yes, I was over there first thing this morning.'

'Oh, I just knew you'd go there,' Michael said. They were a bit afraid of each other. By this time they were far out on the water which had a mill-pond smoothness. The town seemed to get smaller, with white houses in rows and streets forming geometric patterns, just as the blue hills behind the town seemed to get larger at sundown.

Finally Michael said, 'Do you know this Thomas Delaney that's dying in the morning?' He knew his voice was slow and resentful.

'No. I don't know anything about him. I never read about them. Aren't there any fish at all in this old lake? I'd like to catch some fish,' he said rapidly. 'I told my wife I'd bring her home some fish.' Glancing at Michael, he was appealing, without speaking, that they should do nothing to spoil an evening's fishing.

The little man began to talk eagerly about fishing as he pulled out a small flask from his hip pocket. 'Scotch,' he said, chuckling with delight. 'Here, take a swig.' Michael drank from the flask and passed it back. Tilting his head back and saying, 'Here's to you, Michael,' the little man took a long pull at the flask. 'The only time I take a drink,' he said still chuckling, 'is when I go on a fishing trip by myself. I usually go by myself,' he added apologetically as if he wanted the young fellow to see how much he appreciated his company.

They had gone far out on the water but they had caught nothing. It began to get dark. 'No fish tonight, I guess, Smitty,' Michael said.

'It's a crying shame,' Smitty said. 'I looked forward to coming up here when I found out the place was on the lake. I wanted to get some fishing in. I promised my wife I'd bring her back some fish. She'd often like to go fishing with me, but of course, she can't because she can't travel around from place to place like I do. Whenever I get a call to go some place, I always look at the map to see if it's by a lake or on a river, then I take my lines and hooks along.'

'If you took another job, you and your wife could probably go fishing together,' Michael suggested.

'I don't know about that. We sometimes go fishing together anyway.' He looked away, waiting for Michael to be repelled and insist that he ought to give up the job. And he wasn't ashamed as he looked down at the water, but he knew that Michael thought he ought to be ashamed. 'Somebody's got to do my job. There's got to be a hangman,' he said.

'I just meant that if it was such disagreeable work, Smitty.'

The little man did not answer for a long time. Michael rowed steadily with sweeping, tireless strokes. Huddled at the end of the boat, Smitty suddenly looked up with a kind of melancholy hopelessness and said mildly, 'The job hasn't been so disagreeable.'

'Good God, man, you don't mean you like it?'

'Oh, no,' he said, to be obliging, as if he knew what Michael expected him to say. 'I mean you get used to it, that's all.' But he looked down again at the water, knowing he ought to be ashamed of himself.

'Have you got any children?'

'I sure have. Five. The oldest boy is fourteen. It's funny, but they're all a lot bigger and taller than I am. Isn't that funny?'

They started a conversation about fishing rivers that ran into the lake farther north. They felt friendly again. The little man, who had an extraordinary gift for story-telling, made many quaint faces, puckered up his lips, screwed up his eyes and moved around restlessly as if he wanted to get up in the boat and stride around for the sake of more expression. Again he brought out the whiskey flask and

Michael stopped rowing. Grinning, they toasted each other
and said together, 'Happy days.' The boat remained motionless on the placid water. Far out, the sun's last rays gleamed
on the water-line. And then it got dark and they could only
see the town lights. It was time to turn around and pull for
the shore. The little man tried to take the oars from
Michael, who shook his head resolutely and insisted that he
would prefer to have his friend catch a fish on the way back
to the shore.

'It's too late now, and we may have scared all the
fish away,' Smitty laughed happily. 'But we're having a grand
time, aren't we?'

When they reached the old pier by the power-house,
it was full night and they hadn't caught a single fish. As the
boat bumped against the rocks Michael said, 'You can get
out here. I'll take the boat around to Smollet's.'

'Won't you be coming my way?'

'Not just now. I'll probably talk with Smollet a
while.'

The little man got out of the boat and stood on the
pier looking down at Michael. 'I was thinking dawn would
be the best time to catch some fish,' he said. 'At about five
o'clock. I'll have an hour and a half to spare anyway. How
would you like that?' He was speaking with so much eager-
ness that Michael found himself saying, 'I could try. But if
I'm not here at dawn, you go on without me.'

'All right. I'll walk back to the hotel now.'

'Good night, Smitty.'

'Good night, Michael. We had a fine neighbourly
time, didn't we?'

As Michael rowed the boat around to the boat-
house, he hoped that Smitty wouldn't realize he didn't want
to be seen walking back to town with him. And later, when
he was going slowly along the dusty road in the dark and
hearing all the crickets chirping in the ditches, he couldn't

figure out why he felt so ashamed of himself.

At seven o'clock next morning Thomas Delaney was hanged in the town jail yard. There was hardly a breeze on that leaden gray morning and there were no small whitecaps out over the lake. It would have been a fine morning for fishing. Michael went down to the jail, for he thought it his duty as a newspaperman to have all the facts, but he was afraid he might get sick. He hardly spoke to all the men and women who were crowded under the maple trees by the jail wall. Everybody he knew was staring at the wall and muttering angrily. Two of Thomas Delaney's brothers, big, strapping fellows with bearded faces, were there on the sidewalk. Three automobiles were at the front of the jail.

Michael, the town newspaperman, was admitted into the courtyard by old Willie Mathews, one of the guards, who said that two newspapermen from the city were at the gallows on the other side of the building. 'I guess you can go around there, too, if you want to,' Mathews said, as he sat down slowly on the step. White-faced, and afraid, Michael sat down on the step with Mathews and they waited and said nothing.

At last the old fellow said, 'Those people outside there are pretty sore, ain't they?'

'They're pretty sullen, all right. I saw two of Delaney's brothers there.'

'I wish they'd go,' Mathews said. 'I don't want to see anything. I didn't even look at Delaney. I don't want to hear anything. I'm sick.' He put his head back against the wall and closed his eyes.

The old fellow and Michael sat close together till a small procession came around the corner from the other side of the yard. First came Mr. Steadman, the sheriff, with his head down as though he were crying, then Dr. Parker, the physician, then two hard-looking young newspapermen from the city, walking with their hats on the backs of their heads, and behind them came the little hangman, erect, stepping out with military precision and carrying himself with a strange cocky dignity. He was dressed in a long black cutaway coat with gray striped trousers, a gates-ajar collar and a narrow red tie, as if he alone felt the formal importance of the occasion. He walked with brusque precision till he saw Michael, who was standing up, staring at him with his mouth open.

The little hangman grinned and as soon as the procession reached the doorstep, he shook hands with Michael. They were all looking at Michael. As though his work were over now, the hangman said eagerly to Michael, 'I thought I'd see you here. You didn't get down to the pier at dawn?'

'No. I couldn't make it.'

'That was tough, Michael. I looked for you,' he said. 'But never mind. I've got something for you.' As they all went into the jail, Dr. Parker glanced angrily at Michael, then turned his back on him. In the office, where the doctor prepared to sign a certificate, Smitty was bending down over his fishing-basket which was in the corner. Then he pulled out two good-sized salmon-bellied trout, folded in a newspaper, and said, 'I was saving these for you, Michael. I got four in an hour's fishing.' Then he said, 'I'll talk about that later, if you'll wait. We'll be busy here, and I've got to change my clothes.'

Michael went out to the street with Dr. Parker and the two city newspapermen. Under his arm he was carrying the fish, folded in the newspaper. Outside, at the jail door, Michael thought that the doctor and the two newspapermen were standing a little apart from him. Then the small crowd, with their clothes all dust-soiled from the road, surged forward, and the doctor said to them, 'You might as well go home, boys. It's all over.'

'Where's old Steadman?' somebody demanded.

'We'll wait for the hangman,' somebody else shouted.

The doctor walked away by himself. For a while Michael stood beside the two city newspapermen, and tried to look as nonchalant as they were looking, but he lost confidence in them when he smelled whiskey. They only talked to each other. Then they mingled with the crowd, and Michael stood alone. At last he could stand there no longer looking at all those people he knew so well, so he, too, moved out and joined the crowd.

When the sheriff came out with the hangman and two of the guards, they got half-way down to one of the automobiles before someone threw an old boot. Steadman ducked into one of the cars, as the boot hit him on the shoulder, and the two guards followed him. The hangman, dismayed, stood alone on the sidewalk. Those in the car must have thought at first that the hangman was with them for the car suddenly shot forward, leaving him alone on the sidewalk. The crowd threw small rocks and sticks, hooting at him as the automobile backed up slowly toward him. One small stone hit him on the head. Blood trickled from the side of his head as he looked around helplessly at all the angry people. He had the same expression on his face, Michael thought, as he had had last night when he had seemed ashamed and had looked down steadily at the water. Only now, he looked around wildly, looking for someone to help him as the crowd kept pelting him. Farther and farther Michael backed into the crowd and all the time he felt dreadfully ashamed as though he were betraying Smitty, who last night had had such a good neighbourly time with him. 'It's different now, it's different,' he kept thinking, as he held the fish in the newspaper tight under his arm. Smitty started to run toward the automobile, but James Mortimer, a big fisherman, shot out his foot and tripped him and sent him sprawling on his face.

Mortimer, the big fisherman, looking for something

to throw, said to Michael, 'Sock him, sock him.'

Michael shook his head and felt sick.

'What's the matter with you, Michael?'

'Nothing. I got nothing against him.'

The big fisherman started pounding his fists up and down in the air. 'He just doesn't mean anything to me at all,' Michael said quickly. The fisherman, bending down, kicked a small rock loose from the road bed and heaved it at the hangman. Then he said, 'What are you holding there, Michael, what's under your arm? Fish. Pitch them at him. Here, give them to me.' Still in a fury, he snatched the fish, and threw them one at a time at the little man just as he was getting up from the road. The fish fell in the thick dust in front of him, sending up a little cloud. Smitty seemed to stare at the fish with his mouth hanging open, then he didn't even look at the crowd. That expression on Smitty's face as he saw the fish on the road made Michael hot with shame and he tried to get out of the crowd.

Smitty had his hands over his head, to shield his face as the crowd pelted him, yelling, 'Sock the little rat. Throw the runt in the lake.' The sheriff pulled him into the automobile.

The car shot forward in a cloud of dust.

Waking in Eden

•

Seán Virgo

I.

All stories are ritual. They form the same pattern, and share it with memory and love.

Tadeusz believes this without knowing it. He throws porcelain clay upon his wheel and waits another day for Helena to come home.

The winter jasmine blossoms outside the studio window. It is the eleventh time it has flowered since she came back into his life, the third time since she was taken away.

Helena sits in the library, away from the windows. She has a new parcel of books from the outreach programme. The words and ideas she devours, shortsighted, with passion, are as unforgiving, as coy, as the material Tadeusz works with.

Her parole hearing comes in two days. It is her second. She knows and believes that all stories form the same pattern. A weight, a gulf, a desire.

II.

To begin with. A savannah or plateau: the forest above or below, the hills, snow even, to the West. The landscape of innocence.

This is the home of Peking Man, of Australopithecus, of the yet undiscovered, undreamed of, fossil man of the Pampas.

Our man is wandering, alone. No need to have him an outcast, or utterly lost. He has wandered, simply, alone: a child on a Sunday afternoon so long that it has stretched for months.

His mind is not crowded like ours. It remarks, and remembers, everything. Sometimes he sings to himself, sometimes the land sings through him. At night he dreams of conjunctions.

Pain is a strange kind of pleasure. Fear is a style of excitement.

He carries a weight without knowing it. He carries a stone,too—a perforated orb which spoke to him out of the world's fabric. It has grown warm in his palm.

It is itself, and him. It might become a weight for a fishnet or spindle, a missile, a fetish. It is loaded with programmes beyond his knowledge. He touches his lips to the hole in the stone. He holds it between his thighs when he sleeps.

There is a line of trees to his left. Shelter, food, the summons of novelty. Behind the trees is a canyon. Noise, energy, the river a hundred feet below surging between stone walls, down from the hills towards the forest.

The water white, and green. The canyon deeper than wide. He could throw the stone in his hand across it, easily. He will.

A gulf, a weight, a desire.

On the other side of the ravine stands a man. No, a

woman.

They watch each other. They mock each other. Their mimicry becomes a dance. Without that gulf they might have run from each other, or killed, or touched too soon.

They watch each other. It is the beginning of loneliness.

The man throws the stone, which was part of him, across the ravine. To relieve his feelings.

The woman searches in the thicket, and retrieves it. Still warm from him. She holds it, smells it, tastes it.

She throws it back. Her aim is more deliberate. He catches it, bruises his finger, puts her in his mouth.

The stone has grown wings, it is a messenger, it flies back and forth across the gulf.

On the fourth day, their dance has reached its full elaboration.

On the fifth day he slips a red and yellow feather through the stone and sends it to her. She threads it into her hair, and sends him a flowering twig. The yellow buds smell of desire.

On the ninth day she is whirling the stone around her head on a length of braided grass. It whistles and hums in the air. She throws it to him, he makes the same music, the dance has become a language. It rains for three days. They huddle across from each other, staring through the prisms of the mist, listening to the river shaking the rocks beneath them. She has the stone now. She sleeps, holding it between her thighs. They are both cold, and cold is a style of sympathy.

The rain clears, and the world is reeling with scent and color. She sends him the stone. He repairs the grass twine, ties a sweet fern-root to it, and sends her breakfast.

On the sixteenth day they sit plaiting grass across from each other, chewing the fibres, weaving with delicate, eager fingers. With each journey the messenger's tail grows longer. It whispers across the divide.

On the seventeenth morning he throws the stone and keeps hold of its tail. She gathers the stone, and holds the rope in her teeth. He does the same. They pull the rope taut, they can feel each other hum down the line.

They learn they can strum the rope with their fingers, an armslength in front of their mouths. They share the making of music, comical, doleful; they are so delighted that they dance and strum till the line breaks, and they both fall backwards, waving their legs extravagantly at the sky, almost utterly happy.

On the twenty-eighth day the messenger's tail is attached to a vinerope, as long as the gulf is wide. It drags a cable of braided creepers, thick as their wrists. Desire has found its way.

On the thirty-first day the man walks out on a two-rope bridge. One for his feet, one for his hands. The loud snakeskin of the river squirms below him but his eyes are on her, as hers are on him. The stone has been lost, or forgotten somewhere. She hesitates to go out to him on the bridge, but her desire draws him across.

He steps from the bridge. His right hand goes to her cheek. Her right hand goes to his cheek. They are smiling. They are crying. They are shouting and dancing together.

It might be that mind and desire are the same, and that nothing may stop that leap across emptiness. It might be that mind is the weight of desire, or desire the weight of emptiness.

They comprise the story, they dream of conjunctions.

III.

Helena rehearses the riddles of Xeno.
Are they more than a game for children? Is this really

the root of philosophy?

She is not equipped. She hoards the encyclopedias, she always takes the table beside their shelf and piles the table with the maroon volumes. She has the big Collins dictionary, and her own English-Slovak besides. But she depends for direction on what she can get from the outreach programme.

These were her husband's favorites, therefore she tries.

He loved to air them whenever his students came round. Their Friday evenings. She had thought them a game then, too. She brought tea and vodka, and Turkish sugarcakes, and coached the children in their goodnight songs before the fireplace. It added to Anton's mystique; he depended on her.

To be one of those students. Young again, frivolous, wise in a world that seemed safe at last. She wishes she had listened more. She can smell their apartment.

It had something to do with a "number line," she can see him, his arm on the mantlepiece, explaining. His velvet jacket, that smile that came over him, as though truth and jesting were one.

A number line, how crowded it was, whether Achilles is known, in fact, to have finished the race. But she cannot apply this, somehow.

The archer looses his arrow toward the target. The arrow crosses half the distance, then half of the half remaining, then half of what's left. The halves are endless: how can the arrow ever arrive?

Was that Time or Space?

And the athlete who circles the track, through the same endless sub-divisions. Is he not, in effect, slowing down? How can he reach his goal? Is it Time that the athlete competes with, or Space?

Achilles allows the tortoise a certain handicap, and

races after him. How can he ever catch him? Two moving targets? Is that Space, or Time?

What does it matter?

How could a man become a martyr for playing such games?

It vexes her mind. She turns to the dictionary.

So many "lines," though—base-line, deadline, faultline, Green Line, mainline, party line—this crazy, promiscuous language. "Pure line" it tells her: A plant or animal breed in which certain characters appear in successive generations as a result of inbreeding or self-fertilization. How can an animal fertilize itself? Can it be true? There is nobody here to help her.

The library trusty raps on her desk: "Time's up, Jemsky. Move it!"

"I am given an extra hour, this week," she says.

The trusty shrugs and turns back to her harlequin. "Your funeral" she says.

Helena feels dizzy. She reaches for MUN to PIC.

IV.

The wheel's harsh whisper, impelled by the stroke of Tadeusz' bare foot. He will not use an electric wheel—one more remove, through sorcery, between the thrust of his calf-muscle and the spinning plinth, the clay in his hands.

He dips his right fingers into the soft mound. A lathe of flesh. He has made a shape, now he shapes a vacancy. As always, he thinks of his fingers, two, three, in Helena's vagina.

The familiar rippling walls. Formed by her lovers, the birth of her children, rape, solitude, age. By Anton.

The unforgiving clay.

One floor above, the trundle of kittens down a hallway. Voices conjured by the fridge, the waterpipes, the night-settling of the old building.

Gleaned exclamations of love, or self-love, or the simple utterances of a woman living alone?

Pain or joy, or mundane punctuations into the telephone. The machine which he hates above all others.

But nowhere silence, even as darkness comes in.

He abandons the clay. He washes and dresses himself, and goes out on the street. The curtains are drawn, dull pink, in the windows above his studio. The air is tense with frost and exhaust fumes.

In the flat pool of a streetlight, maple leaves lie glued to the sidewalk. They look like the mud-tracks of gulls, beside the Duna.

He walks three blocks, down back streets, and waits for a streetcar. All the way downtown he stares at his own reflection past the people who face him. Yet he knows his stop; he steps down into the street and heads across, through the crawling traffic, to the blue neon gates.

It is early yet. Some of the men have dropped in on their way home from work. One has brought his own sandwiches in a brown paper bag. There are only two girls on the floor.

But it is still, for Tadeusz, the anteroom to Hell.

The dreadful sounds pound from the overhead speakers a fast, goose-step march with jiggling puppet-strokes stringing the beats together. It is all the same, and the spotlights flush on and off in the hues of hallucination while it plays. Not one heartbeat of stillness—the waitress cannot even hear you; it's a world that murders and outlaws language.

And they are so pretty, the children of the free world who parade in the spotlights, with the skin and the forms of angels, and the painted masks. Too young still to show the scars of this slaughter of innocence.

Who are their parents?

The men at this hour are middle-aged like himself. Passive to flesh and lust, as if to TV. Voyeurs without the drive to prowl the back alleys in longing.

No sin. No joy.

Yet knowing this is here he's drawn once or twice a week, to the heart of the city, to watch.

He sees how the dancers, who cannot dance but just throw their limbs into the cage of sound, look down on the girl behind the bar as a lesser breed. And how she just smiles and serves them, and sees with her private eyes, saving up, perhaps, for her school fees.

He knows how *he* seems to her. The sullen regular in the corner, nursing his beer. A shadow-watcher who never smiles, or shows his eyes, or spends one penny on the dancers. He has imagined talking with her, in a coffee bar somewhere. If he were rich, he would leave her money, anonymously.

Two tables away, a girl sets down a stool, and steps out of her dress. The man with the brown paper bag has laid down five dollars. She arches, naked, back onto the table, her knee on the stool. Her hand brushes over her breasts, down her stomach, and caresses the inside of her outstretched thigh.

Tadeusz stares across at the private show. He watches the slender hand on her thigh, lingers on the light pubic curls, the final taboo for his generation.

The girl swings around and kneels over the table. She mimes a Hollywood pout and holds her young breasts just inches from the man's face. The man watches, impassive.

This is where Tadeusz stops watching the girls and focusses, with disgust and fascination, on the men.

She turns her back on her client. Kneels and bends over. Her hands reach back and spread her buttocks. Her fingers reach in to her vulva. The man watches, his hand feels its way into his brown paper bag and pulls out a sausage roll. It goes up to his face, and he chews, slowly, his blank gaze fixed on her anus and the flesh of her birth canal. Flakes of pastry cling to his lips.

Tadeusz sips at his beer. *Nazi,* he thinks to himself, *commissar, sloven.*

The waitress steps in front of Tadeusz. She points at his near-empty glass, mouths through the sound and light a question, contempt in her eyes.

He nods in shame. She stalks back to the bar.

V.

Helena hears rumors the world is the work of angels.

At night as the radiator shunts and groans and carries messages on its flaking skin. From other numbered cells along the hall they murmur and moan, cry out and curse in their dreams. Or laugh, sometimes, like children surprised.

She lies in the darkness, below the judas window, and envisions the ateliers of Time and Space like the galleried levels within which she floats, suspended. The children of light, labouring on our Creation.

Cartoons, maquettes.

Thumb prints upon clay.

Forges and kilns.

Baroque elaborations, rococo extravagance, romantic departures.

She ponders the Mongoose, the Mamba, the Garfish, the Paradise Bird. She considers the Mantis, the multiple Tapeworm cyst, the Karoo moths which cluster together and describe a perfect flower.

The angelic craftsmen extending endlessly the symmetrical blueprint, the two-eyed halves-made-whole, decreed for the animals.

Her fingers count out, on her belly, the ranks of Legumes. The Peas which extend from the manifold vetches to the towering timber-stack of the Brazil Tree.

The fourteen possible lattices in the crystals of lava.

Leucippus' grains of matter.

Time and Space removed from *then* and *now*, from the linear.

Are there recruits, to the angels? Do our dead sometimes aspire to make new connections?

Within this Creation, she senses other ateliers, and studios. The minds of artists, or Anton's beloved philosophers, maybe. Receptive minds, pregnable, fertile. In one sense, female.

Is this where the Sons of God lay down with the Daughters of Men?

She perceives that the world is a work of art. That works of art are sometimes the work of angels.

She is not sure at all that she wants to go home. She is not sure, at least, if she really wants to leave.

She reaches down, under her bed, to her locker. Feels through her clothes for the jar which Tadeusz brought for her. Her fingertips touch the cool porcelain flesh. The unadorned, almost translucent gift has become her icon for the workshop, the divine marriage chamber that his inarticulate mind must be.

VI.

The nature of porcelain is a human miracle.

Its discovery was an act and conjunction of Providence. It is clay combined with the matter that turns into clay—the dissolute, weathered flesh of earth's oldest rocks. Porcelain is the stages of earth's decay, combined and reversed, passed into water and fire, and transformed into permanent harmony. It is translucent. It sings when it is struck. The clay is *Kaolin*, the rotting feldspar, *Petuntse*. It has been analysed, copied, perfectly (as a synthesiser "perfectly" copies Bach) reconstructed. But at some point in Time and Place, perhaps in the Hanyong Mountains, a potter discovered a saprolite pocket, where the clay and *petuntse* lay ready, combined.

The Chinese called it "White Jade"; the merchants of Europe tracked it down in laboratories.

At 2650 degrees fahrenheit, the *petuntse* vitrifies, while the *kaolin* holds the form which the potter created. And of all the substances that a master-potter must learn, with all the provisos of accident, good and bad, porcelain is the most intractable.

It is the clay which does not forgive. Because it remembers. It returns from the fire with every error and hesitation in its shaping exposed.

There are scientists who find a radiance in the infinite cells of Evolution which few of the faithful experience, facing Creation, who have come to believe that clay held the seeds of life. Clay had memory, therefore it recognised, therefore learnt, predicted, or guessed at least, therefore at length adapted. Life and intelligence came as one.

Adom, the red man, was formed out of clay, the dried alluvium of the Euphrates Valley.

Even the great workshops of the Orient used moulds for most of their porcelain.

Tadeusz throws the clay on his wheel.

Out of every twelve pots, he rejects eleven.

VII.

Helena goes down to the showers in a line of twelve. The warders slam back the locks, throw open the doors and call each name. They step outside and fall into line.

They go single file to the end of the gallery. Two warders lead, one comes behind, clanging the cell-door shut as she passes.

They wear grey housecoats, and black canvas slippers. Their towels are white, with a broad yellow stripe off-centre. It is the washbag in each right hand that is individual; and the shampoos inside, the conditioners, safety-razors, bright soaps.

At the foot of the steps they turn in to the shower section. The file breaks up. The guards stand in the vestibule and smoke.

They are the fourth group down this morning. The air is still dense with steam and perfume. The walls and the floor are wet, and warm.

"The end shower's fucked," a warder tells them. "Don't touch it."

Helena lost her shyness long ago. Her heavy thighs, the flattening breasts on her broad chest are no more or less than the other bodies reveal, padding off through the steam. Scars of love and birth and age, of hate and of self-betrayal.

Some are crude and raucous, others keep to themselves.

But number 8 is a new girl.

They fall silent and watch as she hangs up her housecoat, the last. The warders look on, amused.

She lifts her chin and glares back at them. She is young, red-haired. She seems tiny before them. She has breasts that offer no clues—small, upright nipples which might have given suck or might always have been just so.

The steam gleams already upon her skin. It studs her pubic tuft with water-gems.

They snigger, but in the envy behind those sniggers is knowledge, and beneath that knowledge, so Helena believes, is love. In the unblemished skin they see the Fall, and they want that Fall because they know it will surely come, because their envies desire it, because their ugliness has no choice but to taunt. Because the Fall is the affirmation of innocence.

The girl is no innocent. Her eyes taunt back. She parades like a model between them, to the last of the showers.

"Hold it!" a guard snaps out. "You heard me—that shower's off limits." There is a towel hung over the faucet.

The girl's face is a mask against orders. She shrugs and steps toward another shower.

"There's electric current getting to it, somehow," another guard explains. "You could get fried."

The girl turns, stooping a little to conceal the slyness that brings her face to life. This is the real face surfacing—the person who has not dwelt in that flesh long enough to shape it.

She lunges for the last shower, and turns it on. She is screaming.

Do they all have this vision? Of electrical dancers, linked hand to hand, tugging against the current which runs through them, galvanised into death on the concrete floor?

As she flounders toward the shrieking girl, Helena wills herself through what may come, orders her body how to react when she loses control of it.

She is shrieking too, even as she reaches for the girl—she closes in, their screaming is a duet, indistinguishable. Despite her prevision, she hugs the girl instead of grabbing for her wrist. She hugs her against her belly and bears on through, charging into the sudden nausea of the current, her bladder voiding, her screams cut off, as they slam against the far wall and drop, tangled up with each other.

The water keeps falling upon the tiles. The women across the room are frozen, staring. The steam is like dry ice, on a stage.

The lights go out. The guards come in through the

steam with their flashlights. It is mist in the forest, it is smoke in the streets. These are hunters, soldiers, searchlights.

The guards help them up, and lead them across to the doorway. The girl looks up into Helena's face: "Murdering cunt!" she says.

VIII.

The echoes lie in ambush. Ghosts of the ghosts which only death can lay.

The woman is waiting in a car by the far curb. He senses her, something, as he turns in from the sidewalk, fumbling for his key. A shrinking around his ears, then sweat, prickling his shoulder blades.

When the car door slams across the street he stands rigid, on the step, key in hand. Waiting.

The door opens inwards at the same moment as her voice calls his name.

The woman from upstairs, a scarf on her head, is in front of him. Her smile of surprise is unnerved by his expression. The smell of the apartments escapes around her. Her eyes dart at the woman who comes up behind him.

"Excuse me," his neighbour murmurs, and steps around him. The other is right at his elbow: "Mr. Dierrek?" His heart flinches. He turns slowly and stares in disbelief.

She is from the Parole Board: "Could we talk for a few minutes?"

"I just get in from work," he says.

The woman from upstairs adjusts her purse, lingering.

"It's about the hearing tomorrow. Helena, Mrs. Jemsky?"

"Hel*ay*na" he says. "I don't have to talk to you."

"It's in her best interests."

He hesitates. The woman from upstairs walks slowly away. "Okay, then," says Tadeusz. "What you want to know?"

Her face is accustomed to difficult clients, it adjusts itself.

"I really have to come inside," she tells him. The veneer of civility. "I'm supposed to see where—Mrs. Jemsky would be living. If parole is approved."

The door's still ajar. She follows him in, down the hallway. He lets her in first. "Is the same place she lived in before," he says.

She looks around. "It's a nice apartment," she says "Bright. You keep it very clean." Tadeusz goes in the kitchen and sets his bag down on the counter. He takes off his coat and hangs it at the back door.

The woman unbuttons her coat as she walks round the living room. Her eyes go in at the open doorways. "What's in there?" she asks.

"Is private," he says. "My business, not yours."

"I am not the secret police, Mr. Dierrek." She sits on the arm of the big chair.

"Sure you are," he says. "Will you take a drink?"

"Oh. Well, coffee maybe?"

"Coffee? Sure. You like vodka?"

"No thank you. Not on the job, anyway. Vodka's your drink?"

Tadeusz turns in the kitchen doorway and eyes her up and down. "Sure," he says, "we like to drink, some nights a little, some nights a lot. Friday night we drink, we sing, we have good times there together." He eyes the couch, the rug in front of it, the chair on which she is sitting. He grins, savagely. She is very uncomfortable. "Sometimes we fight, also, too just shout, okay?"

"Well," she begins, "that's not the best—"

"Listen, lady," he says, "don't tell me, okay? Helena can drink all she likes. She don't drive a car no more, ever, you know that, so that's that. You understand nothing."

"You're not helping," she says, to her knees. A brittle, rise-and-fall cadence, like a line from the movies.

"So how can I help?" He takes a bottle from the bag on the counter and pours a shot. "Drink?"

She forms a smile: "No thank you. The coffee?"

"Oh sure, I forget." He turns on the gas.

She crosses her legs in the silence. "It's not often I visit a home with no television." Bright again, professional.

"Is the enemy," he says. "Yes, perhaps. Do you and Helena have much of a social group; friends?"

He sips at the vodka, sardonic. "We are okay. We read, we walk, I work, we are fine."

She looks round again. Her hand touches the bowl on the table beside her. "That's nice," she says. "Yes, it's a nice apartment.

"You see" she starts in again, "we need to know what Helena is coming home to. She may not want to start work again, right away . . ."

"Will she get this parole?"

"I can't tell you that," the woman says. "There's a good chance, though. She's done quite well."

"She will work," he says.

"There's a lot of stress, adjusting after prison, Mr. Dierrek. You must try to understand."

"Lady" he says, "I understand. I been in prison, Helena's husband live half his life in prison, die in prison, now she's in prison. I understand."

She has a small notebook out. "When were you in prison, Mr. Dierrek? We weren't informed."

"Is that so?" he sneers. Then shrugs. "Long time ago, twenty years. In Slovakia."

"Oh I see," she says. "Well, that's different, of

course."

"Is no different," he says. He empties his shot-glass. The kettle is filling the kitchen with steam. He turns off the gas, pours another drink. He leans at the doorway, watching her brown eyes.

"Now, you work as a janitor?"

He nods, slowly: "The Mercorp Building, on Wellesley."

"The thing is, you see, whether Mrs. Jemsky and you can get by on your income . . ."

"*Christ*, lady," he says. He puts down his drink and strides to the one closed door. He opens it, without turning a light on, and reaches inside. He comes back with an envelope: "Here, god damn it" and hands her a bank book.

"Okay?" he demands. "Helena can have what she needs from that. Okay?"

"My goodness," she says.

"So that makes the difference?"

"You didn't make this as a janitor."

"Not the secret police, huh? Everything is your business." He leans on the couch back, glaring at her. He points—"In that room, I make pots, yeah? Pots. Are good pots. I am very good. Very expensive. I am not *mafia*, okay?"

"Pots," she says. "Oh. Well, I hardly thought you were *mafia*, Mr. Dierrek!"

He goes back for his drink. "On the table, by you," he says, over his shoulder. "Look. Pick it up. Look at it."

She does so. "You're very talented," she says. "It's very plain, but it's beautiful."

He comes round behind her: "Yes, beautiful." He leans over and flicks the bowl with his finger nail. It rings through the room, the note hangs.

"*D Sharp*," she says.

He laughs, she too. "You are in wrong job, maybe,"

he says, and his finger touches her arm, just inside the wrist, and traces the skin up softly to the pulse in her elbow. "If I could make porcelain that colour, Smokey, Caffee, Black."

"That's only skin deep, Mr. Dierrek."

His hand tightens on her arm. "Turn around," he says quietly.

He holds her hand, with the bowl, up to the window. She can see her fingers, like x-ray shadows. "With porcelain," he tells her, "you see through the skin."

IX.

It was Anton's conviction that language, at heart, was national, specific and unexportable.

Stories, in their simplicity, could be told, and altered like folktales where they travelled.

Ideas, to a point, could be grafted to alien stock, since the evolution of language is the cumulative theft of ideas.

But though poetry was closer to mathematics and music than all other word-structures, it defied translation. You could never learn a new tongue well enough to understand things that illiterate natives would know. "The poets," he said, "are not only sublime, but their wisdom stalks through the speech of their peasantry."

There were more reasons than Plato's for exiling the poets.

The room was packed whenever he gave that lecture. "Here is a foreign religion," he started, brandishing volumes in turn of Goethe, Dante, Baudelaire, Whitman. "We can not be converted; we will never be true believers." A spare prose rendering of the liturgy was his prescription. That, and a knowledge of the language's sounds and cadences, might approach a communion.

Toward the end he would ridicule brilliantly Dante's

beseiged malevolence, and then he'd break out in the passage that ends *Ben son, ben son, Beatrice'*, so that tears came into his own, and the students' eyes.

As to their own language, he spoke of the Frenchman's *correspondances*. Correspondences everywhere which could become conjunctions. "But how," he'd conclude, "how shall we ever know if we understand?"

Helena has tried to shake off the assault of misery. Tried to reduce to sadness the girl's vicious privacy.

She chose not to go to the library. She sits on her bed, hands folded between her thighs. The wing is silent. She has come back to the words.

She cannot grasp them in her own tongue, in any of the languages she speaks. They elude her with puns and subtexts, with echoes and imprecisions. Just the words themselves, in her cell.

"Murdering cunt!" "Murdering cunt!" They become waves breaking in a cave. *Murderingcunt, murderingcunt, murdering cunt* . . . It is not her language, the thing become the idea.

The scarred, white wall that faces her is the fabric of her mind. Upon it an image, suddenly playing. A vulva opening up to disgorge another vulva.

Like the fish in Brueghel's "Proverbs."

Not the slit, the crease, the gash. This is the birth-mouth, wider than high, hinged like a shark's jaw, a frog's. Disgorging and swallowing like a lung, like the frog that can only swallow by pressing down on its meat with the blind prints of its eyeballs.

Mouths within mouths, a landscape of mounds that gape and swallow and disgorge each other to eternity.

Her daughter, somewhere, with a daughter perhaps.

Forward and back. Neanderthal, Pithecogyne, Eve.

This is how Tadeusz thinks, in images.

What Anton would not allow, though he understood

it.

The luminosity of a child's nightmare.

Helena weeps silently. Her clasped hands swing from side to side. Her mouth is a stretched hole of pain.

The little girl, on the wet pavement beside the car, blood streaming with the dark rain out of her hair.

X.

Tadeusz shakes out a clean sheet over the bed. He snaps it methodically, from corner to corner, tucking the ends in, folding each side-flap over itself like an envelope. The hospital corners, army corners, the prison's.

The gauze curtains shift, from the draught in the window frame. There's a ragged margin of frost on the storm windows. The city is muffled by a late snow. Vapor plumes from the rooftops across the street, and all over Toronto, like smoke from the chimneys of Bratislava.

He unfolds a pillow slip, and catches its movement in the mirror on Helena's dressing table. He holds the pillow with his chin and eases the slip up around it. He sets it down at the bed-head and turns to regard himself in the mirror. He sits down at Helena's stool, and lays his hands flat on the walnut surface.

For all his vacuuming, and the weekly dust-and-polish, he still finds strands of hair, floated in from somewhere. Shreds of Helena—fine wavey filaments, dark blonde, kept long for his sake.

But her smell has departed. The powders and humble perfumes in her drawer smell of themselves—the alchemy they formed with her skin was vanished.

Only the green wool jacket in the closet, uncleaned, can summon her body still into this room. Sometimes he stands, half in the closet, with his face buried in its lining.

Sometimes he hears her voice in the other room. Calling his name, or singing. Never more than a word or two. When he is half-asleep, perhaps.

When his wheel whispers to a halt in the studio, he imagines he'll hear her moving as the birds would be suddenly crying in the birch woods when the guns stopped firing.

He hears a siren, moving slowly two blocks away. A table scrapes overhead, a toilet flushes.

He opens the drawer, and feels past the bottles, under the handkerchiefs for the little box that he made her. He pulls it out.

He knows what is in it. She has told him, would have let him see, gladly; but it is her privacy. She would not take it, even, to the prison, for fear of defilement.

Yet he cannot stop himself, now. His hand trembles, and he senses that she, in her cell, must know what he's doing. Or at least she is thinking of the box.

Inside is a folded paper. Beneath that a lock of hair, flaxen, her daughter's. And a baby tooth.

He unfolds the paper, and sees Helena's writing. Within it, three brittle slips, cigarette papers. The faded pencil marks, his brother's words.

They are too faint to read. The folded sheet holds Helena's transcription.

The enlightened man, in the detachment of his irony, faced with the evils of war, oppression, arrest, is in effect a time-traveller.

The interest is less in how easily his poise and assumptions can be destroyed, but in the more abstract question: Are his values false, or simply relative or, in the end, literary?
He has one recourse only—Madness. He is

Hamlet in the prison of Denmark, but is not in control: hence his disease is not feigned. But being released, by whatever means, Can he come back? Can his irony?

Tadeusz folds the papers back into the paper. He returns the box to its nest, and closes the drawer.

The words mean less to him than they had to Helena. Delivered one night by a man who had shared Anton's cell. She had turned away and read them at once, and had been filled, she said, with anger. What had this to do with her? She was enraged at the man who had locked himself out of her, becoming a monument more than a man. His cellmate had stayed, and in her grief and anger and her reaching for the one who had spent three years with this man's naked-ness, she had made love to him that night on the couch, and again in her bed at dawn while the children watched from their bunks, stoical already, wakened by her cries.

Tadeusz leaves the bed unfinished and goes out to his studio. There are tasks you can do when creation's unthink-able. The mechanical craft that refinishes or prepares. There are two pieces he's resolved to have done, if she gets the parole, if she comes home—when?—next week?

He turns on the radio. Knows the piece within two bars. It's a day of connections. Is it possible Helena is hear-ing this too? *The Sly Little Vixen.* He hums along with it, as he takes down the high-shouldered vase and begins to wipe a damp cloth across its skin. There's a burst of static on the radio, the wavelength buckles: the chatter of a taxi or ambu-lance dispatcher, then Janacek again, drowned in the buzz-saw arpeggios of electric guitars and free-world male scream-ing . . .

Tadeusz hurls the vase against the wall, and reaches for another.

XI.

"You were sent to prison *as* punishment, not *for* punishment."

Helena sits in the high-backed chair, facing the table. Her hands grip the seat, beside her thighs. She knows two of the four women here. One was at her last hearing too, unfriendly. There is no man, this time.

"Our job would be much easier if you had agreed to counselling."

The assistant warden leans sideways, to catch Helena's eye. She wears pearls over her jersey blouse, her eyes are concerned. "We've talked about this before, Helena. We offer professional help, and—well, Mrs. Johnstone's quite right—how can we feel that you're helping yourself, when you won't co-operate?"

"Do I speak now?" asks Helena. Three heads nod. "I tell you before—I am not crazy."

"You certainly have a problem, Mrs. Jemsky. Let's be brutally frank about this—you had two convictions for impaired driving before . . ." Whether her voice tails off out of tact or for greater effect, it is hard to say.

It is hopeless. Helena shrugs. The assistant warden intercedes again. "Helena, this must seem like a trial to you, another trial, but it isn't. We are here to help you, to help you get on with your life. You have been a model prisoner, I have stressed that to the board. They also know about your very brave actions yesterday, in the shower room." Even Mrs. Johnstone nods. Helena lowers her eyes.

"But you are very withdrawn. We need to know that you understand this punishment, that you will not—break out again into foolish behaviour."

Helena takes a long breath, and exhales. "What words do you want me to say?"

Mrs. Johnstone's voice is tense with opinions: "We

are not to be taken in by words, Mrs. Jemsky. This is not a charade."

"Helena," there's an appeal, complicit, in the assistant warden's grey eyes, "we are looking for an excuse to let you go. Don't you understand?"

"No, I'm sorry—not an excuse, Miss Stasiuk, a *reason*. We need a very good reason, Mrs. Jemsky, why we should offer you the freedom of the streets."

It is hopeless. Helena folds her hands in her lap. "What words do you want me to say?"

XII.

"I used to watch you." Wherever these words occur in a story must be the pivot: the point at which the past moves into the future and is left behind.

Tadeusz has heard the words twice in his life, and will hear them at least twice more.

The stroke-tightened lips of his mother, beside the window: "I used to watch you, fighting on the lawn with Anton—already you were growing stronger than him. I feared so much for you both—I could not stop you fighting, but a woman alone fears to be sentimental. I remember you fighting over your father's green hunting-bag. Perhaps that was your last fight, I don't know." She was only two days from death. He lacked the heart to tell her that Anton had gone before.

And then in Vienna one of the camp guards, in exile himself. They sat in a bar near the station, and shared cigarettes. "I used to watch you take your walk outside in the snow. I came to expect you—you were the only one outside. I used to aim my machine-gun between your shoulder-blades and follow you with it around the yard." He laughed, and placed his hand on Tadeusz' forearm. "I knew then that if another prisoner didn't kill you, you'd get out alive."

But tonight it is Helena's voice on the phone. "Tadeusz, I used to watch you leaving. I could not bear it. I could see you walking out through the gates and I thought in myself that I was killing you. I could not bear it. That's why I said no more visits. And I came to think that I did not want to be with you again, I thought that we should forget . . .

"Tadeusz, they have given me my parole. They want me to leave the prison, tomorrow. What should I do?"

Tadeusz can hear the woman on the pay-phone next to her. "What about my life? You fucking bastard, what about me?"

He leans his head on the kitchen doorway. "Helena," he says, "I have had this phone in the apartment just to hear news from you. All I have got is wrong numbers, and people who try to sell me things. I am waiting for you—come home." He replaces the phone, and then points a finger at it, like a child's make-believe pistol. He shoots it and shoots it and begins to laugh, quietly, crazily. He dances on one spot, in the living room. The world seems twice as big, all at once.

He rips the jack from its socket and goes out in the hallway. He will throw the phone into the street.

The woman from upstairs is checking her mail-box. "Here," he says, thrusting his hands at her. "Here, lady—you want this phone? Is all paid for."

XIII.

Tadeusz is released from sleep with such gentleness that he scarcely believes he was there.

The room is bright. It is still afternoon. He can feel Helena's eyes on his face. He reaches down for her hand before he can look at her.

She is barely smiling. She brings their hands up to her lips, and then to his cheek. The smell of her body breathes over him.

"I used to watch you," she says, "in the garden on Tatry Street. You remember?" His eyes stay on hers. "Such a busy boy, in your own world there, in the corner under the terrace. Always on your hands and knees, for hours, while your brother was practising Chopin."

The gauze curtains rustle, the ceiling shivers with reflected sunlight. Tadeusz looks upwards, his left hand cradles his head on the pillow. "Yes," he says, "the *Fantasie*, the *Etudes*, and me in the dirt by the apple tree.

"It was rich, that earth, black and sweet. There was Solomon's Seal and Lily of the Valley, a thousand snail shells—you could see the light through them, amber. That earth was old, but it wasn't exhausted.

"I collected china. Fragments of plates and bowls. I had hundreds of them, dug from the black earth. Not once did I find two pieces that fitted each other. I would make up the shapes, and the blue pictures, from the smallest evidence."

He smiles. "Now I think I was often right!"

"Are the houses still there?" she whispers.

"Yes," he says, "of course. You remember the sunken lane, between our places, going down to the churchyard?"

"The cobblestones were red when it rained," says Helena. "There were slate gutters to carry the water down. The ivy on the walls was full of honey-bees."

"Yes. I'd look down from my wall onto the heads of the pall-bearers, a few feet below. The bell would be tolling in the tower. I could read the names on the brass plates on the coffins."

He rolls over to face her. "And once," he says, "I saw a girl looking over from the garden across that lane. She was blonde, and taller than me, and she was standing among the goldenrods. I did not see her at first; she thought she was invisible.

"I thought she was beautiful. Her family had just moved in. I picked green apples from the ground by my feet—and pelted her with them!"

Helena stretches her legs, and relaxes them. Her laugh is a child's. "You missed," she says. "Your face was red and your aim was terrible!"

His hand moves from hers and roves across her belly. He traces the blue-grey fissures in her skin, the marks of the children she has lost and which he never knew.

"I still feel invisible, sometimes," she says. He takes her hand again. They lie looking up at the ceiling. The sounds of the city drift in, and are filtered out. They have never been so close to each other, never so far apart. For the moment each is almost entirely happy.

The Victory Burlesk

·

Margaret Atwood

I went to the Victory Burlesk twice, or maybe it was
only once and one of my friends went the other time and
told me about it. I enjoyed it both times. It was considered
quite daring for young women to go to such a place, and we
thought it was funny; it was almost as funny as church.

You got a stand-up comic, a movie and a man who
sang or juggled plates, as well as the strip-tease act. They
used a lot of coloured lighting, red and blue and purple.
Each girl had a fake name: Miss Take, Miss Behave, Flame
LeRew. I liked the names and the costumes, for their inge-
nuity, and I liked the more skillful girls, the ones who could
twirl tassles or make their bellies or buttocks rotate in a circle. That was before they had to take it all off, there was an
art to it, it was almost like the plate juggling. I liked the way
they floated in the pools of coloured light, moving as if they
were swimming, mermaids behind glass.

One woman began with her back to the audience,
the spotlight on her. She was wearing long white gloves and
a black evening gown with gauzy black sleeves that looked
like membranous wings as she stretched out her arms. She

did a lot with her arms and back, but when she finally turned around, she was old. Her face was powdered dead white, her mouth was a bright reddish purple, but she was old. I could feel shame washing through me, it was no longer funny, I didn't want this woman to take off her clothes, I didn't want to look. I felt that I, not the woman on the stage, was being exposed and humiliated. Surely they would jeer and yell things at her, surely they would feel they had been tricked.

The woman unzipped her black evening gown, slipping it down, and began to move her hips. She smiled with her white mask of a face and her purple mouth, inside her lips her teeth glinted, dull white pebbles, it was a mockery, she didn't intend it, she knew it, it was a trick of another kind but we didn't know who was playing it. The trick was that suddenly there was no trick: the body up there was actual, it was aging, it was not floating in the spotlight somewhere apart from us, like us it was caught in time.

The Victory Burlesk went dead. Nobody made a sound.

Making Poison

·

Margaret Atwood

When I was five my brother and I made poison. We were living in a city then, but we probably would have made the poison anyway. We kept it in a paint can under somebody else's house and we put all the poisonous things into it that we could think of: toadstools, dead mice, mountain ash berries which may not have been poisonous but looked it, piss which we saved up in order to add it to the paint can. By the time the can was full everything in it was very poisonous.

The problem was that once having made the poison we couldn't just leave it there. We had to do something with it. We didn't want to put it into anyone's food, but we wanted an object, a completion. There was no one we hated enough, that was the difficulty.

I can't remember what we did with the poison in the end. Did we leave it under the corner of the house, which was made of wood and brownish yellow? Did we throw it at someone, some innocuous child? We wouldn't have dared an adult. Is this a true image I have, a small face streaming with tears and red berries, the sudden knowledge that the poison was really poisonous after all? Or did we throw it out, do I remember those red berries floating down a gutter, into a culvert, am I innocent?

Why did we make the poison in the first place? I can remember the glee with which we stirred and added, the sense of magic and accomplishment. Making poison is as much fun as making a cake. People like to make poison. If you don't understand this you will never understand anything.

Murder in the Dark

·

Margaret Atwood

This is a game I've played only twice. The first time I was in Grade Five, I played it in a cellar, the cellar of a large house belonging to the parents of a girl called Louise. There was a pool table in the cellar but none of us knew anything about pool. There was also a player piano. After a while we got tired of running the punchcard rolls through the player piano and watching the keys go up and down by themselves, like something in a late movie just before you see the dead person. I was in love with a boy called Bill, who was in love with Louise. The other boy, whose name I can't remember, was in love with me. Nobody knew who Louise was in love with.

So we turned out the lights in the cellar and played *Murder in the Dark*, which gave the boys the pleasure of being able to put their hands around the girls' necks and gave the girls the pleasure of screaming. The excitement was almost more than we could bear, but luckily Louise's parents came home and asked us what we thought we were up to.

The second time I played it was with adults; it was not as much fun, though more intellectually complex. I heard that this game was once played at a summer cottage by six normal people and a poet, and the poet really tried to kill someone. He was hindered only by the intervention of a dog, which could not tell fantasy from reality. The thing about this game is that you have to know when to stop.

Here is how you play:

You fold up some pieces of paper and put them into a hat, a bowl or the centre of the table. Everyone chooses a piece. The one who gets the X is the detective, the one who gets the black spot is the killer. The detective leaves the room, turning off the lights. Everyone gropes around in the dark until the murderer picks a victim. He can either whisper, 'You're dead,' or he can slip his hands around a throat and give a playful but decisive squeeze. The victim screams and falls down. Everyone must now stop moving around except the murderer, who of course will not want to be found near the body. The detective counts to ten, turns on the lights and enters the room. He may now question anyone but the victim, who is not allowed to answer, being dead. Everyone but the murderer must tell the truth.

The murderer must lie. If you like, you can play games with this game. You can say: the murderer is the writer, the detective is the reader, the victim is the book. Or perhaps, the murderer is the writer, the detective is the critic and the victim is the reader. In that case the book would be the total *mise en scéne*, including the lamp that was accidentally tipped over and broken. But really it's more fun just to play the game.

In any case, that's me in the dark. I have designs on you, I'm plotting my sinister crime, my hands are reaching for your neck or perhaps, by mistake, your thigh. You can hear my footsteps approaching, I wear boots and carry a knife, or maybe it's a pearl-handled revolver, in any case I wear boots with very soft soles, you can see the cinematic glow of my cigarette, waxing and waning in the fog of the room, the street, the room, even though I don't smoke. Just remember this, when the scream at last has ended and you've turned on the lights: by the rules of the game, I must always lie.

Now: do you believe me?

When Things Get Worst

·

Barry Callaghan

In the wintertime when the light drops to an hour so still you can hear all the elms along a road crack in the cold, me and Evol were standing at a crossroads beside a snowbound cemetery called Primrose, out on the shoulder of the highway hitching a ride home to the home farm because we'd gone to the city looking for work only to find that no one but the quick and the light-fingered were working and there was no place for a man like Evol who had all the grit and good looks in the world but he had no special skills, which is how the hunky boss sneered and gave Evol short shrift at the auto body shop where he tried to hire on, hoping to spray-paint busted up cars that had been welded and fixed, which he had done in the country in a wrecking lot close by the Crudup's Mobile Home and Trailer Park. So we ended up squatting in a plywood shack under an old iron footbridge alongside a bunch of dipsos and kids with bunged up brains, where we stayed right on through the month of September, the babychild Loanne with us sleeping in a knapsack like it was her own regular sleeping bag, and then when the early winter came on with that whipsnap to the edge of the wind that hits before freezing rain and the following snow, we got a room in a hostel and halfway house where there were druggies and slopeheads living down the hall, all of them deranged most of the time, talking about the molestation and mayhem they'd like to cause and probably did, so that Evol rightly said it was harebrained of us to be living there in that boarding house among people who made ordinary folk like us seem to be common dull, since we had a whole four-and-a-half room frame house, shabby or not, back on the home farm, back on our scrabbly patch of an awkward ninety acres that kept pushing up stones when it wasn't being overrun.by bush.

"Them cursed stones," my daddy used to say, "always pushing themselves up and turning our people crooked and bent into stone pickers," and Evol, scrunching up his eyes over a cup of black coffee in the Future Kiev Café in the city, told me we were going to be smart instead of stupid and go home, which struck me in my funnybone, since my mother had always said before she died, "The world must be flat because no one who leaves home ever comes back," but there we were, bucking headfirst into the winter wind with Evol, though he was a loving man, taking no mind of the child bundled inside my coat against the blowing snow, which didn't please me any about him as we stood stamping our feet and staring down the dark rise of the road between the ploughed snow banks, a hollow lost feeling sucking at me from underneath my breastbone and tears freezing in my eyes since I'd never felt so lonesome and far from anywhere in my life what with the dogs howling off behind a house in a stand of hemlock, the stillness so sharp that Evol said not to worry because all clear thinking takes place only in the cold which was his natural territory, him being a man who didn't take no nonsense of any kind for an answer, from no man, and no animals either, and so he just ignored me when I started to cry but then because an old truck had come sagging around a bend I yelled,

"Is he stopping, Evol? Is he?" and he said, wagging his arms,

"It's hard to see, but I think he's stopping", and then we climbed up into the cab beside a slope-shouldered and long-jawed man with darting eyes, and the moon was up by then, pale over the snow fields as we sat stiffnecked on the high seat and all the empty whiteness we could see out there through the window seemed to contain no promise at all, a stern sight to see and confront after the way things had been with us in the city.

"Just driving on to Dundalk folks," the trucker said, "but that's better than nowhere and besides a bus goes through, and—

"That's right, this here beats nowhere."

"I figure you gotta be crazy and half outa your mind to be standing with your wife and child in the cold as cold as it is."

"Mister," Evol said, "if I don't go crazy I will lose my mind," and Evol laughed, and the old truck bumped up into the air as we crossed a railroad track.

"That's a fine looking child you got there."

"Yes sir, she's a big girl if you like a big girl for a baby," Evol said.

"Hell, me and my wife, we been trying for years to derive a child outa her but she just don't take to it."

"You looking for a child?"

"Matty, that's my wife, she puts her head to the floor and says prayers before we bed down, she wants a child so bad she prayer-walks in her sleep. Not having a child, she says, is like a stone that's a dead-weight in your heart."

"You like this here kid?"

"Sure," the trucker said, who I could tell was really a farmer out trucking on the side, and I went to say something after him but Evol clamped his hand to my knee and squeezed, which is what he always did whenever we got testy together, saying, "When things get worst, how are you?" but I warned him anyway with the slitting of my eyes and by snapping my knees together, I warned him that he could be clever and quick and play the lame wolf with this trucker, but only so long as he didn't get sly and devious with me and my baby girl, but he smiled and whispered for me not to worry which is what he always did, whispered up against my cheek whenever he was stepping out from the home farm door in all his strut, either going to the dog fights or off turkey hunting, and then he'd drop into a semi-squat with his hands on his knees like he was going to leapfrog back at me, and say, "I hear the more sin got big, the more grace abounds," laughing and doing a hambone slap on his thigh and hip, prancing off down the lane to Pandora Road to Crudup's Mobile Home and Trailer Park, whistling. I never heard a man whistle so. He was a whistling fool. Some men like to whittle to pass an hour, he liked to whistle and trill like a bird and while I wiped my hands I watched after him through the kitchen shutters unti he was gone behind the weeping birch on the concession road, and then I drew the sleeve of my dress down over his old family hand-me-down hand-painted sign that we'd hung for a joke and a memory on the wall, a sign back from the time when there'd been bootmakers in his family, long before he was born: KEEP YOUR FEET DRY — BOOTS AND SHOES, back in the olden time when loggers had come from Fergus village along the Garafraxa Road to the lumber camps, and the road was a crooked trail of corduroying through the swamps, all cut and slash through the close bog, and those sweet tough boys had carried the seeds in their cuffs, and their pockets were stuffed with sprigs of lilac rooted in potatoes for the moisture and there it was, "All planted," Evol said, "planted out where the light sits like mirror water on the back of the swamp herons." The two of us crouched on a shelf-stone jutting out of the gravelside of the ravine behind our big hill on the home farm, kicking gravel loose from under the crab-grass, talking and thinning our hopes while looking for the future and how we thought it should be,

"How much you want a baby, mister?"

"Well, hell, I never thought. You mean like money?"

"The truck," he said with his own particular kind of cornering tone, the tone he always took when he was creep-ing up on a thought, canny and hunched forward exactly like he was crouching now, exactly like he crouched silent on the shelf-stone digging his heel down into the gravel, cutting open an apple, prying the seedcase like it was the beginning of where all things began until whatever special thought he was working on wore itself out and he cored the apple and threw the seedcase away, saying, since he was always trying to pronounce something big in words, trying to say some-thing that would save us from the angry sorrow inside he said he felt, "When we throw our seed away no wonder we wonder why we end up where we do," but he hadn't thought that particular thought through to any kind of keen truth because the fact was we were ending up right where our par-ents' parents had begun, we were going back to where my momma and daddy had died, people who had stuck to where they'd been rooted down for life because no single one of them had ever thrown anything away, and had never thrown caution to the winds, but were always looking out the shuttered window for trouble, for God and his angels of rapine who came in all stripes and sizes, Joe McGreevey the crippled tax collector, Walter Skanks the banker in his royal blue suit, and so folks were careful to a fault, digging down and taking hold with their seed, trying to latch on to hope, squatting in the beginning years inside their two-room hutches with some of the families huddling and sharing their own body heat or clustered in the timber churches, chinking and plastering the walls to keep out the swarms of black flies but the flies got them anyway, fly bites festering the way they still fester to this day like stars of pus, the fever that lays down in you like an egg and explodes the way so many dreams and lives exploded, though the log barns they built to barricade themselves and the cattle- beasts from bears and wolves are still standing, standing but empty now, "And we were driven like the driven snow," my momma said, soured by all her years of passing the winter months down snow-locked concession lanes waiting and waiting until the spring thaw came, waiting through my daddy's con- trariness, which is the fund of family hard times that people all too easily want to forget now and let slide out of their lives now, though it was only forty years ago that all this went on that I'm talking about and there were no big yellow school buses making the school boards in the townships plough the lanes, and there was no hydro either, no lights you could just switch on when it gave you pleasure or switch off when it came time to pleasure. It was a dark time until the first spring light leaked in through the trees like a streak of spittle low in the sky. Someone was always found then hanged at the end of their rope, or a woman in childbirth sprawled dead for want of care, and the babies, too, were buried on the home farm, sewn into heavy blankets and put down in the bush that was still so trackless back in those days that women got lost looking for their cows or looking for the mirror in the air that they were hoping to step through so they could disappear and some were found frozen and some were never found, gone, though Armenian gypsies appeared out of the woods instead, right where the women had gone in between the birch trees, selling spice and thread and buying goose feathers and scrap iron from all of us bent over stone pickers who'd cleared the small parcels of land while always dreading any kind of sickness, diphtheria, mumps and measles, scarlet fever, chicken pox, polio, so KEEP YOUR FEET DRY meant something, meant something deep, but not deep enough for Evol, who always took a close-eyed and contentious angle to things, chewing on his anger and his sorrow like it was his cud, because he said it should have been POWDER, it should have been KEEP YOUR POWDER DRY, sniffing around the edge of disaster, always dreaming of disaster or fighting dogs, because he loved his fighting dogs, and he also loved hunting, turkey hunting, and he loved me, but his love for me didn't stop him from cutting the beards off of all the brush turkeys he killed and nailing the beards to all the doors in the house. "Tongues of fire," he called them. "I want to hold on to those tongues of fire." But he really figured that one day he was going to lose us all. He had this doom thing in him. He used to say, "The more you do the more you know there's nothing to be done." Then he'd laugh, and if he had his times of black silence he also had his black laughter, which was beautiful laughter that hovered like a beautiful black bird with a swiveling eye looking to see if there was any more darkness to laugh at, like he always did down on one knee when he was shoeing his foot with the webbed little toe into his boot with a horn of polished deer bone, "Shoeing myself into my grave," he said, "just like all the men I mind and remember who've died with their Greb boots on in these parts." But no matter how grim he got, and he could get grim enough to ghost-dance on your heart, he loved the farms around here and hated seeing them broken up, the driving sheds and the barns caving and falling in, farmers turning their lives into piece-work and second-hand jobs and going out and carting scrap junk and stacking cars in what were their corn fields, heaps of crushed and cannibalized cars littering their land with fenders and rusted hoods, the old split-rail fences strung with hub-caps and looped little bits of chrome, and used-tire mounds piled up

and slipped all askew and swarmed over by hundreds of caw-
ing crows, but the good thing about Evol was that no sooner
did he get his snout down into this gaunt look of things
than he'd come alive with a burst of abounding grace
because he sure could dance, and he sure could play the fiddle to soothe the birds, which is how I first met him one
day, hearing fiddle music from far away, so I went hurrying
over the rise through the dwarf pines and juniper to a clearing where he was slowly dancing by himself in a field surrounded by cattlebeasts and the cattle were spotted black
and white, the sky being an ice-blue that was hard on the
eyes in the sunlight and I set out running at him up the hill
until I stubbed my shoe on a root and stumbled and
thought I saw the cattlebeasts take a gandy step forward and
then a step back in time to the tune he was playing, but
then the sky reeled faster until I heard "Lo Anne," and
everything at the sound of Anne was in an amber light but I
said, "My name's not Anne," and he said, "I was just saying
hello." I saw he was standing over me, sweating himself, and
he said, "You fell down, I want to talk to you."

"I don't want to talk to you."

"Why not?"

"Because I got nothing to say," but we talked all the
long afternoon, and talking to each other was almost the
whole of what we did all year, except make love, which I
must say bewildered my momma and daddy, not that we
made love, but that we talked all the time. They seemed
astonished to hear us talking, almost like so much talking
made our making love okay. "I love you," Evol said, "like a
bone-weary man loves the hour he lies down in," and he
was a do-right man, too, who said, "So roll over woman,
you're up on the rise tonight," sprawled back like he was
feeling loose-jointed and eased free of all his anger and free
to think about how good his life could be, at least good with
me. "You're up top like you're the woman you are, in charge

of yourself," he said, smirking, because he did believe he was giving me the gift of giving him pleasure, "and you can have your fun," which I had, because all of my life as a lone and alone child I had made my own fun. I knew how, even when I was locked in my room for idleness, lying face down on my mattress, I knew how to make fun in my mind and to make my mind the sky the bird flew in, or the earth the worm wormed in and as a child I told my daddy what it was like to be a worm, and then I told him worms could fly if I wanted them to. "That may be okay for worms," he said, liking to keep a hand on me, "but you can't blow your nose if I don't want you to." Years later when I asked Evol if he believed I knew what it was like for a worm to fly, he said, "I'm a believer and I know how to believe. I just got nothing to believe in," and then he rolled over and looked out the window, leaning his head on the white painted sill, the white paint flaking off though my momma had painted it with good semi-gloss in the weeks just before she died, painted it while crying that she could see daddy's face in the sink water every morning in the bathroom, which meant she couldn't bring herself to wash. Wherever it was that she looked into water she saw his face and got all confused about him, saying on end that he was going to die by drowning in the grace of the Lord, when in fact, there he was, he was sitting right opposite her, growling, mumbling that she had turned crazy as a loon, so it turned out that she lived out her last months unwashed and smelly and scented with cologne, haunted by his eyes, she said, his eyes hungering for her in the water, hungering sometimes with lust and sometimes with anger, and Evol lay with his head on her windowsill like a boy-child who'd gone early to seed, so sad, and sadder, as if it had rained all afternoon in his heart and he couldn't go out to play until the moon came up pale like a piece of wet paper and he said, "My own daddy had the gift, he was a horse trader and handyman, good at building barns, who saw visions, an ebony-boned female demon and a cross dragging its slow length along the country-side big enough to crucify us all, redeem us all, but because my daddy's cock went dead on him after I was born, my momma believed that their only hope of reaping an inchful of eternity was through me, her child who would beget a child who would beget,"—

"The truck, you telling me you're willing to trade that child for this here old truck?"

"Sure," and I could feel the trucker get all tense in the dark, gripping the driving wheel hard, sucking little mouthfuls of air,

"Man, that's not right. Naw."

"Don't your wife dream about it, her stone in her sleep?"

But the trucker started bawling out about how wrong-doing was getting too civilized, how you couldn't trust to a world where trucks were traded for children and rape went unpunished, and Evol sat for a long time in silence listening to that trucker hacking for air, a silence so cold I knew Evol could only be thinking clear as clear could be, in the same way that he'd sit beside me staring out the home farm door at the twisted pines down the lane, thinking, thinking, as grim-faced and desolate as he dared to be, all the despair in him dancing in his eyes, since he knew for sure that he could trust me, trust me to let him be as alone and haunted by the sorrow inside himself as he wanted to be, because I always was there and I always came up unafraid by his side, sometimes finding myself laughing out loud for no good reason, laughing at him and his sulks and sorrows. Sometimes, I'd sing him a song my daddy had taught me. Daddy had his own way of teaching songs. All kinds of songs but he wouldn't teach me the tune. He'd say, "Learn the words, make up your own tune." I never did know where he learned all these songwords, but I ended up being able to sing all kinds of songs in any old way I wanted which is how I sang at Evol, in the way I wanted:

> *The whole world's worried about the atom bomb,*
> *No one's worried when Jesus'll come.*
> *But Jesus'll come,*
> *Boom*
> *Like an atom bomb.*

and I laughed and Evol laughed and waved his arms like he was letting something inside himself free, just like I'd laughed and waved at momma and daddy on the day they died, laughed because they were laughing like the loons do when they break water on the lake, the loons who've got the gift of the devil's laugh, which is the word the oldtimers gave the loon's call, the devil's laugh, but Evol said the sound of the birds calling across the water was more like opening up a place somewhere beyond words, "On the other side of the glass, on the other side of the silvering," he said, "where the dead wait to talk to you, all of them sitting cross-legged in a hole that's a great big gap in God's mind like someone, St. Jude maybe, took a cleaver to His thinking and cleaved His brain," and I said the only hole I could call home was the place down the road where our very first settler folks had set down the first village, lightly and gaily calling it Hole-in-the-Woods, with their sawmill on the corner, a post office and the mail carrier, Plumer Dewan, who'd owned good horses and was Evol's grandfather, and a grist mill and a hangman who had two roan geldings and a hansom cab, and two black men, the Souche brothers who'd come up from somewhere in the southern States, being the local honey dippers who lowered their long-handled spoons into the cesspools under the outhouses, carrying a sign on their cart: SANITATION IS SALVATION FOR THE NATION, and they were also sweet singers singing at the first wedding that took place around the Hole because George Tullamore came to the door of grandmother Maggie Brodie asking for work and

Mrs. Brodie said all she could do was offer one of her daughters as a wife, which George took, having nothing else to his name, and also she gave the wedding dinner, my grandmother making sure to tell me of the fresh fish and potatoes boiled in a sugar kettle, raspberries and scones, and then she said their son, my daddy, whose nickname was Wishbone because grandmother said all her life was just a wish on a bone and that's how he got his lasting nickname among his family, my daddy who ended up so curt and counter to everyone because I figure none of his wishes had come true, and because nothing had come true he couldn't stand contradiction. He'd gone to the school the Brodies built with a bell on the roof where the teaching all through the years and up until the thirties was in Gaelic as well as English, until the second big war drew everybody able-bodied off, leaving momma and her jam-preserving and knitting-kind of women behind just like they were silt, and cold winds blew off some of that silt, building up dust in the bedroom corners and dust in the crannies of windows and many bare big stones upstanding in this gravelly land ended up standing in dust, but the schoolhouse and the bell are still there, though Hole-in-the-Woods is long gone and ploughed under for the placing of a hydro pylon that is right now standing on a little island in a springwater pond, the village long gone and leaving behind only wide open space, particularly in the winter when the winds glaze the hills to look like sugar icing on the snow and curtains of blown snow blot the sun into a red wound between the black trees, the black corduroy bark of the sugar maples dusted by frozen snow and the sky a pewter color like grandpa's old spoon.

"I want this truck."

"Right, but I couldn't live, and neither could the baby, without this here truck because our damn farm's not worth nothing, the bloody Mennonites are buying up everything for themselves," the driver said, shying away from Evol while I hunched my shoulder into him so he'd know that if he was playing some weasel game with this guy, then he could count me out, since I wasn't no damn fool deranged enough to trade my baby for a truck, but you never knew what Evol was up to, you had to keep a keen lookout on his left hand while he was working you over gentle with his right, so we all just sat silent and stiff, listening to the rattling motor making a sound like the fan belt was loose, and the child was whimpering in the dark though the dark didn't bother me because me and Evol had always got along in the dark, defiant of the dark, and our defiance, he said, was the one true strength we had, testimony to our being unafraid to walk blindfolded throughout the house in the dark, unafraid of ghosts or the newly dead, or each other, him with his turkey gun racked over the bed, both of us listening for prowlers or maybe an ebony-boned female about to step out of his father's dream vision, though I told him no one was damn fool enough to break in on us to steal something because there was nothing to steal, and he said, "That's right, except some people would steal the time of day," and he turned on the TV, staring, sinking into that strange stunned silence that seeps like drainage water into your brain while it's being swamped by all those TV pictures of faces as polished as a pebble, heads talking and yammering and being pleased as punch about how awful everything is, the kind of stuff my daddy loved, or even better, loved to hate, flashing their phone-in numbers and prayer numbers on the screen so if you are terrified and lonely and want someone to send you a prayer cloth and pray with you over the phone, there's the number and Evol laughed and sneered at that TV prayer business, saying there was only one way to look at preachers and politicians and that was down, so far down until you were looking at the sole-side of your shoe which is where the shit is, so I knew why both Evol and daddy called them all shitheels, but one night when a big roly-poly woman with big wide-open owl-eyes said she was a psychic and you could phone in and find out your future, Evol leapt up and dialed right in to her and whispered into the phone and then he sat stock-still, listening like he was a hard of hearing person, completely concentrated, and then he hung up real smooth and gentle and picked up his gun and touched the barrel-mouth with his tongue the way some folk wet a pencil and said there comes a time when you've got to abandon your principles and do what's right and you have to get rid of what you don't need no more, and he shot out the old Zenith TV saying he hated it more than anything because, he said, stroking the barrel with his forefinger, "It glues you up and gluts your mind, it glues your mind to a whole world of guff, the talk talk talk talk crap of politicians and preacher simps and salesmen," and he put the gun away and started to whistle while I said, because whistling usually meant he was on his way out the door, "We should always lie here naked and let the calm lick at us in the dark because it's the light that hurts." He rested on his elbow and I could feel the angle of his body against me, and he said, "The dark's as true as a grieving woman." Then he sat up on the edge of the bed and played his fiddle for me for so long and so mournful I began to laugh and we made love, his body like a glove, a glove that had held me warm all the way home, yet the hand inside, the hand that held me, I didn't really know that hand at all, I didn't know it at all, though I was dead sure that his dying words would be what he always said,

"When things get worst, how are you?"

"This is it," the trucker said.

"Fine."

"Yes sir, you climb down here," and the driver agreed to step out into the dark and walk us back a piece to show us how and where the bus to Owen Sound would probably come by within the hour and as he lifted his arm to point into the dark, a black steel wrench caught him on the back of the neck and he dropped, his head twisted, and Evol rolled his body into a culvert,

"Jesus takes us one by one," he said, and then he crossed himself because that's what Catholics do and said he didn't mean to kill him, he only wanted the truck, and he smacked me on the shoulder because I was crying again and shaking, and he said, "I said I didn't mean it and what you mean is more important than what you do," but when we were back in the truck driving northwest with the child between us, I burst into sobbing.

"We're gonna get bad luck, I just know we are," so he drove and stared straight ahead because he was so good at staring like that, staring like he was absent from the place where he was and he said staring soothed him, particularly the way he could take a fix on a flame and look right into the blue eye-hole of the fire like he did with the wood fires he made inside the big fieldstones of our front parlor fireplace, stones that had been set so perfect by John Shearer, the local mason, that they floated weightless and I felt, since those heavy stones were afloat in the air, that nothing should or could go wrong in front of that fire, but, "You watch," Evol said, "birds'll come down the chimney in the morning because cold ashes call a bird down and a bird in the house means a death in the family," but why, I wondered when he talked that way with the same grim surety that my daddy did, do men like to call down on themselves all the omens of their own dying?

"Because there are people dying who've never died before," he said and laughed,

"As luck would have it," I said, just as a police car with the whirly-gig roof lights flashing pulled us over and I screamed and screamed and screamed, "I told you. They know, they always know."

The two cops hauled Evol out onto the road.

"I traded this here truck. I didn't do no kinda rape. You want me for rape, I ain't gonna rape no old lady, I never been to Couchiching. I told you, I never been there, it must've been somebody driving a truck just like this who looks like me and you can't leave my woman alone here, she's got her child," but they sure as hell left me alone, plunked down in a short order cafe in a town close by called Knuck, a cross-roads town of scrap dealers and welfare folks hunkering around in their shitkicker boots, singing *Take This Job And Shove It* like Waylon Jennings, and me and my baby, Loanne, we both stood there with me snuffling and her screaming but the cops took no heed of us as they cranked their siren and drove Evol off in the dark to Couchiching which was a lake town to the northeast we had never once passed through, a couple of cops who wore blue-tinted sunglasses with silver rims. I said "What about me, I must have been there, too," but they just laughed and took Evol to Couchiching so he could go eyeball to eyeball with some bed-ridden half-blind old lady, and I have always been rightly afraid of the blind, any blind woman's eyes, all spittle white in the pupil, the shine and color of the end of things, the shine of the underbellies of dead fish, and the old lady, she said, "He did it, he did it," so they decided for sure that he did, and two days later I came to see Evol who was bunked all alone in the Couchiching jail, which was a small red brick squat place if you looked at the outside of the building and all shiny enamelled cinder blocks on the inside, bright bright cinder blocks with fluorescent lights overhead to really light up all the dark brooding and thinking that was supposed to be going on in there, except Evol said he was the only prisoner because there weren't even any drunk drivers, making the place seem empty and abandoned and certainly not ripe with his kind of wrong doing, though the police had not yet put two and two together between the truck and the dead driver who was probably still in the cul-

vert and all Evol could figure was maybe the wife hadn't
reported him missing, or maybe she was glad to get rid of
him, or maybe he had no wife and he had actually stolen the
truck after raping the old lady, all of which left Evol with
that unsettling sly light he always got in his eyes before he
went hunting brush turkeys, sitting with a sideways win-
some tilt to his head like his head was half cocked outside of
the world, and I could see that he was starting to circle
down inside his own head, listening to some silent music
that was all his own, when he told me,

"But after all is said and done the only consequent
thing is that I don't think hardly at all about what happened, or how, or why, or about the truck driver. It was just
worse luck for all of us. Worse luck, that's what my daddy
always said. Worse luck needs no blame, because the laying
of blame is for those who can afford it or are born to it, like
hens get born to lay eggs. It comes with the clucking."

And he laughed, a strange hardly breathing low
laugh from the back of his heart, like I've heard him laugh
right after he's fired his gun,

"It's the joke that gets me down, that's all, the joke
of that scrawny old blind bitch of a woman braying at me
about me being the one who knocked her down and then
she said that I did her, splayed, she said. 'I was splayed,' and
the guard, you see him? He's a goddamn sweating porker
who's got these here rumples of corduroy fat on the back of
his neck, he says they're going to fix a peckerwood like me,
grind me down to a tiny nub of stone with nothing to do
but clatter around in God's head bone, a dry stone in a dry
pod, like a baby-child's rattle, that's what he said, and I was
thinking all night that God's mind must be like that, a
child's rattle full of dry laughter, so all I can hope is that
Loanne, whenever it happens that she's able to get close to
God, why she'll be able to rattle and shake some sense into
His ear but it won't matter to me because by then I'll be

long gone as a bead of light,"

and he stood up and then sat down and winked and said, "You remember that TV psychic woman, she said as bold as brass to me, she said, 'The life you'll lead is all your own, and the life you take will be your own too,' " and he smiled as benevolent as he'd ever looked at me, full of a kind of dark sheen, as if the dark could glow, as if inside the night itself there was light, a seed of light that was always alive there so there could never be a total darkness, and listening and looking at Evol, I suddenly believed there was a whole world in him beyond what I'd ever known, or could ever know, no matter how close we'd been, no matter how we'd cradled into each other, and he seemed like he'd already gone away from me, beyond any horizon we had ever dreamed of, beyond the steel bars where the moon-faced guard's head was suddenly poking, whining at us, all in a sweat, "No more time, you've run out of time," and before they could haul Evol into court to try to hang him for what he didn't do, he hanged himself in his cell, I guess for what he did do, which sort of dovetailed his life because he always did have a hungering for death, almost doting on death, the way he suddenly blurted out to me one day, "I am an accomplished man that's what the dead man says," I guess getting rid of whatever principles he had to do what he thought was right, and he probably did it as calm and subdued as we'd been on that sunny afternoon when I laid down sideways on our bed to sort my little boxes that I kept for his shirt studs and tie clips, but also, those boxes were filled with dried wild flowers, the white petals of field daisies that curled around the dark heads, heads like pin cushions, which I also collected, and hat pins, pins for my hair, old pressed glass jars and satin sofa cushions with needlepoint names in fluorescent thread . . . Loanne, Evol . . . and my momma's name, Sabina, my sad sad momma with all her old tonics for sleepless nights.

The whole heavy load of sleeplessness that I had to stare wide-eyed into while lying in bed hungering for Evol after he died, and I still did miss him, desperately, and I did need to hear his voice, but I remembered how my momma had told me to hold two small stones in my mouth until any and all dread abated, so that you took the weight of the dread in the mouth and not in the heart, a weight which you could then spit out so the dread ended up becoming only a daily drone of emptiness, a drone that had hold of me by the heart strings because toward the end of spring my baby had also gone down into nowhere, my Loanne, a child born flushed and feverish, suddenly taken to bed by the whooping cough not a month after Evol was buried, and she was a real honest-to-God whooper though they said it was pneumonia, my big-boned baby girl going blue-faced from too small a heart, so the doctor told me, and she hung on and hung on to her little life, but at last gave out and the day she died was a terror, like a long-tailed cross dragging itself over my heart, a worse pain than when I buried Evol, because I really did feel on the day she was lowered down in the June heat, I did feel that some live thing ticking inside me had stopped, just stopped like a dead clock looking as empty as a dead clock looks, so in a yearning kind of way I didn't want to ever let go of the ache of that emptiness because the ache kept the echo of her alive in me, which was a consolation, like whenever I needed to get consolation from the ache of the absence of Evol I went out to our old clearing, ducking through the dwarf pines and junipers and I talked to him inside my own mind, wishing he would talk to me, out there alone among the trees that have got their roots curled and humped out of the ground and one time I saw a spider in the throat of one of the roots which I took to be a sign of some new on-coming grappling in the heart, so I up and swallowed mother's tonic for the blood along with my Orifer Multi-Vitamins, swallowing hard on her sulphur and molasses, and I had all her other remedies, too, for ills and aches, my best being for Done Feet, taking one tablespoon of salt, one fig of tobacco, one pint of urine, all simmered and sponged on at bedtime, which was always good for a big laugh because anybody I knew of in town or down at Crudup's Mobile Home and Trailer Park, who was brought up with any brains at all and watched TV, was busy popping all the pills that they'd seen sold to them on television, Carter's Little Liver Pills and Templetons' TRC's, and Tylenol and Excederin, but Evol's cure for done feet was the best of all, and that was to sit down and do absolutely nothing and drain your mind of all distraction, an absolute draining until this light that was not a light you could see anything by began to well up in your body, a light like you get when you close your eyes completely shut, shut tight on a bright summer day, and you stare up toward the sun, and all that heat is full on your face and there's suddenly a bright light inside your eyelids but you can't see anything except your own little veins across the light. You just know that there's heat alive in you, the same way Evol came alive in me, and Evol also had his very own cure for the deadfall of loneliness, too, because he'd say,

"You just squat yourself down in the woods with a deck of cards and lay out a hand of solitaire on an old stump and sooner than you can say the word Solitude, somebody will lean over your shoulder telling you to put the Black queen on the Red king," Evol laughing and getting down on his haunches on the hillside that was ripening with rapeseed, naked and wearing only a long greatcoat in the spring, with tufts of sweet grass under the wild plum trees and pine cones that had fallen like charred birds with circles of windblown sand around their skeletons, and small white fists of flowers growing between the skeletons, and Evol said, "In the years gone by people were luckier, they knew that when awful things were done there were demons all over the place, creatures with eyes instead of breasts and one with only a huge foot and he slept in the shade of his foot, but we've got so damned well smart about ourselves that we no longer know who the demons are. Keep your eye on the owl. When he closes one eye he's the killer no one sees. The owl's got his eye on us. We can't blame anybody else for what happens, we can't blame anybody else because we've created death." He was sitting in the brush willows like a bird-watcher, except his eyes were fixed on a clump of clay as if he'd found a clue down there between his feet, a clue to what was troubling his mind. "It gets so bad," he said, "thinking about your own thoughts, that you can hear birds walking inside your own skull," and he was expecting me to be surprised, but I said birds inside your skull is nothing new to me because my grandma who'd married a Catholic had told me all about it, how the Holy Ghost had come as a bird who flew right to the inside of Mary's head through her ear and the Holy Ghost's words were His seed and what He said was the Word Jesus, and Evol said that that sure gave a whole new meaning to bird seed and bird calls and all the seed of all the birds calling around us, all the hawks and buzzards and bobolinks and redwing blackbirds down by the stream behind the hill, a stream that we'd dammed to make a wetland, a shallow black-colored lake full of stumps and fallen trunks where the bush thickened, always thickening around us, claiming back what was cleared years ago, the stones and gravel pushing up as fast as Hole-in-the-Woods and Sackett's Corners disappeared, and trying also to claim Mount Zion church, though I hadn't been in it for years, but had only seen it across the road from the trailer park, the bush claiming the old closed up cemetery and all those bones of our people who'd been sent back into the land, the cemetery cornered and confined by the growing junk pile fields and mobile homes jacked up on concrete blocks behind them, fields that became a smear, an ugly wide snail's smear of what's becoming lost to us all, the sweet land and the scrub land also gutted, with Evol lost and my child lost, my sweet Loanne who we'd called Loanne because of what I'd heard Evol say the day I first saw him when he said, "Lo Anne," as if that was my name, so we'd made it hers when she was born, but now all I had was the things bequeathed to me, the boon from my momma and daddy, this scrabbly patch of farm with its gravelly hill and mounds that sometimes seem to be a place where all the birdseed has been aborted and all of my hopes abased, this farm that was nonetheless the nearest I could come to the breathing lives that were lived and long since forgotten around here, and when I wanted to get close to those who were forgotten I walked back through the woods following the markers in the map of my mind, walking a branch of the Saugeen in the shallows, flushing chipmunks and coons and a hare, until I got to a closed-off stand of gleaming white dead elm trunks in a marsh that Evol had found for me, a blind in the woods that had been flooded out one year by beaver dams but now it was dried so the ground was covered by a thick weave and braiding of bleached rushes and long grass, a windless place, the black water in the pond just past the marsh heavy with lilies and floating pollen and wrecked drifting trees, and dragonflies pocked the air and some days I'd sit there till it was night wondering how far beyond welfare and the little bit of life insurance left to me through death, how far was I going to be able to go to make the ends and intentions of my own life meet, but still I felt calmer than ever before, strangely consoled by everything wrecked and windless around me, like it was a stillness of angels, and I remembered my daddy who'd always felt cornered telling me his favorite song, "If I had the wings of an angel, over these prison walls I would fly, I would fly to the arms of my darling and there I would willingly die," but it wasn't until just after Loanne died that the foundation at the corner of the house suddenly showed up sopping wet, what with under-ground water sweating through the stone, and Burly Crudup, who'd built the mobile home trailer park down along the town line road where Evol had sometimes worked, Burly came by because he is a witcher, carrying his apple branch, and he set to witching for the water. It wasn't till then that I truly felt in my marrow how much I longed to be here despite all the deaths now fastened to me and to what he rightly called my crabbed land, watching the branch in his hands wrench and dip to the earth and he said, "There's a crick, a source down there," and he handed me the branch, saying just like Evol had said about his daddy, "Some have the gift," as I held it out from my belly and it whipped down and the bark tore in my hands. "I mind you don't need me," he said, "at least not to tap into your own springwater," laying his hand on my shoulder, and I laughed and laughed and the next day I walked the whole puzzle of clearings, crisscrossing and tracking the veins that were a web of water, reading the map of the land's body, and later in the evening sitting at home watching the fieldstones float weightless in the air around a fire in the fireplace, I felt at last a real yielding to all my scrub acres, a yielding to my own stone picker dead, like I was saying a prayer of sorrow that made me joyful, a prayer for my own poor child who had shed this world with a whoop, and for Evol too, who was always trying to get the hang of things so that he could have his way with how he lived, have his own sweet way with his own life, which is what he did at last, creating death where he stood, but the place I had to stand, planted now on my own two feet, is where I learned exactly how I am when things get worst, because I learned that a grace abounds in the earth where darkness lies and is held in a crystal web of water, a web that I can see clearer than clear which means the light in my mind is as cold as cold can be.

The Salem Letters

·

Diane Keating

April 6, 1692
After the waggon left for Jail

To my Mistress Elizabeth Proctor,
    I be out on the stoop scraping plattes into the slop
pail when I heerd the wheels clanging over the froz'n mudd
& dung of the barneyard. Shading my eyes from the sun I
stood in the doorwaie to watch you & Mr. Proctor drive off.
While I be staring at the back of your hooded cloak & his
huge shoalders my week'r eye began drifting upward so at
the same time I be glimsing tops of trees & blue skie.
    Thats when th'Angels appeer'd at the edge of my
sight. Thousands of them. Dancing acrosse th'Heavens.
Dancing like a path of sunlight across water.
    I fell to my nees. Cover'd my face with my armes.
But 'twas as tho I be seeing with my Soule. Befor me rised
up a bull bigg'r than Gallows Hill with hornes the shape of
new moons. Chained to his shoalders a mightie bird of prey
be ripping at his flesh.
    Then it all disappeer'd in a whirlwind of fethers &

blood & I fellt words like handes of the Lord being laied upon my hed — Feer not, Mary, they saied, thou hast found favour with the Lord. Thru thee the unseen shall be seen. Thru thee the bound shall be freed.

Next I remember I be lieing on my back in a puddel from the overturn'd slop buckett & staring up at the skie thru chinks in the roof.

Rite awaie I know'd 'twas a Revelashun cuz of the dazzeling dark befor my eyes. Also I know'd, Mrs. Proctor, that the bull chained to the bird of prey be Mr. Proctor chained to you. Husband to wife. Erthe to Hell.

With my heart pounding hard as hoofs I pickt up my sopping skirt & ran outside. I want'd to warn Mr. Proctor to wait for the Constabul. Not to take you by himself to Jail. Altho I ran all the waie to the gate the waggon be too farr downe the road for him to hear me calling.

After much thot & pray'r I hav decided, Mrs. Proctor, to tell you of my vishun. 'Tis a warning to you as much a promise to me. Take heed. Tho I am only eighteen and your servant I am speshull. The Lord has chosen me to reveel your witchcraft.

When my left eyeball comes unbound I hav seconde sight. I can see th'invisibel world bulging in from th'edges of thinges. You be scared of what I will find out. Thats why you beet me 'bout the hed saieing eyes must work together same as ox'n in a yoke. That why you tell everyone my eye be a signe of weeknesse in the hed and not to take serieusly what I be seeing.

But now I am not alonne. Them other girls hav cried out at you. Now they will beleev that when you be lifting your arme to beat me I truely didd see a brown growth like a nippel in your arm pitt. Abbie saies while you be in Jail it will be prick't with a needel & if there be no sensashun that proves 'tis a witches teat for suckeling imps & demons.

For a long time peepul have suspecked that magpie

of yourn, Mrs. Proctor, be a demon helper. 'Tis unnatural for a wild bird to swoop out of nowhere & perch on a personnes shoalder.

My Soule shivers to think of it. The waie it glares with them round black eyes — lifeless as beeds sewn to the sides of its hed — while chatt'ring in your ear a language without words. A language only you understand.

In a few daies there will be a Heering to decide if the evidence against you warrants a trial at the Court of Oyer & Terminer. Altho I am one of those you torment Mr. Proctor will not allow me to go. He saies us girls be acting madd as March hares to get attenshun & if tied to our spinning wheels we will be cured fast enuff.

Since you both refused to attend the Heering for them oth'r three witches you did not see how we swoon'd & writh'd & howl'd when the accused be brot in. The magistrates called us bloodhounds of the Lord.

Soon everyone between Salem & Boston shall know who I am. Then the Governor himself shall listen to me. Even Mr. Proctor. Tho since you be accused of witchcraft he does not speek but lookes unutterabel thinges at me. Eech time I feel kikt in th'head.

> In truth & trust
> I remain your servant
> Mary Warren

April 9, 1692
After Morning Prayers

To my mistress Elizabeth Proctor,
Now that Mr. Proctor be taking a pacquet of vitalls every daie to the Jailhouse 'tis eesy to slip in your letters. He warn'd me not to tell anyone — not even the littel

ones — so he must hav brib'd the guard. I hav much to saie & you best not laff like you alwaies donne when I spoke the truth to you. Speshully I hated how — if Mr. Proctor be 'round — you would roll your eyes & chuckel so it seem'd you be indulging me. And that soft hollow chuckelling, Mrs. Proctor, be like an echo of your magpie. 'Tis not a human sound.

Abbie agrees with me. She been here yesterdaie for tea the haires on her armes stood up when she herd the magpies evil laffing in the branches of the bigge elm. That bird deserves to be hanged she cried out. Without a dowt,

Mrs. Proctor, you will soon be hanged & I donn't want you crying out at me when meeting the Lord, face to face, for your Final Reckoning.

Since the Revelashun I no longer feer you. With the help of th'Almightie I shall stopp you from destroying Mr. Proctor. I know how much you feer him. His animal strength. His animal lawes. Being almost seven feet high he alwaies gettes his own waie. Peepul shake their head & saie he be more like Samson than Solomon.

I beleev them. I beleev he be the strong'st man next to God. Not alwaies good but then why should he be? God be not good. God be God. And you Mrs. Proctor? You be like Delilah. You want to find the secrett of his power. Thats why you be pacting with the Devil tho Mr. Proctor donnt beleev it. He beleevs only what he sees.

I remember the first time I seen your specter self. 'Twas last summer after you rode off to a Quilting Bee on the Meetinghouse Green. An xcuse, Mr. Proctor saied, for gathering heersaie from the other goodwives. Tho I had not left the farme for som months you told me to staie with the babee who be weak'nd by the Bloody Flux.

While heeting water in the bigg iron cauldron to wash its clouts & coverlettes my wand'ring left eye cawt somethinge moving. I thot your cloake hung by the open door be blowing in the wind. But no, Mrs, Proctor, 'twas your specter. Same as you but loos'r looking as tho your bones be made of jelly.

As you slid toward me I seen your eyes be emptie holes. Your face twist'd & white like it be burnt by acid. My holl'ring brot Mr. Proctor running from the barne. As I throw'd myselfe into his armes I fellt you strangeling me. Your handes on my neck greesy & cold as intestines pull'd from a fresh kill'd goat.

Mr. Proctor must hav been standing on the hem of my skirt cuz when he tried to push me awaie he rippt it. I lost my balance & fell to the floor with him on top of me. Thats when your specter self crosst my legges with so much force they poppt out of joint & Mr. Proctor for all his strength could not uncrosse them. Not without breaking them he saied.

Even then he wouldn't beleev me. Even when I point'd to your specter standing beside him he saied 'twas his shaddowe. Threten'd to ram a hott pok'r down my throate if I diddnt stopp screeming your name.

Thats why now I be too scared to tell him 'bout the Revelashun. For sure he would wopp me. Perhaps send me awaie.

Later
After Cockshut

I am sitting near the winddowe listening for Mr. Proctors hors. The only sounds be the bull kiking at the slattes of his small stall & the calling of a whip-poor-will down by the creek. Makes me bone lonely to hear it.

Mr. Proctor saies its wisiling be an omen the frost has gon from the ground. Time to start plowing but he & the two old'st nev'r be here. They ride farr as Ipswich trying to gett persons to signe a petishun saieing you be a dilligent attend'r upon Gods Holy Ordinances.

Wonnt do no good, Mrs. Proctor. Again this after-noon th'Almightie reveel'd He be on my side by helping me find that strawe doll of yourn.

I be in the smoakhouse unhooking a legge of bacon for dinner when I seen it wedg'd in a crack between chimney & wall. 'Twas wearing clowthes made from Mr. Proctors shirt & the pinnes thru its body be winded with his graye haires.

I wager you leern'd the Black Artes from your Grandma who be accus'd of witchcraft twentie yeares ago. Tho the charge be droppt many people in Salem remember & saie — where theres smoak theres fire.

Perhaps thats why Mr. Proctor wonnt lett me com to the Heering & see you xamined by them Magistrates. He hates their high-fallutin waies. Powder'd pigges in wigges he calls them.

He must be scared I will cry out in publick just like that starkel'd nitwitt daughter of Reverent Parris cried out on their slave & then fell into a fitt. Abie tell'd me she laie on the floor gasping & writhing like a long white fish thrown up on the shore.

Since you be taken to jail, Mrs. Proctor, the wave of afflict'd girles growes bigg'r. They saie it be cuz erly April comes midwaie between winter & summer solstis when the influence of the moon be the great'st.

Mrs. Proctor save yourself. Admitt to the blastings. The worst being Goodwife Putnams babee who died in the womb. The midwife told Goodwife Jacobs who told her ser-vant Sarah, my friend, that while she be pulling the babee out by the legges they broke off — shrivell'd as the forkt root of mandrake — but the wee blind face be perfect as a pansy. And that blue.

Everyone agrees 'twas you who blasted it. Or else why at the Burial did that magpie of yourn keep chatt'ring

& chorteling from high on a neerbye tree. No one could stopp themselves from listening. Like in a waking dream they forgot what they be doing & follow'd it from tree to tree. Reverent Parris & Goodwife Putnam be left alonne to low'r the coffin. Confess, Mrs. Proctor, that Satan took you for his bride. The Lord shall forgive you. So shall I. So shall all of Salem — town & village. Confess & they shant hang you. They knowe we be born damn'd. All of us lost from the Lord. Lost as leeves that loosn'd from a tree be blowing forever in the wind.

> With trust & hope
> Mary Warren
> Bloodhound of the Lord

April 10, 1692
Forenoon
Sitting on the stoop

To My Mistress,

The first warm breezes be coming from the West. Day & Night I heer them slith'ring thru the willows & now the budds be the sise of a mouses ear. Your littel ones be on the creek bank cutting branches to feed the bull. I can heer 'em laff abov the peep of froglings and the faroff ringing of an axe. Must be Mr. Sheldon cleering land on the other side of Gallows Hill.

Erly this morn while hanging out the wash I pegg'd my petticoat to Mr. Proctors breeches. As I be watching them cling & sway in the wind — dancing togeth'r as we nev'r can — I glim'st out of the corner of my week eyeflashes of hellgreen flammes by the back steppes. Turn'd out 'twas crocus leeves poking up from dirty crusts of snowe. As I pickt the wee purple blooms I thot of them sleeping curl'd in their bulbs all winter. Then I thot of my heart sleeping curl'd in my body. Waiting like these flow'rs donne for the warmth of the sun. Waiting for Mr. Proctor.

Since you be in jail eech time I put my hand on my conshence it comes out black as pitch. I must confess I love Mr. Proctor. Thats the truth. Last week I tell'd him when he looks at me I go week as a rained-on bee. He laff'd & laff'd & ask'd me if I tell'd you.

I donnt care, Mrs. Proctor, I knowe he loves me even tho he donnt showe it. He cannt help him selfe. The Lord ordain'd it. Diddnt He give me the gift of seeing the visibel & th'invisibel meeting at th'edges of my sight? That be so I could reveel your witchcraft.

Take heed Mrs. Proctor. 'Tis no sinne to cheet the Devil. Old Hornie, Mr. Proctor calls him.

Yours truthfully
Mary Warren
Bloodhound of the Lord

April 11, 1692
Spring Feest Daie

Dear Mrs. Proctor,

All night I toss't & turn'd like butter in a churn. Theres no relying on a starrie evening to giv one plesant dreems.

Donn't recall much xcept the wind singing save him save him as I soared abov the treetops. 'Twas night but the moon had stopp't shining. The starres be round white stones & I pluck't one out of the skie as I flied bye. In front of me Gallows Hill rise into a dark platform. Perching on top of the Hanging Tree I seen your littel ones tied to a low'r branch. Their naked white bodies dangeling like geese with broken neckes.

On the ground beneath them you be squatting, Mrs. Proctor, gnawing on a dogge bone. Just as I reech't out to droppe the ded starre on your hed the tree start'd to shake & I woke to Mr. Proctors footsteppes on the stairs. Even in his stockings he qwakes the howse. That heavy menacing walk of his'n alwaies seems 'bout to gather into a rush.

This be the third morn Mr. Proctor has rode awaie befor the cock crow'd. So farr twentie-seven persons sign'd th petishun on your behalf. But nobodie from Salem village. They saie Mr. Proctor ownes 4 howses & 700 acres of the best lands & still he donn't paie his ministrie tax.

Two daies ago Reverent Parris stopp't him on the Village Green & saied to xpect a heavy fine. They argued & Mr. Proctor lost his temp'r. Poking the Reverent in the chest with his forefinger he saied no man whose eyebrows meet could be trust'd. Not even an ordain'd Minister.

After the Reverent yell'd that he be a devilish churl-ish uncivil dogge Mr. Proctor accus'd him of being mor interest'd in his salarie than in saving Soules.

Then the Reverent clasp't his handes togeth'r & throw'd back his hed crying O Lord protect us from blas-feemers. At that moment he be shat on from above by a big pidgin. Nobodie could stopp themselves from laffing. Abbie who been there saied the Reverent grow'd greenlooking as an erly apple & seem'd 'bout to vomitt. Todaie she tell'd me he plannes to file for sland'r. Being the Reverents neece she knowes all 'bout the goings-on at the Parsonage. And being best friends we tell eech oth'r everythinge.

Did you remember, Mrs. Proctor, this be the annual Spring Feest Daie to celebrate the end of our long winter & the incoming of shippes with salt & sugar & foreign news? They saie Governor Phipps return'd after five yeares of per-swading King James to giv our colony a new charter.

I am longing to go to the Meeting-Howse but Mr.

Proctor saies the maddness of one be making many madd. He forbiddes me to take the littel ones.

Since you be gon they keep crying off & on. They paie me no heed. Mor like littel caged animales they eet what they will & sleep where they fall. They cann't be missing you, Mrs. Proctor, cuz you never be 'round. You staied all daie in front of the house overseeing the Taverne Room. Gossiping with the men.

I nev'r told you this but Abbie overherd Mrs. Parris saie your licents as a taverne keep'r might be revoked even tho the front roome be the only Ordinarie to wet one's whistle between town & village.

Did you knowe Mr. Ruckes report'd you to the town council? He tell'd them when he couldnn't paie for his fifth pint of cider you demanded his gold tooth. Made him yank it out. Abbie saies Mrs. Parris claims you be lowe as a Sodomite woman who did nothinge but eet & drink & sell & plant & build.

Mrs. Proctor why donnt you paie attenshun to what peepul saie 'bout you? Speshully to what I saie. You never com to the Meeting-Howse with Mr. Proctor & me & the littel ones. On Lecture Daies you be too busy in the Ordinarie. To Labour be to pray you alwaies saied.

On the Sabbath you be too tired xcept it be a Feest Daie. Then you would gett gussied up in that wool'n cloak you order'd from Boston & them leather gloves with the pearl buttons.

Do you knowe what Abbie tell'd me the goodwives saied when they seen you gathering up the front of your skirt & flouncing up the steppes to the Meeting-Howse? They saied ill-gott'n, ill-spent.

There still be time to sav your Soule. Confess, Mrs. Proctor. Confess that the Devil holds you in the hollow of his hande. Confess befor his hande closes into a fist & you be broken to bits like a clod of erthe.

In truth & loyalty,
Mary Warren
Bloodhound of the Lord

April 12,1692
After boiling up
deer fat for candels

Dear Mrs. Proctor,

For over two winters I hav been living in your shaddowe under the roof of a man who be neither my father nor
my husband. Alwaies I be in the back of the housedoing a
wifes chores. Waiting for Mr. Proctor. Waiting since the daie
I arriv'd & he lift'd me out of the waggon. Staring at me
with them eyes — black & wild as any hunting animal —
while my heart flippt-floppt like a scaredbird in a cage.

Do you remember the first winter, Mrs. Proctor? In
the evenings after th'Ordinarie closed & the littel ones been
in bedde I would quilt on the bigg frame in the corner of
the middelroom while Mr. Proctor & you sat in the warmth
of th'inglenook. He in his deep chair whitteling them flee
trappes we wear'd 'round our neckes. You in your rocker
clucking over the book where the tavern ernings be recorded.

You wouldn't knowe how I used to stare at Mr.
Proctor. Outlined in the crimson glowe of the fire he be so
strong & solitarie & solem looking. Like the Angel who
pour'd the Lords Seeds into Marys ear.

Do you remember Mrs. Proctor? How you would be
clapperclawing about something that happen'd in the
Taverne when he would reach over & tapp your nee.
Elizabeth, he would saie, you could talk the Devil out of a
witches howse. Then you would look at eech other & smile.
You diddnt knowe Mrs. Proctor how that look — that smile

— splitt my heart in two. Just like one of them aspens behind the howse splitting in the cold. Its dry crack echoing from tree to tree.

Even after all this time when I heer his stamping outside the backe door — three times with eech boot to knock off the mudd or snowe — I cann no mor stoppe my heart from pounding than a dogge upon his masters return cann stoppe his wagging tail.

Specially in winter when he has been hunting cuz then I gett to rubb polecatt oil onto his feete to cure the rheumatisme. Who would guess with his face weather riven'd as a hilltop that his feete be so pink & smooth & warm. Like fresh skinn'd rabbits in my handes.

I wager you haven't seen the scarr — shaped like a wee clov'n hoof — on the outside of his left foot. Nobodie but me knowes he be born with six toes. His Mama birth'd alonne while hiding in a root cellar during an Indian raid. Feering they would saie she been diddel'd by a demon she bit off the xtra toe. Easie as eating pie she tell'd Mr. Proctor.

Mrs. Proctor, do you remember the Feest Daie last New Years? We be going to the Corys pigge roast but the sleigh been too full. I saied that I would ride ov'r with Mr. Proctor when he got backe from deer hunting.

Upon heering his hounds I closed the shutters & lit the candels. Then I took off my bonnet & lett out my haire. I knowe you warn'd me to keep my head cover'd cuz my haire be redd. You alwaies be saieing Judas had haire redd'r than fire.

But I donn't care. Mr. Proctor cann nev'r keep his eyes off me when my haire be sett free. This be specially true last News Year Feest. When he came in I be standing with my back to the fire. My haire falling 'round me soft & heavie & long like a shawl. All the time he be taking off his cloak & hat he stared at me. Ask't me what happen'd that my eyes had grow'd mor green than a catte stalking a mouse. I giv'd no reply. Just smil'd.

Soon as he sat in his chair by the hearth I nellt to pull off his bootes & stockings. Then hidd'n by my haire I slowly caresst his feet while I rubb'd in the warm oil. He paied no heed. The only sound been the crackel of the fire & the wethercock screeking as it turn'd on the roof.

Thinking how Mary show'd her love by kissing the feet of Jesus I began gently to run my tongue along his soles. And then to mouthe his toes as I snugell'd his feet like a newborn babee to my breasts.

I thot the moaning been the wind coming thru the keyhole of the doore but 'twas Mr. Proctor. Suddenly he giv'd a slite shudder & grabbing my haire yank'd back my hed. I remember how he kept mutt'ring so sweet an evil ov'r & ov'r as he be spitting in my face & then covering it with kisses. It fellt as tho a burning arrowe peerc'd my heart — melting it like hott wax into my bowelles. Darling, I wisper'd, pressing clos'r to him. He jumpt up. Kickt me awaie. I be scared cuz his face had gon white as leprosy. When I start'd crieing he pickt up the spinning wheel & smash'd it against the wall.   You be the gatewaie to Hell, he yell'd, charging out of the howse.

When I heerd his hors galloping awaie I be certain he had gon to sign a warrant for my arrest as a harlott. I tried to pray for my sinne but when I closed my eyes I seen flammes. And the mor hot it grow'd the mor I want'd Mr. Proctor.

At sundowne he return'd with you & the littel ones. Tho he pretended nothinge had gon on I could feel his coal black eyes burning into me with all the pent up force of Lucifers last look at the Lord.

You nev'r notis'd but ever since that daie, Mrs. Proctor, I havnt been abel to look you in th'eyes for feer you would see how I yearn'd for him. But now that I hav been bless'd with the Vishun I need not feer breaking the Ten

Commandments. In my armes — with my lippes — I shall comfort Mr. Proctor. Yea, tho he be made to walk thru vallies of dry bones & dust I shall be with him. For the heart, Mrs Proctor, the heart cannot be divided from the flesh.

Yours truthfully
Mary Warren
Bloodhound of the Lord

April 13, 1692
Moon on the rise

Dear Mrs. Proctor,

All daie I diddn't gett a minute to write. Besides my usual duties I steep'd peppermint leaves to make a Poshun Physick cuz the littel ones be taking a Cold.

I heer them now snuffeling in their sleep like piggelettes with their snouts in a troff of corn meal & lopper'd milk. Mr. Proctor be restless too. I heer him abov my hed thrashing about the bedde like the bull in his stall befor the Spring mating. Three more daies 'til your Heering, Mrs. Proctor. They saie you shall hang befor the first reeping of oats.

Since you be tak'n awaie Mr. Proctor wont staie alonne with me in the same roome or even look at me when I ask him something. He alwaies hunches forward with his hed lower'd as tho about to charge. How powerful his emoshuns be. Like beests inside him. Fierce black beests pacing the cage of his loins.

Now that the Lords power has broke forth in me I cann make my own lawes. Thats why tonight I shall concockt a Lov Poshun. 'Twas Tituba who taut me. At her Heering last week she confess't to being a witch. Must be you, Mrs. Proctor, who forc't her to sign the Black Book. Mr. Proctor saies 'tis a lie she made up so not to be hanged.

All she donne last Fall when I secretly vissit'd her with Mercy & them other maidservants been to tell our fortunes with cards. Thats why when I saied I wanted som magic to put fire in the loins of an old'r man she shook her hed & spatt into the hearth. I can still see the tobacco jus dribbeling out of the corners of her mouthe as she hiss't old love cold love, calf love half love.

However she chang'd her mind when I show'd her the prettie bodkin I found on the Taverne floor. Grabbing it out of my hande she lock't it in a carv'd ebonie box which once belong'd to her Pappy when he be King of a Southern Sea Island.

Tituba saied the Lov Poshun must be made at midnight when the moon be rising. To begin I must protect the place where I will make it with a circul of small white pebbels. Next I must prick my finger & let seven droppes of blood fall on a peese of clowthing upon which I hav sweat'd. Then I must set fire to it & while it be burnning sprinkel in a lock of my haire & nail parings from my fingers & toes. Finally — befor the moon rises againe — th'ash must be mix't into the food of the desired one.

Shivers my Soule to think that once Mr. Proctor eets the Lov Poshun part of me shall be inside him. I shall be clos'r than you hav ever been, Mrs. Proctor. Clos'r than touch even tho I cannt touch him.

A few hours lat'r
The same night

While waiting for th'ash to cool I thot to finish this lett'r so I cann hide it in the food pacquet Mr. Proctor will bring to you tomorrowe. He would whopp me for sure if he found out about the Lov Poshun. He would saie to leeve that crazie flimflam for the Papists & Quak'rs.

However you knowe bett'r, Mrs. Proctor. You knowe

my making of the Lov Poshun be not witch'ry cuz it comes out of lov. Perhaps I should not reveel so much. I alwaies be talking to you inside my hed but the wordes echo like they be in a empty cavern & I cann't think strait. When I write the wordes down it all comes cleer & I knowe I be doing the Lords Will.

Anywaie you cann't show these letters without divulging that you be getting illegal pacquets. Then peepul will turn against you & Mr. Proctor will get no mor signatures for his petishun.

Much later
The same night

Unabel to sleep I trimm'd a candelwick so I cann add a note to this letter.

Befor going to bedde I went out for an armfull of wood to bank the fire. For the first time this Spring I cot the odoure of appel blossoms. In th'orchard the patches of moonlight sparkel'd like fresh fall'n snowe.

Out of the corner of my loose eye I glims't figures in graye capes dancing widdershins 'round th'orchard. I couldn't see any faces but your flatt feet giv'd you awaie Mrs. Proctor. Made you clumsie as a hoofbound mare. For sure it be a Witches Sabbat.

I start'd yelling as lowd as I could. Mr. Proctor came running with his muskett but when he seen where I point'd he cuff'd the side of my hed 'Twas nothinge but mist, he saied, wafting in & out of the trees. Thats when I began to choak, Mrs. Proctor, as tho I be breathing in smoak & I know'd 'twas you smoth'ring me.

I must hav lost my senes cuz next I recall Mr. Proctor be lifting a candelstick to look at me as I laie on my bedde. Elizabeths right, he saied, your eyes be so week I am surpriz'd you can tell a tea pott from a chamber pott.

I paied no heed cuz at leest he be looking & speeking to me. While he scolded I could see abov the candels flamme the crease — jagg'd as a lightning bolt — cutting downe the middel of his forhead. The crease he saies came the daie he marry'd you, Mrs. Proctor. Thats why I grabb'd his arme & pointing at his browe cried — Beware the mark of the Devils bride. But he jerk't awaie. Stomping out of the room he shot a look over his shoalder that almost destroy'd me. As tho it be me not you, Mrs. Proctor, who has becom the embodiement of Evil.

Tomorrow morn I shall visit your jailer & ask that irons be placed on your armes & legges to stoppe your specter from coming to torment me. Remember I hav an eye that never sleeps.

> Yours truthfully
> Mary Warren
> Bloodhound of the Lord

April 14, 1692
Erly Afternoon
Gloomie but no clowds

Dear Mrs. Proctor,

'Tis a qweer daie. The skie ting'd yellowe. The sun turning the coloure of brass while wolves on the farr side of Blind Hole Swampe howl as tho it be a full moon. You should see Mr. Proctors dogges — tether'd to the gate post — barking & straining on their ropes when they heer them. Makes me laff to see them lunging 'round & 'round on their hind legges. Like dwarves with long pointy noses dancing the Maypole. Soon as Mr. Proctor left this morn I rode into Town to speek to the Jailor 'bout chaining you. He tell'd me at dawne you & five oth'r accus'd women be tak'n by oxcart to the Boston Jail. Seems th'outburst of witchcraft has ris'n to such a tidal wave that the Salem Jail be filled. Since it be a halfdaie ride to Boston I am sure Mr. Proctor will not vissit as often. Fortunately the Jailor saied the condishuns be bett'r in a larg'r jail.

When I return'd from town the littel ones tell'd me the horses wonnt eet & the hennes be flapping 'bout refusing to laie. John Junior saied the cowes in the back pasture be wandering in circuls with their tongues lolling out in the most frightfull manner. He thinks it comes from a witches malice. The littel ones be afraide. But not me. I am too blythsom.

This morn Mr. Proctor ate the Lov Poshun. I mix't it in his porridge & then put on xtra creem & sugar. As usual he rode off without looking or speeking to me. Dont matter cuz he only likes talking to his hors & hounds anywaie. Tonight will be different. I will witness the manifestashun of his lov. Thinking of it I cannt stopp hugging myselfe & dancing 'round like them roped dogges. Happiness be bursting out all over me. Same as Spring bursting out of th'erthe. Same as the time Mr. Proctor slapp't my bottom while I be picking up the milk pailes. Called me his buxom bonnie maid.

Afterwards at the dinner table — do you recall Mrs. Proctor? — you ask't why a flow'r garden be blooming in my face. Accus'd me of sneeking off with one of them Porter boys. Then wisper'd to Mr. Proctor that it be xpect'd from someone father'd by the wind. I grow'd so angry I diddn't notis that under the table I be stabbing a fork into my arme. Not till I seen the bloode.

Some daies later when I be visiting Abbie at the Parsonnage Reverent Parris seen the marks on my arme. He thot they came from your specter self biting me. I tried to tell him the truth, Mrs. Proctor, but he wouldnt listen. Saied I be too valuabel a witness to talk gibb'rish.

Since I be the first you afflict'd heds turn when I enter the Meeting-Howse. Now peepul talk to my face. Not to my backe.

I am telling you this, Mrs. Proctor, cuz I want you to understand that I would not be your servant if I be not orphan'd. I com from a proper family. I can read & write. Altho Pa died befor I be born I know'd his Grandpa been a Knight in Old England.

I hav made it cleer to everyone that no member of my family ever practis'd the Evil Artes. Not here or in Old England. Whereas everybody saies you be resembelling mor & mor that Grandma of yourn who been accus'd of witch-craft. 'Tis your laff, they saie, so lowe & fullsom. And the waie you till't your hed. Admitt it Mrs. Proctor. The seeds be in your bloode.

Later
After the quake

When it happen'd I be working in the herb garden cuz Tituba once tell'd me that plantes hav mor power if planted at th'houre when daie & night divide.

As I be poking holes to droppe in the seeds of colts-foot & sweet cicely it turn'd so quiet I almost heer'd the worms creeping. Even the sparrows pecking in the hors dung stoppt titt'ring & every new leef on the willow by the stable door hung heavy & dull as a nail.

Thinking 'twas the stillness befor a storm I look'd up. Th'underheaven be cleer & dark purpel. All the breath seem'd suck'd out of th'aire so smoak from the citchin chim-ney rolled along the roofe.

Suddenly my wondering eye cot a slite movement in the woods at th'edge of the pasture. I thot 'twas the Devil com to tempt me but 'twas Mr. Proctor staring at me while branches sprout'd like antlers from behind his hed. Over his shoalder a ded boar be slung. Bloode dropping from its mouthe. Carefully Mr. Proctor laied it downe. All the time he be staring at me. His face pinch'd & white with some kind of inn'r agony.

As tho a giant hand be drawing us togeth'r we moved slowly acrosse the pasture till we be standing so close I fellt his breathe on my face. Then his lippes be on mine. His fingers digging into my armes. Thats when the ground trembell'd. A kind of shudder like the flesh of a cowe just as it be kill't.

I clung to Mr. Proctor while the hounds cring'd against us wimpering. The shaking grow'd worse & I thot for sure the ded be fighting among themselves. I closed my eyes & try'd to pray while Mr. Proctor held me so hard I heerd his heart pounding. Pounding fast as the hooves of the cowes stampeeding passt us to the barne.

Then from far awaie I heerd the groaning and snapping of branches. The thrumming of winges. Thousands of winges. As tho all the saints be bringing Heav'n down to erthe.

Pressing my eyes mor tightly shutt I tried againe to pray. But Mr. Proctor be biting my throat. His handes under my skirt sqweezing my thighs. Spreding them apart as we tumbel'd downe. Beneath us the ground swell'd into waves as tho we laie on the deck of a shippe during a storme.

Suddenly clowthes be pull'd awaie. O the paine as he broke into my body. An Angel in flammes. Fire flowing out of his mouthe. Nev'r have I fellt mor alive. Blood running in a stream of hot lava. Our bodies burning togeth'r. Our Soules one.

Being outside all feeling I diddn't knowe wheth'r I be ded or alive. On erthe or in Heav'n.

When at last I open'd my eyes 'twas night & I be lieing alonne in the long grass at th'edge of the pasture. The qwaking had stopp't but still there be the thrumming of winges like the distant rumbel of thund'r.

Looking up I seen every bird everywhere had tak'n to th'aire in a whirling clowd that cover'd the skie so it be dark as a night with no moon. Dark as th'Abyss belowe th'erthe. But when I tried to get up I found my bones cold & heavy as chaines piled upon the ground.

In the distance Mr. Proctors white shirt be floating like a ghost in the direcshun of the howse. I could heer the wailing of the littel ones.

For som time I laie like a Zombi with my hed bury'd in Mr. Proctors stain'd coat. In the rich smell of the boars blood mixt with his sweat. Then as the whirlwind of fethers rushing abov me grow'd less my mind cleer'd & I recall'd the Revelashun. Now it be coming true.

I struggel'd to my nees to giv praise to th'Almightie. I donn't knowe how long I be praying but when I open'd my eyes the skie been empty xcept for a lone starre blinking abov the roofe & the smoak rising from the citchin chimney. Rising strait as a pillar of stone.

As I walked back to the howse everythinge 'round me giv'd off a kind of rainbow glowe. Like I been the first that the Lord created. My body so bursting with His Glory Seeds that eech foot cried out Halelujah as I pick't it up & Amen as I plac'd it downe on the firm unmoving ground.

Donnt worry, Mrs. Proctor, no harm came to the littel ones. The only damage donne to the farme be brok'n winddowes caws'd by stones falling out of the chimney & the brass sundial in the garden that splitt in two. Mr. Proctor saies 'tis a sign that Eternity be all that matters. But now that our Soules be merg'd what importance can time hav?

Most truthfully yours
Mary Warren
Chos'n by the Lord

April 15, 1692
Evening
Waiting for Mr. Proctor

My Dear Mrs. Proctor,

Everyone be wond'ring what it means that th'erthe only qwaked along the coast between Reading & Topsfield. The worst calamity occur'd in Salem Town where two peepul and a dogge be kill't by falling bricks. Beware, Mrs. Proctor, cuz they saie the next qwake will run south thru Boston.

Reverent Parris call'd for an alldaie religious service. The whole village turn'd out. Even Mr. Proctor. Seems people like animals flock together when they be afraide.

The Meeting-Howse been crowded & hot. Stank of feer like a tub of rancid butter. Tho the Reverent preeched for two houres in the morning & three houres in th'afternoon not once did the Tithingman hav to wacke the back of that wiggeling Porter boy with his long staff or tie a foxtail on th'end of it to tickel the face of dozing ole Goodwife Nurse.

During the dinner break at Ingersolls Taverne everyone be dismal. Shaking heds & talking lowe they agree'd nothinge could be mor awefull then th'erthe crumbelling to peeses beneath their feet. 'Tis wors, they saied, than the news from a travelling tink'r that 15 hundred Iroquois & French be discover'd on our back borders.

Reverent Parris warn'd us from the pulpitt that an ertheqwake has portenshus significance. Diddn't it occur when Christ died on the Crosse & againe when He be Resurrect'd? They saie an ertheqwake be caws'd by the Hand of the Lord striking the Heavenly Bells. The sound vibrating thru th'aire be what makes th'erthe shake. And yesterdaie at sundowne I knowe as sure as I be sitting right nowe in your rocker, Mrs. Proctor, that them Heavenly Bells strike for Mr.

Proctor & me.

Altho we been in the same company all daie not a look or a word passt between us. Nonetheless there be a kind of force drawing us together. At the socialls between sermons we would be pull'd 'round peepul till we stood backe to backe. But if by chance we turn'd & brush'd shoalders we would be flung apart. Then slowly drawn together againe.

'Tis well after cockshut & Mr. Proctor hasn't return'd. I hope the moon be brite enuff to light his waie. He stay'd behind at the Meeting-Howse to join a gath'ring of Selectmen. They will decide if the village militia needs mor ammunishun in case of an Indian attack.

It seems everyone in Salem be too panick't 'bout th' ertheqwake to consern themselves. Everyone but me. What do I care if theres solid ground beneath my feet. Mr. Proctors my world. All else be fleeting. Just like the shaddowes I be watching flick'r along the citchin wall when the fire flares.

The littel ones be in bedde. I cannt sleep. Tonight when Mr. Proctor & I be alone we shall speek to eech other. Touch eech other. Writing these wordes fans the flammes of my lov. My heart calling out. Singing like a robin after a rain. Singing cuz it knowes where theres lov, Mrs. Proctor, theres no difference between good & evil. Or else why would the Pillars of Heaven be based in the Abyss. The Abyss that Mr. Proctor & I open'd up. And ov'r which our rainbowe be curving.

Much later the same night

When I heerd Mr. Proctor pulling off his boots in the stoop my handes began to shake so bad I couldnt light the candels. Soon as he enter'd I knowed somethinge be wronge. He stumbel'd passt me. Hed bent. Right arme folded acrosse his chest with his hand covering his heart.

I want'd to speek but my hed went stupid as a cabbage & I diddn't knowe what to saie. Without glansing toward me or taking off his hat so I could see his face he moved stiff & slowe as a sleepwalker acrosse the citchin & up the staires.

All night he be pacing up & downe the bedderoom xcept when a small thud tells me has fall'n to his nees to pray. Not once has he call'd for me.

All night I be sitting here in your rocker, Mrs. Proctor, thinking 'bout the Heering tomorrowe. In the morn I must reveel to Mr. Proctor how the Lord chose me to sav him from your Evil Arts. He must allow me to giv witness.

While planning my wordes I be ripping apart & remaking that bodice of yourn with the French lace. You tell'd me you would nev'r wear it againe when Mrs. Putnam after a Service saied you be putting on so much wate you look 'bout as combly as a cowe in a cage.

Do you remember that daie Mrs. Proctor? 'Twas when a Quak'r man be lock't in stocks on the Meeting-Howse Green & Reverent Parris preech'd from a fameus book that saied if th'invisibel world cannt be prov'n we shall hav no Christ but a light within & no Heav'n but a Frame of mind. The Quak'rs, the Reverent tell'd us, be blasfemus Sadducces cuz they donnt beleev th'invisibel world be real & feelabel to the flesh.

Since you be gon I hav much time to think. If I could just laie out all the thinges that hav happen'd to me just like I be laieing out these peeses of your bodice then perhaps I could make somethinge of it.

The thot keeps coming that I cann prove the real invisibel world cuz my wand'ring eye gives me a second sight. Wish't I could perswade Mr. Proctor but whenever I try to speek to him my tongue goes week as a hook'd fish.

The fires dying downe. 'Tis almost dawne. Still Mr. Proctor be pacing. I long to go & comfort him. Why am I afraide? 'Twas only yesterdaie the very ground on which we stood stirr'd & heev'd to bear witness to our bless'd consummashun.

The next daie
Very erly

I must hav dozed off in your rocker Mrs. Proctor. When I open'd my eyes the winddowe panes had faded from black to graye. Your magpie be hopping up & downe on the sill & flapping its winges like a fether duster being shak'n cleen. When I open'd the winddowe to shoo it awaie it dared me with them cold shiny eyes befor rising over the barne roof. High'r & high'r till it disappear'd into a pink bank of clowd.

I be lighting a candel when I heer'd Mr. Proctor coming downe the staires. My hande shook as I held it up to show him the waie. He still moved slow as a sleepwalker with his hande over his heart as tho he had somethinge to hide or a hurt.

I stared at his face. It be blank & white & wax'n looking as the candel in my hande. The crease cutting even deep'r into his browe.

I want'd to ask him why he be pushing me out of his life but it seem'd an invisibel noose dropp't titen'd 'round my neck so I splutter'd & coff'd & couldnt let out the wordes. He stoppt at the bottom of the staires. Staring at me but not seeing. Staring strait thru me to the wall behind. In feer I lower'd my eyes.

We stood silent & unmoving. The first raies of the sun streem'd thru the winddowe into a poole on the floore. The logges sang in the hearthe. A cock crow'd & then another much clos'r. Still we stood. On the floore between the fire & the sunlight I watch't our shaddowes slipping in & out of eech other. Slipping in the waie th'unseen world slippes thru our lives. In the waie our Soules slippt thru our bones to be merg'd into one by the Lord. O why then can our bodies not follow?

Without a word Mr. Proctor walk'd passt me. The candel in my hande flick'rd out. I want'd to tell him that it wouldnt be that eesy for him to snuff out his lov for me but the noose titen'd sqweezing my throat so I start'd to coff. Without a worde Mr. Proctor turn'd & left. The slamme of the door set your cloak swaying on its hook & a cold wind blowing thru my bones.

I open'd the door & ran out calling to Mr. Proctor that he must take me with him to the Heering. When I tried to seez his armes he push'd me awaie saieing he would rather take a dogge with rabbies. Push'd so hard I tripp't over th'endd of my skirt & fell to my nees.

I staied there watching him walk towards the barne. How slowe he be moving. His hed downe. His shoalders bunch't. 'Tis strange, Mrs. Proctor, but when he be close theres somethinge enormus 'bout him. Somethinge too bigg to see. As he walk'd awaie he came mor cleer. Seem'd like I be looking at him for the first time. He has grown old since you be gon. The pow'r of his body leeking out as tho it be a sack of corn meal with a hole chew'd in the bottom by a mouse.

Forenoon the same daie
After gath'ring fiddelheds

Not wanting to think of you or the Heering, Mrs. Proctor, I decided to go downe to the creek & look for fiddelheds to serv with the boars hed I be cooking for supper tonight.

On the muddy path thru the woods I found prints

that I recogniz'd be the soles of Mr. Proctors boots. Carefully I placed my foot in eech of his steppes. How deep & sure & even they be. How I lov the ground he treads. Lov seeing what he seen. The dogwood blooming like starres at dusk. The wild turkeys mating in the undergrowth. 'Twas here last Fall that Mr. Proctor shot a sixty pound turkey sitting in the fork of a beech tree. It be so heavy, he saied, when it struck the ground it splitt open. Gobs of yellow tallow rolling out.

In the heel of one of his footprints my wand'ring eye catch't a littel pool of water. Gold & shimm'ring in the sunlight. At first I thot 'twas a mottelly stone plashing into it. Then bending downe I seen it be a toad. Signe of a demon lurking near. I grabb'd it & tear'd off its back legges eesy as if it been a tiny cook't phesant. Then I throw'd them over my left shoalder saieing very lowd Protect me in the name of ArchAngels Michael & Gabriel.

Mr. Proctor would smack me for this. He beleevs it be evil to kill anythinge 'cept for food. Even if it be an imp or a demon. Com to think 'tis a wond'r Mr. Proctor nev'r has whoppt me like them other farmers whopp their maids. He just stares at me.

As I follow'd Mr. Proctors boot marks deep'r into the woods it grow'd gloomy & dank as a cellar with vines thick as thighs creeping along the ground or flinging themselves to gripp the top of giant trees. I know'd as long as I follow'd in his steppes I would never be lost but I grow'd afraide picturing a savage behind every tree — a child of Satan with paint'd face & naked body slith'ring in bear grease. Mor & mor it seem'd a nightmare.

Forgetting 'bout Mr. Proctors footprints I start'd to run. Thats when I came upon a small cleering blankett'd in mayflowers. You knowe them wee pink blooms, Mrs. Proctor. You been the one who tell'd me they brot a message of hope to our forefathers after their first dizasterus winter.

Tucker'd out from running & lac of sleep I throw'd myself downe on the flow'ry bedde & doz'd till a frighten'd screech curdel'd the stillness.

Thats when my loos eye glimpst a clump of matt'd browne haire on a fork't branch of pine. Looking hard I made out what seem'd bits of dry'd blood & brain & skinne. Suddenly something rised up & I screem'd. As it clatter'd thru the branches I start'd laffing & crying cuz I realized it be a bird & what I thot be an Indian scalpe 'twas only a nest of twigges & mudd.

And the bird, Mrs. Proctor? The bird been that magpie of yourn. It follow'd along while I be gath'ring the fiddelheds among the roots & moss of the creek bank. I couldnt see it but I heerd its chortling. So dark & deep from the throat I could hav sworn it be you laffing.

Som later
Just befor cockshut

All afternoon I work't in the garden planting the seeds of gourds & onions & pees. By the time the shaddowe of the howse creept over me my armes be aching.

Leening on my hoe I watch't the littel ones playing with the ball their Papa made by blowing up a pigges bladder. John Junior be chinking new logges in the smoakhowse. When he seen me looking at him he smiled — the same crook'd smile as his Papa — & once againe the burning arrowe peersed my chest & my face be cover'd with his kisses & spittel. Then I fellt my body breaking apart while a voyce thrumm'd go back to the fire. Go back to the sacred spot where your body be forg'd to his'n.

Putting downe my hoe I went into the howse & gather'd together the remaining ash from the Lov Poshun & the white pebbels that mark'd the magic circul. Then I call'd the childrun inside & tell'd them to studdy their catachisme till I returned.

As I cross't the back pasture the furrowes of clowd be ting'd with pink & my shaddowe be growing long'r & spreding befor me in the shape of two twined figures. As I watch't it wav'ring ov'r the grass & mud & stones I pictur'd Mr. Proctor & I being pull'd out of th'Abyss.

On the farr side I neel'd where we had lain. First I giv'd thanks to th'Almightie for choosing me for the Bless'd Consummashun. For binding my Soule to Mr. Proctors so now & forever I am the cowe to his bull — the henne to his cock. Afterwards I bury'd the Lov Poshun & mark'd it with a mound of the white pebbels.

Walking back my eyes be burn'd with light from the sun slipping behind the barne roof. Half blind — teers running hot as blood from my eyes — I began daydreaming I lov'd Mr. Proctor so much that for the rest of my life my body be casting two shaddowes. Peepul coming farr as Connecticutt to kiss the ground where they spred.

Later
Supper Time
Waiting for Mr. P

The boars hed — stuff't in the French fashion with stale bred & butter & basil & minc't chestnut — be roasting for houres. When I open the oven doore its brisselly pink snout be steeming same as the spout of a tea ketel. Soon its bulging eyes will turn the gray'sh white of hard boil'd egges & the meat cann be carv'd. The last time I be serving one of the cheeks to Mr. Proctor he pull'd me to him by the apronne stringes & pinch'd my bottom wisp'ring that these be the cheeks he desir'd. 'Twas over a year ago but I still remember how he throw'd back his hed & laff'd. Th'edges of his teeth gleeming.

Right now I wish I could remember how you made

that rich gravie Mrs. Proctor. I think the Madeira be what turn'd it red & thick as ox blood. Mr. Proctor loves to sopp up the drippings with bred. Carefully licks the end of eech finger. How he loves to eet. I lov to watch him. His mouthe opening so wide that once — to tees the littel ones — he put a whole appel in it.

While waiting for Mr. Proctor to return from your Heering the littel ones be settel'd 'round the citchin tabel copying out the Ten Commandments on their slate boards. Thats when Annie ask't what covet meant. Gazing up at me with them black greedie beed eyes. Just like yours, Mrs. Proctor.

I smack't her acrosse the hed & lifting the front of my skirt ran up the stairres to the back roome winddowe to look for Mr. Proctor. From there 'twas eesy to see for miles downe Ipswich road. Usually someone be hurrying to get indoors befor the bad aire of nightfall but this evening the road laied empty. Reminding me of a silv'ry river in the waie it be winding between light'r & dark'r shades of fields & woods.

As I be leening out the winddowe to wish upon the first starre I catch't a white light out of the corner of my eye. Twas the moon rising full from behind Gallows Hill. Then my heart giv'd a lurch cuz there be a weerd blackshape on the face of it that I thot be the silhouettte of Satan. Then I realiz'd it for a tree. The only one on that rocky hill. You know, Mrs. Proctor, the Hanging Tree.

And what do you think it be signifying? That gigantic oak with its huge twisting lims cawt compleetly inside the moons circul of light. In all truth I knowe. It be a signe of you, Mrs. Proctor, cawt between death & the Devil.

Later
After the visit
by the Constabul

While writting th'abov I heerd the grumbel of cart wheels. I thot Mr. Proctor be back at last. But 'twas Constabul Williams asking for a cup of tea. Abbie thinks he has the face of an old hors cuz of his bigge long nose & sunken cheeks & high forhed. He be taking the Reverents daughter to staie with her uncle in Town. Littel Betty be the first in the village to becom possessed &, they saie, after the Devil had his waie with her she be drows'd as a mouse dragg'd in by the catte.

As the Constabul carry'd her into th'ingelnook I notis'd how meg'r she look'd. How her butyful blonde haire has turn'd pale & thin as watery milk. Soon as he putt her on the settee she start'd screeming Mama Mama while her eyes be fix't on the boars hed keeping warm on a platt'r in the hearth. The draft when I open'd the doore must hav blow'd the embers into flammes & nowe the boars eyes be melting & sliding slowly downe its cheeks.

It brot to mind them white sticky blobbs of snails I used to gath'r from inside the rainbarrels & boil into a porridge. The littel ones hated it but it stopp't the ricketts. The only waie Constabul Williams & I could stopp Betty from screeming be to pull a pillow casing like a hangmans hood over her hed. Soon as she quiet'd downe I ask't the Constabul if he had any news of your Heering, Mrs. Proctor. He shook his hed but saied if it be the same as oth'r witch-craft Heerings the Meeting-Howse would be pack'd as a bar-rell of herrings.

It seems Reverent Parris has been consern'd for som-time that th'afflicted wouldn't take the stand. Most be maid servants, he tell'd the Constabul ov'rawed by the crowd & speshully the presiding Magistrates cuz they be fameus men from Boston. Thats why befor your Heering the Reverent made sure eech of the torment'd giv'd sworn statements to the Constabul.

I already know'd 'bout the one sign'd by Abbie

claiming your specter flied thru a keyhole & offer'd her a pockett of gold sovereigns to becom a handmaiden of the Devil. But I diddn't knowe you also torment'd Titubas husband. The Constabul tell'd me John Indian has swear'd twice that he woke to find your specter standing naked by his bedde. He claim'd it had the same body as you, Mrs. Proctor, but with no skinne. And when you tried to laie on him he saied it fellt like raw red meat.

While the Constabul be getting ready to leeve — wrapping the simp'ring littel Betty in the folds of his bigge black cloak — I ask't him if the date of your hanging be set at your Trial or afterwards by the Governor. The Constabul look'd at me aslant saieing by lawe a pregnant woman couldn't be hang'd.

Not a worde mor did I saie to him — not even good-bye but I knowe you be lieing, Mrs. Proctor. Trieing to gain time so Mr. Proctor cann take the petishun to the Governor & ask for a repreeve. If only Mr. Proctor would com home. Why has he been so long at your Heering? And this forboding deep inside me. Why be it spreding shade upon shade — like th'aire thats dark'ning outside the winddowe.

Som later
Not to you Mrs. Proctor
This be different

I sit & stare into the fire. My mind dissembeling. No mor will I be waiting for Mr. Proctor. No mor will I be writting to you Mrs. Proctor. So much has happen'd. I must make som order in my hed by putting downe worde for worde what John Indian tell'd me when he stopp't for a dram of whiskey on his waie back from the Heering.

He start'd by saieing he been the first to take the stand when they call'd for witnesses to your witchcraft & 'twas while he be giving testimony that he seen your specter sitting on a crossbeem. He point'd it out to the Magistrates & then it swoop't t'attack the girles. Been awesom, he saied, to see Annie crawling on all fours & biting the ankels of the Magistrates. Mercy choaking on the floore cuz her throate be puff't as tho a fist be inside it.

Then John Indian tell'd me how the crowd screem'd & push't up to the pulpitt. Sweating body press't so close to sweating body that when a goodwife faint'd there be no room for her to fall. No waie to remove her from the Meeting-Howse till after your last test which be the repeeting of the Lords Prayer.

And then John Indian tell'd me when you saied Hollow'd be Thy Name instead of Hallow'd be Thy Name the crowd began screeming Witch Witch & he could feel the pow'r of peepuls feer as they strain'd forward.

I wond'r how it fellt having the Magistrates begg for order. Having Reverent Parris fall to his nees in pray're while Mr. Proctor suddenly be at your side. I cann pictur him standing there with his hed lower'd – like he be 'bout to charge – & the fureus damn-the-world look on his face. I can pictur him pointing at th'afflicted & yelling bitch witches they make Devils of us all. The girls, John Indian saied, began blatt'ring like hennes that sens a wolf behind the barne. It been him that had to stand up & name Mr. Proctor for what-they saie he be – the most dredfull wizard this side of Boston.

'Twas while John Indian be telling these wordes that my mind start'd dissembeling. Everythinge 'round me changing. Not cuz my week eye be rolling but cuz the citchin dwindel'd as tho I be falling asleep. The walls – even the howse itself – fading. My body no longer me. I dreem'd it into being.

And I must be dreeming still for I cann see John Indian sitting on the stool in th'ingelnook. A dirty-looking dried-up littel man searching for lice in his haire while he be talking & talking. Saieing me how Abbie stood up & tell'd the court that one night Mr. Proctor flied with the wind downe the chimney of the Parsonage. That he spred his specter self ov'r her. His body growing into her body. His mouthe into her mouthe. On & on he be talking. His rasping voyce. I cann feel it cutting thru me like a sawe thru wood as he saies Mr. & Mrs. Proctor be tak'n togeth'r to the Boston Jail to await trial. I cann hear myselfe saieing Abbie my best friend while watching him fold into a muddy graye cloak & skuttel out into the night. And I cann still hear myselfe saieing Abbie my best friend while list'ning to the fading sounds of his waggon wheels . . . list'ning to the gusts of wind following behind him like the wheels of fate turning & turning.

Mor late

With every gust the fire flares up & the sealskin dressing trunk be chang'd into a hump't sea monster sliding across the floor. The four turkey-work't chaires with the bowed legges becom dwarfs dancing a jig.

In the flick'ring spurts of flamme the picture of yourselfe Mrs. Proctor abov the mantel stirrs & comes alive. Eyes blinking & following me 'bout the roome. Sometimes she speeks like you to tell me taint a babee inside but the Devil himself bigge as a woodchuck. Tonight be the witches Sabbath & she will send her demon bird to steel the littel ones so their fleshe cann be eet'n at the midnight feest.

While I sit rocking & praying I heer a swishing sound like wind outside the howse but I knowe it be broom-sticks sweeping th' aire. The weth'rcock turning on the roof screeks kill kill kill & somethinge black blasts out of the chimney & flies past my ear. It be the Devil that changes from a huge bat to the demon magpie cover'd in soot & ashe.

Sprinkeling kernells of Indian corn at my feet I watch the demon bird walk on stiff splinterlike legges towards me. Soon as it starts pecking at the corn I lunge & dropp my apronne over it. Then I scoop it into an empty flour sac. Xcept for a few soft sniggerings it nev'r struggels or speeks as I smash the sac with the fire poker.

The limp bundel under my arme I rush out of the howse. A heavy clowd covers the moon making the starres bigg'r & mor bright. The demon magpie must be buried outside Mr. Proctors land. I run & run. The gusts of wind ripp my breathe awaie. Yank at my haire & clowthes. Running acrosse the farr'st corn field I tripp over some-thinge like a logge that be a fall'n scarcrowe cover'd in ded leeves. Then I see 'tis a ded savage woman. Must be here a long time. Clowthes rott'd awaie. Skinne hanging in tatters from her bones.

As I run back the wind cries God O God O God & blowes thru me as tho I be not there. Blowes & blowes. And the only thinge not moving be the starres.

A sudden mightie blast like the Fist of the Lord smashes the citchin winddowe & scatt'rs the glasse into petals of flow'rs. The wind rushing in snuffs out the fire. Not even th'afterglowe of ashe. It be so dark I cannt see my hand in front of my face. There be nothing round me but aire blowing. It nuzzels my neck. Pulls up my skirt. Cold fin-gers pinching my thighs & forcing them apart. Presses into all my openings. The pain intens as knives thrusting deep'r. I want to wake up. I want to crie out but cannt. My eye like a scared bird flies up into my skull. Into a place immens & silent & curv'd. Like the night skie with starres the coloure of blood.

Now I knowe eternity. Now my Soule has chang'd places with my body & everywhere be God. The wind be His Breathe rushing thru my seven openings. His Shaddowe so bright be Mr. Proctor letting go his bones & slipping inside me. I can see him like the moon floating thru my darkness. He be a thousand times clos'r than my own skinne. Than my own breathe.

What do I care if we be witches or Gods Chos'n. If I be asleep or awake. Mr. Proctor be the Light within me & togeth'r we take the shape of Heav'n. Now & eternally one.

Bless'd be the Lord
Mary Proctor

"The Salem Letters" is an excerpt from a novel in progress entitled *The Crying Out*.

The Heart Must From Its Breaking

•

Leon Rooke

1.

This is how it happened that morning at the church.
Timmons was speaking on a topic that had us all giggling,
"What You Do When and If You Get To Heaven and Find
It Empty," and we were all there and saw it. How suddenly
before Timmons got wound up good the wood doors burst
open and there in the sunlight was someone or something,
like a fast-spinning wheel made up of gold, though it
couldn't have been gold and was probably some funny trick
of the light. Anyway, there it was, and beckoning. Must have
been beckoning, or calling somehow, because two children
got up from their seats at the front and quiet as you please
marched right out to him—to him or it—and went through
the door, and that was the last any of us ever saw them.
Then a second later that other kid—Tiny Peterson was his
name—went out too, but his mama was in time to save him.
Now I'd lie about it if I could or if I knew how, but it was all
so quiet and quick and then over that I wouldn't know how
to improve on the actual happening.   Out that door and

then swallowed up, those two kids, and that's all there was to it.

2.

He can say that's all if he wants to. Roger Deering sees an affair like this the same way he sees his job, which I would remind you is delivering mail. He drops it through the box, if he can be troubled to come up the path, and then he's gone. What he's left you with don't matter spit to him. But I live in that house now, my sister's house, and I can tell you the story don't end there. They were my sister's children, Agnes and Cluey. Sister was home in bed sick so I'd taken little Agnes and Cluey to church to hear Timmons give what we hoped would be a good one, and right after the second song, with Timmons hardly begun, Cluey who was on my left stood up and whispered "Excuse me," and brushed by my knees, then Agnes on my right stood up, mumbled "Me too" and they went on down the row, scraping by people, getting funny looks, and then going on down the aisle pretty as you please. I thought Cluey had to go to the bathroom. He was always doing that, never going when you told him to and it embarrassed me. But you do get tired of telling a boy to wait wait wait when he's squirming and crossing his legs, trying to hold it in. I don't mean he was doing it that day, I'm only saying that's what I thought he got up for. He'd been nice as pie the whole time, both of them, both while walking along with me to church and while sitting there waiting for Timmons to get primed. So I was in a good mood and bearing them no malice, though they were a longshot from being my favorite nieces and nephews. Sister had been ailing for some while and they were feeling dopey about that, we all were. That was the day Sister died, in fact the very minute, some said. Some said they'd looked at their watches when that door burst open and Cluey and Agnes went out never to be seen again and that very second three blocks over was the very second Sister passed on. It was close, that's all I'm saying, and my skin shivers saying that much, especially when I remember about the blood. But I'm not saying anything about the blood on Sister's window, being content to leave that to the likes of Clayton Eaves who is still dunning me for that ten dollars. I don't like to think of any of it is the truth, for I'm living in Sister's house now and I know sometimes I hear her and that she hears me. Sister dies and her two children disappear the same minute and it does make you think. Though I didn't see any whirling light or gold spinning at the door. I felt a draft, that's all. Like most people with any sense I thought the wind had blown it open, and when people say to me there wasn't any wind that day I just look through them, since any fool knows a gust can come up. Still, it's strange. I can't think what happened to the children. No one wanted them. I couldn't, and Sister wasn't able. Their daddy couldn't have come and got them because none of us hardly remembered who their daddy was, or wanted to, because even in his best of days he hadn't been what you'd call a solid citizen. He wasn't right in the head, and not much in the body either, and even Sister knew that. So she had her hard times, raising that pair without a hand from him who hadn't been seen I think in nine years when all this happened. No aunts or uncles would have come for them. We don't have kidnappers around here. No, it defies explanation and I've given up trying. When Sister wakes me calling in the night I sit up in bed and answer back and we go on talking that way until her spirit quietens.

I hope Cluey and Agnes are all right, wherever they are, that's all I hope. I don't agree with those who say they're long-since dead, nor those who say they're in heaven either. Timmons might.

3.

Sure they're dead. I don't know how, or how come, or why, not having the divine intervention on it, but you can't tell me two children dressed for church and without penny or snotrag between them are going to get out of this town without anyone knowing it. There are just two ways for entering or leaving and that's by the one street that leads off to Scotland Neck at one end and Enfield at the other, and they didn't go either of those ways. Couldn't have, because a hundred people rocking on their porches that fine Sunday when they should have been at Spring Level hearing my sermon on The Empty Hell would have noted their progress and likely turned them around.

So they're dead. Yep, and their bones plucked by now. Dust to dust and the Lord's will abideth.

Somebody picked them up right off the church-grounds, I'd say, right there at the door, and spooked them away. Why I don't know. They were ordinary children, no better or worse than most. Funny things go on in this town the same as they do anyplace else and I figure those two are buried this minute down in somebody's cellar or in a backyard where a thousand things hidden go on day in and day out. I've preached till I'm blue in the face, the same as one or two other ministers have, and it's done no good. Not a lick. You can't stamp out the devil's work for he's like a mad dog once he gets going. That's what it was, of course. The old devil keeping his hand in. If it hadn't been those two children it would have been something worse.

We searched the woods, every rock, weed, and clover.

Nothing. Not a hint.

About that door. I saw *something* but *what* is something else. It wasn't gold, though. It was more like a giant black shadow had spun up over the stairs and filled the doorway. I remember remarking to myself at the time: it's got so dark in here so suddenly I'm going to have difficulty reading my text. I was going to ask Minny at the organ to turn more light on, when Cluey and Agnes got up and distracted me. A second later it was light again. If I'd known what was to happen I would have called out. But who knew? That's how you know it's the devil's work, I say, because you don't. You just don't. You never will.

4.

Timmons is right. I was at the organ. I didn't want to be, having a bad cold, but I was. They couldn't get anybody else. My nose was runny, I told them, and I had aches—but so what? 'Minnie, now Minnie, you come on down.' So I did. Yet it's the same story everytime and nobody ever even bothering to keep up. I've heard cows mooing in a meadow had more rhythm and feeling than the people in that church. But I saw nothing. Saw and heard nothing. No light or gold. No shadow. No children either. It takes a lot in that church to make me turn around. Back trouble, leg trouble, I wore a neck brace for ten years. I keep my back to that lot and that's how I like it. One time a curtain caught fire back there when Orson Johnson—the crosseyed one—was playing with matches. I looked around then. That's about the only time.

5.

My name's Orson, I'm the one she's talking about. What I wished I'd done that day was burn the whole building down. But I didn't and I growed up and I was back there the day those two walked out. Back there whittling on a stick with this Fobisher knife I have. With the wife and hoping it would wind up early, though I knew it wouldn't, so I could go home and have dinner, maybe grab some shut-eye. But, yes, I saw them. and I felt my neck crawl too, before they ever stood up, because something was behind me. Maybe not at the door, but behind me certainly. My skin froze and I remember gripping my wife's wrist I got that scared. I thought it was Death back there, Death calling, and He was going to lay his cold hand over my shoulder and speed me on off. "What date is it?" I asked my wife. "How long we been married?" Now I don't know why I said this, but I know it scared her too, though she just kept shooshing me. I didn't want to die. Hell, it seemed to me I'd only started living. But "shoosh" she says, so I shoosh. I shoosh right up; I couldn't have said another word anyway. I sat there with my knees knocking, waiting for Death's hand to grab me. Then I see the kids coming down the aisle. They got their faces scrubbed and that ramrod aunt of theirs, Gladys, she had slapped some worn duds on them and got their hair combed. Death's hold on me seemed to loosen a bit and I thought how I might slip out and ask them how their mother was doing—whether she was still in her sick bed or out of danger yet, that sort of thing—maybe slip them a quarter because I'd always felt pity for those kids—and I tried to move, to wiggle out the side and sort of slink to the back door, but what it was I found was I couldn't move. I couldn't stir a muscle. And a second later my hair stood put on my head because a voice was hissing in my ear. "Don't go," it said. "Don't go, Orson, it will get you too."

Though I didn't think then that "too" business was including the kids. I might have got up if I'd known that. I might have headed them off, tried to save them. If anyone could have. I don't know. Oh they're dead, no question of that. I think they were likely dead before nightfall. Maybe within the hour. It's too bad too, especially with their mother going that same day.

6.

I felt Orson stiffen beside me. He looked like death warmed over and he started jabbering beside me, shivering

so hard he was rattling the whole row. I put my hand down
between his legs and pinched his thigh hard as I could but
he didn't even blink. He was trying to get out. So I put my
hand up where his man parts were and I squeezed real hard
and told him to hush up. "Hush up, Orson, stop playing the
fool"—something like that. He was freezing cold. He had
sweat beads on his brow an inch thick. I brought my heel
down on his foot, trying to get him quiet, then I heard him
say "Death, Death, Death." And "Don't go, don't go." He
didn't know he was talking. I saw Aaron Spelling, in front
of us, lean over and say to Therma that Orson Johnson had
a briar in his behind. Therma turned and looked at us. Her
mouth popped open. Because Orson was such a sight. I got
my hand away real quick from where it was; I just clamped
my fingernails into his thigh and kept them there the rest of
the service.

Later on we had to get the doctor in, I'd hurt him so
and the infection must have lasted a month.

I didn't notice the kids; I had my hands full with
Orson.

It was three whole days in fact before I so much as
heard of the children gone missing or dead and of their
mother's death.

7.

I was nursing Tory when she took her final breath.
By her bedside I was with a tea cup in my lap and watching
the window because I thought I'd heard something running
around out there. Like a galloping horse it was. But my legs
were bothering me, and my sides, so I didn't take the trouble to go to the window and see. I sat sipping my tea, listening to the galloping horse.

It was a day like many another one up to that time
except that the house was empty, it being a Sunday, and
other than that horse. A few minutes before, when I got up

to get my tea, I'd put my head down on Tory's chest. I was always doing that, couldn't help it, because although I've sat with hundreds of sick people I'd never heard a heart like hers. It was like water sloshing around in a bowl; she hardly had no regular heartbeat is what I'm saying. So I'd put my head down over her chest and listen to it slosh like that.

I couldn't see how a human being could live with a heart beat like that. The horse it keeps right on galloping. Now and then I'd catch a whir at the window, whiteish, so I knew it wasn't no dark horse. Then all at once my blood just stops, because something has caught hold of me. I look down at my wrist and there's the queerest hand I ever saw. Thin and shrunk and mostly bones. The hand is all it was in that second, and I shrieked. The china cup fell to the floor and broke. Saucer too. Tea I splashed all over me, so I afterwards had to go in and soak my dress in cold water. There were the long red nails though. A vile color but Gladys said Tory liked it. That she wouldn't feel comfortable in bed, sick like that, without her nails painted, because how would you feel to be in bed like she was and looking like death, in case anybody came in. So let's keep her looking civilized, Gladys said, and one or the other of us kept her nails freshly painted. So after my minute of fright I knew it was Tory's hand, her who hadn't moved a twitch in three months, suddenly sitting up with a grip like steel on my arm. It was practically the first sign of life I'd seen in her in the whole time I'd been minding her. She was sitting bolt-up, with her gown straps down at her elbows so her poor little bosom, the most puckered, shrivelled little breasts I ever hope to see, was exposed to the full eyes of the world.

She had her eyes locked on the window.

And there went the horse again, gallop, gallop.

I got hold of myself, got her hand off me, and stooped down over her. I was about to say, "Now little lady let's get that gown up over your bosom before you catch your death"—but then that word caught in my throat so I said nothing. And I'm glad I didn't or I might of missed what she said. Her eyes were on fire and she was grabbing at something. At the very air, it seemed to me. "You'll not get my children!" she said. "No, you'll not get them!" Well my skin crawled. I don't know why, don't know to this day. Just the way she was crying it. "You'll not get them, not my Cluey and Agnes!" She was screeching that out now, as frightened—but as brave too—as any soul I hope to see. "You *can't have my children!*" On and on like that. And she was twisting around in bed, flailing her arms, striking at something with her poor little fists. "*No, you can't!*" she said. Then this even worse look come over her face and for the longest time she wasn't making human sounds at all. Half-animal, I thought. Like something caught in a trap. I thought she'd finally bit the noose—that her mind had gone. I kept trying to get that gown up over her breast works—you never knew who would come barging into that house without knocking or breathing a word, even her sister has crept in sometimes and scared me out of my wits. And she's fighting me, not letting me get her back down in the bed. She's scratching and yelling and kicking—her whose legs the doctor claimed was paralyzed—and she's moaning and biting. Then she shrieks, "*Run! Run! Oh children, run!*" And this perfect horror comes over her face, pure agony it is, and torture worse than I've ever known a body to feel. "*No!*" she screams, "*No! Please! Please don't!*" and the next second her breath flies out, her eyes roll up, and she sags down like a broken baby in my arms. I put her head back on the pillow and fluff it some. I pull her straps back up and smooth out her gown over her chest's flatness. I pat the comforter up around her neck. I get her hair looking straight. I close her eyes, first the left then the right just as they say you ought to do, and I root in my purse and dig out two pennies. I go in and wash them off and dry them on my dress, and I put them nicely over her eyes.

Then I sit watching her, trembling more than I ever have. Wondering what has gone on and thinking how I'm going to have to tell her sister and those poor children when they come in from the church. Not once giving mind to that broken china on the floor. I reckon I never did. I reckon someone else must have come in and cleared that mess up. Maybe Gladys did. Or maybe not. I plumb can't guess, because one second I'm there sitting looking at my hands in my lap and the next second I'm thinking What about that galloping horse? Because I don't hear it any more. No, it's so quiet you can hear a pin drop. And I hear it too. Pins dropping, that's what I think. This shiver comes over me. I have the funny feeling I'm not alone in the room: that there's me, a dead person, and something else. I look over at the bed and what do I see? Well it's empty. Tory ain't there. I hear more of these pins dropping and they seem to be coming from the window so I look there. And what I see is this: it is Tory, come back to some strange form of life, and sliding up over, over the sill and out of that window. That's right, just gone. And I guess I fainted then, that being the first of my faints. The next time I open my eyes my sight is on that window again and this time Tory is coming back through it, sliding along, and her little breasts are naked again, she's all cut up, and blood has soaked through her and she's leaving a trail of it every inch she comes. "Help me, Rosie," she says. Well that's what I'm there for. So I get her up easy as kittens—she hardly weighs an ounce—and I get her back into bed. "They're safe," she says. I say, "Good." I say a lot of comforting words like that. "Don't let anyone see me like this," she says. "I'm black and blue from head to toe." It's the truth too, she sure is. "Have Gladys quietly bury me," she says. "Closed coffin. Can you promise that?" I said sure. She patted my hand then, poor thing, as though I was the one to be comforted. Then she slips away. She slips away smiling. So I get the pennies back on. I straighten the covers. Then I sit back in the chair and faint away a second time. I'm just waking up when Gladys comes in from church to tell me that Agnes and Cluey have gone and there's been a mighty mess at the church and some are saying the children are dead or gone up to heaven. I pass out my third time. I can't help it. I fold down to the floor like a limp rag and I don't know what else is going on till there is a policeman or a doctor at my elbow, I don't know which.

8.

It was me, Sam Clive. Clive, C-L-I-V-E. Officer Sam Clive. I wasn't there in any official capacity. I lived then just two doors down from Tory and that day I felt in my bones how something was wrong. I was out in my yard mowing and this funny feeling come over me. I looked up and it seemed to be coming from her house. It was shut up tight, the house was, but there was this whirring disc in the sky. A flying whatayacallit I at first thought. Anyway, it seemed to sink down in the woods just behind her place. So I strolled over. I saw curtains fluttering at her sick room window and I was brought up real short by that— because that window had always been closed. Every day, winter and summer, on account of Tory was holding on by such a thin thread. Heart trouble, kidneys, pneumonia—the whole she-bang. I stepped closer, not wanting to be nosy and more because of this eerie feeling I had. Well I saw those curtains were dripping blood. It was pouring right off that cloth and down the boards, that blood. And I thought I saw something sliding up over the sill the minute I come up. Flutter, flutter. It was the curtains I guess. Though I don't recollect it being a windy day. But that blood, heck, you can still see where it dribbled down the side of the house, because they never painted it over. They painted the rest of the house, the sister did after she got it, but for reasons known only to them they painted up to the blood and stopped right there. Anyhow, I hurried on over. I looked through the window and there was this fat nurse down in a heap on the floor beside this broken china and Tory in the bed with bright pennies over her eyes.

9.

I done the paint job. I give the old gal a good price and me and one other, my half-brother who was helping me then, we went at it. White, of course, that was the only color she'd have. And she wanted two coats, one put on vertical and one crossways. I said why. She said her daddy told her when she was a kid that's how you put paint on if you wanted a thing to stand up to the elements more'n a year or two. I said I'd never heard that. I said Tom Earl, Have you ever heard that and he said No, no he hadn't. She said Well that's how she wanted it and if I wouldn't or couldn't do it or didn't think I was able then she reckoned I wasn't the only painter in town and a lot of them cheaper'n me. Ha! I said. I said it's going to cost you extra. She said I don't see why. I said because Miss Gladys it will take me a good sight longer painting this house the fool way you want it. You can't hardly git no speed painting vertical because the natural way is to go crosswise following the lay of the boards. She said it might be natural to a durn fool like me but that weren't how her daddy done it and I could do it and at the price quoted or I could shove off and go out and stick somebody else. So I got the message. Two coats? I said. Two coats, she said, Hank Sparrow can't you do that neither? I shook my head a time or two. There weren't any way I was going to make one red cent out of it. I'd be doing well just covering wages and gitting the paint paid for. But her sister had passed on and hide nor hair of her kin had been seen, those two children, so I said well it won't hurt me none to do this woman a favor.

I got Tom Earl and him and me took at it. It went right smooth and we did the same top job we always did.

Till we got to that window. I brushed the paint over them dark red streaks and said to Tom Earl Well it'll take a second coat but that ought to do her. But when it dried, even after the third and fourth coat, them bloodstreaks were still there same as they were when we started. Tom Earl said Well she ain't going to pay, you know that, until we get these streaks covered over. I looked at him and I said You're right there, you done spoke a big mouthful. And I went out to the truck and got me my tools. Got me my hammer and chisels, my blow torch too: one way or the other I was going to git that blood removed.

Well she comes running. She have got her head up in a towel, one shoe off and the other one on, and she's dripping water, but still she comes running. What are you doing, what are you doing, she keeps asking, are you going to take hammer to my house or burn it down? Is this what you call painting, she says. So I looked at Tom Earl and he's no help, he just shrugs his shoulders. I look to her and I say I've painted and I've painted and it's still there. What is? she says. Hank Sparrow are you trying to two-bit me? No'm, I say, but there's something peculiar going on here. There sure is, she says, and it's you two with no more sense that a cat has pigeons. Now hold on minute, I say. So I take her round the house and I show her how we've put on a good seven coats minimum. But still that blood where your sister crawled up over the ledge. You leave my sister out of this, she says. She says, Hank Sparrow I have known you Sparrows all my life and there has never been one of you didn't try to weasel out of work and didn't lie with every breath scored. Now give me that brush, she says.

Tom Earl and me we give it to her. We coat it up good and we wrap a little tissue over the handle so she won't get none on her hand, and we let her to go to it. We stand back picking our teeth and poking each other, laughing, because one, the way she held that brush in both hands with her tongue between her teeth and bent over like she was meaning to pick up dimes, and two, because we knew it was a lost cause and no way in hell that paint was going to do it.

See there? She said. See there? Now is that covered or isn't it?

Give it a minute, we said. You give them streaks about two minutes and your eyes will pop out.

Well she stood right there with us, insulting us up one side and down the other every inch of the way. But we took it. We said nothing hard back to her. We knowed she was going to get the surprise of her life and be walking over hot coals to beg our pardon. And in two minutes, sure as rainwater, those streaks were back. They looked fresh brand-new, even brighter.

She went back and stood under the tree studying it, thinking her and distance would make a difference.

It's this paint, she said. This is a shoddy paint you're using.

Well we saw there was no end to it. So we got her in the truck between us, her with her hair still up in this green towel, and we drove down to the hardware. She got Henry Gordon pinned in the corner not knowing which way to turn but no matter how hard she pinned him he kept telling her that the paint we had was the best paint made and there weren't none no better including what went on the mayor's own house. I'll see about this, she said. And danged if she didn't call the distributor, long-distance, charging it to Henry. What is the best paint made? she said. And he said the very one we'd put on her house. She slammed down that phone. All right, she said, but Henry Gordon you have sold these two so-called working men a bad mix. I want another. Help yourself, Henry told her. She marches in his stockroom, says eennymeenyminnymoe over the cans, and comes out with one. All four of us now go back to her

house. She has me git the lid off and she dabs over that
blood again, so thick it just trickles down to the ground. We
wait. She is now fit to be tied. I have lost a dear sister, she
says, and lost my precious niece and nephew, and now you
are telling me I've got to live with the curse of this blood?

We said it looked like it. Everyone of us did, jumping
right in with it. Because that blood was coming right back
up. It was coming up bright as ever.

Well I never, she says.

So we go inside and stand in her kitchen and she
gives each of us a Coca-Cola. It surpasses meaning, she said.
I don't understand it. I don't guess I'm meant to.

We said Yesmam.

All right then, she said, I will just have to leave it
there. It's meant to be left there. It's meant to be some kind
of sign or signal. A symbol.

We didn't argue with her. I didn't even raise a hand
when she said she was holding back ten dollars paint money
because I never finished the house. There was something
spooky about that place. All I wanted was to git shut of it.
Me and Tom Earl took her cash and I give him some and
me and him went out drinking.

10.

He drank. I didn't because I was only thirteen and
the law wouldn't have it. But I knew Cluey, had seen him
around, and that Agnes too because she was always at his
heels, and I'd heard the stories of how the woman had died
and Cluey and Agnes had gone up in thin air. I had beat up
some on Cluey, being something of a bully in them days. I
had blooded his nose once and left him sobbing. I remember it and know it was him because he threw a rock at me
and got me on the kneecap. And because of what he said:
"My daddy will git you," he said. I was nice enough not to
say "What daddy?" And I was glad I didn't. Because that

night something tripped me up as I was walking home along the dye ditch, and I fell off into that ditch and broke my left leg. It was somebody there all right, that's all I'm saying, and it wasn't Cluey or any other thing with two legs. It tripped me up, then it put a hand on my back, and I went tumbling over. I was with Tiny Peterson. He can tell you.

11.

It's every word true. But what I want to get to is that church. Timmons was being his usual assy self, playing up like he was doing a cameo role for Rin Tin Tin, yammering on about emptiness this and emptiness that, when the wood doors burst open. I was already turned around, trying to smack at a little girl back there, when Cluey come by me. I had my legs up high and he couldn't get past. So he dropped my legs. I'd just got them back up when his little sister tapped my knee. "Excuse me," she said. "Me and him are going out to see my daddy. That's him at the door."

I raised up high in my seat and looked again at that door. People behind me started hissing but I didn't care. There was something in that door all right, but it wasn't hardly human. It didn't have two arms and two legs and it didn't have a face either. But it was beckoning. I saw Cluey and Agnes walk into the thing, whatever it was, and then they simple were not there anymore. There was nothing. I thought it was a vision. Timmons just then got his smart voice back and was saying something about "Heaven is empty." The empty heaven, something like that. I admit it. Goose bumps rose high on my arm as a kitchen window. I was really scared. Now why I did it I don't know to this day, but I went running out after them. I figured that if maybe their daddy was out there then maybe mine was too and he might save me from my empty heaven. I went flying out. I sped out over everybody's knees and trampled on feet and the next second I was outside in the yard. Cluey and Agnes couldn't have been five seconds in front of me. And what I saw there gave me a chill I can feel to this minute. There was this woman there in a white gown which was down to her waist so I could see her nipples and these real wizened breasts. I reckon to this day it's why I like big-bosomed women. But what she was doing was struggling with this creature. Creature is what he was, make no mistake about that. She had her arms and legs wrapped around him, pulling and tugging and chewing—pure out-and-out screeching—while the creature thing was trying to throw her off and still hold on to poor Cluey and Agnes who by this time were just bawling. They were just bawling. The creature was dragging them along and that woman was up on the creature's back, riding him, biting into the thing's neck, punching and clawing. Well it let go of the children. It gave a great howl and tore the woman off itself and practically bent her double. I mean it had her with her back across his knees and it was slamming her down all the while she screamed "Run! Run! Oh children run!" And they streaked off. I've never seen nothing tear away so fast. "Run! Run!" she cried. And they did and it was about this time that I heard this galloping, and a great white horse came out of the woods. The prettiest horse I ever will see. It galloped up to the children and slowed down and Cluey swung on its back, then got Agnes up there with him, and that horse took off full-speed, faster than I'd think a horse could. Then gone, just flying. The creature still had the woman. He slammed her down one last time and from where I was, hiding behind the tree, I could hear it: her back snap. *Snap*, like that, and the creature flung her down. It let out a great roar—of hatred, of pure madness at being thwarted, I don't know which—and then it took off too. But in the wrong way, not after the children. It seemed to me, the longer I looked at it run, that the closer it came to having human form. It had arms and legs and a face, though that face looked a million years old and like it hated everything alive.

That's all I saw. My own momma came out then and fixed her finger over my ear and nearly wrung it off. "Git yourself back in yonder," she said, "and don't you move one muscle lessen I tell you you can. When I git home I mean to put stick to your britches and you are going to wish you'd never been born."

I whimpered some, though not at my ear or at any threats she made. I never told anyone till now. Hell with them.

12.

The horse came by my place. I was out on the porch rocking away when it come by. Mary was in her chair with peas in her lap, shelling them. It was white, that horse was, it had two riders. They were up in the hills though. They were out a good far piece. There was something unnatural about it, I thought that. About how fast that horse was running, how it didn't get slowed down none by tree or brush. I said to Mary how I'd never seen no horse like that, not around here. Not anywhere else either, I reckon. My dog was down between my legs and he got up and took off after them. About a quarter hour later he come back whimpering, his tail drawed up under his legs. He went under the house and moaned. It took me two days to git that dog out.

13.

See that horse? He told me. And he pointed. I went on with my shelling.

Wonder why they don't take the road, I said. Wonder whose it is?

I never saw no children. Didn't see what the dog did either. I didn't look that long. I can't set out on the porch all day like him, watching what goes on. I got my own concerns to look after. Still, it was unusual. In the kitchen washing my hands I found myself staring out at a bluejay in a tree. Was that a horse, I ast myself, or was that a ghost?

14.

I thought when I went out and tweaked his ear that the sobbing Tiny was doing wasn't on account of that ear. He was snow-white and trembling and it was all I could do to hold him up. If I hadn't been so mad and set in my ways I would have known he'd seen something. It wont no way for me to behave, whether its to your own flesh or another's—but my husband had run out on me again and I imagine that had something to do with it.

But I'm sorry for it. I think it was the last time I wrung that boy's ear.

15.

You are all looking at me. Keep looking, then. You've always come to me with you aches and pains, now you're coming to me with this—is that it? I've told you my end before. I've never held anything back, and I won't now. Yes, I signed the certificate. She'd been slipping a long time and we'd all expected her death. I spent more time than most worrying about her. I said to her one day, "Tory," I said, "my medicines are doing you no good. I know you are in terrible pain all day and we both know you haven't got long. If you've a mind to, and want me to, and realize I am only raising this issue because I am aware of your misery, then I could give you something to help you go out easy and gentle and without the smallest pain."

She always told me she'd think on it. She'd let me know, she said. Then one day, after I'd given her every painkiller I could and none of it was helping her the slightest bit, I raised the question again.

"I'd like to go off, doctor," she said, "in a nice and swoony dream just as you describe. But I can't go yet. I've got to hold on for my children's sake because I know one day he is coming back. I've got to stay and save them from him, if I can."

I knew, of course, who she was talking about. You can't live here as long as I have without knowing that. But I said: "Tory, if he *does* come back, we will take care of his hide. You don't have to worry about his harming your kids."

"You don't understand," she said. "There will not be a single thing a living soul can do. No," she said, "I will have to take care of this myself, if I'm able. But I thank you."

I didn't mean to divulge this. Though I don't see how it alters anything. It tells us something of the spirit she had, I suppose, and confirms the love and concern she had for that boy and girl. The rest of it I'd discount. I never saw evidence of anything to the contrary while I was in medical school. Nor since, either. Yes, I signed the death certificate. You know as I do that it was a natural death. The heart couldn't any longer do its job. Yes, she was black and blue all over. Yes, there was blood on the curtains, and not merely her own blood either. I ran a test. The report came back to me and an idiot at the laboratory had scribbled on it, "Please provide more information."

Well, I didn't. I wasn't about to let myself be made a fool of up there.

I'm done. Let Tory and her children rest in peace, I say. Let these stories stop right here.

Knox Abroad

•

Eric McCormack

The voyage is over. John Knox stands, sways a little, with Clootie, his cat, on the forest-ragged banks of the river (more like the shore of the ocean), on land at last. It is October, and this is an alien place. He looks around and smiles. Nothing has changed, even after a wilderness of sea. His shoes touch dead leaves, the discreet vomit of the trees. He observes the paralysis of the rocks. The winds still blast down from directly above, threatening to hammer him, like a stake, into the ground, drive him under, bury him alive. Every night of the voyage, he saw (he has seen the same thing for twenty years of nights) the planets and the stars desert, rush centrifugally away into the outer universe, as though fleeing a plague. In the mornings, as always, the sun searched him out, singed his ever so-delicate grey skin. Again he smiles. Even amongst the trees there is no refuge. He bends over and lightly strokes Clootie's black coat. Together they turn and walk along the beaten path, fade into the forest gloom.

"An etymological footnote on the name

Canada. John Knox, the founder of Scottish Presbyterianism, was apprehended in 1547 by the French and sentenced to serve as a galley slave in the French navy. After eighteen months, he escaped. A Breton legend, however, suggests that before escaping he served some months on an exploration ship to New France. This is not impossible. A less reliable tradition supplies the information that, many years later, after his return to Scotland, one of his disciples asked him for his opinion of the New World, which had now become a refuge for the persecuted. Knox is said to have replied, 'I *canna dae wi'* it, I *canna dae wi'* it,' thus, albeit inadvertently, giving the country its name."

M. Gobert, *Memoires des Ecossais,*
(Geneva, 1897)

In the galleys he was supposed to be the slave, but he was master, he knew it and they knew it. The same on the expedition ship. The mate lacked the nerve to make him holystone the decks alongside the others, for fear of his tongue. No ears could endure the monstrous words (predestination! election! reprobation!) he would hurl against them. Still, he was no burden: when the barber-surgeon drowned in a storm, two weeks out of St. Malo, Knox took his place— no one else had the stomach for the job. Though he loathed the unbearable closeness of other living bodies on the ship. Give him solitary confinement, a narrow dungeon, and he would have been more content.

The captain, knowing his prowess as a controversialist, tried often, on this tedious journey, to entice him to his cabin for dinner, to dispute on matters theological. Knox spat at him as an idolator like all the others, and refused the bait.

Knox jettisoned the statue of the Virgin. It was on a Sunday, and the crew assembled for the weekly statue-kissing, a good-luck ritual, Knox grabbed the statue from its perch by the mainmast and hurled it, head over tail, halo of stars over serpent's head, out into the ocean. Where it sank like a stone. The sacrilege horrified the French sailors, but they kept their hands off him. He joked to his cat: "The Queen of the Sea cannae swim, Clootie." But they kept their hands off him.

Physically, Knox was scrawny. He was an aggressive talker, except to his cat, Clootie, a black creature, sleek, with wicked eyes. The cat was a growler, a hisser, and in the minds of the sailors, was Knox's familiar demon. Knox, too, was a growler, but never growled at Clootie:

"Well, Clootie, my wee man, did you ever see a country so naked of churches? It won't do. I can already imagine a forest of steeples along this river-bank. Churches could make this obscene river a lovely thing." (Knox could speak perfectly good English, ungnarled by "ach's" and "dinnae's," whenever he felt like it.)

The cat would purr its admiration of his voice, winding itself around his narrow shins. The man would squint about. If they were alone, he would allow the rubbing to continue, melting into it. If someone was watching, Knox would boot the cat out of his way, its tail swishing angrily

Thank Christ I am off the ship at last. That fat pig-wife of the captain's spying on me everywhere with her pig eyes. The only favour I ever did for her was to tear the dead baby out of her by the feet. Now she wants me. The black sows farrowing on my father's farm sickened me less. And thank Christ to be out of that stinking fo'c's'le. Filth and corruption everywhere. Men opening their breeches to show off the size of their organs. Ship's boys acting as their fancy-women.

But during the storms, the truth flared up in them. Fear bulged in their eyes, and I taunted them all, every single one of them, with the burning fires of hell. I was on deck during the great storm in mid-ocean, admiring the fury of the waters. They were trying to lower sail when a boom snapped, the sail ripped, and sheets flogged everywhere. A young sailor, the worst balls-strutter of the lot, caught his arm in the grip of a ratchet. The bone was half-broken, like a sappy branch, and all the flesh torn, the muscles severed. I took the surgeon's saw and sawed the arm away from his jerking body, then I carried him below and dipped the stump in boiling tar. For days, I was the one to bite off his rotten flesh and suck out the pus. I even swallowed it if they were watching. They couldn't match me. As long as I can remember, death and sickness, sickness and death have been my allies.

Now the voyage is over. This was a good place to land. All around me, beautiful sites for churches, plain churches, with plain cemeteries, no flowers if I can help it. I have planted already the men nobody else would touch, who died of cholera on the voyage. I've manured the soil with corpses the way we did with the dead cattle on the farm. I buried their sad priest, sick since we left France. Only Clootie and I attended his funeral. We commended his body to the devil. Back on the ship, I cleaned the shit and the vomit of the sick from the decks. It gives me an advantage over them all, they are so concerned about staying alive.

The sailors presented the natives with pieces of coloured broken glass, brown wooden beads, pieces of rope, and scraps of cloth. The natives seemed uninterested. One gift only, an iron knife, they all admired. The captain insisted it go to the chief, Quheesquheenay, to win his favour. They offered the natives pieces of Breton cheese, quite rank after the voyage, which the natives, in turn, gave to their dogs, fried chicken legs (chickens had been kept aboard), which the natives relished; boiled chicken eggs, which they spat out. Wine they treated as contaminated water, and could not understand why the sailors drank it when there was so much fresh water around. They munched cautiously on some lumps of black bread from the captain's pantry.   The natives gave little in return, no gold or silver, which was really what the sailors hoped for. They did give them amulets full of rats' giblets and bones. The sailors objected to the smell and threw the amulets into the river while the natives looked on. They invited the crew to eat a sort of stewed beef that smelt very appetizing, but the sailors were afraid it was made of human meat. Some of them vomited spontaneously at the very sight of it. The natives watched all this impassively.

Finally the chief's council offered, as a special treat to the captain, a bowl full of fresh assorted testicles of forest creatures, from the huge rubbery testes of the moose and the bear to the tiny soft beads of rats and rabbits. The captain hid his nausea and diplomatically accepted the gift. He took it back ship, and, after dark, flung the testes overboard. They caught in an eddy, and floated around the ship for days, swelling grotesquely till they burst and sank.

The male natives were tall, for the most part, well muscled, dressed in neatly stitched animal skins. Sickness was unusual amongst them. There were no wens, no leprosy, no bloody flux, no stopping of the stomach, no gout, no strangury, no fistulas, no tissicks, no spotted fever, no headmould, no shingles, no rickets, no scurvy, no griping in the guts. There were no congenital deformities. There were no pest houses.

The skin of the warriors was bronze and clear, except for battle scars. They had flashing dark eyes, and they all seemed to be superb athletes, capable of feats the puny

Bretons could only envy. They could lope with ease along tangled forest paths, hurl their spears gracefully, paddle their bark canoes at amazing speeds. They wrestled with ferocity, not hesitating to break an opponent's limb if the opportunity offered.

The natives had heard about the French from neighbouring tribes who had been visited by earlier ships, but this was the first they themselves had seen the strangers. Clearly they were disappointed for they found it impossible to respect men whose physical prowess was so defective. But they did respect the power of the arquebuses and the ship's canon, which the Frenchmen quickly demonstrated.

The French sailors learnt to be careful in their approaches to the native women. A warrior's wives were private property and it was death for a stranger to tamper with them. All the other women were available to all the tribe, and were quite free with their sexual favours, even widows and grandmothers. Which was as well for the Frenchmen, since the young women, golden-skinned and lithe, would have nothing to do with them. They had the bodies of dancers. Their clothing was provocative, their breasts dangling loose, their nipples erect when excited, which was often. Their skirts were split to the waist. When they ran, their hairless crotches were visible. Often, while they were relaxing, or were just sitting down, they would finger their groins unconsciously, or sometimes consciously if they saw the Frenchmen squinting at them.

At night the warriors would flit around their bonfires, whooping fearsomely. Or they would stretch on beds of skins moodily sucking on their tobacco pipes with glassy eyes. If the visitors were present, there would be an air of tension. The chief of the tribe, Quheesquheenay, would sit there on his deerskin mat, making no effort to communicate, staring intently at the Frenchmen. The solemn beat of drums would resound, echoed by other drums great distances away across the river.

"Oomhowoomareoomtheoomaliensoom?"

"Oomtheyoomstinkoomouroomvillageoomoutoom."

"Oomkilloomthemoom."

"Oomweoomunlikeoomyouoomonlyoomkilloomworthy-oomenemiesoom."

"Oomcutoomthemoomupoominoompiecesoom."

"Oomevenoomifoomweoomcutoomthemoomupoominoom-piecesoomandoomsewedoomalloomtheoombestoompart-soomtogetheroomweoomstilloomwouldoomno-toomhaveoomaoomreal oomenemyoomforoomtheiroom-penisesoomareoomlikeoomwormsoom."

"Oomuseoomtheiroompenisesoomtooomcatchoom-fishoom."

"Oomtheoomfishoominoomouroomriveroomaroom-toooomsmartoomtheyoomknowoomwormsoomareoomno-toomthatoojsmalloom."

I have the heathen under control. They despise the others but they fear me. I notice the young braves, showing off to each other, throwing their spears at targets, grow silent even when Clootie appears amongst them. Their shaman is terrified of the cat. I am sure he has tried all his curses against me and Clootie in vain, since the time when the daughter of the chief, Quheesquheenay, developed a terrible fever and was clearly going to die. The shaman couldn't cure her, he could only make things worse. The chief was desperate and asked if I could do anything. They believe that those who are indifferent to death have great power over life.

What makes John Knox tick? A question he sometimes asks himself. He tells himself this story:

Once upon a time early in the sixteenth century, a little Scottish boy lived on a farm near Edinburgh. He was a quick-witted little boy, too smart by half for his school-fellows, who hated his guts. He possessed certain time-honoured schoolboy traits: he liked to pluck the legs and wings from insects to see their reactions. He possessed, too, certain other traits not so time-honoured: with an axe, he enjoyed cutting the legs off live rabbits and chickens. From time to time, he would take pleasure in dropping a dead mouse into his mother's stew. On such occasions, he would play sick, and reap the double benefit of watching the others eat the stew, and of being himself considered rather delicate. This gained him additional attention. In short, that was the kind of boy he was. A practical joker.

He had many sisters, some of them quite attractive, and no brothers. His attitude toward his sisters was somewhat ambivalent. He hated their guts and would steal their make-up and pinch their arms quite cruelly. But, he liked to peep at them before bedtime through a crack in his bedroom wall, admiring the breasts and pudenda in their various stages of development. Yes, he found that rather a stimulating part of his day.

His mother and father, it should be noted, were honest-to-goodness farmers, and regular church-goers.

John Knox always likes the story to this point.

One of the practical jokes the boy liked to play concerned rats. He would capture rats in a wooden box. Then, when no one was around, he would head on over to the pigsty, and call out the pigs. There was a small round hole through the wall beside the feed-troughs. The boy would chase the rats out of the box, into this hole, and right into the mouths of the pigs. The pigs had grown fond of such a regular treat. This was one prank the boy really enjoyed.

One thing leads to another. It happened that he was looking after his littlest sister, three months old, while his parents were making jams inside the house. As he wandered past the pigsty, carrying the baby, he wondered how the pigs would deal with a tiny pink infant, rather than tiny pink rats. He gently laid the baby on the muddy floor of the sty, and called out the pigs.

Well, who knows what goes through a pig's mind? Did they even notice the different proportions, the different texture? Four huge porkers seized the baby's limbs, and ripped her to pieces, regardless of her screams, and swallowed her in great slobbering gobbets.

The howls of the baby and the snorting of the pigs attracted the attention of the honest father and mother, and they came running down from the farmhouse to see what was going on. What they saw horrifed them. They saw the bloody mess on the sty floor. They saw their little boy looking at them apprehensively.

At that very moment, just then, quite as if by design, the boy found religion. As soon as he saw the genuine anguish on his parents' honest faces, he began to shout, as if by instinct, "O Jesus, O Jesus," and jumping in amongst the pigs, kicked and slapped at their snouts, shouting, "Begone, Satan, begone," an expression he had often heard from the preachers at the church to which his honest parents took him each Sunday. His father grabbed him by the coat and pulled him out of that sty. The boy said, "I was takin' the babby doon for a walk, when a great hairy black beastie wi' fire comin' oot o' its mooth and its ears pulled the bairnie oot o' ma airms and threw it ower the wa' to the piggies."

He could see that his parents already half-believed him, certain that no human child would be capable of feeding his baby sister to pigs. The boy understood then that all the quirks in himself he had misguidedly thought to be unnatural and perverse were really, if properly perceived, signs of a religious disposition. And so he decided that, as soon as he grew up, he would become a Reformer. And he did. His parents became, in due course, very proud of his achievements, though he sometimes thought he could see a sceptical glint in their eyes. But they all lived happily ever after.

Such is the tale John Knox tells himself: he knows it doesn't cover all the bases, but it is generally quite pleasing. One thing still surprises him after all these years: when alone, religious matters never enter his head. He wonders if the other Reformers are the same, but hesitates to ask.

With my pussy-cat, Clootie, I went to her tepee. As we entered, a sweaty young man left, hitching up his loincloth. The tepee was all shadows and foul smells, the shaman's smoke. The girl lay on a frame bed of stretched skins, staring at the roof. She was naked, and she too was covered in sweat. Her legs were parted and her hand was at her crotch, fingers stroking. The chief, two of his councillors, and the shaman, stood beside the bed. He is a mouth shaman, and was leaning over her spitting some green mixture into her mouth. I saw her spit most of it right back in his face, and vomit up the rest. The shaman looked fierce with his red and white stripes but his eyes were anxious. He shook his rattles and howled, but they all knew, and he knew, he had failed. The girl looked over at me and smiled, the shreds of vomit around her mouth. She lifted her hand from her crotch, and stretched it out to me, her fingers glistening.
She had sweated out her disease, her *furor uterinus* for days, and she would die soon, for they did not know how to save her. All they could think of was to supply her with men to satisfy her deadly appetite and to trust in the shaman's superstitious mumbo-jumbo.

"That hill, over there by the sacrificial stakes, would be a good spot for a church."
"Ah, yes."

"The long-house would be all right as a temporary church, but they'd have to strip away those ornamental scalps and skulls."

"Indeed."

"If we burnt down the whole forest on the peninsula and ripped up the weeds and the flowers, and anything else alive, we could build a whole set of churches, one for every day of the week. Nothing fancy, no ornaments or any of that kind of thing, just plain seats and a stool for the preacher. Cats would be welcome. We'd have plain cemeteries with picket fences for each church.

"Interesting."

"How about a church under that waterfall? Made of fieldstone, very plain. You'd have to carry an umbrella for going in and out. A nice effect."
"Quite so."

I told them I must have absolute freedom in the treatment of the girl or I would do nothing. I ordered the shaman out with his barbarous cures. He mumbled at me, cursing me, no doubt, in his heathen way. I wouldn't let him away with that, but I replied moderately, damning him only according to the Scriptures. Clootie, as ever, snarling at him with hunched back, terrified him, and he hurried out of the tepee, along with the chief and the others. I called in two of the older sailors to help me begin this holy work.

First we forced her hands away from her groin. We lashed her hands and her feet to the sides of the crib to stop her thrashing about. She sweated even more and began screaming. I opened my Bible in my left hand and, from under my coat, I unsheathed my whip, which I had brought with me on purpose.

Everything was ready. I ordered the sailors to stand outside the entrance of the tepee, and allow no one to enter. I began to read from the Book of Psalms in a loud voice, uncoiling my whip slowly before the patient's eyes. Clootie jumped onto the bed and rubbed himself against her.

> My wounds stink and are corrupt because of my foolishness.
> For my loins are filled with a loathsome disease: and there is no soundness in my flesh.
> Thou shalt break them with a rod of iron.
> The heathen are sunk down in the pit that they made.
> Upon the wicked thou shalt rain snares, fire and brimstone, and a horrible tempest: this shall be the portion of their cup.
> Then did I beat them small as the dust before the wind.
> And I smote his enemies in the lower parts: I put them to a perpetual reproach.

I began to read the verses a second time, more loudly. But this time, after each verse, I lashed her naked body. She screamed as the skin lifted, the welts rose across her breasts. Then I aimed lower on her body, across the thighs and the open vulva. She stopped screaming She gave great gasps and whimpers, and it was my turn to roar. I shouted the verses and lashed harder and harder. Her body convulsed, and, at last, the demon rushed out between her legs in a liquid gurgle. Clootie, who had been rubbing himself against her all through this, howled, and his hair stood on end. I myself was roused by that evil in her. To ensure it was completely gone, I lashed her several more times. Then I put my hand cautiously towards her groin, fearful of the bite of the beast. With my fingers I could feel nothing at the entrance, so I slid them into the round, moist cavern. Still nothing to be afraid of. Unsatisfied, I inserted the long sweaty handle of my whip, turning it, moving it in and out, in and out, the sure way to scrape any remnants of the demon away. Her eyes glazed as she looked up at me, thankful for my precautions. I jerked the handle up and down rapidly, she convulsed again, sighed, and immediately fell asleep. I too was drained by my exorcism, but satisfied. I knew that all was well.

I sat for a moment to catch my breath, then I opened the tepee flap and let the chief and his men back in. I sensed their revulsion as they saw on her body the stripes of the lash. Yet she was in a deep, untroubled sleep and her fever was broken. I expected no thanks and received none. The shaman untied the ropes, and covered her sleeping body with skins. I told the chief that somebody must administer the same cure to her each time she fell into that fever. I told him, though I am not sure he understood, that he must build churches, churches, churches, in memory of her cure.

"You tell us we should not eat our enemies, yet the captain says that in France, he and his men eat Jehovah daily. Explain this. "

"Filthy heathen, spare me your quibbles."

"Before original sin, did men still fart and shit after they ate?"

"Filthy heathen, you do not understand."

"What good is heaven if all our tribe do not go to heaven? What good is heaven if my wives and my sons and my dogs are not in heaven with me? What good is heaven if my enemies are not there so that we can all reminisce together in heaven about old battles?"

"Filthy heathen, cease your blasphemy."

"How can you hate the women and yet desire them so much at the same time?"

"Filthy, lying heathen. You are one of the damned."

How ugly the aliens are, their skin is wormy white

and marred by scabs. Boils sprout on them overnight like forest toadstools. Their clothing is clumsy and heavy. Their minds are a mystery. They adore their Book, a collection of dead words. We would have annihilated them long ago, but for their guns. We have never before faced enemies who were contemptible as men, yet could defeat us in battle because of their weapons.

Their shamam, the little man, Knox, is the living death. He has made a few converts amongst our people, even my own daughter. Pain was his gift to her. The captain, a simple man, admits that many like Knox will come to our hunting grounds in the future. Our own shaman has dreamed, for three nights, the end of the world.

"I am curious about the function of your shamans across the ocean. Here, our shaman prays for good luck, curses bad luck, sings songs and tells good stories at our feasts, blesses the penis and vagina of the newly-weds, teaches the children how to bind arrows well, how to be brave in battle. He defies the demons of darkness; in times of famine, he fasts and moves his teepee to the forest so that the rest of us may eat well and live in company in the village. He weeps for all the dead, he rejoices at births. He loves the river, the trout, the moose, the eagle, the pack-wolves, the muskrats, the morning sun, the snow in winter: He is the friend of our friends, he admires the ferocity of our enemies. Nothing that exists disgusts him."

"He is a filthy heathen fiend and is already damned."

Their stay amongst us has lasted only two moons. They must sail away before the winter storms. They have wiped out all game within six miles of the village—we will now face a hard winter. Some of our children have died of a cough we have never known. As a final gesture, the aliens say they will kill for us, with their guns, our enemies in a neighbouring village. I have thanked them and refused their offer. Our shaman is glad they are leaving, but he still whispers to me that he sees only death in his omens.

One night around midnight, while the village fires were still flickering, two huge marauding bears came barging out of the forest. Knox's cat, Clootie, fur on end, charged at them screeching from deep in his throat. The bears, startled, turned and ran. For days afterwards, Knox would wheeze with laughter at the memory. "Ach, Clootie," he would say, "ane wee Scottish cratur is mair than a match for a' the beasties in the New Warld."

Some thoughts on a brief code of behaviour to be followed by converts after I am gone.
A. *Sexual Matters* Strict monogamy is a must, even bestiality is a lesser offence than adultery; sexual intercourse only for breeding; cover the flesh: shirts and trousers for men, underwear and breast bindings for women; absolutely no kissing, cuddling, or touching of the body of the other sex before marriage; the menstrual abomination to be dealt with in complete secrecy by the women.
B. *Other* Hunting needs to be organised on a less seasonal basis to keep the men from being idle for lengthy spells; rites of passage for the boys should not be discouraged, the pain being a valuable discipline; likewise the practice of torturing enemies: it teaches contempt of the flesh (much of these heathens' behaviour may be turned to good account)
C. *Build churches, churches.*

The French captain (his wife was party to it) coaxed one of the older native women to be his mistress. She would then gossip with the other women about his fat paunch and his stinking breath. And about how, with his wife looking on, he always made love to her from behind like a dog.

Whenever the captain appeared in the village afterwards, Knox would trot in front of him, barking as loudly as he could. All the village dogs would join the chorus. Some of the native women, inspired by this, would squat on the ground and urinate, as the captain passed, their tongues dangling like those of hounds.

We will root out the shaman Knox's followers after he has gone. Even my own daughter. We will saw off their heads with the iron knife they gave me, then we will throw the bodies and the knife into the river. Nothing of him will remain. He longs to return to his homeland where his enemies are more like him. We are too innocent for his liking. This alone is certain: we are our only friends.

The day before they were due to sail, a native guide led a group of sailors through the forest and showed them a mound of earth in a clearing. Knox and his cat Clootie went with them, as always when there was the prospect of some hunting. The sailors began digging in the mound, hoping to find some of that elusive treasure. Instead, skulls. Hundreds upon hundreds of human skulls. They presumed they were in some kind of traditional tribal burial place. But the skulls, belonging to men, women and children, all seemed recent. Perhaps some disease was responsible. Then they noted that many of the skulls had been split, pierced with sharp objects. They saw too, that the bone had not been picked clean by worms and ants. The guide told them the mound was the top of a shaft, hundreds of feet deep, and that it was the place where they had, for generations, buried the heads of enemies who had been decapitated. Their heads were boiled, he said, their brains eaten. In the last three moons before the sailors arrived, he said, Quheesquheenay's people had beheaded in this way at least one thousand enemies, and had filled the pit to overflowing. On the basis of that good omen, the arrival of the aliens had been welcomed. Some of the men were appalled, but Knox laughed heartily. They lacked faith, he said: it was clear from the Bible that Providence frequently operated by means of a timely massacre or two. Knox secretly suspected that Quheesqueenay had arranged the "discovery" to deter the Frenchmen from ever returning to the New World.

The coastline of France looms in the distance. Knox alone, of those on deck, does not need to be there. He relishes the ferocious cold, the thin snow falling in a gusty wind. The coastal hills are dappled with it, like leprosy. Or is it, he smiles, heaven's vomit? Clootie would have purred at the idea. Clootie who is not with him. Clootie, who had to be left behind, prowling, he imagines, those forest thickets, terrifying man and beast for years yet, especially that old heathen shaman. Reminding them of something they would not easily destroy. He thinks of Clootie with fondness but with no regret. The New World was child's play. Now the battle will be amongst professionals, like himself. He breathes deeply, fills his lungs with the chill air sweeping over the water from all the chill regions of the Old World. His home.

Chronicle of Anse Saint-Roch

·

Jacques Ferron

I

Between the Madeleine lighthouse and the harbour
of Mont-Louis an unmistakable line separates land and sea.
Because of the height of the cliff the only access to shore is
through one of four gullies, three of them visible from the
water, one quite hidden from view. They are, travelling from
east to west, Manche d'Epée, Gros-Morne, Anse-Pleureuse.
They cut deeply into the cliff, but the coves they feed are
small and exposed to wind and weather. "From Madeleine
to Mont-Louis, pay no heed to what you see and sail right
on," the old-timers used to say. The fourth gully, situated
between Gros-Morne and Anse-Pleureuse, is not easily
detected. Narrow and winding, it runs at a sharp angle into
a deep and sheltered bay. It was christened the Valley of
Mercy. "Don't depend on it," the sailors would say. "When
you look for it you never find it, and you're sure to find it
when you don't." As a result of this reputation, and also
because of the fact that the larger sailing vessels could only
enter it at high tide, its discreet harbour was hardly used. It

was forgotten. And though today you might hear talk of a Valley of Mercy, no-one would be able to tell you where it was. It has become a legend now.

The sailor judges the coast from a distance, aware only of the rise and fall of the land. The fisherman, who sails close to it, concentrates on the shoreline and ignores all that lies beyond. Accordingly, each has his own terms to describe what he sees. Mont-Louis, Gros-Morne bear the mark of the sailor, Manche d'Epée and Anse-Pleureuse are a fisherman's names. When the Valley of Mercy was rediscovered the place was christened Anse Saint-Roch, because the fishermen who spent their summers there came down from Saint-Roch-des-Aulnaies.

In November 1840 a typhus epidemic brought over on an emigrant ship, the *Merino*, swept through the parishes of the lower Saint Lawrence. The Abbé Toupin, the young and conscientious curate of l'Islet, was not in the least surprised, for he had long anticipated this kind of vengeance from Heaven. The epidemic lasted well into February. He had plenty of time to explain it. His preaching gained him immense popularity. People came from neighbouring parishes to hear him. However, as time went on, the Abbé Toupin's sermons grew gradually more somber. One Sunday he rose in his pulpit, a strange expression on his face. "Dearly beloved brethren," he cried, "the end of the world is at hand!" And he fell down dead. The epidemic died out soon afterwards. But its effects were to be felt for a long time. The following spring most of the boats stayed drawn up on the shore. Fishing had lost its appeal. The spirit of adventure had worked itself out at home. From Saint-Koch, only Thomette Gingras and Jules Campion went down to the Gulf.

II

After *brecquefeste* the Reverend William Andicotte

asked his wife what she felt about Canada. Intrigued, she looked down at the table, but there was nothing there to explain the question.

"William, have you had enough to eat?"

The clergyman pushed his plate aside. He was serious. He expected a reply. Canada, Canada . . . . Well, really she hadn't the slightest idea.

"God be praised!" he cried, "then you have nothing against my project?"

"Your project, William?"

"My mission, to be precise. I believe, dear, that Canada has need of us."

Reverend Andicotte was vicar of Liverpool Cathedral. A mournul looking man with red hair, he could, if occasion demanded, leave off his mournful mien and laugh. Though thin, he had the appetite of a band of fat friars, and while he preached asceticism, he hardly practised it. He was a man of contrasts, unintentionally disconcerting, an eccentric and quite forbidding in his way, yet a good minister for all that, and an astute theologian. The Lord Bishop had named him his successor.

His wife loved him. He loved her in return, as much and even more. For this her love grew stronger still, and time, thanks to this steady increase, had brought them both together. As they never had been very far apart, they were now extremely close indeed. This did not prevent them from having separate worlds. He lived for his church, she for her home. They had three daughters. The eldest resembled her father, without quite managing to be ugly.

The others were like their mother. All three were accomplished young ladies.

"But what about the episcopate, William?" Reverend Andicotte had been waiting for this episcopate for ten years. The Lord Bishop had promised it to him. When the old man died it would go to him. Only for ten years now it had not been the Lord Bishop's pleasure to die. In fact he was looking fitter every year and, if things went on this way, he would soon be celebrating his centenary.

"Fie on the episcopate!"

"Let's wait a little longer."

"The old boy will bury us. No, believe me, dear, it's best we go to Canada."

She believed him, just as she had always done. Besides she was still young enough to find the fervour of mission life more appealing than episcopal decorum. It was with a deep thrill of emotion, wholesome and utterly commendable, albeit unrecognized by the Church of England, that she gave him her consent. She had once been as ignorant of marriage as she now was of Canada, and marriage had not disappointed her.

"Shall I wash the dishes?" she enquired.

"No, no. Just break them, dear."

She did not dare. After twenty years of frugal living some actions were unthinkable. In the end she washed them. It was a bad omen.

III

One month after the fateful *brecquefeste*, the minister, his wife and their three daughters boarded the *Merino*. The day before, on hearing of their departure, the Lord Bishop had died of rage. They were still laughing about it. Seagulls darted above the girls' heads with shrill cries. The Reverend himself showed more restraint. He was escorted by an old and taciturn gull, with neck drawn in and wings starched stiff, belching from time to time just to prove it had a voice. The mother followed behind, slightly dazed by all these birds.

The captain was shaving. He heard the commotion. "What's all that?" He was told it had to do with some clergyman. He rushed out of his cabin and stood in their path, one cheek pink, the other black, his razor in his hand. Against the pink, the black stood out, and the razor became a scimitar. The seagulls fell silent. The old gull, hearing the laughter fade, thought he had gone deaf. Holding back the sound he would no longer hear, he hung there, motionless, above the silence.

"Who are you?" the Reverend asked the apparition.

"And who are you?"

"I am the Reverend Andicotte."

"And I the captain of this ship."

The two men looked each other up and down, then, wheeling suddenly about, the captain disappeared again inside his cabin. Followed closely by his females, the clergyman carried on to his.

"What did you think of him, William?"

"Dear," he replied, "we'll meet with worse than that in Canada."

The *Merino's* captain was not a church-going man. He had a strong dislike for clergymen, believing that they never laughed. And now it seemed they did. His curiosity was piqued. When he had finished shaving, he went to the Reverend's cabin. His appearance was much improved. They listened to him. He explained himself, and everyone was happy.

"But what were you laughing about?" he asked.

"About the Lord Bishop dying," explained Mary, the youngest.

The captain slapped his thighs. From now on, he decided, he would be an Anglican.

IV

The *Merino* was a former slave ship. Once the emigrants had boarded, the anchor was weighed. The emigrants forgot their woes and set their sights on the promised land. They left behind them a trail of human wreckage, of torn bellies, petrified children, demented souls and severed hands. The sails were hoisted. They were white. The ship left Liverpool, a black hulk borne on by hope.

"I'm the one who gives orders around here," the captain grumbled. Her Majesty's regulations prevented him, at least while in England, from taking on more than two hundred passengers. Gracious Majesty, perhaps, but stupid regulations; he had already taken two thousand negroes across.

"We might as well sail with no cargo at all, just to amuse the crew."

They set sail for Hamburg. There, another three hundred emigrants embarked. The captain's mood improved: with any less than five hundred passengers on a vessel built to carry a hundred, he would have felt lonely.

"I like having souls, lots of souls, in my charge," he confided to the minister.

The minister praised his zeal, although the overcrowding it occasioned did seem to him decidedly un-Anglican. He did not wish to complain, however. It is advisable not to press a convert too hard. "Besides," he thought, "we'll meet with worse than this in Canada."

V

Jules Campion and Thomette Gingras sailed out at the beginning of May, and two weeks later they reached Mont-Louis. The next day dawned on a sea of infinite calm. It was no good hoisting the sail: it takes more than a piece of cloth at the end of a mast to get a boat on its way. The two fishermen waited for high tide before moving out of the bay, then, when they were in open water, they shipped the oars and let the ebb-tide carry them east. Below Anse-Pleureuse they came closer to shore. A few huge icicles still hung from the cliff, a sure sign that they were too early to fish for cod. They were in no hurry to get there. They got there just the same. A long bright streak, like a shadow cast by the jutting cape above, stretched before them out to sea. Here and there the swirling waters warned of submerged rocks. The tide, though ebbing, was still high. They moved in among the reefs. The hull of the boat scraped a flat rock. Campion stood at the bow and pushed with an oar. The rocks dropped suddenly out of sight beneath them, and they were in the harbour. The valley came into view. Then a single detail caught their attention: from a cabin near the shore, a pale whiff of bluish smoke rose up and disappeared without a trace into the still air.

"Christ!" shouted Thomette Gingras, "they're burning our store of hardwood!"

VI

The joy of departure lasted only as long as the departure. As soon as land was out of sight they began to be sick.

"Bah!" said the captain. "No-one dies of seasickness!"

On the fifteenth day of the crossing four emigrants died. They were Poles. The captain shrugged his shoulders: they had paid their passage.

"They're not negroes. They can die when they like. After all, they're free men, aren't they?"

Besides, they had no doubt died of some Polish malady that would not affect British subjects.

VII

In her comfortable cabin on the upper deck, Mrs.

Andicotte was overcome by a malaise that seemed to rise up from the hold. If she ventured out, the reeling sky descended on her with harsh, discordant cries, and she was obliged to go back inside and lie down. Elizabeth and Mary stayed with her. She wept for their youth. Jane, the eldest, accompanied her father. She put the word of God before all else and paid little heed to proprieties.

VIII

Typhus is better than the plague. It brings with it a gentle resignation. Violent shivers, with scarlet spots, grip the patient. His tongue is paralyzed. He can no longer articulate his pain, but sings it, softly, sadly, without resisting. He can be thrown overboard before he is dead.

IX

Jane learned one day that Tom, the captain's negro slave, was dying in the hold. She went down to talk to him of God and fell into the hands of four sailors, who left her, bruised and streaked with tears and grime, alone with the negro. He crept over to her and, with a trembling hand, wiped her face. Then Jane, observing his charity, was touched. The captain found them together.

X

The spotted shivers took hold of the minister's wife. The *Merino* had been tacking back and forth in the Gulf for a week. She died off Gros-Morne. Her body was brought out onto the deck. Above it Tom the negro hung from a yardarm. The captain placed a lifeboat at the disposal of the bereaved family, and the *Merino* sailed on without them to Quebec.

XI

At the sight of the smoke Thomette Gingras was seized with great indignation. He threw himself down inside the boat, rummaged about in the gear, reappeared with a loaded shot-gun and shouted to his mate: "Bring 'er in, Jules!"

Jules worked the oars and the boat ran up on the beach. Gingras jumped ashore. Campion got up to follow him. A girl came out of the cabin, young, red-headed, well-built, but very scantily clad. Campion froze in the bow like a figurehead. The girl, just as taken aback as he was, stared, her mouth agape, forgetting to do up her bodice. This oversight by no means worsened things. Campion caught up with his mate.

"Don't shoot," he said. "She looks pretty tame to me."

"What'll we do?" asked Gingras, whose gun was getting him excited.

"Go take a closer look," suggested Campion.

They made as if to step forward. But at that very moment two more girls suddenly rushed out of the cabin, leaving them completely hamstrung. Gingras, now mightily impressed, shook his gun. "Christ! I'll shoot! I'll shoot!" he yelled, so as to keep himself from shooting. Campion did his best to calm him down.

"Easy now, Thomette! Easy now!"

Just then the girls, who were clustered in front of the door, parted, and a huge figure of a man, dressed all in black, with a shock of red hair, stepped out, a Bible in his hand.

"Christ! What's that?" The figure advanced. It was coming straight for them. Gingras fired. The man opened his mouth, as if he had swallowed the bullet, then pitched forward and fell to the ground, his nose buried in his big book.

XII

At Saint-Roch-des-Aulnaies autumn came and went. The village had waited in vain for the two fishermen. They were presumed drowned. Two years later a boat from Cap Saint-Ignace brought back news that they were still alive, healthy in body but in peril of their souls, consorting with three she-devils. The following spring fishermen in great numbers sailed out from the Lower Saint Lawrence to fish the Gaspé cod. On their return they all confirmed the news: Gingras and Campion had settled in Anse Saint-Roch, each with the girl of his choice and the children born to them out of wedlock, happy, healthy, and perfectly disposed, should the opportunity arise, to take the holy vows of matrimony, and not, by any means, in peril of their souls. Their women were two magnificent creatures, with skin as white as milk and flame-red hair, distinguished ladies, who spoke English like fine society folk. As for the devilry, it was all the work of the eldest sister, a strange, thin girl, red-haired but without the milk, who spent her time reading from a big, black book, while around her hung the black child she had had by Satan before the fishermen had come.

XIII

A single bird a sea-lit day
One lone gull wheeling low

It spins and dives to skim the spray
What you are I do not know.

Yet surely it is a sign to me
This ocean rose this stemless bloom
Showering its petals over the sea
And your love makes my senses swoon.

A shimmering veil this dizzy flight
As tenderness reveals its fate
And a wing-tip traces in the light
Your own emerging shape.

You rise new-born from the waters' motion
Wrapped in a mantle of silent wings
Bearing the mark of the ocean
And your name my heart now sings.

Let the lone bird still spin and turn
While God trembles far above
I glimpse your body's nascent form
And know you, Goddess of Love.

XIV

Man is a wanderer. Woman holds him back. A land
without a woman, fit only for passing through, a country
uninhabited because it lacked a place to plant the stake the
restless animal is tethered to. Such, for many years, was the
north coast of the Gaspé. Fishermen from Montmagny,
from Cap Saint-Ignace and l'Islet went down there every
spring, but they returned home at the end of the season.
No-one ever wintered there. The adventure of Gingras and
Campion marked the end of an era. The French Canadian

woman who triumphed over the squaw, her rival, in whose arms lay a whole new continent for the taking, was not the kind to give up her men. She would let them go as long as she could be sure of their return; otherwise she would go with them. And this was what the women of the Lower Saint-Lawrence did. Since the Gaspé was no longer safe, they said farewell to the older parishes, to their serene and Catholic countryside. They came down with their men, not for one summer, not to live out some dream of late afternoons beside the sea, but, bundled up to the neck, prepared for all seasons, to give life to the country. Before long, from Méchins to Rivière-aux-Renards, every cove was settled.

XV

Under the cliff, facing out to sea, your house is not large. Your man is brave, but he is not the master. Giants hover over you at night. At dawn the wind cuts down in all its force from the cliff-tops. It passes over your roof like a thousand shrieking birds. You shiver, even in normal times, when you have nothing to fear. But when a child stirs in your womb, you are filled with dread. Why did you leave the old country, where man is master, where the houses are large and the lands small? Why did you follow the fisherman's call to this wild, forsaken bay?

XVI

Jane came to a stop on the beach. She hesitated, her own question taken up for a moment in the harsh cries of the gulls and the unsteady motion of the air. Then she recovered. She had caught sight of her son, playing with shells, surrounded by a flock of ragged and familiar crows.

She had arrived here in great distress; then a child had been born and with its angry cry had reassured the whole world.

When the little black boy saw his mother, he left the shells and crows. She took him in her arms and rocked him. She was tired. She would have liked him to go to sleep, but his laughing eyes never left her. Soon afterward his uncles' boat came in. The men threw their catch up onto the shore, then climbed out themselves, happy as children. Jules Campion picked up a stone and threw it. To his surprise it hit a crow. The bird stayed where it was, its wing outstretched, its neck drawn in, its beak half open.

Jane had cried out in an attempt to stop Jules. She jumped up now, but it was too late. Misfortune had already struck. She took the bird in her hands. It stared at her fixedly. She tried to say she was sorry, but she knew that she would never be forgiven. So she let the bird go, and it hobbled off, dragging its broken wing. Jules and Thomette laughed at her distress. Two days later the little black boy cut his foot on a shell. The cut festered, the woolly head was soaked with sweat. All night the fever raged, and at dawn the shrieking birds swept down from the cliffs to carry off his soul.

Several weeks passed and Jane did not recover from this final blow. One morning, as the sun came up, she was sitting on a log, holding in her lap the huge Bible she no longer read, when she saw the wounded crow. She got up. The bird ran off toward the path that leads to Anse-Pleureuse. She followed it. Every now and then she lost sight of it, but whenever she stopped it would reappear. The path is steep; it veers up over the mountain to avoid the jutting capes. Jane was soon exhausted; her knees gave out. She had come to a burnt clearing that stretched across the path. She looked around her and saw the entire crow nation assembled there to judge her.

XVII

The Abbé Ferland, a professor at the college of Sainte-Anne-de-la-Pocatiere, a giant man with a heart of gold, spent that summer ranging up and down the north shore of the Gaspé, baptizing, confessing, marrying, bringing with him the peace of God. At Madeleine, with a single stroke of an axe, he silenced the Brawler who had been terrorizing the village. When he left Anse Saint-Roch, Jules Campion and Thomette Gingras had each one taken an English girl, with skin as white as milk and flaming hair, to be his lawful wedded wife. They were the happiest men alive. And they had many more children. As for Jane Andicotte, the Abbé found her half dead on the footpath to Anse-Pleureuse. He took her back with him. She found her final rest in the convent of the Ursulines in Quebec.

This chronicle records facts that may appear unseemly, but life itself is not always seemly. What counts is that in the end events all fall into place, and around the wild, forsaken bay, little by little, the gentle customs of the old country triumph over pagan fear, softening the cries of the birds that pass in the gusts of wind that sweep down off the land.

Translated by Betty Bednarski

What I Learned from Caesar

·

Guy Vanderhaeghe

The oldest story is the story of flight, the search for greener pastures. But the pastures we flee, no matter how brown and blighted—these travel with us; they can't be escaped. My father was an immigrant. You would think this no penalty in a nation of immigrants, but even his carefully nurtured, precisely colloquial English didn't spare him much pain. Nor did his marriage to a woman of British stock (as we called it then, before the vicious-sounding acronym Wasp came into use). That marriage should have paid him a dividend of respectability, but it only served to make her suspect in marrying him.

My father was a lonely man, a stranger who made matters worse by pretending he wasn't. It's true that he was familiar enough with his adopted terrain, more familiar than most because he was a salesman. Yet he was never really of it, no matter how much he might wish otherwise. I only began to understand what had happened to him when I, in my turn, left for greener pastures, heading east. I didn't go so far, not nearly so far as he had. But I also learned that there is a price to be paid. Mine was a trivial one, a feeling of mild unease. At odd moments I betrayed myself and my beginnings; I knew that I lacked the genuine ring of a local. And I had never even left my own country.

Occasionally I return to the small Saskatchewan town near the Manitoba border where I grew up. To the unpractised eye of an easterner the countryside around that town might appear undifferentiated and monotonous, part and parcel of that great swath of prairie that vacationers drive through, pitying its inhabitants and deploring its restrooms, intent only on leaving it all behind as quickly as possible. But it is just here that the prairie verges on parkland, breaking into rolling swells of land, and here, too, that it becomes a little greener and easier on the eye. There is still more sky than any country is entitled to, and it teases the traveller into believing he can never escape it or find shelter under it. But if your attention wanders from that hypnotic expanse of blue and the high clouds drifting in it, the land becomes more comfortable as prospects shorten, and the mind rests easier on attenuated distances. There is cropland: fields of rye, oats, barley, and wheat; flat, glassy sloughs shining like mirrors in the sun; a solitary clump of trembling poplar; a bluff that gently climbs to nudge the sky.

When I was a boy it was a good deal bleaker. The topsoil had blown off the fields and into the ditches to form black dunes; the crops were withered and burnt; there were no sloughs because they had all dried up. The whole place had a thirsty look. That was during the thirties when we were dealt a doubly cruel hand of drought and economic depression. It was not a time or place that was kindly to my father. He had come out of the urban sprawl of industrial Belgium some twenty-odd years before, and it was only then, I think, that he was beginning to come to terms with a land that must have seemed forbidding after his own tiny country, so well tamed and marked by man. And then this land played him the trick of becoming something more than forbidding; it became fierce, and fierce in every way.

It was in the summer of 1931, the summer that I thought was merely marking time before I would pass into high school, that he lost his territory. For as long as I could remember I had been a salesman's son, and then it ended. The company he worked for began to feel the pinch of the depression and moved to merge its territories. He was let go. So one morning he unexpectedly pulled up at the front door and began to haul his sample cases out of the Ford.

"It's finished," he said to my mother as he flung the cases on to the lawn. "I got the boot. I offered to stay on—strictly commission. He wouldn't hear of it. Said he couldn't see fit to starve two men where there was only a living for one. I'd have starved that other sonofabitch out. He'd have had to hump his back and suck the hind tit when I was through with him." He paused, took off his fedora and nervously ran his index finger around the sweat-band. Clearing his throat, he said, "His parting words were, 'Good luck, Dutchie!' I should have spit in his eye. Jesus H. Christ himself wouldn't dare call me Dutchie. The bastard."

Offence compounded offence. He thought he was indistinguishable, that the accent wasn't there. Maybe his first successes as a salesman owed something to his naivety. Maybe in good times, when there was more than enough to go around, people applauded his performance by buying from him. He was a counterfeit North American who paid them the most obvious of compliments, imitation. Yet hard times make people less generous. Jobs were scarce, business was poor. In a climate like that, perceptions change, and perhaps he ceased to be merely amusing and became, instead, a dangerous parody. Maybe that district manager, faced with a choice, could only think of George Vander Elst as Dutchie. Then again, it might have been that my father just wasn't a good enough salesman. Who can judge at this distance?

But for the first time my father felt as if he had been exposed. He had never allowed himself to remember that he was a foreigner, or if he had, he persuaded himself he had been wanted. After all, he was a northern European, a Belgian. They had been on the preferred list. He had left all that behind him. I don't even know the name of the town or the city where he was born or grew up. He always avoided my questions about his early life as if they dealt with a distasteful and criminal past that was best forgotten. Never, not even once, did I hear him speak Flemish. There were never any of the lapses you might expect. No pet names in his native language for my mother or myself; no words of endearment which would have had the comfort of childhood use. Not even when driven to one of his frequent rages did he curse in the mother tongue. If he ever prayed, I'm sure it was in English. If a man forgets the cradle language in the transports of prayer, love, and rage—well, it's forgotten.

The language he did speak was, in a sense, letter-perfect, fluent, glib. It was the language of wheeler-dealers, and spoke of people as live-wires, go-getters, self-made men. Hyphenated words to describe the hyphenated life of the seller, a life of fits and starts, comings and goings. My father often proudly spoke of himself as a self-made man, but this description was not the most accurate. He was a remade man. The only two pictures of him which I have in my possession are proof of this.

The first is a sepia-toned photograph taken, as nearly as I can guess, just prior to his departure from Belgium. In this picture he is wearing an ill-fitting suit, round-toed, clumsy boots, and a cloth cap. The second was taken by a street photographer in Winnipeg. My father is walking down the street, a snap-brim fedora slanting rakishly over one eye. His suit is what must have been considered stylish then—a three-piece pin-stripe—and he is carrying an overcoat casually over one arm. He is exactly what he admired most, a "snappy dresser", or, since he always had trouble with his p's, a "snabby dresser". The clothes, though they mark a great change, aren't really that important. Something else tells the story.

In the first photograph my father stands rigidly with his arms folded across his chest, unsmiling. Yet I can see that he is a young man who is hesitant and afraid; not of the camera, but of what this picture-taking means. There is a reason why he is having his photograph taken. He must leave something of himself behind with his family so he will not be forgotten, and carry something away with him so that he can remember. That is what makes this picture touching; it is a portrait of a solitary, an exile.

In the second picture his face is blunter, fleshier nothing surprising in that, he is older. But suddenly you realize he is posing for the camera—not in the formal, European manner of the first photograph but in a manner far more unnatural. You see, he is pretending to be entirely natural and unguarded; yet he betrays himself. The slight smile, the squared shoulder, the overcoat draped over the arm, all are calculated bits of a composition. He has seen the camera from a block away. My father wanted to be caught in exactly this negligent, unassuming pose, sure that it would capture for all time his prosperity, his success, his adaptability. Like most men, he wanted to leave a record. And this was it. And if he had coached himself in such small matters, what would he ever leave to chance?

That was why he was so ashamed when he came home that summer. There was the particular shame of having lost his job, a harder thing for a man then than it might be today. There was the shame of knowing that sooner or later we would have to go on relief, because being a lavish spender he had no savings. But there was also the shame of a man who suddenly discovers that all his lies were transparent, and everything he thought so safely hidden had always been in plain view. He had been living one of those dreams. The kind of dream in which you are walking down the street, meeting friends and neighbours, smiling and nodding, and when you arrive at home and pass a mirror you see for the first time you are stark naked. He was sure that behind his back he had always been Dutchie. For a man with so much pride a crueller epithet would have been kinder; to be hated gives a man some kind of status. It was the condescension implicit in that diminutive, its mock playfulness, that made him appear so undignified in his own eyes.

And for the first time in my life I was ashamed of him. He didn't have the grace to bear an injustice, imagined or otherwise, quietly. At first he merely brooded, and then like some man with a repulsive sore, he sought pity by showing it. I'm sure he knew that he could only offend, but he was under a compulsion to justify himself. He began with my mother by explaining, where there was no need for explanation, that he had had his job taken from him for no good reason. However, there proved to be little satisfaction in preaching to the converted, so he carried his tale to everyone he knew. At first his references to his plight were tentative and oblique. The responses were polite but equally tentative and equally oblique. This wasn't what he had hoped for. He believed that the sympathy didn't measure up to the occasion. So his story was told and retold, and each time it was enlarged and embellished until the injustice was magnified beyond comprehension. He made a damn fool of himself. This was the first sign, although my mother and I chose not to recognize it.

In time everyone learned my father had lost his job for no good reason. And it wasn't long before the kids of the fathers he had told his story to were following me down the street chanting, "No good reason. No good reason." That's how I learned my family was a topical joke that the town was enjoying with zest. I suppose my father found out too, because it was about that time he stopped going out of the house. He couldn't fight back and neither could I. You never can.

After a while I didn't leave the house unless I had to. I spent my days sitting in our screened verandah reading old copies of *Saturday Evening Post* and *Maclean's*. I was content to do anything that helped me forget the heat and the monotony, the shame and the fear, of that longest of summers. I was thirteen then and in a hurry to grow up, to press time into yielding the bounty I was sure it had in keeping for me. So I was killing time minute by minute with those magazines. I was to enter high school that fall and that seemed a prelude to adulthood and independence. My father's misfortunes couldn't fool me into believing that maturity didn't mean the strength to plunder at will. So when I found an old Latin grammar of my mother's I began to read that too. After all, Latin was the arcane language of the professions, of lawyers and doctors, those divinities owed immediate and unquestioning respect. I decided I would become either one, because respect could never be stolen from them as it had been from my father.

That August was the hottest I can remember. The dry heat made my nose bleed at night, and I often woke to find my pillow stiff with blood. The leaves of the elm tree in the front yard hung straight down on their stems; flies buzzed heavily, their bodies tip-tapping lazily against the screens, and people passing the house moved so languidly they seemed to be walking in water. My father, who had always been careful about his appearance, began to come down for breakfast barefoot, wearing only a vest undershirt and an old pair of pants. He rarely spoke, but carefully picked his way through his meal as if it were a dangerous obstacle course, only pausing to rub his nose thoughtfully. I noticed that he had begun to smell.

One morning he looked up at me, laid his fork carefully down beside his plate and said, "I'll summons him."

"Who?"

"Who do you think?" he said scornfully. "The bastard who fired me. He had no business calling me Dutchie.
That's slander."

"You can't summons him."

"I can," he said emphatically. "I'm a citizen. I've got
rights. I'll go to law. He spoiled my good name."

"That's not slander."

"It is."

"No it isn't."

"I'll sue the bastard," he said vaguely, looking
around to appeal to my mother, who had left the room. He
got up from the table and went to the doorway. "Edith," he
called, "tell your son I've got the right to summons that bastard."

Her voice came back faint and timid, "I don't know,
George."

He looked back at me. "You're in the same boat,
sonny. And taking sides with them don't save you. When we
drown we all drown together."

"I'm not taking sides," I said indignantly. "Nobody's
taking sides. It's facts. Can't you see . . . ," but I didn't get a
chance to finish. He left, walked out on me. I could hear his
steps on the stairway, tired, heavy steps. There was so much
I wanted to say. I wanted to make it plain that being on his
side meant saving him from making a fool of himself again.
I wanted him to know he could never win that way. I wanted him to win, not lose. He was my father. But he went up
those steps, one at a time, and I heard his foot fall distinctly,
every time. Beaten before he started, he crawled back into
bed. My mother went up to him several times that day, to
see if he was sick, to attempt to gouge him out of that room,
but she couldn't. It was only later that afternoon, when I was

reading in the verandah, that he suddenly appeared again, wearing only a pair of undershorts. His body shone dully with sweat, his skin looked grey and soiled. "They're watching us," he said, staring past me at an empty car parked in the bright street.

Frightened, I closed my book and asked who was watching us.

"The relief people," he said tiredly. "They think I've got money hidden somewhere. They're watching me, trying to catch me with it. The joke's on them. I got no money." He made a quick, furtive gesture that drew attention to his almost naked body, as if it were proof of his poverty.

"Nobody is watching us. That car's empty."

"Don't take sides with them," he said, staring through the screen. I thought someone from one of the houses across the street might see him like that, practically naked.

"The neighbours'll see," I said, turning my head to avoid looking at him.

"See what?" he asked, surprised.

"You standing like that. Naked almost."

"There's nothing they can do. A man's home is his castle. That's what the English say, isn't it?"

And he went away laughing.

Going down the hallway, drawing close to his door that always stood ajar, what did I hope? To see him dressed, his trousers rolled up to mid-calf to avoid smudging his cuffs, whistling under his breath, shining his shoes? Everything as it was before? Yes. I hoped that. If I had been younger then and still believed that frogs were turned into princes with a kiss, I might even have believed it could happen. But I didn't believe. I only hoped. Every time I approached his door (and that was many times a day, too many), I felt the queasy excitement of hope.

It was always the same. I would look in and see him Lying on the tufted pink bedspread, naked or nearly so, gasping for breath in the heat. And I always thought of a whale stranded on a beach because he was such a big man. He claimed he slept all day because of the heat, but he only pretended to. He could feel me watching him and his eyes would open. He would tell me to go away, or bring him a glass of water; or, because his paranoia was growing more marked, ask me to see if they were still in the street. I would go to the window and tell him, yes, they were. Nothing else satisfied him. If I said they weren't, his jaw would shift from side to side unsteadily and his eyes would prick with tears. Then he imagined more subtle and intricate conspiracies.

I would ask him how he felt.

"Hot," he'd say, "I'm always hot. Can't hardly breathe. Damn country," and turn on his side away from me.

My mother was worried about money. There was none left. She asked me what to do. She believed women shouldn't make decisions.

"You'll have to go to the town office and apply for relief," I told her.

"No, no," she'd say, shaking her head. "I couldn't go behind his back. I couldn't do that. He'll go himself when he feels better. He'll snap out of it. It takes a little time."

In the evening my father would finally dress and come downstairs and eat something. When it got dark he'd go out into the yard and sit on the swing he'd hung from a limb of our Manitoba maple years before, when I was a little boy. My mother and I would sit and watch him from the verandah. I felt obligated to sit with her. Every night as he settled himself onto the swing she would say the same thing. "He's too big. It'll never hold him. He'll break his back." But the swing held him up and the darkness hid him from the eyes of his enemies, and I like to think that made him happy, for a time.

He'd light a cigarette before he began to swing, and then we'd watch its glowing tip move back and forth in the darkness like a beacon. He'd flick it away when it was smoked, burning a red arc in the night, showering sparks briefly, like a comet. And then he'd light another and another, and we'd watch them glow and swing in the night.

My mother would lean over to me and say confidentially, "He's thinking it all out. It'll come to him, what to do."

I never knew whether she was trying to reassure me or herself. At last my mother would get to her feet and call to him, telling him she was going up to bed. He never answered. I waited a little longer, believing that watching him I kept him safe in the night. But I always gave up before he did and went to bed too.

The second week of September I returned to school. Small differences are keenly felt. For the first time there was no new sweater, or unsharpened pencils, or new fountain pen whose nib hadn't spread under my heavy writing hand. The school was the same school I had gone to for eight years, but that day I climbed the stairs to the second floor that housed the high school. Up there the wind moaned more persistently than I remembered it had below, and intermittently it threw handfuls of dirt and dust from the schoolyard against the windows with a gritty rattle.

Our teacher, Mrs. MacDonald, introduced herself to us, though she needed no introduction since everyone knew who she was—she had taught there for over ten years. We were given our texts and it cheered me a little to see I would have no trouble with Latin after my summer's work. Then we were given a form on which we wrote a lot of useless information. When I came to the space which asked for Racial Origin I paused, and then, out of loyalty to my father, numbly wrote in "Canadian". After that we were told we could leave. I put my texts away in a locker for the first time—we had had none in public school—but somehow it felt strange going home from school emptyhanded. So I stopped at the library door and went in. There was no school librarian and only a few shelves of books, seldom touched. The room smelled of dry paper and heat. I wandered around aimlessly, taking books down, opening them, and putting them back. That is, until I happened on Caesar's *The Gallic Wars*. It was a small, thick book that nestled comfortably in the hand. I opened it and saw that the left-hand pages were printed in Latin and the right-hand pages were a corresponding English translation. I carried it away with me, dreaming of more than proficiency in Latin.

When I got home my mother was standing on the front step, peering anxiously up and down the street. "Have you seen your father?" she asked. "No," I said. "Why?" She began to cry. "I told him all the money was gone. I asked him if I could apply for relief. He said he'd go himself and have it out with them. Stand on his rights. He took everything with him. His citizenship papers, baptismal certificate, old passport, bank book, everything. I said, 'Everyone knows you. There's no need.' But he said he needed proof. Of what? He'll cause a scandal. He's been gone for an hour."

We went into the house and sat in the living-room. "I'm a foolish woman," she said. She got up and hugged me awkwardly. "He'll be all right."

We sat a long time listening for his footsteps. At last we heard someone come up the walk. My mother got up and said, "There he is." But there was a knock at the door.

I heard them talking at the door. The man said, "Edith, you better come with me. George is in some trouble."

My mother asked what trouble.

"You just better come. He gave the town clerk a poke. The constable and doctor have him now. The doctor wants to talk to you about signing some papers."

"I'm not signing any papers," my mother said.

"You'd better come, Edith."

She came into the living-room and said to me, "I'm going to get your father."

I didn't believe her for a minute. She put her coat on and went out.

She didn't bring him home. They took him to an asylum. It was a shameful word then, asylum. But I see it in a different light now. It seems the proper word now, suggesting as it does a refuge, a place to hide.

I'm not sure why all this happened to him. Perhaps there is no reason anyone can put their finger on, although I have my ideas. But I needed a reason then. I needed a reason that would lend him a little dignity, or rather, lend me a little dignity; for I was ashamed of him out of my own weakness. I needed him to be strong, or at least tragic. I didn't know that most people are neither.

When you clutch at straws, anything will do. I read my answer out of Caesar's The *Gallic Wars*, the fat little book I had carried home. In the beginning of Book I he writes, "Of all people the Belgae are the most courageous . . . ." I read on, sharing Caesar's admiration for a people who would not submit but chose to fight and see glory in their wounds. I misread it all, and bent it until I was satisfied. I reasoned the way I had to, for my sake, for my father's. What was he but a man dishonoured by faceless foes? His instincts could not help but prevail, and like his ancestors, in the end, on that one day, what could he do but make the shadows real, and fight to be free of them?

Tanganyika

•

Brian Brett

After Jim Luster died he went to Tanganyika. He woke up at the wheel of a new car, and the long, black roll of road unravelled into the valley below like a big snake. The landscape was brown, its hills undulating and peppered with stick trees.

He woke up hot and thirsty, his hands on the wheel, his eyes fixed on the nearby trees that were the colour of a deer's hide. The trapped air within the car was suffocating, so he unrolled the window. The heat swept by.

He was tired already.

He noticed the trees on the surrounding hills were twisted—too much wind.

It was an Africa without lions; at least it resembled the Africa he had always dreamed, and Luster was disappointed because there were no lions. If he was going to be dead in Africa, he should have been given lions. But there weren't any animals moving in the valley or the mountains. There wasn't even a bird.

His clothes felt dirty, his mouth dusty, his head full of insect sounds. Yet, he drove on. He wanted to talk, tell himself he was alive, but a squall of crystal-like insect wings drowned out everything, ticking against the windshield and obscuring the route.

He drove for hours down that empty road in the empty valley.

Finally, Luster saw a man gathering hay, and he steered the car onto the dirt shoulder, breaking open a cloud of dust like birds.

The man leaned on a long, wooden rake-thing, waving away the dust from the car with his straw hat as Luster climbed out and slammed the door. The sound of the slamming door echoed in a world that was silent now that the motor was no longer running. It reminded him of when his head hit the rock.

The stranger had dark skin, tanned by years under the sun. A strand of rope held up his baggy trousers. Smiling toothlessly, he resembled a Mexican peasant standing among piles of golden hay.

"Have you died?" the peasant asked, polite, unsure of either the words or perhaps the crazy death they shared in nowhere. He was as solid as stone; big and full of the flesh a man carries in his prime.

"Yes." Luster's ears roared with the sound of the locusts rising from a devoured field. At least something else was alive out there in the empty land. "Where am I?"

"In the valley of Tanganyika."

It sounded logical, and Luster didn't wonder until later if the peasant meant this was a valley in Tanganyika or a valley named Tanganyika. By the time he realized he still didn't know where he was, the man had been left far behind.

Standing lamely in front of him, Luster couldn't think of anything else to say. He wanted to ask the man if he was also dead.

Luster realized the bright hay piled beside the rake

wasn't grass. It was the product of huge trees spotted throughout the valley—deadlimbed giants without leaves, burdened by the yellow straw which drifted to the ground at every gust of wind.

"Are you infested?" the peasant asked.

Luster's heart began to pound. His body felt awkward, his thoughts seated above it, as if he were an outsider examining himself. Infested? No, it wasn't disease, unless the disease was too much life. The conclusion was violent and abrupt, but strangely, he didn't regret it. To lie in her arms, his blood leaking onto her, staining the wet stones by the pool, her damp belly cushioning him as the cold seeped from his fingers, up his arms, to the back of his neck. Infested? Is death a disease? Luster looked into the sun. "No." His eyes filled with black spots, so he focused on the peasant, and the spots turned green. The sound of the locusts returned.

The peasant bent to his knees in the straw, searching for something invisible on the ground, ignoring Luster who was still considering infested. There are two kinds of infested. Those who break down, give up, and wait for disease to tag them, and those who fall by chance, get caught by luck and circumstance . . . like him. No, that wasn't a disease. How could he deny the touch of her fingers or that smooth skin on her belly?

The stranger's hand darted forward; he caught something, cupped it in his palm. He stood up and showed it to Luster. It was a silver toad.

"If you're not infested—then you can watch." The man admired and stroked the amphibian in his open palm, held it up to the sun and whispered at its head. The toad didn't move. It knew it was in trouble. He took a small knife from the pocket of his well-used trousers, and with the knife poked out one of the toad's eyes, rolling the tiny ball in his palm as if it were a sacred object. He beckoned for Luster to follow as he walked across the road to a dirt lane while Luster trailed behind like a sick man.

After studying it for a moment, the peasant set the silver toad on the lane and dropped the eye six inches in front of it. The toad sat stupidly in the dirt; then lunged forward and devoured its own eye.

"Let that be a lesson. Never allow anyone to put out your eyes." The peasant shuffled back across the road to his interrupted haying. Luster couldn't move. The locusts were hungry in the field. It beat at the back of his eyes, that sound like the wind of broken wings, telling him he was going to lose something, and he wanted her arms again, wanted to knead her flesh with his fingers. Alive.

The toad bounced sloppily across the dirt and fell into a pond of clear black water; giant, mossy branches interwove with each other beneath the surface. Green turtles rested on the mud bottom.

One lurched, almost too quick for such a lethargic animal, and its beak engulfed the toad's leg.

Luster turned away, ran to the car, and jumped in, driving off without waving goodbye. He knew he had a long way to go, even if he didn't know where he was going. And the rock kept rising out of the deep water. Alive. Childhood lovers, they'd come to the same pool and swum naked through the summers for fifteen years, falling more in love each year. The pool. That clear aquamarine water. Cold. The surface rippled around the waterfall. Her naked skin gliding beneath the reflection. It was too beautiful. Why did he jump? Because she had surfaced and cried: "Come in! Come in!" And he had always jumped. Only this time God had moved the rock.

So he drove down that singing, hellish road for what seemed like eternity. His ears were pounding with locusts. His head was looking for all the memories—those that he loved and those he hated, but mostly those that he loved—

the cottonwood trees rising above the river where the steelhead ran, the perfect cup of coffee in the morning, the satisfied leap of joy when the right thing falls into the right place. Her long hair spreading around her underwater. And for the first time Luster realized the insufficiency of life. He was grateful for what he had taken, yet he wanted more. He wanted everything.

She killed him. No, he killed himself. He always had to jump. Take that extra step. More love. More height. There wasn't enough life. His fist split the water and the icy world of the pool engulfed him in silence. Down. Down. The boulder rushed toward him. A black iceberg five feet from where it should have been. And he shuddered at the memory of the contact. His hand knocked aside in slow motion, his forehead striking and bending back. It was a dream, the dark bulk filled his vision, the crack that echoed underwater and his back corkscrewing.

He was lying on the stony bottom of the pool, his eyes open, watching her naked body dive towards him, the bubbles streaming behind her, and he wanted to touch her thighs even though he couldn't move.

When she dragged him onto the shore, crying, holding him, her skin clammy against his, he couldn't tell her that God had transplanted the rock the night before. He couldn't embrace her, say good-bye. But he could see. The blood on the stones, on her. She picked up his bathing suit. She didn't want to leave him naked on the beach. She looked so awkward staring at it, wondering what to do in that pained way he'd learned to love over the years. It didn't matter. He wouldn't be alive by the time she found somebody to take him back to town. He'd just be a body beside a pool in a forest. His eyes filled with blood.

The road veered, and at the curve was a large white house. It was square, lined with small, odd windows, something a cubist painter would design. The walls were made of whitewashed stone.

A young girl, perhaps seventeen years old, stood on the roof, leaning against a stone ledge, waiting for someone. When she saw Luster driving towards the house, she waved.

He stopped the car and got out. Not knowing what else to do, he waved at her. It was then he realized he still didn't know where he was, and worse, he had the vague fear that Tanganyika no longer existed. For a moment he wanted to go back and ask the peasant again.

The dark girl clapped her hands over her head and sprang high into the air.

She started to dance, moving slow, banging her open hands against her body and the stone ledge in a manner that told him she knew of locusts and toads and what they meant on this road.

He could only see the upper half of her body behind the ledge. Soon she was joined by another girl who was smaller but also lovely. They danced and hurrahed and threw themselves into the air.

A young man moved alongside them with a mandolin, playing a song that reminded Luster of the insect wings and hay the colour of gold.

The three sang and laughed and danced while the tears burned rivers down Luster's dusty face as he leaned on the car, one hand resting against the hot metal, one hand held to his mouth.

They shouted for him to join them. He was thirsty and tired, and they were so beautiful he found himself sucked towards the door at the side of the house.

The first girl skipped down the stairs and embraced him at the door. He let his hand rest on her waist, and smiled when she kissed his cheek.

Inside the house there were animal noises, the sound of lions at their kill, and he thought, "At last I'm getting somewhere."

The other girl appeared beside him. She ran her hand over his shoulder as if greeting a lover returned from a long journey. Behind her, the young man strummed his mandolin, half-way down the stairs, pretending he was in a trance. Luster could tell he was a fake, and began wondering about the girls. Luster had done his share of dancing—the boy didn't have it. And for a sweet moment, he wanted to show him how to dance.

Then the first girl swung open the oak door, and he peered into the belly of the house. There was a party taking place. The darkened interior was filled with people laughing and dancing and talking. Luster could make out no faces.

She smiled and pulled his ear gently. His hand was still around her waist. "Are you infested?" she asked.

And Luster knew that being infested wasn't a disease, no blistering and corruption of the meat. It didn't have anything to do with the body. It was time and chance. It was life. The rock. "Yes." The locusts drummed under his clothes, all around his body. He knew what was going to happen next.

"Do you want to come in?" He was tired and thirsty. "Yes."

"You must give us your eyes."

He moved backward, dropping his hand from her waist. He'd been warned; the old peasant had told him what was going to happen when he'd been lucky enough to make the wrong answer. "No, I won't give you my eyes."

"But," she pouted, her hands held tight against her chest, "everyone is here; if you take the road you will never find them again."

"Everyone?" That awful lump was in his throat—the knowledge that he was caught on the hook of his dying. The road, he knew it went on forever, lifeless and lonely. The worst kind of death. Inside the house there was no sun. It was shadowy, yet the party was endless.

"Of course." She pointed to the dim interior. The crowd moved aside and he saw his father seated at a long table, drinking and laughing, pounding his glass on the wood. One by one, he saw them: family, friends—drinking and enjoying themselves, but it was dark and he couldn't see if they had eyes.

"You must go in," the mandolin player insisted.

Luster didn't know what to do. He looked at the sun, that huge black wave of locusts moving towards the edge of the valley. Then he contemplated the murky room. She was there.

"Come in. Come in!" she shouted from inside the house. She was naked, as beautiful as ever, covered with blood, holding the silly bathing trunks in her hand. And the rock was behind her.

As Birds Bring Forth the Sun

•

Alistair MacLeod

Once there was a family with a highland name who lived beside the sea. And the man had a dog of which he was very fond. She was large and grey, a sort of staghound from another time. And if she jumped up to lick his face, which she loved to do, her paws would jolt against his shoulders with such force that she would come close to knocking him down and he would be forced to take two or three backward steps before he could regain his balance. And he himself was not a small man, being slightly over six feet and perhaps one hundred and eighty pounds.

She had been left, when a pup, at the family's gate in a small handmade box and no one knew where she had come from or that she would eventually grow to such a size. Once, while still a small pup, she had been run over by the steel wheel of a horse-drawn cart which was hauling kelp from the shore to be used as fertilizer. It was in October and the rain had been falling for some weeks and the ground was soft. When the wheel of the cart passed over her, it sunk her body into the wet earth as well as crushing some of her ribs; and apparently the silhouette of her small crushed body was visible in the earth after the man lifted her to his chest while she yelped and screamed. He ran his fingers along her broken bones, ignoring the blood and urine which fell upon his shirt, trying to soothe her bulging eyes and her scrabbling front paws and her desperately licking tongue.

The more practical members of his family, who had seen run-over dogs before, suggested that her neck be broken by his strong hands or that he grasp her by the hind legs and swing her head against a rock, thus putting an end to her misery. But he would not do it. Instead, he fashioned a small box and lined it with woollen remnants from a sheep's fleece and one of his old and frayed shirts. He placed her within the box and placed the box behind the stove and then he warmed some milk in a small saucepan and sweetened it with sugar. And he held open her small and trembling jaws with his left hand while spooning in the sweetened milk with his right, ignoring the needle-like sharpness of her small teeth. She lay in the box most of the remaining fall and into the early winter, watching everything with her large brown eyes. Although some members of the family complained about her presence and the odour from the box and the waste of time she involved, they gradually adjusted to her; and as the weeks passed by, it became evident that her ribs were knitting together in some form or other and that she was recovering with the resilience of the young. It also became evident that she would grow to a tremendous size, as she outgrew one box and then another and the grey hair began to feather from her huge front paws. In the spring she was outside almost all of the time and followed the man everywhere; and when she came inside during the following months, she had grown so large that she would no longer fit into her accustomed place behind the stove and was forced to lie beside it. She was never given a name but was referred to in Gaelic as *cù mòr glas*, the big grey dog.

By the time she came into her first heat, she had grown to a tremendous height, and although her signs and her odour attracted many panting and highly aroused suitors, none was big enough to mount her and the frenzy of their disappointment and the longing of her unfulfillment were more than the man could stand. He went, so the story goes, to a place where he knew there was a big dog. A dog not as big as she was, but still a big dog, and he brought him home with him. And at the proper time he took the *cú mòr glas* and the big dog down to the sea where he knew there was a hollow in the rock which appeared only at low tide. He took some sacking to provide footing for the male dog and he placed the *cú mòr glas* in the hollow of the rock and knelt beside her and steadied her with his left arm under her throat and helped position the male dog above her and guided his blood-engorged penis. He was a man used to working with the breeding of animals, with the guiding of rams and bulls and stallions and often with the funky smell of animal semen heavy on his large and gentle hands.

The winter that followed was a cold one and ice formed on the sea and frequent squalls and blizzards obliterated the offshore islands and caused the people to stay near their fires much of the time, mending clothes and nets and harness and waiting for the change in season. The *cú mòr glas* grew heavier and even more large until there was hardly room for her around the stove or even under the table. And then one morning, when it seemed that spring was about to break, she was gone.

The man and even his family, who had become more involved than they cared to admit, waited for her but she did not come. And as the frenzy of spring wore on, they busied themselves with readying their land and their fishing gear and all of the things that so desperately required their attention. And then they were into summer and fall and winter and another spring which saw the birth of the man and his wife's twelfth child. And then it was summer again.

That summer the man and two of his teenaged sons were pulling their herring nets about two miles offshore when the wind began to blow off the land and the water began to roughen. They became afraid that they could not make it safely back to shore, so they pulled in behind one of the offshore islands, knowing that they would be sheltered there and planning to outwait the storm. As the prow of their boat approached the gravelly shore, they heard a sound above them, and looking up they saw the *cù mòr glas* silhouetted on the brow of the hill which was the small island's highest point.

"*M'eudal cù mòr glas*" shouted the man in his happiness—*m'eudal* meaning something like dear or darling; and as he shouted, he jumped over the side of his boat into the waistdeep water, struggling for footing on the rolling gravel as he waded eagerly and awkwardly toward her and the shore. At the same time, the *cù mòr glas* came hurtling down toward him in a shower of small rocks dislodged by her feet; and just as he was emerging from the water, she met him as she used to, rearing up on her hind legs and placing her huge front paws on his shoulders while extending her eager tongue.

The weight and speed of her momentum met him as he tried to hold his balance on the sloping angle and the water rolling gravel beneath his feet, and he staggered backwards and lost his footing and fell beneath her force. And in that instant again, as the story goes, there appeared over the brow of the hill six more huge grey dogs hurtling down toward the gravelled strand. They had never seen him before; and seeing him stretched prone beneath their mother, they misunderstood, like so many armies, the intention of their leader.

They fell upon him in a fury, slashing his face and tearing aside his lower jaw and ripping out his throat, crazed with blood-lust or duty or perhaps starvation. The *cú mòr glas* turned on them in her own savagery, slashing and snarling and, it seemed, crazed by their mistake; driving them bloodied and yelping before her, back over the brow of the hill where they vanished from sight but could still be heard screaming in the distance. It all took perhaps little more than a minute.

The man's two sons, who were still in the boat and had witnessed it all, ran sobbing through the salt water to where their mauled and mangled father lay; but there was little they could do other than hold his warm and bloodied hands for a few brief moments. Although his eyes "lived" for a small fraction of time, he could not speak to them because his face and throat had been torn away, and of course there was nothing they could do except to hold and be held tightly until that too slipped away and his eyes glazed over and they could no longer feel his hands holding theirs. The storm increased and they could not get home and so they were forced to spend the night huddled beside their father's body. They were afraid to try to carry the body to the rocking boat because he was so heavy and they were afraid that they might lose even what little of him remained and they were afraid also, huddled on the rocks, that the dogs might return. But they did not return at all and there was no sound from them, no sound at all, only, the moaning of the wind and the washing of the water on the rocks.

In the morning they debated whether they should try to take his body with them or whether they should leave it and return in the company of older and wiser men. But they were afraid to leave it unattended and felt that the time needed to cover it with protective rocks would be better spent in trying to get across to their home shore. For a while they debated as to whether one should go in the boat and the other remain on the island, but each was afraid to be alone and so in the end they managed to drag and carry and almost float him toward the bobbing boat. They lay him face down and covered him with what clothes there were and set off across the still-rolling sea. Those who waited on the shore missed the large presence of the man within the boat and some of them waded into the water and others rowed out in skiffs, attempting to hear the tearful messages called out across the rolling waves.

The *cù mòr glas* and her six young dogs were never seen again, or perhaps I should say they were never seen again in the same way. After some weeks, a group of men circled the island tentatively in their boats but they saw no sign. They went again and then again but found nothing. A year later, and grown much braver, they beached their boats and walked the island carefully, looking into the small sea caves and the hollows at the base of the wind-ripped trees, thinking perhaps that if they did not find the dogs, they might at least find their whitened bones; but again they discovered nothing.

The *cù mòr glas*, though, was supposed to be sighted here and there for a number of years. Seen on a hill in one region or silhouetted on a ridge in another or loping across the valleys or glens in the early morning or the shadowy evening. Always in the area of the half perceived. For a while she became rather like the Loch Ness Monster or the Sasquatch on a smaller scale. Seen but not recorded. Seen, when there were no cameras. Seen but never taken.

The mystery of where she went became entangled with the mystery of whence she came. There was increased speculation about the handmade box in which she had been found and much theorizing as to the individual or individuals who might have left it. People went to look for the box but could not find it. It was felt she might have been part of a *buidseachd* or evil spell cast on the man by some mysterious enemy. But no one could go much farther than that. All of his caring for her was recounted over and over again and nobody missed any of the ironies.

What seemed literally known was that she had crossed the winter ice to have her pups and had been unable to get back. No one could remember ever seeing her swim; and in the early months at least, she could not have taken her young pups with her.

The large and gentle man with the smell of animal semen often heavy on his hands was my great-great-great-grandfather, and it may be argued that he died because he was too good at breeding animals or that he cared too much about their fulfilment and well-being. He was no longer there for his own child of the spring who, in turn, became my great-great-grandfather, and he was perhaps too much there in the memory of his older sons who saw him fall beneath the ambiguous force of the *cú mòr glas*. The youngest boy in the boat was haunted and tormented by the awfulness of what he had seen. He would wake at night screaming that he had seen the *cú mòr glas a' bhàis*, the big grey dog of death, and his screams filled the house and the ears and minds of the listeners, bringing home again and again the consequences of their loss. One morning, after a night in which he saw the *cú mòr glas a' bhais* so vividly that his sheets were drenched with sweat, he walked to the high cliff which faced the island and there he cut his throat with a fish knife and fell into the sea.

The other brother lived to be forty, but, again so the story goes, he found himself in a Glasgow pub one night, perhaps looking for answers, deep and sodden with the whiskey which had become his anaesthetic. In the half darkness he saw a large, grey-haired man sitting by himself against the wall and mumbled something to him. Some say he saw the *cú mòr glas a' bhais* or uttered the name. And perhaps the man heard the phrase through ears equally affected by drink and felt he was being called a dog or a son of a bitch or something of that nature. They rose to meet one another and struggled outside into the cobblestoned passage-way behind the pub where, most improbably, there were sup-posed to be six other large, grey-haired men who beat him to death on the cobblestones, smashing his bloodied head into the stone again and again before vanishing and leaving him to die with his face turned to the sky. The *cú mòr glas a' bhais* had come again, said his family, as they tried to piece the tale together.

This is how the *cú mòr glas a' bhais* came into our lives, and it is obvious that all of this happened a long, long time ago. Yet with succeeding generations it seemed the spectre had somehow come to stay and that it had become ours not in the manner of an unwanted skeleton in the clos-et from a family's ancient past but more in the manner of something close to a genetic possibility. In the deaths of each generation, the grey dog was seen by some—by women who were to die in childbirth; by soldiers who went forth to the many wars but did not return; by those who went forth to feuds or dangerous love affairs; by those who answered mysterious midnight messages; by those who swerved on the highway to avoid the real or imagined grey dog and ended in masses of crumpled steel. And by one professional athlete who, in addition to his ritualized athletic superstitions, car-ried another fear or belief as well. Many of the man's descen-dants moved like careful hemophiliacs, fearing that they car-ried unwanted possibilities deep within them. And others, while they laughed, were like members of families in which there is a recurrence over the generations of repeated cancer or the diabetes which comes to those beyond middle age. The feeling of those who may say little to others but who may say often and quietly to themselves, "It has not hap-pened to me," while adding always the cautionary "*yet.*"

I am thinking all of this now as the October rain falls on the city of Toronto and the pleasant, white-clad nurses pad confidently in and out of my father's room. He lies quietly amidst the whiteness, his head and shoulders elevated so that he is in that hospital position of being neither quite prone nor yet sitting. His hair is white upon his pillow and he breathes softly and sometimes unevenly, although it is difficult ever to be sure.

My five grey-haired brothers and I take turns beside his bedside, holding his heavy hands in ours and feeling their response, hoping ambiguously that he will speak to us, although we know that it may tire him. And trying to read his life and ours into his eyes when they are open. He has been with us for a long time, well into our middle age. Unlike those boys in that boat of so long ago, we did not see him taken from us in our youth. And unlike their youngest brother who, in turn, became our great-great-grandfather, we did not grow into a world in which there was no father's touch. We have been lucky to have this large and gentle man so deep into our lives.

No one in this hospital has mentioned the *cù mòr glas a' bhais*. Yet as my mother said ten years ago, before slipping into her own death as quietly as a grownup child who leaves or enters her parents' house in the early hours, "It is hard to not know what you do know."

Even those who are most sceptical, like my oldest brother who has driven here from Montreal, betray themselves by their nervous actions. "I avoided the Greyhound bus stations in both Montreal and Toronto," he smiled upon his arrival, and then added, "Just in case."

He did not realize how ill our father was and has smiled little since then. I watch him turning the diamond ring upon his finger, knowing that he hopes he will not hear the Gaelic phrase he knows too well. Not having the luxury, as he once said, of some who live in Montreal and are able to pretend they do not understand the "other" language. You cannot not know what you do know.

Sitting here, taking turns holding the hands of the

man who gave us life, we are afraid for him and for ourselves. We are afraid of what he may see and we are afraid to hear the phrase born of the vision. We are aware that it may become confused with what the doctors call "the will to live" and we are aware that some beliefs are what others would dismiss as "garbage." We are aware that there are men who believe the earth is flat and that the birds bring forth the sun.

Bound here in our own peculiar mortality, we do not wish to see or see others see that which signifies life's demise. We do not want to hear the voice of our father, as did those other sons, calling down his own particular death upon him.

We would shut our eyes and plug our ears, even as we know such actions to be of no avail. Open still and fearful to the grey hair rising on our necks if and when we hear the scrabble of the paws and the scratching at the door.

Circe

•

Michel Tremblay

I who am speaking to you have ploughed the seas and been to countless different countries. I've even seen a country that perhaps doesn't exist. That's as true as I'm sitting here. You don't believe me? Listen . . .

We had set sail from Liverpool one 24th of June and were making for . . . I don't remember exactly which port we were headed for. Anyway, it was the 29th of June and it was hot. I had chosen the evening watch because I like to see the sun disappear into the sea. Every evening, around half past eight, I used to settle down at the bow of the ship, just behind the figure-head that represented a mermaid with golden hair and inviting breasts, and watch the sun shrink, go down into the sea and then disappear completely. Once the last rays of the sun had disappeared I used to look at the mermaid and . . .

It's silly, but I used to have the impression that the two of us were feeling the same thing. A kind of nostalgia, a kind of tightening of the throat . . . well. Then I would go back to my post and it used to take me at least three or four pipes to calm down again.

Well, it was the evening of the 29th of June. The heat had been overpowering all day long and the sea was as flat as the palm of a nun's hand. I was leaning over the rails quietly smoking a pipe, waiting to see the sun go down. I was alone on the bridge. I stress this because later I tried to find someone who might also have witnessed what happened, but I never found anyone and everyone said I had been dreaming. But do people dream with their eyes open? I'm not a poet and when I see and hear things, I see them and hear them!

The sea was orange and the sun was almost touching it when I heard a distant voice. It was as though a woman were singing away in the west. I looked up at the sky, but there were no birds. Anyhow, seabirds don't sing like that. It really was a woman's voice. A languorous voice, a voice that took you by the entrails and told you things without even uttering words. I had just taken up a position below the figure-head and I raised my telescope. Far away, just alongside the sun, there was an island. I knew quite well there was no island in this part of the ocean and that we shouldn't see land for another three or four days . . . I almost shouted "Land ho!", but something prevented me. I think it was the voice that prevented me from shouting.

No, don't laugh and listen to what followed.

The island seemed to be quite big and, surprisingly, it seemed to be moving. That's to say, after a few seconds I noticed that it was approaching our ship a bit too fast. Our ship couldn't be doing more than fifteen knots and the island was approaching at—well, let's say thirty or forty knots. I was frightened, but the woman's voice, the woman's voice I could hear more and more distinctly, conveyed some peace to my soul. I don't know how to put it—it calmed me down or something. And I wanted to see who was singing like that.

When the island was quite close to the ship I saw in

a small cove . . . Listen, you mustn't think I'm mad. I can swear that I really saw this creature. I wasn't dreaming. In a little cove, sitting on a rock level with the surface of the water, I saw our ship's mermaid, our beautiful figure-head, and she was singing and smiling and thrusting out her breasts to me. She was beautiful. If you had only seen her. She was gently squeezing her breasts and seemed to be inviting me to leave the ship and follow her I don't know where—perhaps to her country, to her world that isn't like ours, a world in which the women are always singing, always singing and smiling at you . . . Excuse me, every time I tell this story I can't help being moved. This country of song and happiness only appeared to me once, as the sun was setting; it only lasted a few seconds, but it caused me such pain. You see . . . No, you wouldn't understand. Forgive me.

Translated by Michael Bullock

Today is the Day

•

Carol Shields

Today is the day the women of our village go out along the highway planting blisterlilies. They set off without breakfast, not even coffee, gathering at the site of the old well, now paved over and turned into a tot lot and basketball court. The air at this hour is clear. You can breathe in the freshness. And you can smell the moist ground down there below the trampled weeds and baked clay, those eager black glinting minerals waiting, and the pocketed humus. A September morning. A thousand diamond points of dew.

The women carry small spades or else trowels. They talk quietly to each other, but in a murmuring way so that you can't make out the words; all you hear is a sound like cold water continuously falling, as if a faucet were left running into a large and heavy washtub.

At one time the blisterlily grew profusely on its own. By mid-May the shores of the two major lakes in the area were splashed with white, and the slopes leading up to the woods ablaze. It must have been a beautiful, compelling sight, although a single blister blossom is nothing spectacular. It springs up close to the ground like a crocus, its toothed cup of petals demurely white or faintly purple. The small, pointed, pale leaves are equally unprepossessing. By ones or twos the plant is more or less invisible. You'd step right on it if you weren't warned, crush it without knowing. It takes several million of the tiny blisterlily flowers to make an impact. And once, according to the old people of the village, there really were millions.

No one knows for sure what happened. Too much rain or not enough, that's one theory. Or something poisonous in the sunlight, radiation maybe, from the nearby power plant. Or earth tremors. Or insect pests. Or a drop in the annual mean temperature. All sorts and manner of explanations have been put forward: a vicious fungus of the sort that attacks common potatoes or a newly evolved, unkillable virus. Also mentioned is crowding by larger, more aggressive species such as the distantly related bluewort, or the towering caster plant with its prickly seed pods, or the triple-spotted tigerleaf. There is only so much root room available at the earth's surface, and the root, or bulb rather, of the blisterlily is markedly acquiescent. To the eye it may look firm and reliable, an oval of slippery pearl under a loose russety skin, like a smallish onion or a French shallot, but it is actually soft-fleshed and far too obliging for its own good. Under even minimal pressure it shrivels or blisters and loses moisture, that much is known.

All the women of the village take part in the fall planting, including of course scrawny old Sally Bakey. Dirty, wearing a torn pinafore, less than four feet in height, it is Sally who discovered a new preserve of virgin blisterlilies in a meadow on the other side of the shiny westward-lying lake. There, where only mice walk, the flowers still grow in profusion, and the bulbs divide year by year as they once did in these parts. Sally lives alone in a rough cabin on a diet of rolled oats and eggs. Raw eggs, some say. She has a foul smell and shouts obscenely at passers-by, especially those who betray by their manner of speech or dress that they are not of the region. But people like her smile. A troll's smile without teeth. In winter, when the snow reaches a certain height, the men of the village take its measure by saying: The snow's up to Sally Bakey's knees. Or over Sally Bakey's bum. Or clear up to Sally Bakey's eyebrows. No one knows how old Sally Bakey is, but she's old enough to remember when churches in the area were left unlocked and when people could go about knocking on any door and ask for a chair to sit down on or for a cup of strong tea.

From the railway bridge you can see the women fanned out along the highway in groups of twos or threes. Some of them work along the verge and others on the median. Right up to the horizon they go. In this part of the country, because the land is low lying and the sun reluctant, the horizon exercises an exceptionally strong influence. It presses downward like a punishing lintel. Every inch of pasture or woodland feels its weight, but roofs and chimneys and porches take the brunt of it, making the houses look squashed and stupid, thick-walled and inhospitable. It never lets up. But today the women, bending and patting their bulbs into place, then standing upright and placing their hands on their hips, taking a moment's rest, bring about a softening of the harsh horizontals. They scatter the light and, from a certain distance, the flexed silver of their bodies appears to pin the dark ground to the lowering sky, the way tablecloths and sheets are pinned to a slackly hung clothesline. There's ease in it, and merriment. Sally Bakey can be heard singing in her crone's cracked voice, a song she invents as she goes along—except for the refrain that is full of ritual cunning and defiance.

The women wear comfortable, practical clothes that are widely dissimilar in style and variously colored. Bright sports clothes. Fringed deerskin. Pants wide and narrow, reaching to the thigh, knee or ankle. Pleated skirts, leather tunics. Rayon blouses. Knitted cardigans. Aprons of terry cloth or linen. Dresses of denim, challis or finely shirred woven cotton. Age and inclination account for these differences.

Those women who are married have removed their wedding rings, and these rings are strung like beads on a length of common kitchen string that is securely knotted to form a necklace. This necklace or wreath or garland, whatever you choose to call it, has been attached to a low branch of a particular blue beech tree—not at all a common tree in the region—situated on a knoll of land north of the overpass. All day long, while the women bury the blisterlilies in the ground, this ring of gold shines in the open air, forming an almost perfect parabolic curve. Birds dive at it, puzzled. Spiders creep on its ridged surfaces and attempt to wrap it with webs. Often they succeed. The younger unmarried girls, happening near it, glance shyly in its direction, imagining its compounded weight and how it would feel to slip such a necklace over their heads. Unthinkable; even the strongest breezes barely manage to stir it.

The midday meal is taken in the shade of a birch grove, a favored spot. Birches are clean, kindly trees, particularly at this time of year, early fall, with the leaves not quite ready to let go, but thinned down to a soft old chamois-like dryness. There's plenty of room between the trees for the women to spread their blankets, and around the edges of these blankets they sit, talking, eating, with their legs tucked up under them. Everyone brings something, sandwiches, roasted chicken, raw vegetables and flasks of ice water or hot tea. The meal ends with dried apricots, eaten out of the hand like candy. Every year it is the youngest girls who take turns passing the apricots—Sally Bakey is served first—carrying them in a very old wooden bowl that has acquired a deep nutmeggy burnish over time. Some of the women reach up and stroke the slightly irregular sides of the bowl with their fingers, exclaiming over its durability and beauty.

The planting of the blisterlily continues until late afternoon. Between the red-stemmed alder bushes and Indian paintbrush, wild carrot, toadflax, spotted dock, milkweed, Michaelmas daisies, blue chicory, and stands of rare turtlehead lie thousands of newly nested blisterlily bulbs. A few good inches of black soil have been packed on top, enough to give protection through the winter months—seven months in all, for nothing will be seen of the blisterlily until the first week of May, perhaps later if the winter is particularly severe, perhaps not at all if things go badly.

The women, dispersing at the end of the day, resettle their rings on their fingers. Since morning they have been speaking in the old secret language of which, sadly, only eight verbs and some twenty nouns remain—but these they string together inventively, weaving a stratagem of potent suggestion overlain by a wily, votive grammar of sign and silence.

Now they revert to their common tongue and set off for home. Despite their fatigue they go on foot. They feel a chill breeze, notice a graying of the air, field stubble burning somewhere not far off. All that is ordinary and extraordinary about the day converges the minute they cross their separate thresholds. Necessity and order rush together, providing a tent of calm while they go about preparing the simplest of suppers, envelopes of soup and soda crackers, or plain bread and jam.

Sally Bakey, brewing her solitary tea, has an attack of the yawns. She's tired, more tired than anyone who knows her would believe. Shadows move on the wall behind her. Her old bones complain, whimper, and her yawning shades away into an unconscious sifting of images, one burning into another, stubborn and curious. An onion trying to be a flower. A long sleep in the frozen ground. Misgivings. Dread. Unbearable pressure. Cracked earth. The first small faintly colored shoot, surprised by its upright shadow. A hard round waxy bud. Watchfulness. More than watchfulness, a strict and willing observance.

Saint Augustine

•

Alexandre Amprimoz

His mother died during the winter. Her last words were, "Continue your research and you won't be lonely."

The idea of courting one of the eight girls who lived down the street with their mad father crossed his mind. It would be easier now, with the house all to himself, his mother no longer there to check up on him.

But he'd never thought women were essential. He had other ways of fighting his loneliness. He decided to get a rattlesnake.

It was a pleasure, coming home with a few rodents for Saint Augustine. That was the name he gave his pet (a thing he would never confess to anyone). He never tired of watching the "snakedance and song of death" and when the reptile finally sank his fangs into a rat, he felt shivers of pleasure travel up his spine. The same game with mice had been a lesser thrill.

Spring. One evening he was too tired to read even a few pages of *The City of God* before retiring (though he hadn't yet reached forty-five). In his sleep, in his dream, he spoke to his mother. "Mother, on the purple hill, you left me alone, by the first gate where the river boils, but thank you, Mother, for the two mermaids. I will chew them properly. Then I will take the train that drips down from the moon like a slow slug and . . ."

The next day Saint Augustine had two heads. He didn't mind going to a funeral home with the madman and his six daughters. Two of them had just died in a car accident.

"The party at the funeral home is for them. I'm bringing a bottle of Cold Duck, get it?" asked the madman.

That night, he gave Saint Augustine a rat and went to bed. Then in his dream he spoke to his mother. "You should see Augustine. For a long second it is too beautiful. You should see, Mother, the way he swallows the two witches ..."

The next morning the snake had four heads. Two more of the madman's daughters had died during the night, drowned in the lake.

There are no more dreams and Saint Augustine has eight heads. He is rather happy: four of the girls are still alive. That proves that there is no relation between his snake's extra heads and the madman's daughters' deaths.

"It was only a coincidence!" he murmurs.

He is sitting in his living-room looking at Saint Augustine.

"I should have bought an octopus." He falls asleep. *The City of God* drops from his hands. Saint Augustine bangs one of its eight heads against the glass, the terrarium begins to break ...

Back on April Eleventh

•

Hubert Aquin

When your letter came I was reading a Mickey Spillane. I'd already been interrupted twice, and was having trouble with the plot. There was this man Gardner, who for some reason always carted around the photo of a certain corpse. It's true I was reading to kill time. Now I'm not so interested in killing time.

It seems you have no idea of what's been going on this winter. Perhaps you're afflicted with a strange intermittent amnesia that wipes out me, my work, our apartment, the brown record-player . . . I assure you I can't so easily forget this season I've passed without you, these long, snowy months with you so far away. When you left the first snow had just fallen on Montreal. It blocked the sidewalks, obscured the houses, and laid down great pale counterpanes in the heart of the city.

The evening you left—on my way back from Dorval— I drove aimlessly through the slippery empty streets. Each time the car went into a skid I had the feeling of going on an endless voyage. The Mustang was transformed into a rudderless ship. I drove for a long time without the slightest accident, not even a bump. It was dangerous driving, I know. Punishable by law. But that night even the law had become a mere ghost of itself, as had the city and this damned mountain that we've tramped so often. So much whiteness made a strong impression on me. I remember feeling a kind of anguish.

You, my love, probably think I'm exaggerating as usual and that I get some kind of satisfaction out of establishing these connections between your leaving and my states of mind. You may think I'm putting things together in retrospect in such a way as to explain what happened after that first fall of cerusian white.

But you're wrong: I'm doing nothing of the kind. That night, I tell you, the night you left, I skidded and slipped on that livid snow, fit to break your heart. It was myself I lost control of each time the Mustang slid softly into the abyss of memory. Winter since then has armed our city with many coats of melting mail, and here I am already on the verge of a burnt-ivory spring . . .

Someone really has to tell you, my love, that I tried twice to take my life in the course of this dark winter. Yes, it's the truth. I'm telling you this without passion, with no bitterness or depths of melancholy. I'm a little disappointed at having bungled it; I feel like a failure, that's all. But now I'm bored. I've fizzled out under the ice. I'm finished.

Have you, my love, changed since last November? Do you still wear your hair long? Have you aged since I saw you last? How do you feel about all this snow that's fallen on me, drifting me in? I suppose a young woman of twenty-five has other souvenirs of her travels besides these discoloured postcards I've pinned to the walls of our apartment.

You've met women . . . or men; you've met perhaps one man and . . . he seemed more charming, more handsome, more 'liberating' than I could ever be. Of course, as I say that, I know that to liberate oneself from another person one has only to be unfaithful. In this case you were right to fly off to Amsterdam to escape my black moods; you were right to turn our liaison into a more relative thing, the kind that other people have, any old love affair, any shabby business of that kind . . .

But that's all nonsense. I'm not really exaggerating, I'm just letting myself go, my love, letting myself drift. A little like the way I drove the Mustang that night last November. I'm in distress, swamped by dark thoughts. And it's no use telling myself that my imagination's gone wild, that I'm crazy to tell you these things, for I feel that this wave of sadness is submerging both of us and condemning me to total desolation. I can still see the snowy streets and me driving through them with no rhyme or reason, as if that aimless motion could magically make up for losing you. But you know, I already had a sedimentary confused desire to die, that very evening.

While I was working out the discords of my loneliness at the steering wheel of the Mustang, you were already miles high in a DC-8 above the North Atlantic. And a few hours later your plane would land gently on the icy runway of Schipol—after a few leisurely manoeuvres over the still plains of the Zuider Zee. By then I would be back in our apartment, reading a Simenon—*The Nahour Affair*—set partly in a Paris blanketed in snow (a rare occurrence), but also in that very city of Amsterdam where you had just arrived. I went to sleep in the small hours of the morning, clutching that bit of reality that somehow reconnected me to you.

The next day was the beginning of my irreversible winter. I tried to act as if nothing had changed and went to my office at the Agency (Place Ville Marie) at about eleven. I got through the day's work one way or another. While I was supposed to be at lunch I went instead to the ground-floor pharmacy. I asked for phenobarbital. The druggist told me, with a big stupid grin, that it called for a prescription. I left the building in a huff, realizing, however, that this needed a little thought.

I had to have a prescription, by whatever means, and information about brand-names and doses. And I needed at least some knowledge of the various barbiturate compounds.

With this drug very much on my mind I went next day or the day after to the McGill medical bookstore. Here were the shelves dealing with pharmacology. I was looking for a trickle and found myself confronted by the sea. I was overcome, submerged, astonished. I made a choice and left the store with two books under my arm: the *Shorter Therapeutics and Pharmacology*, and the *International Vade Mecum* (a complete listing of products now on the market).

That night, alone with my ghosts, I got at the books. To hell with Mickey Spillane, I had better things to read: for example this superbook (the *Vade Mecum*) which has the most delicious recipes going! Your appetite, your tensions, your depressions—they are all at the command of a few grams of drugs sagely administered. And according to this book of magic potions, life itself can be suppressed if only one knows how to go about it. I was passionately engrossed by this flood of pertinent information, but I still had my problem of how to get a prescription. Or rather, how to forge one that wouldn't turn into a passport to prison. A major problem.

His name was in the phone book: Olivier, J. R., internist. I dialed his number. His secretary asked what would be the best time of day for an appointment and specified that it would be about a month as the doctor was very busy. I answered her with a daring that still surprises me.

'It's urgent.'

'What is it you have?' asked the secretary.

'A duodenal ulcer.'

'How do you know?'

'Well, I've consulted several doctors and they strongly advised me to see Doctor O.'

'Tomorrow at eleven,' she suggested, struck by my argument. 'Will that be convenient?'

'Of course, ' I replied.

I spent forty-five minutes in the waiting-room with the secretary I'd phoned the day before. I flipped through the magazines on the table searching for subjects of conversation to use on this doctor friend I hadn't seen for so long.

He appeared in the doorway and his secretary murmured my name. I raised my gloomy gaze to greet this smiling friend. He ushered me into his overstuffed office.

After the usual halting exchange of memories from college and university days I took a deep breath and, talking directly to Olivier, J. R., I told him straight out that I was having trouble sleeping. He burst into laughter, while I crouched deeper in the armchair he kept for patients.

'You're living it up too much, old boy,' he said, smiling.

Just then his intercom blinked. Olivier lifted the phone.

'What is it?' he asked his secretary.

(I had been hoping for something like this.)

'Just a second. I have something to sign. You know how it is. They're making bureaucrats out of us.'

He got up and went out to the reception room, carefully closing the door. At once I spied on his hand-rest the prescription pad with his letterhead. I quickly tore off a number of sheets and stuck them in the left inside pocket of my jacket. I was trembling, dripping with sweat.

'Well, bring me up to date,' said Olivier, coming back.

'Is she running around on you?' He obviously found his own humour as irresistible as I found it offensive and our chat didn't get much farther. We fell silent and Olivier took his pen. Before starting to write on his prescription pad he looked up at me

'What was it, now? You wanted some barbiturates to get you to sleep?'

'Yes,' I said.

'Okay, here's some stuff that'll knock out a horse.' He tore off the sheet and held it out to me.

'Thanks, thank you very much.' I suppose I was a bit emotional.

'I've put *non repetatur* at the bottom for these pills have a tendency to be habit-forming. If you really need more after a couple of weeks come and see me again.'

I folded the prescription without even searching out the *non repetatur,* an expression I had learned only a couple of days before. The intercom blinked again. Olivier, annoyed, picked up his phone but I paid no attention. I was already far away. Afterwards Olivier started telling me how his wife complained—or so he said—that she never got to see him any more.

'I'm working too hard,' he said, hand on brow. 'I probably need a holiday, but there it is. My wife's the one who's off to Europe. And it's only a month or so since she did the Greek Islands.'

In my mind I saw you in the streets of Breda and The Hague. I imagined your walks in Scheveningen, your visits to the Maurithuis. I wasn't sure any more just where in Europe you were: at the Hook of Holland, the flying isle of Vlieland, or the seaside suburb of Leiden at Kalwijk aan Zee . . .

I was out again on the chilly street. The sky was dark and lowering. Black clouds scudded by a rooftop level, presaging another snowstorm. Let the snow come to beautify this death-landscape, where I drove in a Mustang while you moved in the clear celestial spaces of the painters of the

Dutch school . . .

Back in our apartment I analyzed the prescription I had obtained by trickery. Twelve capsules of sodium amobarbitol. I had no intention of remaining the possessor of a nonrepeatable number of pills and began practising Olivier's handwriting. On ordinary paper. I had stolen ten sheets of his letterhead but that precious paper must not be wasted. In two or three hours I'd managed four good prescriptions. I fell asleep on the strength of my success.

It took me some days to accumulate a *quoad vitam* dose with the help of my forged scribbles. But I wasn't satisfied with the *quoad vitam* dose indicated in the *Vade Mecum*. I went on accumulating the little sky-blue capsules, each with its three-letter stamp—SK&P. There were nights when I slept not at all rather than dip into my stock of precious sodic torpedoes.

Quite a few days passed this way. Strange days. Knowing that I had my stock of death in hand I felt sure of myself and almost in harmony with life. I knew that I was going to die and at that moment it would have been upsetting to receive a letter from you, my love, for I had come too close to the end of living.

When your letter came on November sixteenth it in no way disturbed this harmony, as I had feared it might. After reading it I still wanted to end my life by using, some evening, my surprising accumulation of sodium amobarbital. You'd written in haste (I could tell by your hand) from the Amstel Hotel, but the postmark said Utrecht. So you'd mailed it from there! What were you doing in Utrecht? How had you gone from Amsterdam to that little town where the treaty was signed ratifying the conquest of French Canada? Symbol of the death of a nation, Utrecht became a premonitory symbol of my own death. Had you gone with someone? A European colleague, as you usually describe the men you meet on your travels? Are there many interior decorators in Utrecht? Or perhaps I should ask if they are friendly and charming. I imagined you sitting in the car of a decorator colleague, lunching on the way and perhaps spending the night in Utrecht. I grew weary of calling back so many memories of you, your charm, your beauty, your hot body in my arms. I tore up your letter to put an end to my despair.

By the twenty-eighth of November I'd heard nothing more from you. My days grew shorter and emptier, my nights longer and more sleepless. They finally seemed barely to be interrupted by my days and I was exhausted. Recurrent insomnia had broken my resistance. I was destroyed, hopeless, without the slightest will to organize what was left of my life.

For me an endless night was about to begin, the unique, final, ultimate night. I'd at last decided to put an arbitrary end to my long hesitation, a period to our disordered history; decided, also, no longer to depend on your intermittent grace, which had been cruel only in that I had suffered from it.

That day I made a few phone calls to say that I was not available and spent my time tidying the apartment. When it was evening I took a very hot bath copiously perfumed from the bottle of Seaqua. I soaked for a long time in that beneficent water. Then I put on my burnt-orange bathing trunks and piled a few records on our playback: Ray Charles, Feliciano, Nana Mouskouri. I sprawled on our scarlet sofa, a glass of Chivas Regal in my hand, almost naked, fascinated by the total void that was waiting for me. I put Nana Mouskouri on several times. Then I finally made up my mind and swallowed my little sky-blue capsules four at a time, washing them down with great gulps of Chivas Regal. At the end I took more Scotch to help me absorb the lot. I put the nearly empty bottle on the rug just beside the couch. Still quite lucid, I turned on the radio (without getting up) so that the neighbours would not be alerted by the heavy breathing which, according to my medical sources, would begin as soon as I dropped into my coma.

To tell you the truth I wasn't sad but rather impressed, like someone about to start a long, very long, voyage. I thought of you, but faintly, oh, so faintly. You were moving around in the distance, in a funereal fog. I could still see the rich colours of your dresses and bathrobes. I saw you enter the apartment like a ghost and leave it in slow motion, but eternally in mirror perspective leading to infinity. The deeper I slipped into my comatose feast the less you looked my way, or rather the less I was conscious of you. Melancholy had no grip on me, nor fear. In fact I was blanketed in the solemnity of my solitude. Then, afterwards, obliteration became less complex and I became mortuary but not yet dead, left rocking in a total void.

And now, you ask, how are you managing to write this letter from beyond the tomb? Well, here's your answer. I failed! The only damage I received in this suicide attempt resulted from the coma that lasted several hours. I was not in the best condition. My failure—even if I had no other devastating clues—would be proof enough of my perfect weakness, that diffuse infirmity that cannot be classified by science but which allows me to ruin everything I touch, always, without exception.

I woke up alive, as it were, in a white ward of the Royal Victoria, surrounded by a network of intravenous tubes that pinned me to the bed and ringed by a contingent of nurses. My lips felt frozen and dried and I remember that one of the nurses sponged my lips from time to time with an antiherpetic solution.

Outside it was snowing, just as it had been on the day you left. The great white flakes fell slowly and I became aware that the very fact of seeing them silently falling was irrefutable proof that I was still, and horridly, alive. My return to a more articulated consciousness was painful, and took (to my relief) an infinity. As soon as I reached that threshold of consciousness I began to imagine you in the Netherlands or somewhere in Europe. Was there snow in Holland? And did you need your high suede boots that we shopped for together a few days before you left?

Suddenly I feel a great fatigue: these thoughts, returning in all their disorder, are taking me back to my stagnant point again. . .

It was really quite ironic that your telegram from Bruges should have become the means of your tardy (and involuntary) intervention on behalf of my poisoned body. I suppose the message was phoned first. But I didn't hear the ring and Western Union simply delivered the typed message to my address. The caretaker, who has no key to the letter boxes in our building, felt the call of duty and decided to bring me the envelope himself. There is something urgent about telegrams, you can't just leave them. Lying around. People can't imagine a harmless telegram that might read: HAPPY BIRTHDAY. WEATHER MARVELLOUS. KISS-ES. And yet that's exactly what was written in that telegram from Bruges.

I suppose the caretaker rapped a few times on our door. He probably couldn't see how I'd be out when the radio was blasting away. Finally, his curiosity must have got the better of him. He opened the door with his pass-key and stepped in to leave the envelope on the Louis XV table under the hall mirror. It's easy to imagine the rest: from the door he saw that I was there, he noted my corpse-like face, etc. Then, in a panic, he phoned the Montreal Police who transported me—no doubt at breakneck speed—to the emergency ward of the Royal Victoria. I spent several days under an oxygen tent. I even underwent a tracheotomy. That, in case the term means nothing to you, involves an incision in the trachea, followed by the insertion of a tracheal drain.

I must tell you everything, my love. I'm alive, therefore I am cured. The only traces are an immense scar on my neck and a general debility. While I was surviving one way or another in Montreal, you were continuing your tour of Europe. You saw other cities, Brussels, Charleroi, Amiens, Lille, Roubaix, Paris . . . Bruges had been just a stopover where you perhaps had dinner with a stranger, but no one hangs around in Bruges when the continent is waiting. Though God knows Bruges is a privileged place, an amorous sanctuary, a fortress that has given up a little terra firma to the insistent North Sea. I feel a soft spot for that half-dead city which you left with no special feeling. I stayed on in Bruges after you left, immured beneath its old and crumbling quays, for that was where you wished me (by telegram) a happy birthday.

There is no end to this winter. I don't know how many blizzards I watched from my hospital window. Around the fifteenth of December some doctor decided I should go home, that I was—so to speak—cured. Easy to say! Can one be cured of having wanted to die? When the ambulance attendants took me up to the apartment I saw myself in a mirror. I thought I would collapse. As a precaution I lay down on the couch where I had almost ended my days in November. Nothing had changed since then, but there was a thin film of dust on our furniture and the photos of you. The sky, lowering and dark, looked like more snow. I felt like a ghost. My clothes hung loose on me and my skin had the colour of a corpse. The sleepless nights again took up their death march but I no longer had my reserve of suicide-blue amobarbital pills. And I'd used up all my blank prescription forms. I couldn't sleep. I stared at the ceiling or at the white snowflakes piling up on our balcony. I imagined you at Rome or Civitavecchia or in the outskirts of Verona, completely surrendered to the intense experience of Europe.

From my calendar I knew that you were coming back to Montréal on April eleventh, on board the *Maasdam*. If I went to meet you that day at the docks of the Holland-American Line I would be in an emotional state. Too emotional, unable to tell you about what I did in November or about my disintegration since. Of course you'd give me a great hug and tell me all about those marvels, the fascinating ruins in Bruges, the baths of Caracalla, the Roman arches of triumph: the Arch of Tiberius, of Constantine, of Trajan, and so on. And all through your euphoric monologue I'd feel the knot at my throat.

It's for that reason—and all sorts of others, all so related to cowardice—that I'm writing you this letter, my love. I'll soon finish it and address it to Amsterdam, from which the Maasdam sails, so that you can read it during the crossing. That way you'll know that I bungled my first suicide attempt in November.

You'll understand that if I say 'first' it means there'll be a second.

Don't you see that my hand is trembling? That my writing is beginning to scrawl? I'm already shaky. The spaces between each word, my love, are merely the symbols of the void that is beginning to accept me. I have ten more lucid minutes, but I've already changed: my mind is slipping, my hand wanders, the apartment, with every light turned on, grows dark where I look. I can barely see the falling snow but what I do see is like blots of ink. My love, I'm shivering with cold. The snow is falling somehow within me, my last snowfall. In a few seconds, I'll no longer exist, I will move no more. And I'm so sorry but I won't be at the dock on April eleventh. After these last words I shall crawl to the bath, which has been standing full for nearly an hour. There, I hope, they will find me, drowned. Before the eleventh of April next.

Translated by Alan Brown

Cut One

•

Victor Lévy Beaulieu

((It happened when he stepped onto des Récollets Street: he
could tell something was different all of a sudden. A cloud
hovering over him like a dusky wing and right away this feeling of oppression. His legs were hurting. Goddamn creaky
knees! He lifted a foot and set it down slowly. He took off
his cap. His curly, matted hair. Damn sweat! He wiped his
forehead. If at least I had a car. He saw himself at the wheel
of an old convertible tearing through the streets of Morial
Mort. He'd put on seat covers to hide the rips and the cigarette burns in the worn leather. The tires squealed on the
asphalt; he'd slam on the brakes at red lights, and the
Hollywood mufflers made a hell of a racket when he took
off again. The fox tail fixed on the antenna was an occult
trophy, some strange symbol of virility. He had the radio
turned up all the way: it was blaring, really blasting out of
the back speaker. Think I don't know how to handle cunt,
motherfucker! And there sure are some out on the prowl
this mornin'! Truth was, there were lots of them—girls on
the street in summer outfits—You know, the kind of clothes

that show everything without showing anything, those scanty things that show off the navel and the place where mongoloids are made. Hey, get a load of those big, high-class asses in those shorts! He must have been walking for an hour now, long strides beneath a leaden sun. The arm holding the overnight bag'd gone to sleep a long time ago. Even his bad leg was growing numb. Good thing there were plenty of taverns along the way for old Joseph-David-Barthélémy Dupuis! He yawned the time to let the novelist see his nicotine-stained teeth and that tongue he could wag as fast as a nervous foot—and wasn't it wearing a sock right now! It was the beer, it had knocked him out: KO, CHA-O . . .S. But Joseph-David-Barthélémy Dupuis didn't give a damn! The house wasn't far, and soon, sucking his Jeanne D'Arc's tits, his barometer'd show fair weather again. Yeah, sure, he was out of work—so what? There're more than enough people workin' already! He hawked up phlegm and spit it out on the sidewalk, then cleared his throat. Somethin' stunk. Too many women on the rag, most likely. He figured Jeanne D'Arc was parked naked in front of the television set watching some crummy film, holding her heavy, brown tits in her hands. His hand tightened into a fist; he couldn't help it: I don't trust her, an' I got good reasons not to. Hers ain't the most Catholic cunt in the world, the lousy bitch! He might have added that he didn't do much to help her there, and that he wasn't exactly a model husband. But what would be the point? Everybody in Morial Mort knew that, starting with his Jeanne D'Arc. (You're a no-good bum, understand? That's what bugs me!) He would pinch one of her tits, laughing a manly laugh. Usually it worked: all he had to do was tickle a tit and she'd calm down. But this mornin' it didn't do any good: she slapped shit outta me and me too stupid to slap her back. I took my cap off the nail an'—ahhh! What he had done was simple enough: he had slammed the door, slammed it so hard a pane of glass tumbled out onto the floor and broke all to pieces. And Jeanne D'Arc screaming when he jumped over the fence—Bastard! You're nothing but a coward, a drunken bum! He'd shrugged his shoulders. Women always scream the same thing. First of all, I'm not a drunk. I have a small Labatt's every now and then but you gotta wet your whistle when it's hot like this, eh? He laughed. He liked being a holy terror with his Jeanne D'Arc. Get fed up? Her? Come on! Was anybody gonna hump her any better than him in his old parents' big bed? Yeah, well, that's what worries me: Jeanne D'Arc's got fuckin' on the brain an' maybe she says, another prick that'll keep the juices flowin'. He saw her stretched out in the middle of the old parents' big bed, her legs spread for Christie to feed her one mean sandwich. He chased the thought away in a hurry—Till I'm shown different my Jeanne D'Arc eats the same kind of sandwiches as everybody else. Joseph-David-Barthélémy Dupuis was thinking too much and had hardly noticed things as he passed them, so he was astonished to discover he was almost home. The house's gable was a white maw in the green surroundings. He had just trimmed the trees, whose branches were beating against the upstairs window and keeping Jeanne D'Arc from sleeping. I worked a lot this summer. Yes, he had. He had butchered the hedge of spirea in front of the porch trying to fashion green figures and a cross. Yeah, well, I was bound to mess it up, I got no experience with that sort of thing—I ruined the fuckin' hedge, if you wanna know! He had even hoed up the pumpkins his Jeanne D'Arc was growing by the fence in the back yard. She must really like those big, green balls warmin' their bellies in the sun! Damn if the little woman ain't vulgar! It comes from watchin' TV with all those programs full of nothin' but sex! He laughed again. He laughed a lot lately. Laughter would simply bubble up in his body like witches' brew in a cauldron. He was beginning to enjoy it. He was perfecting his laugh, thickening it and rounding it out.

Because soon he was going to undertake something noble;
he didn't know what yet, but he was sure he would go down
in history. I'm gonna have my fine car an' then my Jeanne
D'Arc's gonna be in trouble, then she's gonna get it, but
good. Now des Récollets Street had changed while he was
gone. What was it all about? You're too tired, probably from
walkin' and drinkin' too much. Is it because you just got
outta Dorémi, old Joseph-David-Barthélémy Dupuis? An'
you're gonna go home and hug and squeeze your Jeanne
D'Arc? He didn't really believe it, there was too much noise
on des Récollets, too many helicopters circling around and
landing somewhere behind the houses in huge clouds of
dust with their long, sweeping propellers, too many police
sirens and red bubblegum machines on top of the patrol
cars, too many soldiers with long carbines on their shoulders. And des Récollets Street closed off by a wall of cops.
Joseph-David-Barthélémy Dupuis stopped. His heart. Out of
breath. Hey, what's goin' on? For a second he thought it was
him they were after, they were going to haul him in because
his Jeanne D'Arc had reported him. He punched his cap. It
was that hypocrite Jeanne D'Arc's face he was pounding. She
sold me out, crossed me. Now what's gonna become of you?
He moved forward a bit; he had to go past the police if he
wanted to get home. The street was full of people. Big,
greasy faces, wide mouth-faces belching out left and right:
Can't get through! Can't get through! Turn around! People
were crowded together on the hill in the direction of
Monselet. They were afraid of the rifles and of the motorcy-
cles coming from every direction. Barthélémy thought of
big, buzzing flies, black and wingless. A chill ran up and
down him. Those bastards crammed me full of dope. A
hand landed on his shoulder. He turned around. You were
told to move back. Don't you see you can't get through? He
jumped out of the way of a motorcycle. The white cop hel-
mets were golf balls with red eyes and ears. Barthélémy

started to run. What is this? The end of the world, or a war, or what? He jostled men and women alike because he wanted to get away as fast as possible from that swelling, threatening sea. On the bare shoulders of sun-blackened men, children were crying. (Could he really know there was no time left to recreate the world, to ring the past around with a heavy palisade of pious folk, a fort of sorts, to protect it against sly, slinking procedure and savage words flying at the skull with tomahawk fury? There was to be no future for him, perhaps; not even a present; for he was already condemned to what had never been, to what would never be, living out his life in dank obscurity, in a rubber snake world coiling and uncoiling around him, motion almost mechanical, banal, the randomness of mere process, the dumbness of a thing overflowing, emptiness' pure lack which sucked at his spine, leaving him only his purposeless wanderings through Morial Mort—to make sense if he could out of the phoney world of Steinberg supermarkets, Laura Secord shops, Smoker's Corners, snack bars, alleyways, cars parked in no-parking zones, houses jammed up against one another to find warmth, making sure nothing and no one holed up in those decorated wombs should ever be lonely or sick or without a telephone to call the doctor when he was ready to die. Did God alone know that the future was to be found cowering in the narrow folds of the steadily shrinking present?) Oh, push open the tavern door so that darkness might take him and bind his hands behind his back and lead him below and leave him for dead. (God almighty. Oh, God almighty!) Barthélémy's ears were still ringing with the sounds of life outside. His eyes were watering. He was an old hound who was going to die far from his bitch, she with life still beating in her. He was the same as he always was when he got out of Dorémi. Which meant he was scared. So he slapped himself hard on the forehead several times, trying to get hold of himself. But he was far gone already, water was cascading now somewhere behind his eyes and only the traditional invocations could do anything for him—Jesus fuckin' Christ! You becomin' afraid of your own shadow? Damn ugly bitch! Jeanne D'Arc's not gonna eat you. Just because you slugged her doesn't mean you oughta have the shakes. Take it easy, old buddy, take it easy! But he couldn't help himself, his teeth were chattering and hot tears fell from his eyes. He had these attacks more and more often and he was powerless against them. He was definitely going to die. He was definitely through. He kicked a table leg. His wrists came free at once. He downed his beer, stood up, then took off running between the tables and through the opening the door suddenly offered. Outside it seemed to him he was a big, unruly horse hightailing it down the street. (Whoa, whoaaa boy!) He pulled on the reins and the taps on his bootsoles sent up sparks off the asphalt. You wanna break your leg and get sent to the glue factory? He laughed once again. He never thought he could be so crazy. To celebrate, he took an old harmonica out of his pocket and began to play, to the delight of the passers-by, Jeanne D'Arc's favorite reel, the one she asked for when she was happy and in love with him. She'd rub up against me and take hold of my prick. Or keep time with her foot. With the very first notes he shivered violently. And those bastards at Dorémi, they hid my harp—he blew hard into his mouth organ and danced on the sidewalk, happy, so incredibly happy. But Jeanne D'Arc's waitin' for me, I gotta hurry. (Maybe she'd put perfume between her legs and in her ears. Am I ever gonna go at that with my tongue!) But he wasn't getting anywhere, his house was like a target seen through field glasses: if he went another five hundred feet he wouldn't be able to turn back, he'd have to open fire. (All this was taking place at the hour when the wild animals go down to drink in the Rivière des Prairies. All this was taking place at the hour when the mighty males stand watch, backside to backside, while the females contemplate their antlers in the still water.) Barthélémy's lungs were spitting flames. The old harmonica had turned red in his hands. His fingers were twisted with pain, his charred nails were bloody spots. Barthélémy threw the harmonica on the ground and stomped it furiously. His lips were bleeding, the eyes in his face, he knew, were burning embers. (I hate your guts. God, do I hate your guts!) Once the instrument was demolished he fell to his knees and saw the poor, squashed thing crawling along the sidewalk. He was full of remorse then, and of fierce anger against Jeanne D'Arc, who must have been waiting for him, secure behind the living room curtains. (It was no longer at watering time that this was taking place now, but at the silent hour, the hour of inner lamentation and of the sun closing its red eye behind the houses along Monselet Street. Barthélémy carefully picked up what had been his harmonica, looked at it tenderly, kissing it before putting it in his pocket next to his heart—I'm losin' my grip. I gotta get to the house before I can't find my way at all! He started walking fast, straight ahead. It was like being in a train: the coach window was distorting the lines of the houses. At least doors were opening to let him through. They know I'm in a hurry an' Jeanne D'Arc's pining for me. He'd never liked houses as much as now. He stammered out his thanks, raising his hand high, two fingers forming the ritualistic v. He was beside himself with joy. For the moment, he had to forget Dorémi, his internment, the judge's threats, Jeanne D'Arc's false witness, the night in the cell, the cops brutality, the drugs injected into his thigh, and a lot of other shit that would come back one of these days and occupy his heart. Finally, here I am! When he reached the gate his legs were shaking. He was exhausted, as though all his energy had seeped out of the wound in his foot. He waited a while so he could catch his breath. He held on to the fence. Didn't somebody have him by the legs trying to drag him away?

Weren't the devils gripping his ankles, warning him how important it was not to move an inch? He punched at thin air, then lifted the gate latch. He began to mutter to himself. A sort of song came out of his mouth, one that he must have heard on the radio, though he didn't remember the real words. He was walking now; the sound of his voice had calmed him. He was approaching the house, his paradise regained after all too much suffering. He pictured to himself Jeanne D'Arc's beautiful face as she let him caress her at the head of the stairs, her eyes glassy, her body not moving, her thoughts elsewhere, in a beery coolness, or perhaps nowhere at all, floating peacefully in darkness, an evil demon pacified by his patient aloofness. The stairs creaked under his feet The sweat. His large checkered handkerchief was soaking wet. He had dropped his bag to stop the muscles in his arm from twitching. He breathed deeply and walked to the other end of the porch looking at the stars, his nostrils open wide to the familiar odors they'd deprived him of for too long. Then, coming back to the door he stumbled over something and fell. He lay silent. He hoped Jeanne D'Arc hadn't heard him fall—I open the door, she doesn't know I'm there an' lookin' at her, she's got a finger in her mouth, is she ever nervous, that Jeanne D'Arc, it must be because of TV, she must think she's in the movies but she's pretty, I can't wait to put my hand on her head. (He was standing up now.) Wanna tell me what it was I tripped over, for God's sake? He reached for whatever it was that had toppled him and ran his hands over it, astonished to discover it was his old overnight bag. It's not hard to recognize it, it's missin' a handle. Jeanne D'Arc must've filled it full of bricks it's so heavy. He unzipped it and plunged both hands inside. At Dorémi I hid under the bed so I could fool around in the bag without bein' bothered. Sonsabitches, they'd want to stick me while I was asleep an' the next day there I was with my mouth hangin' open. I'd keep noddin' out all day an' I couldn't even talk 'cause my jaws wouldn't move. An' they thought I'd take it without sayin' a word. OK, I ate damn good, I'd've been fat as a pig in no time, but those pills, oh no, well, they weren't gonna get me with that. Hee-hee-hee. I fixed 'em when I began to take 'em with coke. Like walkin' into a stone wall; I'd go off my damn nut, I might've killed everyone of 'em; I was highflyin'. Hee-hee-hee-hee. Joseph-David-Barthélémy Dupuis began to empty his bag. Ah, Jeanne D'Arc put everything I own in there. He might have added: including my memory, but he didn't know the word, that is, what he was in the process of doing, laying out his personal effects, the various pieces of his past that he was anxiously, frantically, dragging to the surface—it left him feeling so unreal that he forgot Jeanne D'Arc. The bag. A catch-all. That is, a trap. And he could never reach the end, there were too many things he considered irretrievably lost, sunk, crushed, undone under barrels and barrels of small Labatt's. Suddenly coming face to face with all this terrified him and made him almost delirious. Breath—Hey, have I ever been around! Damn, have I ever been through it or not! He looked at the Westclox hands, the phosphorescent numbers. He put it to his ear and shook it because he didn't hear the tick-tock. Not surprisin' it ain't runnin' it's been so long since it was wound. He had completely forgotten he was supposed to go inside and take Jeanne D'Arc in his arms. He wound the clock and listened to the noise the springs made. I'd have really liked to work in a clock factory! Of everything from his past it was the old Westclox he liked most, the old dented and rusted body which was just like him, you couldn't wear it out, its stubbornness kept you from ever really getting at it. It was the world he was holding against his ear, his whole existence he held on to so tightly. The metal's hardness. The cracked glass he had never replaced because dust couldn't hurt those rock-solid works. He set the clock down on the chair beside him and stayed a long time watching the progression of its hands. It was to remember, that was why he was doing it. As a form of homage too, no doubt. Because the clock had saved his life lots of times. Too often when he was completely drunk he just couldn't stand it any more: he would see hordes of demons, monsters would leap at his face trying to disfigure him. He didn't know how to talk about those things, there were no words for what he saw, he'd have had to draw a picture. (But the big hippopotamus had reached the foot of the bed: it was breathing ferociously and soon was going to jump on him and crush him beneath its weight.) Hey, Jeanne D'Arc! Hey, damn it! He leapt to his feet. The evil spell had turned into a whirlwind, lifting dust, dead leaves and scraps of paper in the yard. It's time for me to go in an' take Jeanne D'Arc in my arms an' talk to her once and for all. I got so much to tell her, it's been three months now that I been keepin' it all inside me. A blown up balloon full of words, a long series of sentences which would flow from him the minute he opened his mouth lying at Jeanne D'Arc's side in his old parents' big bed after they'd had a good fuck. He'd be delivered from all that was afflicting him, he'd be soft and humble like in those easy, early days. Oh, the little house. The scratching of a clothes line. High banks of snow. An ass like an offering for the eye. Where and when, all of that? In what dream? Before which decisive swig of beer that had destroyed everything? He coughed softly so as not to alert Jeanne D'Arc, then he tried the door. (Locked, damn it.) He fumbled in his pockets but found nothing he could use to force the lock. He thought of the bag; he knelt down and unzipped it. There's gotta be an old piece of wire in here somewhere. His hands burrowed into his life's debris. (Casting aside the dice, the thin chains, the worn-out shoe, the medallions, the handkerchiefs, the false nose and fake eyeglasses, the doll's head, its eyes hanging out of its sockets, finally coming up with this narrow metal rod with small plastic wheels at both ends which still turned.) Barthélémy unscrewed the wheels and tossed them in the bag. The Kodak. The muffled noise (Jeanne D'Arc peeking out from behind the window?) He slid the metal pin into the lock. Easy, easy, don't scare away the birds that've built their nest in there. The sound of breathing through the nose. (And that big draught-horse stepping sleepily through the potato plants. Whoa boy, don't bolt on me now, damn you!) Joseph-David-Barthélémy Dupuis was nervous, you see. And I got no patience, my nerves ain't so hot these days. He kept at it, slowly working the little truck axle into the lock. The springs (he knew there were no springs but he liked to say that word that sounded so nice, that made him think of motion, something like the wild flight of two terrified beasts down des Récollets)—so the springs, then, gave: there was a sort of click, and when he turned the door knob there it was, the long hallway of paradise regained running straight up to him. He was overjoyed, his head full of scenes of the time before Dorémi, only the nice ones, and leaning with his hand against the white plaster wall he understood how close he'd come to dying and losing his Jeanne D'Arc. (No. A mole no more. No more to roam dark holes. No more to be surrounded by stray dogs, their paws bloodied from scrabbling in ice-encrusted snow. No more. No. He was full of fine resolutions, full of tender words he was finally going to say to himself as much as to his Jeanne D'Arc.) To keep from speaking yet he closed his mouth and sealed his lips with adhesive tape. It was thus that he wandered through paradise regained, invisible in the shadows, and silent, and terribly troubled by what was welling up inside him, all of it somehow constituting his affection for Jeanne D'Arc. I should have taken a bath before I left. And if I had my suit. And my good polished boots. And my tie with the shiny stickpin. Or if I was naked. You can't tell I'm ugly when it's dark. The scars disappear, an' the sores on my foot, too. I'm presentable then. He was sweating profusely and talking to himself in his head because inside things were churning. One wrong move an' I'm caught. Jeanne D'Arc'll be at me tooth and nail. (The truth was he didn't dare admit he was worried, that a knot of anguish had come to his throat the minute he stepped onto des Récollets Street. At a certain point I'm gonna open a door and then—Jeanne D'Arc.) He saw her naked on the sofa, her neck broken, her head, its long blond hair like a torchlight, hanging over the side, soaked in warm blood, her belly open, the smell of piss and shit. That obsession again! He was trying to calm down; he leaned against the wall and closed his eyes—Sickly, pale infant in a stroller with rusty wheels. Then battles with baseball bats somewhere along the Rivière des Prairies. And big caved-in bellies with pieces of intestine sticking out like mushrooms. And quick kisses through the bars to make of love something poor and difficult, to make it nothing but two obscene tongues trying to meet. And happiness right at hand when once alone in the huge, white room at Dorémi. (You're a little boy. Everything's big. Steinberg's parking lot is a black sea. You go one mile and you think you're at the other end of the earth. But you're not afraid; you know that what's gonna save you is the fact you're so little and everything around you's gonna get lost in its own bigness. When you get older and grown up then it's not the same at all. You walk down the streets an' think you're taller than the houses an' think the cars are goin' between your legs and think with a flick of your prick you could knock down every single one of the Steinberg's, and think everybody else is a dwarf an' if you wanted to you could scoop 'em up by the handfuls. But you don't use your powers; you wait for your moment an' you're too dumb to realize it's come an' gone an' you're gettin' worn down an' becomin' as little as everybody else which means one fine mornin' you wake up and find your legs limp as dish rags an' the bones broken an' stickin' out everywhere. What're you gonna do then? You go from pillar to post, try like hell to make ends meet and don't, or start yellin' or laughin' till you're out of breath, or else you just sit back an' watch yourself sink under. Don't worry! You're gonna wind up with a little pinhead and tiny arms and no feet an' no body an' no heart especially. No heart; the heart's important. No heart, you got no diamond or club or spade either. You're nothin' but a fuckin' lump of ground beef with raggedy legs that don't run that fast any more.) He'd opened all the doors now. He saw the blind television set in the living room under the plastic palm tree, he saw the monkey hanging from a branch, he saw the hollow coconut shell, he saw the frayed burlap trunk. Jeanne D'Arc had to really be angry for him to buy her a gift like that! (At Dupuis'.) And him drunk. Jeanne D'Arc was going to leave him because of the poke in the eye he gave her, because of the insults, because of the drinking, and him, he'd gone to Dupuis'. The taxi and the tree cost him his whole pay cheque, he must have explained all that to the salesman, who pretended not to hear, turning a deaf ear to those words oozing fear. Hey, listen you, you loaded or what? You don't understand nothin', eh? Then what you doin' here? He was acting that way out of impatience and out of brutal desire for Jeanne D'Arc lying on the sofa with a tiny bag of ice on her eye. Whew! It was a hard job gettin' all that into the trunk of the car, alright. The memory made him terribly happy. He thought of the old taxi, the harsh lights, the screeching of the tires, the swarm of colors, buildings falling away behind the cars, the people, the nice-looking people walking up and down the streets, while the Pontiac was a half-tame animal let loose on Jeanne D'Arc's trail. (Ah, damn, damn!) And now there were just rooms which were too bare because Jeanne D'Arc wasn't in them. The dirt, the smell of burnt potatoes in the kitchen, of milk curdled in the container. And the living room. Jeanne D'Arc must have always watched television in the same spot, snuggled in a blanket in the rocking chair. The chair's rockers had left too many marks on the rug. And the potato chip crumbs, wasn't that proof enough? And the four coke bottles with the lipstick-stained straws. And the cigarette butts drowned in the bottles. Barthélémy remained perfectly still in the doorway. (Like on TV when they freeze the picture.) He felt nothing. His eyes were fixed in a stare and were filling up with water. A cordon of cops made an impenetrable curtain between him and the rest of the world. He was threatened and safe at the same time. If I was two people there'd be no problem. Each of us would have his place. Me, I could be mean an' him good. His ears tingled. The house was filling up with sounds, defending itself after its fashion against his intrusion; it was like a womb about to deliver, gas was escaping from it and it gave off cracking noises. How could Barthélémy not believe that he was once again a prisoner inside the white hospital where the only sounds were of needles piercing skin. He tried to move out of the doorway. Then suddenly everything went black. His knees buckled, his forehead struck the door frame, he fell on his leg (the dressing grew large and heavy with blood and pus and pain). He dragged himself down the hallway, grabbing at furniture. But running away was pointless because the guards were already at the door, the white guards were already blocking the windows—QUEBEC OCCUPIED. It was written in huge letters across the front page of the newspaper the guards brought him following his afternoon nap. (Why?) The nurses wore masks, they were naked but their faces were hidden behind squares of white gauze. The red rubber gloves. The frizzy, black hair below the belly. If it'd been any longer they'd have had real corkscrew curls. That's what he was thinking as the four nurses came toward him, he with a hard-on under the covers. They had tied him down to the bed, straps around his shoulders and knees; the nurses were really kangaroos or bloodsucking vampires. (Nothing escaped from that silent mouth.) Inside he was screaming and sirens were sounding. They took the sheet off the bed and tossed it aside, and the only vertical thing in that horizontal hospital world was his prick. The vampires were definitely going to grab him and plant passionate kisses all over him. Those teeth going into the skin. Those long draughts of blood, that prolonged sucking. Barthélémy doubled his efforts to move his trapped muscles. Warmth, and a heart bursting with love in his breast, and red tattoos on those impotent arms. Satiated, the vampires were perched on the big heating pipes which ran the length of the room. Other metamorphoses were going to take place, the vampires-kangaroos-nurses and the hypodermic needles would penetrate the flesh once again. Once again there would be inaudible cries and intense heat beneath the skin. During all this time Jeanne D'Arc's image pressing upon his eye, so small, so lovely, so pure. (Object of troubled affection rooted in the iris; a spear gouging the socket; blurred, failing sight.) Sphincters relaxing with rotten noises. Shitting and pissing. The white whale had strong breath. All around it a sheet of white, foul water in which the whaling ship was going to sink. The gold piece on the mainmast blinded Barthélémy. Unable to scream, he was crying. So, you like that book? Whales scare me. And cannibals more. The nurse was seated close by on the white chair taking his pulse. Those fingers with their long nails, and those protruding veins at his wrist, reassured him. I'm finished, eh? Why'd you have to kill me? The odor of excrement underneath him and this delicious feeling of buttocks wet with hot piss. He spit out the thermometer. You're acting like a child, monsieur Dupuis. Help us make you well. He kept his teeth clenched. His breath taken away because of the strap, his head like thunder ready to blow up the world. He would have liked to put his hand between the nurse's legs, violate her intimacy, get revenge for the indignities he was suffering. But she wasn't paying any attention to him now; the vampires had come back. They turned him over on his stomach and were holding his legs wide apart. His sex hurt him, his too-stiff prick was pure pain beneath him. Could the hippopotamus have put on the rubber glove the better to get inside him and brutally explore his anus? Don't you know it was time? You'd think there was cement in there. Oh, die of shame hearing the dry turds land in the bed pan. (Let go of me! Fuck, let go of me!) A car's headlights flashed yellow into the shadows, suddenly lighting up the long hallway. Barthélémy rubbed his eyes. He was covered with sweat, his leg was bloody and his heart beat rapidly in his chest. What the hell's happenin' to me? Heyheyhey! He lifted himself up and crawled on his knees to the door and collapsed on the porch beside his overnight bag. He was gasping for breath, tongue hanging out of his mouth, face on fire, blind and deaf and wild with excitement. Everything was turning, he couldn't tell where he was, there was too much wind and the flames were shooting out all around him now. He put his hand over his heart. Stop it, for God's sake! Stop it! He needed all his energy, something really serious must have happened while he was gone and if he didn't grab hold of himself he would be broken and destroyed before knowing what was what. He took a package of Forest out of his pocket, licked a Vogue paper, and came up with a pinch of tobacco. He was shaking so hard he lost the tobacco. His lungs were stopped up; there was no more air in the house, everything was crisp and dry. He made a sudden, violent movement with his body to break the spell and fell down the steps. Crying out—Jeanne D'Arc! Where are you, my Jeanne? He tried to get up. The back of his head struck something and all Barthélémy's strength left him. Later, he would understand that his head was stuck between two steps, that the wild grass growing beneath the porch was tickling his chin, and that he needed to laugh—It would rise on its own from somewhere deep within him, or maybe from somewhere outside him, so tired did he feel. Then the machines mounted him, caterpillar tractors flattening his back, jackhammers drilling his head; and, filling half the yard, there sat the grotesque hippopotamus, all smiles, its green teeth bared. Barthélémy couldn't keep from laughing, it made a protective wall between him and the rest of the world. I'll finally go to sleep. He wasn't aware right away of the importance of what he had just thought. He must have vomited before and wiped his lips on his shirtsleeve. Then he understood—that was the important word: sleep. He laid his head on the step and yawned. (Old lion lost in the jungle, mortally wounded, no Tarzan to bring him hunks of beef. Old fatgut, toothless lion who's lost his roar. Go to sleep, damn it. Go to sleep. He knew Jeanne D'Arc would come back at the right moment, that first he had to wait for her deep in the heart of the night before he could take her in his arms. He let the tears flow down his cheeks and closed his eyes. He was floating down the Rivière des Prairies, gasping for breath, drowning in the blood running out of his leg) —))

Deaf to the City

•

Marie-Claire Blais

He stood watching the busy traffic in the street from the window of the Hôtel des Voyageurs, wearing the apron he wore at lunchtime when he helped his mother in the restaurant, his face pinched in the sallow light, his restlessness frozen for a moment in meditation, so that he looked at that instant like the very countenance of pain captured by Munch in *The Scream*; like that anonymous figure whose silent cry fills the painter's canvas, Mike rested his heavy head on his frail hands and with his wide-eyed questioning gaze, his pupils enlarged with concern, he challenged the world, or rather the various silhouettes that made up his world at that instant—the people passing by out on the street, his mother, the men she was waiting on at the bar, Tim the Irishman who was standing near him unfolding his newspaper, all the strangers going in and out of the hotel, each and every one of them—just when it seemed as though his quavering, half-open mouth was about to emit an endless scream to remind the indifferent human mass gathered there, crouching or musing over a glass, a sunbeam, or some other scant dose of morning pleasure, that even if it were not

a shame to live as they were living, as tranquilly and incon-
sequentially as flies—although flies had been blessedly
spared those human cravings that weigh down so many
good and wicked men alike—even if this were not cause for
shame, it was scandalous to live and die without ever managing to strip away the damning halo that branded their fore-
heads with the sentence: "You shall suffer on earth . . ." It
was engraved on all things, Mike thought, even on old
Tim's flabby face as he muttered in English, his nose in the
paper: *"Do you believe everything you read in the paper, Gloria,
do you? Hé, the kid wants to go to the movies, hé, a blue movie,
Mike, what's the matter with him, Gloria, anyway? They all took
their money out, they're crazy . . ."* Day after day the same
sounds came stumbling from the wrinkled, bitter mouth: "
*What a bastard he is, hé, what a bastard, take care of your
heart, my Gloria, take care of your heart . . .,"* and Gloria
responded to the fetid murmur of the bar with a haughty,
ferocious sensuality that would have struck them dead in a
single glance if her body had been as hateful as her soul, but
her body was bored and it gave in, gave in with the softness
of her handsome, languorous arms and the curve of the
placid, voluptuous breasts she offered up to all, her body
yielded despite herself to the torpor, to the somehow
unclean fondling of so many fingers, "and that's OK"
thought Mike, "Just so long as she doesn't start pawing them
all over and getting them excited . . . if it rains Tim will take
me to a dirty movie . . . three orders of spaghetti in the
oven, yes, just so long as Mom's hand doesn't slide any
lower . . ." lethargy, the first caress of the day, Gloria
thought, "if you don't like it you don't have to look, Mikey,
don't forget your father wasn't just anybody, he was the great
Luigi, we'll go to the hospital for your treatment and then
we'll take in all the movies you want, *stop it, Tim, you could
kiss my royal ass,* OK? Why don't you go fetch me the porno
slicks at the corner, na, not for the kid, for me, he don't read

much, that one, his head hurts too much . . " "How'd it all
start?" asked Tim, his lips slobbering against Gloria's face,
"there's always a beginning, hé, always a beginning . . . " "It's
nothing!" Gloria snapped back, "nothing at all, he's OK,
they got rid of his tumour, going to take him all the way to
San Francisco on my bike this summer, *shit* won't it be a
pleasure not to see your holy mug, you damned Irishman!"
"Well, what if his father turned out to be just an ordinary
Italian," said Tim, *"or just me, your old lover, just an ass like
me, hé?"* "You holding that spaghetti up for Easter, Mike? Get
a move on, and wash some cups for coffee while you're at it,
what're you standing there like that for with your tongue
hanging out?" Mike, with an anguished look, avoided his
mother's glance and hid his head in his arms. "It's nothing,
Mom, nothing. I feel hot." "The doctor told you it's normal
to feel hot, that spaghetti's going to be burned to a crisp . . ."
It was a cool day, the street bright with sunshine, and before
long the student who ran down from the mountain would
break into the street then the park with his long-limbed
weightless flight, and in a moment Mike would be left only
with a sense of the perfection of the runner's muscular life,
the spirited body dashing forward toward life itself, he
would be no more than a long back stiffened by effort and
the tight clothes binding it, a scarlet blob about to disappear
around the corner, "Tell me now, Tim, what d'ya know
about the role of sex in life? Nothing, cause it's up to us
women to know about those things . . ." As for me, I'm a
mother, first and foremost a woman and a mother, and mistress all round, or lover, if you prefer *my old boy* . . ." The
Irishman's big fist was resting on Gloria's chest, the runner
was coming down, still coming down, and he must get a bit
winded, Mike thought, the whole city was running out of
breath bit by bit, noise and light dilating it, the aroma of coffee was invading the dimly lit kitchen and Mike said to Lucia
who was staring at the burned spaghetti, "Hurry up and

take care of Jojo and we'll go out, it's a nice day, we can take a walk in the park . . ." "I don't want to be late for school," Lucia replied, "I'm afraid I'll miss my bus. Why don't you feed her yourself?" "I don't know how," Mike answered. "Just put the spoon in her mouth, see, like this—Mom feeds you stuff that's nothing but juice when you can't swallow! You know who her father is, Mike?" Lucia's tiny shadow went bouncing through the yard and disappeared. "Eat up now," Mike said to Jojo, "then we'll go out in the sun . . ." but Jojo refused the spoon Mike tried to slip into her mouth, she was laughing and crying at the same time and then all of a sudden a question seemed to fix itself in her black, uncannily knowing eyes. "Do you know why I was born," she seemed to ask Mike, "what I'm doing here?" Mike went on feeding her patiently with the kind of dreamy, slightly far-off gentleness that had come over his movements in the past few months. "Let's go play in the park, Jojo . . . but stay away from the horses, sometimes they get mad if you bother them", the grass was coming up in the park, it was spring, "this summer we'll go to San Francisco" said Mike as he set the child down in a patch of light and warmth, and Jojo immediately began to run every which way with Mike running after her, laughing, laughing because it was nice out at long last and in winter you couldn't see or hear anything when the snow and the wind blinded you, and now, as he went skipping along in the path of his sister's fragile destiny, Mike listened to his heart beating in his chest, "where I'll be next year, maybe I won't hear it any more." Jojo went on laughing, falling down and scrambling to her feet, thinking to scare Mike by hiding behind trees. Mike let her whirl about him, stronger for the kind of glow he felt in her presence, as if not even the mighty, unsightly cathedral that dominated the city could protect the child as he could just by letting the back of his hand brush over her hair, this was life, this was living and the people walking

and scurrying around him didn't know it, none of the people spilling out of the subway in groups or emerging from
the station and the banks knew it—or were their hearts making as much noise as the furious cascade that seemed to roar
in his veins, yes, perhaps . . . It was a bright day, but Gloria
had forgotten about the electric sign and the red letters
sparkled with their nocturnal fire: *"Come as you are, day and
night, chez Luigi."* Tim would come staggering out of the
hotel, others would stop in for a beer or a coffee, Gloria had
a man in the house but he was bad, Mike thought, she also
had dogs to protect her and they were bad too, "but it's better than being alone," he reflected, and the sky was so blue
you saw it a lot closer, without fear. "Look, Jojo, the birds
are back. . ." but the small ball of life wouldn't nestle long in
Mike's hands, it drew close only to run off elsewhere, far
away, already far away, leaving in its place a waft of perfume,
a breath, now it was just a curly head of hair, curly like
Gloria's, a big head for a child, thought Mike, a head set
atop a bundle of woollen clothes since Gloria hadn't noticed
that spring had arrived, and inside this coloured package
there was life, life that knew how to walk and run unaided
toward a goal that didn't yet seem at all obscure although it
would cloud over eventually, maybe even the very next day.
The runner, Mike thought, must have turned the corner a
long time ago, as if sucked up into the blue sky, for it was
already time for the girl—he didn't know her, but he had
become used to seeing her—to come down the mountain for
a cup of coffee, to sit at the bar while Gloria hissed, mocking
and impious, in her ear, "Say, love, what's your name again?
Judith Langenais . . .That's right, you told me yesterday,
Judith Lange, Judith Angel; you'll wake up in the gutter one
day, all the same, the cappuccino's on the house today cause
it does me good to see you, it's a welcome change from Tim,
you're a professor, hé, must be tough going sometimes what
with the brats you got in schools today . . What d'you teach?

Philosophy! Well, then, you ought to be able to answer my question: what's the role of sex in life?" Leaning against a tree while Jojo toyed with some pebbles at his feet, Mike observed the woman, his mother, from a distance, he was steeped in her, in her shamelessness, in her benevolent lewdness, so benevolent for herself and for others; he didn't hate her, he respected her, even loved her sometimes, especially when the weather was nice and you had the illusion of suddenly seeing her face and the eager movements of her features very close up, when the words she pronounced every day resounded in your ears as if they were rising from her entrails, the stream of lewdness that was also Gloria, that was Gloria and nobody else, for it wasn't just any woman who was willing to be called Gloria and to have had a husband murdered in the street, and a bar that might also become a bloody stage from one night to the next, what kind of a life was it after all, being called Gloria and having dyed hair and a sick child, "and others who aren't doing so bad but that's just it, you've got to feed them, all the same the best part of the T-bone's for my dogs in case we're attacked one day, you understand, love? You still haven't answered the sex question, should be a cinch for you, being into that philosophy stuff you should know all about it!" Judith didn't answer, Mike knew Judith never answered Gloria's questions, he had seen her coming down from the street's golden summit, Judith, Judith Lange, the Angel, as his mother called her, although nothing about her made you think of an angel, she walked with her books under her arm, she had a class at two, she taught philosophy, her shiny raincoat was open at the collar and a gold chain glittered on her bare neck, a rather buxom girl, that was how Mike saw her approaching in the distance, first recognizing her head, then her neck that she never covered, not even in winter, and he recalled that when spring came she suddenly seemed lighter, slimmer, as if everything floated around her, maybe it was just the shiver of the air, unlike the runner who flew along with the current of the buildings, of the houses, Judith Lange drew near with a slow, heavy step, her feet sank into the ground and then she came back up toward you, maybe it was her slowness and the invisible weight of her gait, stealthy as a cat's, that stirred the air, she said nothing when Gloria asked her an indiscreet question, only smiled, but Gloria thought she heard her say, "But Gloria, sex is everything, life, death, everything, Glori.a." But she never said anything, Mike thought, it was the kindness of her smile that traced on her lips the words Gloria alone could really understand, then Gloria, appeased, would say, "*Love*, you wouldn't think, seeing me like this behind my cash register, that I had an ancestor who came from Norway like me, she was the first woman doctor received by the Academy . . . And even me, Gloria, my eldest daughter, Berthe, is studying for the bar, not the alcoholic kind, mind you, no, she's in law school, it's a change for us but the girl's got a heart of stone, won't have anything to do with us, even disowns her father! But I've still got my Mike, my Michel, and I swear you'll see us take off on the bike for San Francisco this summer! They won't keep him at the hospital, he's my little boy, after all. You've got time yet, have another coffee, at your age I was always shacked up with one guy or another, didn't give a damn about school, you see I've had sex on my mind for a pretty long time now . . ." But maybe Judith Lange wouldn't be coming today, Gloria said Mike pretended to be deaf when she spoke, deaf to her groans of pleasure, to the wrenching sighs of her revolt, deaf to everything, she said, and yet he heard her when she spoke of "life, sex, and death," and again of "sex, death, and life," those words that churned about freely in Gloria's mind and perhaps hers was the only mind in the world that harboured them, thought Mike who wanted to be like Gloria, working late into the night, sometimes seeking out her clients in funeral parlours, she would tell Judith about that, too, some day, sex was Gloria's legend, she would tell it all to Judith one day, but Jojo was living her own life under the tree, the tree Mike was fondling with his moist palms, you could tell when you leaned against it that it was a tree that still had many years of life ahead, Mike thought, yes, the day would come, tonight or tomorrow, it might be fiercely violent or sweetly murderous, the soul just took off, all the souls of the dead were wandering in the sun, looking for someone to understand, someone who would let them into his or her thoughts, even Gloria's thoughts about sex, life, and death, one day Mike would understand everything, everything that was dormant in Gloria, on Judith's lips, the delivered soul went elsewhere, went to all those places to which it had been denied admittance during its joyous but often terrible captivity, and it might be only a short time before Mike's soul would also know that flight, that dance deep within the hearts that were now closed to him. Mike, still leaning against the tree, suddenly forgot about Judith as he noticed three boys in the park lying in the sun, spread out on a bed of grass that seemed to have been made for them at that instant; Jojo had probably run around them, chirping, but the boys, dozing, remained aloof in their wholesome non-chalance, each of them resting his head on the other's leg, and in the moment of unexpected languor in which sleep had caught them off guard, in such a rigid, three-sided pose that one might have taken them for statues, thought Mike, the only thing that still recalled their existence or the fact that they had been alive ten minutes earlier—and they had been, they'd spoken loudly, they'd quarrelled—was a pair of running shoes; one of the shoes that no longer served to walk and run had been separated from its twin, and during the battle that had brought the three boys together the shoe, harassed, molested at the hands of the enemy, tossed up like a ball, had landed close to the tree and Mike, and if in the distance the flash of blue and yellow T-shirts added a bright touch to the triangular tomb the boys seemed to form, only the battered, saddened shoe appeared, as Mike contemplated it, to claim an existence proper; broken, subjugated by its owner, it knew, better than Mike, the boy it had shod and protected against the cold, it had soaked up his joyous and grieving Sweat, it had loved, cried, laughed, and suddenly it was just an obsolete thing that would soon be cast aside for another and it lay there, close to Mike who watched it living its final moments of revolt in the sun. Eternal Gloria, celestial Gloria, thought Gloria of herself, she gave all men their bottle, there could be no higher philosophy than the one Gloria dispensed to all, her body's fluids drenching the arid earth where everything one loved would die tomorrow; it was Friday, Judith was having lunch at her parents' house, Madame Langenais was asking her daughter "what she was going to do later on", she was an attentive mother and Judith had every reason to be proud of her, Marianne, Gisele, and Micheline were wearing their school uniforms "but they're not severe enough", Madame Langenais informed her husband, "the skirts are too short this year . ." and she hardly dared let her gaze slide over her daughters' splendid thighs—the stockings stopped below the knees and all the rest was on display, the healthy, silken flesh and the pleats of the navy blue skirt not quite covering it, Marianne, Gisele and Micheline would go off to play tennis this afternoon as usual rather than study, and of course, Madame Langenais explained to her husband, their studies took a back seat to everything else, and Judith asked her father if he had been afraid before performing that morning's operation, no, he hadn't been afraid, "strangely", he told Judith, it was afterwards that fear really gripped him, "even when the operation had been successful", the soup was served and Madame Langenais suddenly wondered, as if it were a fact she'd never noticed until this particular Friday, why her daughter had green eyes when nobody else in the family had green eyes, teaching philosophy, it was no career for a woman, what would become of her later on, Good God, she had surgeon's hands like her father, she would rather not know what Judith did with her hands, hands so firm yet delicate, there was no way of knowing anything about Judith since she no longer lived at home, as for Marianne, Gisèle, and Micheline one knew just about all there was to know, Madame Langenais still decided what books they read, or practically, but Judith's soul eluded her completely and for a mother there was something obscure in that, an irritating, wilful secret, they had finished eating, Gisèle and Micheline could be heard trying to find their tennis rackets "in their mess of a room," remarked Madame Langenais while Judith silently ground a piece of fruit between her small, cat-like teeth, thought her mother, Marianne went to sit on her father's lap, her knees red and so bare, so bare, she was too big to sit on her father's knees now anyway, at her age, thought Madame Langenais, thinking at the same time about the gardener, she'd have to look after that, Judith had asked why Gilbert didn't eat with them and Madame Langenais had firmly replied: "Gilbert prefers eating alone in the kitchen," that's the way things were, she wasn't going to give in to Judith's whims, to that communist, she mused, staring at her with her round eyes, Judith, she had to keep reminding herself that this was her flesh, her blood, Marianne was addressing her father, "you don't know anything, Papa, no, you don't know anything, you told me you knew everything but you don't know anything at all," her father explained that mathematics had changed a lot since his youth but Marianne wasn't listening and Madame Langenais, while carefully watching her family, was casting furtive glances toward the garden where Gilbert was coming and going with a shovel, the tip of his cap just visible beneath the window, social classes no longer existed, a shame, was there a place left on earth where people still respected them, of course everybody has a right to his or her political ideas, but how did Judith spend her nights; the word "night" sprang up like a sudden menace in Madame Langenais' mind, the word was the very essence of insubordination, night, sumptuous night, secret night, no, better to ignore what Judith did at night, the word was so heavy with sighs, with abandonments, and these easy-going girls thought their parents had ceased loving each other, but the night, nights, and all of a sudden Judith had risen and wound her giant arms around her mother's shoulders and Madame Langenais had heard the hissing of her raucous voice in her ear, a voice that was saying, insidious, loving, "Maman, dear Maman, Josephine, I love you in spite of everything . . ." Madame Langenais, accustomed to her daughter's affectionate outbursts, hadn't budged, the tip of Gilbert's cap could still be seen bobbing up and down beneath the window as he passed, and Madame Langenais was overcome by a kind of sinner's sadness, she realized she'd been lacking in charity, Judith's warm breath against her cheek evoked the latent fault, the fault that was so ancient, irreparable, a habit already, it was too late, even if Judith was a communist, she had no proof of that but where Judith was concerned it was fitting to imagine the worst, she thought, it was already too late to ask Gilbert in to share the family's meals, Madame Langenais had no reason to complain, didn't she have affectionate, maybe over-affectionate daughters—there was Marianne still cuddling up against her father—yes, but how did Judith spend her nights, and Gilbert kept passing back and forth with his shovel, his piles of earth, we'll have beautiful roses this year, Josephine, I love you in spite of everything, the "in spite of everything" ringing in Madame Langenais' ear, there was a rebuke in it or at least a hint of rebuke, Madame Langenais pushed her daughter off gently, saying, "I've already told you I don't

want you calling me by my name . . . not in this house . . .
ask your father if I'm not right . . ." and suddenly, while
Judith's arms were still resting on her neck, a young couple
Madame Langenais had noticed that morning on her way to
the bank came to her mind, they had been waiting at a street
corner and suddenly, in an amorous impulse, looking each
other over, they had brusquely grasped each other in a long
embrace, passionately intertwined right there on the sidewalk where they stood, Marianne's bare knees flashing
before her were suddenly confused with the enchanting yet
dangerously sensual explosion of the two young people clad
in coloured shorts, each giving the other, without any particular reason, this entangling of knees and tongues, drowning
in broad daylight, they'd yielded to the moment without
shame or reproach, each so lost in the other as long as the
hypnotic embrace lasted that Madame Langenais had felt
herself a witness to their bodies' most intimate movements
beneath the transparent, multicoloured shorts that offered
such scant protection on such a cool morning. Suddenly
Judith was no longer there, Madame Langenais was alone in
the empty house with its blue drapes, out in the garden, on
the mountainside, you could see the whole city, where was
Judith now, what was she doing, a class at two, Madame
Langenais was going to go out and offer Gilbert a bit of
advice, red roses or white roses, Judith's breath was hot,
before long the whole city would be in blossom, fragrant, so
fragrant, and Mike had dozed off vaguely while his sister
played at his feet, he was still standing against the tree,
"don't put that poison in your mouth, Jojo . . ." old Tim
came out of the drugstore with his porno papers under his
arm, his old dog trailing after on a rope, Tim and the dog
staggering towards their bench under the brotherly hundred-
year-old tree that awaited them, the tree, the bench, these
were their shores and neither Tim nor his dog noticed Mike,
flotsam in the sun, they went on, kept going, they didn't

fall, they were walking almost straight, the entire city was feverish with men and sounds but they were still headed for their bench, the old dog was also called Tim and he too was Irish, you could no longer tell which of the two was at the end of the rope, the one with the logger's jacket or the one with tattered fur and unsteady gait, both were hungry but once at the bench they would share the crumbs of the same sandwich, they would watch the women together, their desires coming through in identical fashion, two muzzles dripping with drool, old Tim and his old dog, they were close to Mike now, running out of breath together, but they didn't see him leaning shakily against a tree, you couldn't really buckle under with pain or sadness, you could only give in, give in slightly on such a good day, weighed down by that something, maybe it was ecstasy, the ecstasy of being alive, and suddenly the vision of his mother came back to Mike in the whirl of old Tim and his dog, of the plaid jacket and the haggard dog at the end of the rope, flotsam in the sun, but they were still on their feet and so was he, slackening a tiny bit as he leaned against the tree, the tree that would always be there, tomorrow or later, in rain or snow, Mike saw again his mother, saw old Tim pinching her hip that morning, slipping his shifty hands into Gloria's armpits, so old Tim didn't know that at night Gloria was transformed, that she became for her son something terribly severe, the image of crucifixion, the Mother of Sorrow, that was Gloria, she had a man or several men with her in her room, they were all bad like the five police dogs in the yard, that night she was sleeping with Charlie, "my goddamned hooligan on probation, you don't even know how to make love," she shouted, "leave the door open in case my kid calls me . . ." "What did Charlie do, Mom?" "Nothing much, he killed someone one day, he was too young, he doesn't even remember . . . ." Charlie had killed, maybe he'd kill again that very night, Lucia, Jojo, and Luigi 2 were downstairs, all the people Gloria knew had killed, but it was time to sleep, nothing had been written on sleep, not yet, and sleep, white as a snow field, was calling Mike, come, come, and Mike would not be slow to obey, love and sleep also belonged to those who had killed, Gloria and Charlie would soon sleep just like everybody else, "All the same leave a light on in the hall, just in case he calls me, first time I've ever heard of a guy getting homesick for prison, never saw the likes of it!" Sleep was still as pure as a sheet of blank paper but in the feeble light coming from the hall it seemed as though an unknown, detached hand had come to write on it, yes, a hand was writing by itself, drawing on the wall, the design was imperceptible, the work of an ant, the written expression of the terror that crept along the wall, something was pursuing Mike, hunting him down even when he hid under the sheets, or maybe the devastating parasite was lodged in his own body and it was nothing but his own shadow that he saw on the wall, it was his head, his thronging head that had become a refuge for these larvae; and his heart that usually throbbed so wildly, pounding with fever, was suddenly beating noiselessly, without echo, maybe it wasn't a parasite after all but that formidable She, maybe the Unnameable had just entered his body, and surely this deaf heart, this voiceless heart was no longer his own; and yet, though he heard no sound rising to his lips, his moan too low to be perceptible, it was she after all, Gloria, who now bent heavily over his iron bed, she, Mother of all Sorrow, of the crucified: "Stop screaming, come on, I'm right here . . ." and cradled in her breasts, he had watched it all flee, even the ghost of his terror, the hand writing by itself on the wall, the worm of his own destruction nestling into the purity of the night, and his heart had taken up its own rhythm and song once again, "But why do you give your mother such frights?" Not even old Tim who was so proud of being a Catholic knew that the saints were no longer in heaven but among us on earth, in the lightning flash of our pains, he was stretched out on the bench with the panting dog, still holding on to the end of the rope although there was no need to hold the old dog who had been Tim's master for such a long time now, old Tim saw the sky through clouds of alcohol, it wasn't a sky full of angels furious because he'd had too much to drink, it wasn't a sky so blue that it was like blue lake-water passing over his eyes, pained by visions, no, it was the sea, his own country's sea, he only had to dream a bit and he found it again, a pale sea waiting for him on the other side of a pine-covered mountain, then it slipped out of sight and came back again with a tumultuous clamour, his native sea that had thrown him up here on this bench with an aging dog for company, he no longer knew how many years had passed, if he let the dream continue the bench became soft dunes under his back while the sea moved by with perfect, rigid tranquillity, a woman was coming down toward him, Gloria, the woman who had been the village schoolteacher during his child-hood in the suburbs of Limerick, a nun hiking up her skirt and leaping over boulders—old Tim's dog had sneezed and the spell was broken, old Tim was back on the bench and would have to wait until tomorrow to find his native sea again, he grumbled, grumbled *"those bastards, those bastards,"* moaning when a boisterous gang of adolescents, trampling the new grass with an insolent, dancing tread, began to bark just for a laugh, "woof woof,", tossing the "woof woof" to old Tim and his dog more as a mock homage than as an insult; it so stung the drunkard's delicate soul that he spit with scorn, but they went on barking, "Hi, woof woof," and old Tim began to dream, he was gunning them all down with his rifle, it didn't matter if his hand was a bit shaky and he had no rifle, only Tim's old dog was touched by the music and suddenly light-hearted under his tattered coat he perked up his nose and ears and answered with drawn-out echoes the amused barks which, just this once, had been aimed at him, one had so few laughs with old Tim, they would wind up in the city pound or the poorhouse sooner or later, yes, better enjoy it while it lasts, *"will you shut up, you monster!"* said the Irishman, kicking his best friend, *"you bastard, I'll kill you!"* and the dog, surprised, sad again, thought that yes, the city pound or the poorhouse, that was their future, but old Tim had had too much to drink, he was "stiff to the very roots," as Gloria put it, better stop barking, quiet down, submit, since old Tim still held the end of the rope. "All the same, some have it easy, sweet Jesus," muttered Tim, noticing a taxi driver who was taking a nap in his car, "look at that bastard!" He was a thin man and seen in profile he looked like a corpse, as though the solemn stiffness of rigor mortis had allowed him to relax and listen to the call coming in over the radio without slouching in his seat: *"It is an emergency test, only, it is an emergency test, when you hear this sound . . ."* then he'd fallen asleep and Tim saw him thus from a distance, with his corpse's profile and the nervous line of a last little smile that persisted, flouting Tim and his dog, the taxi driver telling Tim *"Look how lucky I am, you dog!"* Two images lingered still between the taxi driver's eyelashes, one of a Spanish star—at any rate that was how he imagined her—wiggling her hips on the street corner while waiting for a man, followed by the apparition of a Greek pope, or a person who bore a striking resemblance to a Greek pope with his black tunic and purple bonnet, accompanied by a businessman, nobody knew where they were all going like that, the mysterious convoy of the street coming and going, it doesn't matter, thought the taxi driver, it was time for his nap, the rest of the world was thrashing about in vain in a swamp full of footsteps and sounds; perhaps it was at that very moment that Judith Lange, who was explaining Descartes to her students, suddenly noticed in the college yard, which was otherwise bare and ugly, a lone branch of white lilac trembling at the window, hovering alone as if the wind had blown it off the bush; it was probably an illusion, the yard was ugly and bare, but someone had nevertheless thought to plant the white lilacs that lined the wall, it was Judith who had been blind to their presence for so long, and suddenly the lilacs were alive again in the warm spring sun, and the quavering wind that was a foreboding of summer gales and storms parted the branches of lilac; their white intoxication floating in toward Judith's nostrils so sweet that she put her book aside—it was daylight, a radiant day bathing the students in the classroom and Judith herself in its generous, fragrant light, and silence had hushed the din of life, yet Judith thought of night, nights full of love and all those fragrances, and that light too, but night was when one was apt to give in to despair, "and what did you do last night?" her mother had asked, she had been to see Florence, she was the visitor who broke into lonely nights, but her students to whom she went on explaining Descartes knew nothing about that side of her life, who was this Florence, after all?—a woman she'd met in a train station, a deserted eighteenth-floor apartment in a big city, Florence, a woman alone, where was her husband, where was her son, both dissolved in an ocean of memories, "No, you must not die," Judith had told her, and now the lilac branch seemed to confirm her statement which was suddenly truer than ever, the lilac branch whipped the windowpane, the sun flooded the classroom, springtime, spring, and summer before long, and Florence had not forsaken the joys of life, not yet, not that night, but now it was day again and a dull light fell on her furniture, on the pictures of her husband, of her son, all that wrenching apart of the past frozen on the wall, Judith, a stranger, who was she after all, perhaps nothing more than a dream with which she'd consoled herself, the apartment was deserted once again, inhabited by so many bourgeois victories, Judith had said, maybe she was an anarchist, a revolutionary, inhabited, yes, with treasures, with china, but it was a distressing place since Florence had thought about dying there, Judith Lange, friend of suicides, sister of the inert martyrs of existence, where was she now, Florence wondered, why had she come to save her, for one night, for a few hours, when the fatal act was already stamped on her being, tonight or tomorrow, what was the sense of hanging on, respecting life when she was bound to it by nothing more than a young woman's smile illuminating the night, the apartment was deserted once again, Judith Lange was no longer there, the same nauseating sense of life rose in Florence's breast, and perhaps in thousands of other breasts at that very moment this same sensation was working its way into the thousands of gloomy, silent hearts in spite of the glorious light that flooded the white lilacs in the college yard, into hearts that had already settled into silence as they advanced in their own solitary company toward that eternity of silence of which we know nothing; Florence was already dead, she thought as she cast an indifferent glance at her hands resting on her knees, dead hands resting on icy knees, Judith Lange had tried to warm them between her own but they were no longer fit for the reasonable task of living, how sweet it must be to belong to the community of the living, to love and live as they lived, deliciously and weightlessly; dying was a malady that weighed you down so, it was so heavy that even two frail hands on your knees felt like lead, and wasn't the painful light pouring from the sky spilling all over you and your paleness only to strike you down? This heavy heart was dead, and yet it kept on beating loudly in Florence's chest, it was a knell, a strident wail that nobody heard and it went on repeating, "soon everything will be all over!" but time was passing and nothing was over yet, time was passing even more heavily today than yesterday, it passed with the sudden lulls and flashes of recovery that come to the condemned: that was when Judith's mag-

netic smile held the night hour at a distance, but the people
of death remained close by, they were all gathered just
beyond the fragile door, pressing against each other in these
attics of time and silence: it was the city of the dead, the
great faceless refuge, and if there was also a human presence
lithely calling her back to life with warm breath and smiles,
it was only Judith, a passer-by of whom Florence knew nothing except that she might never come back, and Judith at
that moment noticed a student couple walking under the
canopy of white lilacs; they looked like an ordinary boy and
girl, perhaps their only asset was the awkward charm of
youth as they walked along close to each other, their hands
barely touching, and Judith read in their features the desire
of love, or love about to blossom even if they themselves
were still all shyness and disorder; it was as though the
brightness of the white lilacs, the radiant headiness that
filled the air had caught them off guard in this uneasy
enchantment without their quite realizing it; maybe they
were holding their breath, maybe their pulses were slowing
down as their eyes searched the other's and yes, perhaps the
wind shivering amongst the lilac, this barely perceptible
movement of nature, was all that was needed and the boy
and girl, separated now by the trembling shyness of their
desires, which seemed as they glanced at each other cautiously as impenetrable as a wall, would be united, the slightest
breath would suffice and they would find themselves uniting
in each other everything which at that moment cut them off
from all the rest, Judith would see them embrace during
that moment of peace, the luminous veil would close in over
them as the veil of death would close in over Florence
tonight or tomorrow; but they were shy, the boy made an
awkward move that brusquely detached him from his companion and then they disappeared as they had appeared,
gentle and magic, and Judith took up her book again,
Descartes, Descartes, but they weren't listening, they were

all staring at the lilac branch at the window and Judith's body panted with the simple joy of being alive, she felt their gaze, their impatient caresses all around her, life was the only sacred philosophy we had, the words were still ringing in Florence's ears but she was on her own from now on, her sad face and the memory of her hands on her knees lingered still in Judith's soul, at long last she was going to go away she'd told Judith, one can also die a bit further on, in another city or in a hotel room, while preserving in one's home the still tepid appearance of everyday life, the car parked at the door, the light burning in the bathroom, those who passed by would think you were still caught up in life's traps, and the track left by all the gestures accomplished day after day—open a door, close it, read a book, put a glass away—this trail of gestures and objects would linger a long time after you had gone, haunting those who survived your absence, Judith Lange, friend of suicides, but you could not bypass the road to your own death, it was lurking in some sinister place, in a sinister light, preparations for the dull, fetid ceremony were already under way and it was close by, so close by; the person to be condemned walked listlessly or hurried along toward his place of execution, toward his livid shroud, and there were thousands of people like Florence shuffling across the face of the earth, coming and going at death's threshold, all stunned by a bruising, incomprehensible adversity; the arrows of misfortune never missed their mark and each victim wandered, wandered like Florence, stumbling again and again into the walls of the city, and all that could be seen of Florence was a grey spot, her body against the vast, grey sky, and the heavy suitcase she was carrying dragging her entire being down, down toward the bottomless pit of the world, it was a bright green suitcase which seemed huge compared to the woman carrying it, and Florence had filled it with old letters as if the weight of words written and delivered during a lifetime could help her take her leave and enter the earth again; in the meantime she wandered amidst the other travellers, dragging with her the enormously heavy suitcase that perhaps contained nothing more than ashes, like the others she stumbled against the walls of the city, her soul exhausted and drained; sometimes she stopped walking and sat on a bench; she shared a yellow bench with another woman, a woman silent like herself, but the other woman wasn't going anywhere, her destiny was to wait for a train that would get her safely home to her family and her own kind by evening. Florence had envied the unknown woman, had even envied the woollen folds of her coat, for beneath the coat, beneath the leather gloves and the small handbag there was a woman, a living woman and her world, instead of the stray, dispossessed spirit, instead of the anguish that had become Florence's world ever since she had left her apartment and her memories, and yet everyone would think she was still there, the light burning in the bathroom, the car at the door, still back there, yes, and she wandered, wandered, perhaps her soul had already left her body, she thought, yes, perhaps that was it, the almost weightless feeling she had beside this burden, can one possibly get lost in a city while dragging around such a weight, a heavy green suitcase pulling you towards the ground while all around there's nothing but vast, grey silence, while at the other end of a bench there's a silent woman who doesn't hear your breath, your lamentation, your cry, for she'll soon be home among her own, and the trains, their whistles and wails, trains coming in, going out, for the first time Florence noticed all the others she had barely had a glimpse of through the grating at her window, suddenly they were all there, they existed, someone had said "Nice day today, isn't it?" and Florence observed, stupefied, the silent form that was no longer there, the woollen coat, the leather gloves, the small handbag, none of it existed now, the other end of the bench was suddenly occupied by a girl wrapped in misery, an extremely poor girl smelling of wine, and Florence was confronted with the filthy apparition of two bare legs that had been cold all winter; through the grating at her window, from her apartment that was so close to the sky that Florence had never seen legs that had been cold during an entire winter this close up, the legs were still young, the socks and the boots that protected the benumbed feet had the look of wear, the transparency of old rags, but the creature abandoned there on the bench, who seemed to breathe the very breath of abandonment, was courageously saying to Florence, "Nice day today, isn't it?" Florence didn't answer as she contemplated the face and the legs that had endured the stigmata of bitter cold: injustice and evil were everywhere on earth, go away, leave it all behind, and the girl who had been cold all winter was saying, "On nice days like today I sure feel like taking off on a trip, but no money, no trip . . . ." Florence didn't answer; she was accustomed to silence, one didn't speak to other people, they were there but one didn't speak to them, the sensation of fear only grew worse at their contact, and suddenly an old man who also seemed to come in from a wintry, nocturnal path appeared in the light, he looked as though he was walking but he was in fact trotting in one place, no, he wasn't walking, he moved his feet slowly, guided by his blind man's cane, the feet, the man, old age followed the cane but he didn't move, or barely, he must have come a long way, thought Florence, like the poor girl who had been cold all winter, maybe he was a man who thought about nothing, who had a hard time just existing, sweat running down his spine, his cane guiding him, blind, blind, like any object that moves us to pity he wandered blindly, adrift in the world and seeing nobody, neither Florence sitting on the bench nor the other woman; his blind memory held fast to the crude forces that had been crushing him for such a long time, cold, hunger, misery, it all moved along slowly

with him and, like Florence, he could find no refuge anywhere, like Florence, he was bitter, bitter, sapped and blind,
and he scorned the brutal forces that had debased the digni-
fied man in him, of whom there wasn't a trace left, nobody
even vaguely remembered him, that was what living was,
when men were slain before their time only their ghosts
remained and Florence thought, "Why doesn't he fall, he
hasn't an ounce of strength left to continue," but like a
worm the old man clung stubbornly to the surface of the
earth and Florence felt fear stirring in her, it was all part of
the same thing, her fear, his stubbornness, what's the use,
what's the use—if this particular fear was intolerable it was
because it carried other familiar sensations in its wake, and
yet Florence, her heavy suitcase at het feet, remained calm,
staring at the ridiculous hands resting on her knees, they
were all alive, all of them, they were going to go home, eat,
love, sleep, and she stayed on, the fear in her cutting her off
from everything, even from their habits, and yet she remembered, yes, it was a familiar sensation, maybe one even felt it
in the company of the powerful of this world, when she was
with her husband for example, who was an influential man,
a physicist, people respected him, the sensation of fear floated all around him, even if it was something invisible it was
there lurking behind the malicious, enchanting screen of
pleasure, everywhere, fear beneath the pure, tranquil sky, he
was powerful, bent over sheets of paper lined with frigid figures and saying, "You're afraid, darling, but what are you
afraid of?" When she moved it all moved with her, an
immense, terrible chaos and dread and he knew nothing of
it, he went on writing, meditating, sipping his cognac, they
travelled first class, they were somewhere over Africa, alone,
agitation seizing her high above the black abyss, and what
would become of him now, she had no idea, the old man
was still pushing his cane along before him, he had taken a
few steps, with great difficulty but he had taken a few steps

and this gave Florence an oppressive sensation, she had no idea how much longer it could go on this way, the old man with the cane, the girl who had been cold all winter, each of them passing before Florence like a sublime figure of her own life's throes, both of them, like herself, had fallen into the life-trap and were now struggling, frenetic and humiliated, with the duties imposed at birth, the obligation to enjoy life or suffer; they all had the impression they were wandering, advancing, but every one of them was bound up in his own torment, like Florence sitting on her bench and there could be nothing more terrifying than just being there, motionless against the grey immensity of the sky, being nothing more than that, Florence, a shapeless human being imprisoned by the evil forces of life, pain and solitude were driving them all out of their minds, why weren't they screaming, but their screams froze in the icy air, her husband had told her that there were "so many things we will only understand when we're about to die" and she was ashamed because she still didn't understand anything, Judith Lange was no longer there to listen to her moan in silence, other suicides were expecting her in the night and while the lilac branch whipped the window Judith told her students about the throngs of Austrian schoolchildren who, forty years after, still filed through Mauthausen every day, all the horrors of Nazism were still in evidence there, they had to learn all about it, become fully conscious of it all, they had to see the executioner's instruments, drink the victims' blood, and Judith Lange's eyes were full of tears when she said you too must remember, must not forget, and all they saw was the canopy of white lilac out in the college yard and Judith Lange, sitting there so beautiful and serene, and they couldn't see the sense of resurrecting such a dim morbid scene on such a beautiful day, a hundred and ten thousand people had died there, said Judith Lange, you'll never be able to forget it, not tonight, not tomorrow, never, some exe-

cutioners were jovial, others were gentle, who knows, perhaps in eternity the tormentors were placed alongside their
victims, perhaps a voice full of self-pity went on comforting
those who were being led to the gas chamber: "If you only
knew how it makes me suffer to see you suffer this way!"
There had been nice, friendly tormentors who were good
husbands and fathers, generous lovers, and yet they had left
their descendants a monument to Cruelty at Mauthausen;
they had beaten, killed, massacred their fellow men with
great pleasure, they were, Judith Lange said, God's skulking
criminals, sometimes the executioners were so gifted they
could assume the supplicating credibility of their victims;
they too lifted their frightened faces to the sky as if to ask,
"Can this possibly be happening to me?"—they had felt fear
in the face of the incomprehensible cruelty that drove them
to drunken orgies of blood, and even the tottering victims
they nudged on toward the stairway of death had the nerve
to sharpen that fear with a touching, pitiful cry, the victims
dared to rise from the scalding nest of torture to face them,
and when the sensitive executioner, who was a man just like
any other, but an aesthete of pain, fearfully approached the
neck that offered no resistance to his hands, something hovered in the bloody, moan-filled fog, something that was the
very secret of agony, of death, and the sensitive executioner
understood that he in turn, maybe tonight or tomorrow,
would become that same feeble victim he had stunned with
his blows and his hatred, and he was afraid, suddenly the
perfection of his crime didn't seem to matter, he took his
victim in his arms, sighed and stroked his head: "Don't be
afraid, I don't want to hurt you," and the bewildered victim
gazed up, a final glimmer of gratitude in his eye, it was
almost love . . . but there were other executioners who were
so sensitive that one never saw them; lacking the courage to
kill with their own hands, they dispatched their invisible
armies, their invisible massacre machines, and Judith Lange

told them about it all, they stared at her without understanding, like the schoolchildren who visited Mauthausen day after day; Judith Lange also told them that everything had changed, that when trains passed near Mauthausen or any one of the other torture sites, a bloody steam rose from the ground, no, nothing was as before, the traveller comfortably seated or dozing in the train suddenly noticed the bloody vapour rising from the earth, and the victims' anguish was still so great that it shook the cars on the tracks and the passengers, suddenly oppressed, were covered with sweat and anguish, the anguish of a hundred and ten thousand victims clammy against their bones, they asked themselves why and where did it come from after so many years, but nothing was as before, the houses, the fields, the form of the trees, spring and summer alike it was winter in Mauthausen and wherever else a river of blood had run over the ground, forty years later you could still hear their cries and in the freight cars their emaciated bodies were still shrivelling up, but why, so long after, was it still going on, the countryside seemed as beautiful as ever, especially in spring and summer, you would have expected Austrian school children to be picking flowers and running in the fields as before in spite of what had happened there, but the schoolchildren, even if they didn't understand why, also felt fear rising in them when they drew near the site, they came in buses with their teachers, their brothers, their friends, they came to Mauthausen in order not to forget, they looked, they touched the instruments that had lacerated and crushed frail adolescent bodies, that had cut up the gleaming flesh that had been hands, arms, or cheeks, and the bloody vapour rose up and slowly seeped into the intact, triumphantly living flesh of the Austrian schoolchild who was only passing through Mauthausen, and the horror of all the evil inflicted on the victims, was in him, and Judith Lange spoke of those who had been separated from each other, death was the greatest of pains but death had been preceded by the throes of separation, very often death closed in like something blind and deaf, sometimes it even came at the hands of a blind, deaf executioner, but those who watched their mothers, sisters, children, loved ones, or some part of themselves being taken away, went on living and breathing, still afflicted by the light of consciousness, the sharp awareness of what they were going to leave behind and lose forever, and that light, that consciousness, was something inexorable, who knows, said Judith Lange, maybe consciousness even preceded us in death, maybe it arrived before us to initiate us into the white light of nothingness that awaited us there, Judith Lange admitted that she too was afraid sometimes, for her consciousness always led her on, even drove her to consider sterile promises of eternity although she expected nothing from them except, maybe, that the executioners and their victims, united by divine justice, would find themselves face to face in the barren light of consciousness, but was that knowledge something to rejoice in? No— so if there were any happy expectations, they were to be found in life, in life as it was given us, we were life's path and refuge, our passing days were no more than that, Judith Lange referred to moments of separation, the moment when the soul left the body, when people were separated from each other, the moment when the knife of ultimate torture severed all ties and the stray soul took off by itself, still under the shock of a terrible, savage evil, mothers wailed as their children were wrenched from their arms, the body perished when it was left deprived and thirsting for the one it was meant to love, and even those victims who were already marked for the gas chamber, already consumed by hunger and illness, began to tremble, for these final ties with the world, yes, the real world, these ties were also going to be taken from them and they would have absolutely nothing left on this earth that had already become unrecognizable, and as the day declined and the immensity of the grey sky turned harsh and furious, Florence rose laboriously, rose with the weight of the green suitcase still pulling her toward the ground, each step dragging her farther down and, far from everything, from everyone, she thought she could perhaps go on walking a little more in the city, wandering, wandering, and she thought, "but it could happen to me, too, being cold all winter, having to look at my frozen legs every night . . . . ." she still had time to change, between that moment and the time of her death, time to transform herself Judith Lange had said, but how and why, and suddenly she noticed the shabby hotel, the Hôtel des Voyageurs, one of those places where you had to carry your own suitcase up to the twelfth floor, no elevator, she was now buoyantly giddy at having fallen so low, she had never really had an existence of her own, living in the shadow of her powerful husband, but now she was aware of a kind of intensity, playing out the role she had assigned herself, advancing alone to realize the end of a life, even if it was just a life like hers that gave the appearance of being so middle class and Gloria told her she had a sick child who screamed sometimes but it was nothing serious, he'd get over it, "Go right on up, Ma'am, make yourself at home, just follow that rag of a rug, it's just about worn through . . . .

Translated by Carol Dunlop

Sometimes,
a Motherless Child

•

Austin Clarke

She went back on her knees beside the bed. But the words did not come. "I can't commune with you this morning, Lord." She got up, rubbed the circulation back into her knees, pulled the pyjamas leg from sticking to her body, passed her hands over her hips, promised to eat less food so late at night, touched her breasts for cancer, said, "Lord, another day, another dollar!" She walked out of the bedroom and into the cold hallway, four paces long, passed through the living room which served also as a dining room and kitchen, and into the tiny bathroom, colder than the short hallway. She looked up at the color print of a man with a red beard grown into two points, strong piercing eyes, thin face and sallow complexion. The man's heart was not only bare, but exposed. Something like a diadem, or a crown made of two strands of branches, thick and plaited with thorns sticking into the man's head, was causing drops of blood to fall from his skull. The color print was above the sink. "Father God," she said. She closed her eyes and continued to pee. The man's hand was raised, the right hand, in a salute like that made by a boy scout, or like a gesture giving benediction. It was this gesture which made her say, "Thank you." And with that, she felt better. But the words they were saying and the words written about the Jamaican; and the sad memories that the snapshot of her husband brought back; and the drying up of her own words so necessary to begin the morning with; and the snoring behind the wall, all these worries passed from her mind, and made her step light and carefree as she stepped into the shower. She hated showers. But they were quick. And this morning, in her hurry to be happy, she pulled out the new-fashioned circular knob, and the water, cold as winter, pounded against her body, as if it contained small pellets of ice. She shrieked. And before the scream died down, she was on the telephone to her landlord, who lived above her head. She hated that more than she hated showers.

"*Mister* Petrochuck!"

"Yes, my dear?"

"Am I paying you rent for this place? And I can't take a proper bath in peace, without the water turning cold, cold, cold as Niagara Falls, and freezing my blasted body?"

Through the receiver she heard his hearty laugh, and words in some foreign language which she hated next to having to take showers, which after five years she still did not know the origin of; and when his laughter abated, and her anger lowered, she heard Mr. Petrochuck explaining the difficulty.

"I tell you two times now, Mrs. Jones," he was saying, no longer with laughter in his voice, for in a way he both feared and respected her. "Two times I explain it now. You turn knob to left for the cold. And you turn knob to the right for the hot. And you turn before you pull out knob."

She felt ashamed to have to be told these explanations again. "So, how the hell am I to know that? Where I come from, you turn to the left for the hot. *To the left!*" She tried to imitate his accent, to diffuse both her frustration and her anger. "And you turn the knob to the right for the cold."

"That's right!" It was her time now to laugh, and to laugh and talk as she teased him.

"Thanks, Mister P."

"Thank you, Mrs. J."

"*Sometimes, I feel like a mother-less child!*" She was already in the shower, and the water was warm, and her voice was beautiful and clear above the sound of the water which came out in jets, as if it was mixed with marbles that had been taken from a furnace, and mixed in cold water. "*Sometimes, I feel like a mother-less child . . .*"

When she was dressed, she started to prepare a sandwich, using Wonder Bread and canned salmon. She put a slice of tomato and a leaf of lettuce between the soft white slices. She wrapped it in a large white napkin, then into grease-proof paper, then into plastic. She dropped it into a brown paperbag. She placed a five dollar note on the paperbag, and secured it with a paper clip.

She pushed the door of the small room behind the wall where she was standing in the kitchen, and looked at the large body curled in the shape of an embryo, on his left side, breathing heavily through his mouth. She looked down at the sheet and the blanket torn away from his body. And she admired his smooth black body, muscular in the places where men his age are muscular; and with his hair cut in that odd style which she never liked, with two things that looked like lightning marks shaved deep into his short hair; and after she had taken in all this, as she does every morning during the week, she turned the light on.

"You!" she shouted.

This is the way she greeted him every morning, the

way she chose to rouse him from his sleep. There was a smile in her shout, as she stood by the door, blocking it, sturdy as if she was a prison guard. "You!"

Her voice penetrated the sleep that had been embracing, and it might have penetrated also the nightmare that his sleep had wrapped him into, for with the second call, he sprung upright, and started to tremble in terror. She noticed that he had a hard-on. But she was his mother.

"Don't shoot, don't shoot!" There was terror in his pleading.

"Who shooting you? Boy, who are shooting you?"

"Sorry, Mom."

"Is somebody shooting you? Look, fix yourself in front of me, do!"

He pulled the sheet up, and covered his nakedness.

"School isn't this morning?"

"Yes, Mom."

"Well, get up, you!"

"Thanks, Mom." And she laughed, and hugged him tight, as if it was a farewell of love. He wrapped his strong black arms round her body, and she could feel his heart and she was sure she could feel his blood. Then, she released him. She turned the light off. She closed the door. She shook her head from side to side in profound satisfaction at the way he was getting along, making plans for him and for herself, but more than anything else, making plans for his future. She was so proud of him. So proud. And he was growing so well. She gathered up her purse. She selected a large bag. She folded it and put it into the leather bag in which she carried her purse and other things. She turned the lights off in the rest of the apartment. But she was worried about something. Why would he say, "Don't shoot, don't shoot?" But just as soon, she put it out of her mind. He was such an obedient boy. She began to hum, and before she closed the front door, and before the clock on the mantelpiece chimed seven times, she heard him say, "Bye, Mom. Have a good day."

Her shower this morning was warm and embracing, and the water soaked her body as if she was still bathing in the waves of the sea. She was feeling better. She would manage her work today, and not complain. She would even change her mind about taking showers.

"Life is so good!" she said, turning the key in the lock. When she walked down the short path, covered with snow with ice beneath, her steps were gingerly, and she didn't mind the winter. *"Some-times, I feel, like a mother-less child . . . ."*

"BJ! BJ! Hey ,man! It'sMarco, man! BJ!" He waited as usual, until he was sure, until the caller had identified himself by name, before he even moved from the chair where he was reading a book, *The Autobiography of Malcolm X.* He wanted to be sure. He had to be sure that he was opening his mother's door to the right person.

"Hey, BJ! It's Marco, man!"

Years ago, when he skipped school on the smallest pretext, and felt he was clever in doing so, his mother got the landlord, Mr. Petrochuck, to check on him; and Mr. Petrochuck asked her how he would check on her son, and she told him how. "He can't fool me, Mr. P., so don't let him fool you. Just look along the alleyway between my place and the house next door, and see if you see if my son left. Make a note of the footprints in the snow, and I sure, Mr. P. that a man with your experience in the Second World War, as you always telling me you was in the Alpine Batallion with skiis and a gun on your shoulder, that you would know what time my son passed through the alleyway on his way to school." The landlord's laughter, and hers, and his remark that she was a better spy than any he had faced in the Russian Army, lasted throughout the rest of the conversation that ended with her giving him her number at work, with the instruction to call her back. She spent that morning, with her hands in the rich foamy water in the double sink, washing crystal glasses from the party the night before. But her laughter turned to anger and violence when she heard Mr. P's report; and when she got home at seven o'clock that night, she was tired and blue with fuming, but her energy came back to her, just as she was revived from the morning shower, and she stood over him, ten years old on that cold Monday night, and she counted twenty-one times that the leather slipper was raised and landed on his back, and she stopped counting and did not hear her words, as she drove the slipper across his back, ripping away one of the thongs, and shouting and muttering and screaming as she flogged him, "Let me tell you something, you hear me? Let me tell you something, young man. If you don't want to go to school, I will take you myself, to the nearest police station, and let them lock you up, you hear me?" And it went on that way, the sharp blows from the slipper rising in their unsatisfied anger, and her voice piercing the peace of her place which she kept clean and in which she made no noise, careful to be decent and respectable, ". . . . and, and-and, living in this place with all the things happened to black people, to men and boys like you, and you wanting to turn out like them?" And it stopped only when there was a pause in her energy, and in her anger, and she heard the pounding at the door. At first she thought it was the police. And she got scared. And then she felt grateful that they had come to take her son away. "Serve you damn right!" And then she was terrified. She saw herself in handcuffs, taken out to the police cruiser, and placed in the back seat, with the road of neighbors watching, and led into the station, the same police station she was going to take him to, and have her fingers placed on the ink pad, and in ten small spaces, printed as a criminal, and the charge of assault, or bodily harm, or violent assault whichever charge they wanted to lay on her. And then, she recognized Mr. Petrochuck's voice. "Are you going to kill this boy?" And the relief, and the protection his presence brought, as if he was still in the Alpine Batallion and had rescued a detachment of his men ambushed and encircled by their own loss of control and of nerves, she did not lower the broken leather slipper again, but held it in her right hand, as her eyes filled up with tears. And she embraced Mr. Petrochuck, and she asked him to sit with her for a while, and she remained silent and heavy with her grief which shook her body in spasms from time to time. That morning when they had spied on him, as he explained it to Marco on the telephone, hours later, the snow had betrayed him. It had remained firm and pure, clean and like innocence itself, without a blemish, because he had remained in his room all day, listening to music. Marco had supplied the school principal with a note of excuse, with his mother's signature forged on it. But he learned his lesson and deceived the landlord who continued to report his activities to his mother; and he excelled in class through his brilliance, and because he was bright he had more time to do the things he wanted to do. So, this morning when he heard her leave, as he has been doing for years, he put his coat, a fur-lined jeans jacket over his pyjamas, put on his sneakers, and walked from the back door, his private entrance, through the deep snow, right to the alleyway, and through the alleyway to the front of the house. Then carefully, he walked backwards, placing the sneakers exactly into the footprints going away from the back door, retracing his steps, right back into the house. He had been doing this so often, that he no longer regarded it as a skill. Or as deceit. It was like brushing his teeth as the first activity after getting out of bed. He took off his sneakers, brushed them off on the mat covered with a copy of yesterday's *Star;* he dusted the snow off his jacket, as he had brushed the low hanging branches of the tree in the alleyway, and put it back into the cupboard where he kept his stereo and CD player, and his clothes, and which he had covered with a piece of cloth he had bought from the Third World Books & Crafts store on Bathurst Street. The cloth was Kente cloth. He had read somewhere in his voracious appetite for books that Malcolm X was married in Kente cloth.

"It's Marco, man."

He closed the book, after putting a bookmark between the pages; the bookmark was a sliver of Kente cloth; and replacing it into the shelves which took up two complete walls in his small room. The shelves were crammed with books. All the books were paperbacks. All the books dealt with black people, and were written on black subjects, in fiction, philosophy, religion, art, culture and his favourite, biography. He kept his school texts under the bed, on the floor.

"BJ! Man, it's Marco!"

He was not impressed by the impatience in the voice, and before he went to the door, he rested the Gaulois cigarette into an ashtray, he lit some incense, and he turned down the volume of John Coltrane playing A *Love Supreme*. He put his housecoat on, and went to the door. The ashtray was a square crystal one, which his father had bought eight Christmases ago, and had never used. His father did not smoke.

"Fuck, man!" Marco said, stomping one foot after the other, on the worn coconut husk mat. "It's fucking cold out here, man!"

BJ looked at Marco sternly.

"Sorry, man."

A trace of a smile came over his thin lips as Marco remembered his aversion to foul language. His father had drilled that into him, with a few beatings. So, he opened the door wider, and Marco squeezed between the post and him, and went in, and stomped one foot after the other, although his sneakers were already wiped clean on the mat. He hunched his shoulders, and pushed his hands into his jeans side pockets and said, "It's fucking cold, man!" Under his arm were newspapers.

"You should control your emotions better than that."

Marco looked cowed, and said, "Sorry, man. But it's all right for you, man."

They embraced, touching bodies, and slapping each other on the back three times, as if they belonged to an old fraternity of rituals and mystery. They let go of each other, and did it a second time, with their heads touching the other's shoulders. It was Italian, and it was African, and it was this that joined them in their close friendship for the past nine years. They saw each other every day, either at school or here in BJ's room. Their parents never met. And did not know of their sons' deep friendship. And it never occurred to either of them that they should bring their parents into their strong bond of friendship. BJ's mother went to every school event that required a parent's presence. And Marco's mother and father attended them too. But they never met.

BJ went to the small square table in a corner and with an African print covering it, and on which he had put a large leather-bound copy of the Holy Qur'an. Two glasses and a bottle of vodka were on the table. Ice was already in the glasses. He had been expecting Marco. The ice was already melting.

"Punctuality," he told Marco, "is also not an Italian characteristic, although *we* are blamed for inventing CPT."

"Fuck, man! Gimme the drink!"

And BJ poured two strong vodkas. He had not forgotten the orange juice, but he could not risk taking it earlier out of his mother's fridge, just in case. He did this now, and when he returned, Marco was sitting in a straight-back chair, with his drink already at his lips. He poured each of them some orange juice.

Coltrane was at the stage in his song, chanting "a love supreme," over and over. Marco joined in the chanting. His voice was deep for his age, eighteen, similar to a bass

"A *love su-preme, a love su-preme,*" he chanted. "Nineteen times, fuck, you say he does that. Sometimes, you don't know, BJ, but I feel he's gonna sing it maybe twenty times, or eighteen times! Fuck."

"Unless your concentration diminishes, Coltrane won't."

"Fuck!"

BJ went back to the table, brushed a piece of ice from it, and ran his hands over the cover of the Qur'an. It was covered in brown paper, cut from a bag from the Liquor Control Board of Ontario, weeks ago when he went to pick up his weekly supply of vodka. He was seventeen then. But he looked older. He always looked older. This did not fool the manager at the LCBO store around the corner from his home, and he knew it; so to save the embarrassment, he used forged identification, including a school mate's birth certificate. He felt guilty about doing this, on the first three occasions; but it was the style of the times. Only last week he read in the *Star* that the police had caught five immigrants working illegally under false names and with forged social insurance numbers. It was the way of the times. And he was a born Canadian, so, "Fuck!" Marco consoled him, and himself. On the brown paper cover, he had printed HOLY BIBLE. On the bedside table, beside his single bed that had an iron bedstead, he had placed the Bible, just in case. He read the Bible, too. His mother had given him the Bible. But he devoted his devotions to the Holy Qur'an. Coltrane was now into the second part of his song. The music came out at them with equal balance, and power, even though he had turned down the volume, out of the four speakers. The speakers were four feet tall and more than one foot in width. He had built them himself. The other components in the stereo, he and Marco had reconditioned from spare parts and odds and ends thrown out by neighbors in his district in the Bathurst Street area, and in Marco's neighborhood up in North York. Every piece but the CD player, they had reconditioned themselves.

"Did you check out the things for me?"

"Yeah, man," Marco said. He was almost perfect in the speech of black people. It came out easy and almost natural. "I got me the Form, man."

"Well, let's spend a few moments scrutinizing the entries, and adding to our fortune."

"All these books. Fuck. Man, you's something else! All these books!" Marco would busy himself by taking out a book, flipping its pages, replacing and repeating this until he had touched almost every book in the shelves. And he did this to allow BJ to concentrate on the Racing Form. "You're like, like a walking 'cyclopedia, man. And also a genius at the track. Fuck!"

"All it takes is concentration, Marco. I've been telling you this for years. Concentration. *And* dedication."

"I gonna give you something Italian to read. You know anything about Italian classics? Man, I gonna lay some Italian literature on you, one o' these days. Like *Dante*, man."

"Third shelf, sixth book from the right. Second bookcase."

The book Marco picked out was *Seven Systems of Dante's Hell.*

"Fuck! I didn't know he wrote this, too!"

"Imiri Baraka wrote that, Marco. That's a different inferno," BJ said. "My mother is fine. She didn't ask for you this morning."

"Fuck!"

"This morning, she pushed my door and greeted me in her usual way, "You!" I pretended I was sleeping but all the time I could see her face, and the worry in it, and the worry in her body about her work, and I was pretending I was sleeping. I was up all night, reading."

"This black power shit?"

"As a matter of fact, Marco, I was reading Shakespeare." Marco got up from his chair and went to the bookcase. He knew this one. This one, was in a way, his favorite bookcase, for it contained books he too liked. The bookcase was made from unpainted dealboard, sawed and cut by him and BJ; and it occupied the space in the wall between a window and a cupboard. It ran from the floor to the ceiling. BJ liked everything in his room to run from the floor to the ceiling. It had something to do with perspective, he said. Marco did not understand, and said, "Fuck!" to show his sentiments. If his room were larger, BJ knew that they would have built the speakers, from the floor to the ceiling. In this shelf in the bookcase were books by Shakespeare which Marco liked, and did well in, in school, preferring *Romeo and Juliet*, "Fuck! Not because I'm Italian, man!"; and As you *Like It*, and *The Merchant of Venice*, which they stopped studying in his school the term before he reached that grade. BJ preferred *Henry IV* and *Othello*, "because you're black, right? Fuck!." But BJ told him, "because it contains the best and perhaps, the most noble of Shakespeare's noble poetry. I don't even like the character Othello. Iago is a more realistic character. I see Iagos every day in class." And to all this, all Marco said, years ago when they had this conversation the first time, was "Fuck!" They have had this same conversation many times since. And Marco uses the same single word to express his sentiments.

"Today is the last day. I suggest we go out with a bang. But how many classes would you miss if we got there for the first?"

"Lemmesee. Biology? Physics? English? And basket-ball practice."

"I will do your Biology and Physics assignments for you. Or we can do them together at the track."

"Fuck!" Marco said. He rubbed his hands as if he was cold. He poured himself another vodka and orange juice.

For young men, for eighteen-year-old boys, really, they had an enormous prodigity for alcohol, which is the term BJ used laughingly, when they would sit in his small room, and consume half of a twenty-six once bottle of imported Absolut Vodka; and if his mother had returned home and had seen them, she would shake her head in plea-sure at their hearty liking for orange juice, "You two boys don't know how good I feel to see you drinking orange juice, instead of all this damn Coke and Pepsi!" And after these long bouts, their speech was not even slurred, afterwards.

"Did you remember the *Globe?*" BJ read the *Globe* everyday. He read the racing tips first. He read the sports section second, the editorial third, and the foreign news sec-tion fourth. He read nothing else in this newspaper.

"Woodbine, here we come!" Marco said. *"They're at post!* Fuck!"

"Should we invest a hundred each? What is your opinion, Marco?"

"A hundred bucks? Fuck! Why not, man? I deposit-ed yesterday's winnings in my account. Those tellers're *weird,* man. She look at me with all that bread as if I was a drug dealer! Fuck, man."

"Today's the last day," BJ said. Marco noticed the tone of his voice.

"You all right, man?"

"You have to do something with the money in your bank account. Something. *Something.* And we have to think about the car, too."

"Today is the last day, man. So, if we lose . . ."

"Don't say it!"

"Sorry, man."

BJ went to his dresser, a narrow, tall piece of furniture which his mother had bought at the Goodwill Store on Jarvis Street, to save money, and which he had stained to make it look like mahogany. It looked like a mahogany antique piece of Georgian furniture, although he did not know that. It had five drawers. In the top drawer, under his handkerchiefs which his mother starched and ironed and folded into four, he kept his cash, arranged in denominations in ascending order, inside a box that contained cheques from the bank. He opened this drawer now, and took from it a metal box that had a key. He brought the box to the bed, and unlocked it. There were four boxes that used to contain cheques in the metal box. They were full of bank notes. No note was smaller than a ten. He did not count his money every night, but his memory was good, and he knew that with the withdrawals and the deposits into his private "safe," that he had five thousand, three hundred and five dollars in it. He could not tell his mother about this. He could not offer to lend her money, not even when he saw her moaning and crying and cursing his father for having abandoned them; not even when her rent of four hundred dollars a month was in arrears. And sadly, not even when she had to postpone her registration for one month, and never caught up, in the Practical Nursing course at George Brown College. She would kill him to learn that he had so much money, in her house, in all the time she was seeing misery, in all these days when she had to cut and contrive. But he had prepared for her. At such a young age, it seemed ominous, too adult, too final a thing this preparation by someone so young. He had opened a savings account in her name, at a different bank from the one she used. Marco put his winnings in a chequing account. But he kept his in cash.

"Here's twenty tens, Marco. I'll take twenty, too. This is the last day, so I'm staking you. What we win we keep. What we lose, well."

"Fifty percent of our winnings should still go in the kitty, man. Fuck!" It was their business arrangement. And they stuck to this code, like members of a gang. "And look for a longshot, man!"

"There's no such thing, Marco! No such thing. My father went to the races every day. Faking illness from work. And family crises and emergencies. He had to be there. In summer and winter. He even walked there, once. Not to mention the times he had to walk home. And he betted on longshots, because he was a gambler. He was a gambler. And was greedy. He was a fool. A damn fool. He thought he could get rich from the track. We are different. We are investors. Don't ever let me see you betting on a longshot! Longshots are for racetrack touts."

"Why can't we use the car?"

"How many times do I have to tell you it's not safe to be driving that kind of car in Toronto? It's safer to drive it in Montreal."

"Oh man! What's the point of having the wheels, and not using it? Fuck!"

"Have you told your parents you own a white BMW? Or more correctly, a fifty percent share in a 1992 white BMW?"

"Well, fuck no, man! For them to execute me?"

"Exactly! My mother doesn't even know I can drive. As long as our friend respects our confidence, the car will remain parked in her underground garage in Scarborough. Now, I have to make my *salats*."

"Make your salads, man. Make your salads. Fuck."

"Are you going to respect my religious principles? Or are you leaving?"

"I'll respect your salads, man. I'll respect your praying, man."

The Timex watch on BJ's wrist began to buzz. It was the hour for prayer. Marco poured himself a vodka quickly, wanting to stop the racket of the ice cubes in his glass, and the sound of the vodka pouring out of the bottle, now almost empty, before BJ began his prayers. BJ pulled a cheap Persian rug from under his bed, unrolled it, and placed it in front of the table on which were the Absolut Vodka imported, and the Holy Qur'an. He placed the Qur'an on the floor, in front of him, and he placed his hands before his heart in the demeanor of prayer and concentration.

All this time, Marco was looking into the pages of *Plutarch's Lives,* which he had taken from the bottom shelf of the narrow, unpainted bookcase that contained only classical literature. And he sucked on the vodka straining it through his teeth and the melting pieces of ice cubes, as his friend *ommmmmmmed* and *ommmmmmmmd,* and intoned *"alla hack-bar"* which is how Marco understood the pronunciation of the Muslim prayers. Fuck, he said to himself, this motherfucker is real serious. If I didn't know he was serious, fuck! It was nine o'clock. The morning was crisp and cold and clean.

The boy flung the newspaper, aiming for a different spot, and it banged against the window where she was with her hands in the thick, white dish water, foaming like the waves that banged against the rocks near the Esplanade, and then retreated back into the calm, blue sea. She was thinking of home. She had seen him. "You little bastard!" And the boy jumped back on his bicycle, and sped out of the circular driveway over the crunching snow. It was ten o'clock. The morning was cold. When she had got off the subway and was walking to this mansion, the wind ripped into her body, and made her think of going back home the moment she made herself into a woman, meaning when she had money; and it made her feel as if she was naked. The wind had the same brutal touch as *his* fingers on her backside that day when she was bending over the vacuum cleaner. He had not touched her. She imagined it was his intention. And imagining it, it made it real. The wind swept up her legs, right between her thighs, clawing at her pantyhose with such force that she thought she had left home without putting on her underwear. She felt the shame in the touch of the wind. "I should have been born a man," she said, to the boy disappearing over the smashed snow, but really not for his ears. Men didn't know how lucky they are, she said, continuing her thoughts; they don't know how damn lucky they are to be wearing pants to get more greater protection from this damn cold. "And in other things, too!" Her thoughts went back to her son. For she had seen the photograph of the Jamaican family on the front pages of the *Star* newspaper many weeks ago, and now this morning, when that damn boy pelted the paper that almost broke the window where she was, here was another one. She wiped her hands in her apron, and studied the newspaper. It said that the young man was seventeen, and it said that he was living with his mother in a big house in the suburbs, and it said he was in the car with another young man about his same age, and it said that he was not going very fast and that the traffic policeman didn't have to follow him with the sirens on, and it said he was shot in the back of his head. She felt sad. And wanted to cry. She was leaving her own son at home, so often, by himself, before the dawn broke, in bed, and she wondered if he was safe. "But praise God, he doesn't have any car. A car is the surest thing to make a police shoot a black man dead. Praise God for that!" And she wanted to take up a cause, and hold a piece of stick with cardboard stapled on to it, and a message written on the cardboard, in thick black letters: THIS COUNTRY RACIST. THE POLICE TOO! "Yes! And put an exclamation mark after it, too!" She wanted to cry. She wanted to scream. But who would listen to her? A simple woman like her? That's why, she said to herself, a man has it better; for "I am the least amongst the apostles."

The young man's face, and the face of his mother, wringing her body in tears, filled the space of the double sinks, as she returned to her work. Her employers were having a party at five. And when the image of the mother and the son evaporated like the foam of soap from the two sinks, in their place were the faces of her own son, and his no-good father. She pulled the plug in the second sink out, with force, and the face of that bastard disappeared. She began to hum, "*Sometimes, I feel like a mother-less . . .*"

BJ got out casually, and with self-assurance, from the taxi, at the front of the tall apartment building somewhere in Scarborough; and as he walked across the lawn, he passed a blue car in which two men were sitting. The men were watching the same entrance BJ took. They had been there for the past three hours; and they had started watching the door since last Sunday. BJ paid no attention to the blue car. He walked straight to the panel of names, and pressed one of the buzzers. It was a buzzer beside the name, G. Harewood. He did not know G. Harewood. He could have pressed any buzzer. It was only two o'clock, and his school friend who allowed him to use the underground parking without her mother's approval and knowledge, was still in school. This was the only way to retrieve the car.

"Who's it?" a woman's voice, mangled by the malfunction in the speaker system, cried out. The voice came through louder then he expected, and he made a start. It stirred him more than usual. "Who's it?" The voice was now irritable. "Is it George?"

"Yeah!" BJ said, trying to change his voice to George's voice, with knowing George's voice.

"Come on up!" the woman's voice screamed. It was less irritable. "Come on up!"

And when BJ entered the lobby, he could still hear the voice saying "Come on up!" and the buzzer on the door to let him in, was still being pressed.

He pressed the button in the elevator to P2, and went down into the bowels of the building. Three women were in the elevator with him. The three women stared at him. When the three women were tired staring at him, they stared at the floor. Pools of water from melted ice were on the floor. When the three women were tired staring at the floor, they stared at the illuminated numbers on the panel in the elevator. When it came to P2, the three women stood where they were. It seemed to BJ that they were standing in such a way to suggest that they had taken the wrong elevator. BJ got out. BJ walked straight to a corner of the large dimly lit underground parking area. Glimmering in the bad light of the dull fluorescent bulbs, was the white BMW. He stood beside it. He looked at the front tires. He looked at the hood. He looked at the windshield. The elevator door was still open. The three women were watching him. He went round to the front of the BMW and he looked at the bumper. He looked at the cap which covered the hole to the gas tank. He screwed it tight. It was already tight. It was locked. One of the three women got off the elevator when it reached the main floor, and walked straight to a door marked superintendent. The superintendent answered at the first ring. He was eating a salmon sandwich that had bits of green things in it. The woman started talking to the superintendent.

BJ looked at the license plate. He passed his hand over it. He was about to brush the dust from the plate onto his trousers, but he remembered in time. He was wearing expensive clothes. His trousers were black. They were full in the leg, and narrow at the ankle. His socks were white. And the shirt and jacket fitted him as if they were three or four sizes larger than his weight and size. He took a handkerchief from his pocket. The handkerchief was white, and folded into quarters. He wiped his hand, and then he passed the handkerchief slowly over each letter of the car licence. When he was done, the licence plate was glimmering almost as much as the BMW itself. The licence plate was, BLUE. His beeper was beeping. So, he got into the car, with the doors locked, and the engine still turned off, and he checked the beeper. It was Marco.

He turned the engine on. Gradually, the interior of the black leather got warmer and warmer until he felt he was as comfortable sitting in it, as he was in his room surrounded by all his solid state stereo and CD equipment and books. In this car, he had installed an equally expensive system. John Coltrane was playing. He had left the cassette in the tape. A *Love Supreme*.

The car was warm. BJ's two large eyes filled up the rear-view mirror, and he could barely see, in periphery, the elevator door open, and a man and three women; and the women were pointing in his direction as they talked to the man; but the BMW was warmed up, and it moved without noise over the caked ice in some parts of the underground parking; and he manoeuvred it through spaces left by bad and careless drivers, past large concrete pillars, and mounted the incline to the exit door, in no hurry, and all the time speaking to Marco on the telephone, and he had to repeat himself two times, for the aerial struck the top of the last exit door, and finally he emerged into the brilliance of the winter afternoon, bright in the sun but still cold. The women had just told the superintendent, "I'm sure he looks like one 'of those drug dealers, and I feel he is, not because he's . . ."

The two men in the blue car saw the white BMW. And the two men made a note of it. And they registered

BLUE in a notebook. And they made a check on their computer. And they began to talk on the telephone. BJ was heading for Victoria Park and Kingston Road to pick up Marco at the subway station. He was in a good mood. The last racing day was something else, fuck! as Marco put it. They had won and won and won . . .

Facing her now was the most magnificent slender white sculptures of branches on the trees in the backyard. She had seen these trees change their form for three years now, and she still did not know the name of one of them. But this afternoon, around three, with the dear light and the brilliance of the sun which gave no heat, she marvelled at the beauty and thought of men travelling in olden times, over this kind of landscape, walking in shoes made from skins; and following in the tracks of wild animals they had to kill to stay alive. It was as if an artist had applied pearls and other kinds of jewels, with precision on the branches of the trees. But she was not happy inside herself. Something was bothering her. And she picked up the telephone and called her landlord.

"Did you really see him?"

"Yes, I tell you, Mrs. J."

"Go out, dressed? In his school clothes? In time for school?"

"Everything."

"You sure it was my son? You didn't mistake somebody else for him?"

"Sure!"

"Well, thank you, then." And to herself, she said, "I don't know why I am in this mood."

She had selected the crystals and the silvers and the plates, and all she had now to do was choose the serving dishes, and put the place mats on the shining mahogany table. She checked the roast beef in the oven, and shook her head at the amount of food she cooked, with most of it being thrown away the next morning, since neither husband nor wife liked to eat left-over food; and with all this damn food wasting day in and day out, and so many people on the streets of this city starving with nothing to warm their stomachs, and that blasted boy I gave birth to, refusing this good rich food, saying he is a Muslim. What a Muslim is? Is a Muslim a person who doesn't have commonsense inside his head, that he would refuse all this richness. And she laughed to herself. It was a joyous laugh. A hearty laugh. A laugh from the bottom of her belly. She looked round to see if anyone was close by, to mistake her for a fool, that she was going out of her head, laughing and talking to herself, like this. "And come telling me that he is fasting. *Fasting?*" And all this food, all this food going to waste. I wish I knew somebody on my street, without foolish pride that I could leave a plastic container full of this food! And she began to hum. *Some-times, I feel . . . .*

As BJ pulled off from the curb in front of the subway station in the East End, with Marco strapped in beside him, and laughing and turning up the volume of the saxophone solo, the BMW was so loud with the music contained within it, that Marco himself felt his head was about to explode; and BJ himself was becoming nervous that perhaps the BMW would become conspicuous with the two of them in it with so much noise. The windows were rolled up. The BMW took the first entrance on to the 401 West doing 80. BJ settled behind the wheel, with a Gaulois unfiltered cigarette at the corner of his mouth, one eye closed against the smoke, and he put the car into fourth gear, and the car still had some more power, and moved like a jungle animal measuring its prey, and receiving additional power because of the certainty of devouring its prey. The prey in this case was their destination. But they did not have any anxiety of time and distance to reach that destination. It was simply that BJ liked to drive fast. That was why he convinced Marco to buy the BMW instead of the Thunderbird. And that was why he got it with standard transmission. They had won the money at the race track, one afternoon when Marco made the mistake of buying the three horses in a triacta race for ten dollars, instead of five which was the custom. The name of the horse that won, that went off at 50 to 1 odds, was Blue. BJ knew he could not keep all that money in his room; and he knew that he could not open an account, without questions asked. He knew he could not give it to his mother, even with the explanation that he had won it at the track. What would he be doing at the track? Why was he at the track on a school day? So, he bought a white BMW. He paid a friend of his, a real estate salesman, three hundred dollars to cover for him. Real estate was at rock bottom at that time, and the salesman was more than happy to keep his mouth shut, and to pocket this unearned commission. But BJ knew all the time that he had to be careful, and that a time might come when the real estate salesman, still at the bottom of the unsold rocks of houses on the market, would need more help in keeping his mouth closed. He had to be careful.

He turned the music down a little more, and he reduced his speed to 80. As these thoughts entered his head, he had been doing 150. He had just spotted a marked police cruiser, with 52 painted on its white side, parked alongside the 401. But he did not know that as soon as he had pulled off from the subway station in the East End, that at that precise moment, a blue sedan with two men in it, had pulled off too, and had followed him until he entered the 401 going West. The marked police cruiser was expecting him. And as he had swooshed by, the traffic policeman was on the radio to another one, somewhere farther west, along the 401. Conversation passed between the policemen in the cars. "Drug dealers for sure!" And through another system, came "Question of being armed and dangerous." And the two policemen in the parked blue car up in the suburbs of Scarborough added their contribution, "We were hoping for a red Camaro but you never know with these drug dealers, they have the money to change cars . . ." And Coltrane was playing his ass off, as Marco would say, still fond of the way he thought BJ talked, and should talk. "Trane's playing his ass off!" he said, eventually. He said it three more times. BJ grunted something. In his rear view mirror he saw the police cruiser pull into the same lane as his, tailing him. He knew this stretch of the 401 like the palm of his hand. He was west of the Allen Road, approaching on the highway a little north, the area in the city known as the habitat of drugs and guns and gangs, and called by two names, one the name of a woman, a whore: the other name of a bird, which may also be a woman and a whore. Jane-Finch. He knew this stretch of road well. He knew he could get into the express lane within twenty kilometres. The cruiser was gaining on him. Marco was oblivious to this, as he listened to Coltrane. The cruiser's red light was still not on. But BJ surmised that any time now, it would be. And the siren would start. The lanes ahead of him were crowded with slow drivers who had themselves seen the cruiser. All four lanes heading west were crowded. But that was what he wanted. He put the BMW into third. He was gearing down to stop; and the car was not so noisy with the music, and that was when Marco had commented about Coltrane's mastery of *Love Supreme*, when BJ changed his mind about stopping, to face the consequences. For how would he know the cruiser was following *him*? Of the hundreds of cars on the highway, why should a police cruiser pick him out because he was driving an expensive car, and was a young black man? He told himself he must not be fooled by the logic of a man, or of a woman, or of a time, a better time than was taking place in this city; he remembered that logic had absolutely nothing to do with it. He was intelligent in the ways of the hunter, and in this case, the hunted. He was relying upon his instincts. Somewhere in his vast reading, he had come across something about this. He was not quite sure, nor could he remember the exact quotation; but it had something to do with instinct and emotion and gut feeling. His mother lived by her emotion. So, he geared up to third, and the BMW lurched forward. Marco said, "Fuck!" and tightened his seat belt. "Let her ride, let her ride!" It was already in fourth. And in and out of traffic, from the slow lane to the middle, to the fast lane, and when the fast lane was not fast enough, and the entire width of the four-lane highway seemed to be creeping, the white BMW swerved like a top spinning near the end of its revolutions. "Fuck!" Marco said, when they were safe, for the time being, in a secondary road, somewhere near Dufferin. "What the fuck was that all about?"

BJ smiled. He turned Coltrane up. The car was filled once more with the beauty of music, with the pulse of emotion and with the feeling of the time; and they remained quiet in the waves of this melodious tune they both liked so much, and argued about. BJ insisted, because of his new religion, that it was a religious chant. Marco equally insistent, said it was a love song.

"A love supreme," he began chanting. "A love supreme. Nineteen times the brother says *a love supreme!* Nineteen times, BJ!" He never lacked enthusiasm about this aspect of the song. "Fuck!"

"Nineteen times," BJ said. And he turned the music up even louder. They were cruising along Eglinton Avenue, passing record stores from which reggae and dancehall blared out upon them, past barber shops and restaurants and shops which sold curry goat and fish and ox-tail and peas and rice, and they felt they could smell and taste the food even in this breathless afternoon so cold, and so uncertain. Young men, some younger than either of them, walked with a patience that came closer to loitering along the lively street, stopping now and then to place their hands on the parking metres, as if reassuring themselves and the ugly pieces of metal that life was still going on, even in this cold aftenoon when it was difficult to breathe; in this heart of West Indian life, when there was no attention paid to the depth of the fall in the coldness and where life remained constant: the laughter and the lightness of dress and manner. "What about lunch?"

"Yeah!"

"Curry goat? Or Oxtail?"

"Fuck! Goat *and* oxtail!"

BJ and Marco were driving around. Listening to Coltrane and taking in the sights. It was about four in the afternoon. The white BMW had just been washed at the car wash on the corner of Bathurst and St. Clair. And the music was sounding better it seemed, now that the car was spotless. As they handed in their chit, the four car washers who were polishing another car, paused in their work to admire the white BMW. And they looked long at the car and then longer at the two teenagers, and said something with their eyes and said something to themselves, and went back polishing an old black Pontiac. BJ was accustomed to people looking at him and then at the BMW. And when Marco was with him, they looked at Marco, at him, and at the car. And sometimes, if it was in the parking lot of a supermarket, or in a mall, they would go through the order of looking and staring a second time in reverse. They were cruising along Bathurst now. It was Friday afternoon about five. And the traffic was heavy. And BJ was driving within the speed limit. And as he turned left into the street before Dupont, to tack back on to Dupont because there was no left turn there, from under a low-hanging tree came a police cruiser. BJ and Marco were alone on this stretch of road. And the cruiser came close to them, and BJ understood fast enough, and pulled over and stopped.

"Get out! Get out!"

"Yes, officer."

"You too! Get the fuck out!"

"Yeah, officer."

The policeman was out of the cruiser, and he had his hand on the T-shaped night stick. His other hand moved to his gun to make sure, it seemed, that it was still there.

"Out!"

They were already out.

"Okay, okay!"

"Who're you talking to like that? Eh? Eh? Who're you fucking talking to, like that? Eh? Eh?

And with each "eh," he poked his T-shaped stick into Marco's ribs.

"Up against the car! Up against the fucking car! Both o' youse! Both o' youse!"

It seemed that in his training his lecturer had had a hearing problem and he had to repeat each answer two times; for he was now saying the same thing two times, as if it was his normal way of speech. Or as if, he was also accustomed to talking to fools, or immigrants who didn't understand English, and he had to speak in these short, truncated, double sentences.

"Spread your legs! Spread your legs! Come! Open up! Come! Open up!"

And they obeyed him. BJ could feel the dust from the side of the cruiser which needed a wash, going into his nostrils. He could feel the policeman's stick moving around his legs, round his crotch, up and down, up and down. He could feel the policeman's hands, tough and personal, strong as ten pieces of bone, feel his thighs, his chest, under his arms, between his legs, and feel his penis and his testicles; and then the ten pieces of bone spun him round, so that he now faced the policeman. BJ stood silent and calm as the policeman did the same thing to Marco. He thought the policeman was treating Marco more severely.

"Where you get this goddamn car?"

Before BJ could answer, the policeman was talking again.

"Where you get this goddamn car?"

BJ was about to say something, when the policeman cut him off.

"You steal this car! You steal this car?"

Marco opened his mouth to speak, and thought better of it.

"Who owns this fucking car? Who owns this fucking car?"

BJ put his hand into the breast pocket of his suede windbreaker, and was about to pull out his driver's licence, when the policeman came at him. His hand was on his gun. His gun was in his hand. The policeman seemed to see red. The policeman seemed to feel his life was being threatened. The policeman was behaving as if BJ had taken out, or was about to take out, a dangerous weapon. The policeman turned red. He came at BJ with great force, as if he was tackling a running full back, and when he hit him, he had him flat onto the side of the cruiser. Dust rose from the side of the cruiser. The cruiser leaned for a short time off its tires. Marco was about to intervene, when BJ raised his hand to stop him.

"Come on, nigger! Come on, nigger!"

And he slammed BJ into the side of the cruiser, a second time.

He put his hand behind his back, and when he brought it from behind his back, he was holding handcuffs. He snapped them on BJ's wrists. He poked the T-shaped stick into Marco's side, and ordered him into the cruiser. And he pushed BJ toward the cruiser, and threw him into the back seat, beside Marco.

"You could put away those! You could put away those!" BJ's licence and ownership papers were still in his hand.

The policeman went to the white BMW, stroked the tires with his T-shaped stick, and was about to smash the front side window, but something made him change his mind. He turned the engine off, put the key into his pocket, and came back to the cruiser.

He drove off. Voices of other policemen and of a dispatcher babbled on the radio. He seemed impervious to the racket of the voices. He drove south on Spadina and turned right at Bloor; and left on Brunswick, and into a few short one-way streets, and then he was back on Spadina going south of College; and then he turned east onto Dundas. BJ recognized the Ontario College of Art and the Royal Ontario Museum. He visited the ROM twice a month on Saturdays, to study African cultures and art. And Marco went along with him on many occasions. They have been doing this for three years now. BJ recognized Division 52 police station. And his heart sank. He had heard about Division 52. Wasn't it a police officer from 52 who shot a Jamaican many years ago? The policeman moved on to University Avenue, and turned left, and took them northwards on University Avenue. Apart from the crackling of voices from the other invisible policemen and dispatchers, the cruiser was quiet. It was six o'clock and the winter light was fading fast and made the afternoon seem like night. And if night should catch them in this cruiser, alone with this policeman, oh my God! The policeman had not spoken in all this time. He had smoked two cigarettes. They came to Queen's Park, and took the roundabout and were beside Trinity College, and back onto Spadina. Marco had a cousin who was attending Trinity College; and he took BJ there, one Friday night at dinner, and they ate fish that had no peppersauce. BJ loved the huge oil paintings and the black gowns the students wore. In all this time, BJ said nothing. And Marco said nothing. Marco was slapping his trousers' legs. BJ sat with his eyes closed, his teeth pressed down tight, and if you were sitting in Marco's place, you would have seen the slight movement in BJ's jaws.

"Get the fuck out! Get the fuck out!"

It took them a while to realize who had spoken to them. It took them a while to recognize where they were. The policeman came round and unlocked the cuffs from BJ's wrists.

"Get-outta-here! Get-outta-here!"

He had let them off beside the white BMW.

His mother remembered it was a big day on Saturday, a wedding she had to go to, and she rushed from work to get to the hairdresser before he closed. There were many women there, some of them had been there since early afternoon. It seemed that every woman in the place had an important church service on Sunday. Or an important dance date. Or a wedding to go to. She was tired, too tired from a long day, and she dozed off as she sat in the chair. She could barely hear pieces of conversation around her.

"I know a Jamaican man that the cops kill."

"But that was five years ago, child!"

"And in Montreal too. Not here. As a matter o' fact, this particular Jamaican had a daughter who went to school with me, in . . ."

"I mean the Jamaican man. The Jamaican who get killed and brutalized by the police. Those ladies you was having the discussion with, do they know the Jamaican man?"

When she opened her eyes, she realized that the hairdresser, Mr. Azan who was rubbing the grease into her hair, had been talking too. He turned now toward the ladies who were still with their heads over the square sinks, and to the others under dryers. But he did not say anything to them.

"How long is this going to take? I have to get home and see that boy."

"How the boy?"

"Bright as anything. Doing well in school. Someday he going-crown my head with pride and glory. Praise God. But apart from that, sir, he's a boy. And that means he has his ways. How long?"

"Well, let's see. It's going on seven now. Comb. Folding. Gimme a few minutes. You'll be done in no time! No problem. Not to worry. Yeah, man. You'll be out in no time."

And when his mother left, a new woman, years taken from her appearance, years taken from her gait, years taken from her attitude to herself; and with her hair a bright mauve, and shining, and smelling of the lotions and the smell of the hairdressing salon, it was eight o'clock at night. But she was beautiful and looking young; and feeling sprightly and full of life. And that was what she wanted for the wedding on Saturday afternoon.

The yellow police cruiser was stopped a few yards ahead of her. It was a dark night. She had looked up into the heavens a few moments, a few yards farther back, and smiled as she wondered and remembered that in this city, you don't see stars as you see stars back home, when you can become dizzy counting more than three hundred in one raised head and spinning eyes. But when she saw the police cruiser, she became tense and the feeling of paranoia which came to her every time she saw a police cruiser, came to her now. The black-clad police officers always brought a tense, angry tightness into her chest. And the tightness moved swiftly into her guts. And without knowing she always felt that it was a black man, or a black woman, but more frequently a black man, who was stopped by the policeman. In all the time she has been living in this city, she never saw a white man stopped by a policeman. But then, of course, they had to be some white men stopped by the police. All couldn't be so much more better than black people, she said. And she always felt the black man was innocent. She assumed that. He had to be innocent, she figured, because he was black. And she always thought that the policeman stopped him for no reason at all; that he was not breaking the law; but that the police was merely testing him, and anticipating that he would break the law, showing the black man who had power and pull. And the way she always saw the police hold his truncheon, as if it was a long penis, in an everlasting erection, as if he was telling the black man, "Mine is more bigger and more harder than yours!" This is the way she always felt whenever she saw a police cruiser stop a black man in a car.

The night was darker now. She was walking on Davenport Road going toward Bloor Street, and the cruiser was still too far from her for her to see clearly. But she was sure that the man inside the cruiser was black. She hurried her steps. And when she drew almost abreast of the cruiser, it was still too dark for her to see the man's face. The roof light inside the cruiser was not on. But she would bet her bottom dollar that it was a black man, a black youth, a black child. Her stomach became tight. There were two police-men. She remembered the argument in the hairdressing salon. Two? Or three? There were two. And they were stand-ing beside a car. It was a lovely car. She had seen cars like this one all over the Ravine where she worked in a mansion. It was a beautiful car. Many times, standing at the cold, large, picture window, looking out into the blank, white afternoons, with the rhythm and blues music from the Buffalo radio station behind her, she had admired these beautiful cars coming and going along the street in front of the large house. This was a beautiful car like those. It was gleaming. It was white. And it blended well with the snow that was not falling. And she wondered why the license number plate did not contain numbers like other license number plates. All it said was BLUE. What a strange license to have! BLUE? And she was feeling so good just a few moments ago. She understood blues. But what was this blue? He must be in a blue mood. What a strange license to have! BLUE? But she laughed to herself: she herself liked the blues. Rhythm and blues. She stood up to investigate. She was sure there was someone in the back of the cruiser. She had just passed the show window of Mercedes-Benz, when the bright color of mauve in her hair was reflected back to her and showed her bathed and professionally coiffeured, and hennaed. It startled her. The color did. For the instant of the reflection, she could not move. She stood up. She looked at herself in the reflection. She leaned her head slightly to the right, and then to the left; stood erect before the show window and could see not only her reflection but also a salesman in the window looking at her, with his right thumb raised in approval. He had smiled and she had smiled. And then she had moved on, after having stolen a last glance at herself.

This was before she saw the police cruiser. And when she saw it, all that gaiety in the reflection in the show window evaporated. She was beside the cruiser now.

The two policemen were walking away from the cruiser, going to the white BMW; and she caught up with them. She stopped three feet from the policemen.

"Keep moving, ma'am."

She wondered who was in the dark back seat of the cruiser. And she thought of the Jamaican man, the poor man and his two fatherless girl-children. They said that when the policemen burst into the house that Sunday afternoon, just before the peas and rice were dished and served, and the shot was fired, his head burst open just like when you drop a ripe watermelon from a certain height. They said his head burst open, clean clean clean.

"Why you-all always bothering black people? Why you-all don't go and try to catch real criminals, them who molesting children? And women?"

"None o' your business, ma'am."

"Who say it isn't none of my business? I pays taxes. I obey the law. I have a right to ask you this question, young man."

"Move on, lady! Or I arrest you for obstruction."

"Obstruction? Who I obstructing?"

"What did you say?"

She stood her ground. But she was not so stupid to repeat what she had said.

"Lord, look at this," she said under her breath. She felt she dared not pray, appeal nor talk to her God, aloud with the policemen to hear. And the policeman who spoke to her was about to forget about her when she started up again. "I hope you're not taking advantage of that poor boy you got locked up in that cruiser and I hope you read him his rights and I hope he has a good lawyer to defend him, oh God, for if it was me I would surely lodge a complaint against the two o' you with the Human Rights Commission and complain and tell this policeman to please kiss my . . ."

"Lady!"

The policeman knew there was something said, although he did not quite know what was said. He knew there was this bond and agreement which he could not break. And he became uncomfortable, and nervous, and felt threatened, as if somebody, this woman standing in front of him, with nothing in her hands, save her handbag and a plastic bag full of left-over roast beef, was going to take his life from him. And he rested his hand on the side of his waist where he had his gun.

She took a last glance at the beautiful car, and shook her head with some disappointment that she could not see through the heavy tint of the glass to make out the person inside, and satisfy her prejudice that it had to be a young black man. But she was not going to give up so easily. So, she leaned over the bonnet of the car, being careful not to smear its sheen, almost feeling the cold of the glass, as she peered through the obstructing glass. Inside, on the passenger's side, was a young man. She could see that much easily enough. But she wanted to be sure, to be certain that this tinted glass was not playing tricks to the young man's color. Perhaps, he was black, and this tint was changing his color. She could touch the glass now, and feel the coldness of it, and at the same time, the comforting heat from the engine, even though it was turned off. She stared, and saw him. It was a young man. A young white man. And the man inside the car, feeling his own shame for his predicament, held his head aside, as if he thought his profile would hide the identity of his face from this malicious woman whom he had seen five minutes before. He did not know her, could not remember ever seeing a woman with her hair dyed mauve, and sticking up in the air as this woman's hair was doing in the tricky changing light caused by the passing cars. He held his face in a profile against her staring eyes. And felt the curiosity in her eyes, and thought he could feel the love and the sadness in her manner. If he was not handcuffed behind his back, he would push the door open, and invite her in. But what would he say to her? Perhaps, he would call out for help. She moved away, walking backwards for the first few steps, and the smallness of his space, and the fit of the manacles made the car seat large, and it became larger and embraced him in the growing space of his temporary imprisonment. She was walking backwards to get a last glimpse of the license plate, BLUE, which still made her smile at its eccentricity. And when she walked past the police cruiser, her body flinched, and the tightness that she sometimes deliberately put her body into, to prevent the cold from climbing all over her bones, came to her, as she moved beside the cruiser. She could smell no similar smell of polish as she had done standing beside the beautiful car. She could sense no powerful fragrance of leather in the interior, as she had surmised with the white car, named BLUE. And she could feel no warmth from the engine of the police cruiser, as she relished in that short moment when her curiosity challenged her wisdom. The police cruiser was cruel, and ugly and tense and made her feel guilty. And in this shame, in this surrender of self-control, she walked away not being able to tell, should she be asked, what was the color of the cruiser. But she made a note of the writing on its side. Division 52. She would never forget that number. And she amused herself, heading to the next bus stop, and if no bus came to rescue her from the gnawing cold, the subway station at Bay, that if she was a gambling woman, she would play combinations of 52 in tomorrow's Lotto 6/49.

Time, and not the consequences nor the cause of his presence here, this evening where he was, was heavy upon BJ'S nerves. He paced up and down, with various thoughts entering his head, and his panic and isolation made the space much much larger, so that he was buried in its vastness, and the time and the consequences, what they could be, and the cause became real and he could see his life, his entire life in three short hours that had passed. All these things passed through his mind, and for each of them, he had no solution. He paced up and down, not having enough length in the square space to make his pacing more dramatic, and less of pathos. And when he again realized the restriction of the square space, his mind bounded backwards to a time, which he had almost wiped from his memory, recalling a time when he had spent four hours in this same police station, in another cell, alone and not knowing really why he had been locked up, not having had a charge laid against him, not having had a policeman enter the warm cell and interrogate him about the alleged theft of a kid's bicycle that afternoon in August when he and three other kids were horsing around and pretending to be bagmen—they did not play with girls—near the corner grocery store, trying to beg enough quarters to buy ice cream, when his mother was at work down in the Ravine this other kid came wobbly on his bicycle, his first, a present *his* mother had given him for Christmas past; and one of the other three kids took the bike playfully from the little kid and the little kid started to cry and ran home with tears in his eyes and told his mother, and his father returned with sunburnt arms bristling with black hairs and chest like a barrel covered with the skin of an animal with the black hairs punching from under a nylon undershirt and with his underpants showing just above the waist of his green trousers, when the kid pointed at the colored fella, dad; the colored fella is who took my bike; and all hell broke loose with *mama mias* spewn all over the road in white vomit, and as if it was still Christmas and hail was falling, and the cops came screaming down the avenue going against the pointing of the white arrow, two carloads of them, to solve this ghetto delinquency, that began as a small neighborhood kid's prank, "I didn' mean nothing" and slam! into the cruiser, nigger; into the goddamn cruiser, you goddamn nigger, mama mia Hail Marys and BJ not understanding the various languages and accents being vomited against him, no explanation in the eyes of the man who owned the peddling grocery store, no explanation from his three friends who did not know Italian and Greek and were no longer within ear-shot and speaking distance to translate this crime, no understanding from the father with his chest buried in black hairs ripping the air with gestures which BJ thought at first were karate chops, but later knew their meaning even though he knew no Italian and no Greek, and no understanding from the four cops who descended armed and sunburnt like the father, to solve this serious crime, git, goddammit, git! into the goddamn cruiser! no, not in the goddamn front seat, in the fucking back, where youse belong, and they took him down, and did not book him, and put him in a nice large warm cell, large though his age, bigger, goddammit nigger warmer than the piss-small room you and your goddamn mother lives in! you fucking West Indians! and they left him there to stew and to mend his thieving ways, and then, hours later when the time for his supper of plain rice and boiled king fish and boiled green bananas had come and gone, the truth was known and the kind sargeant came with a styrofoam cup of steaming coffee, have a cup, come now, have a cup; and then said, a little mistake, if you can understand what I mean, you being such a little fella to know these serious, big things, a little goddamn mistake and you happened to be the goddamn unlucky one. So, beat it, kid, and don't let me lay my goddamn eyes on you again! Git!

Too young to know what he had done; not knowing what he had done; not knowing what the policeman in the cruiser had done; not knowing the exact shape of his fate this time, but wise enough to know that he was going to have some fate, BJ paced and paced. And then, perhaps because of his Black Muslim sense of destiny, he stopped walking up and down. He decided not to worry. "Let the motherfuckers come!" he said, but within his heart, he was calmed by the small square space, and by his history. And then he worked it out, in detail, and with a logic he was capable of, but which in the circumstances of the steel surrounding him in the four smells of impatience and of no restraint, the smell of vomit and old urine, in the circumstances of an unclear head, he had permitted to elude and overwhelm him. But when he had worked out his plan, he lit a cigarette, all that they had left him, and in his mind, for his mind was clean and not touched by his circumstances, he took out the long-playing record, could see his fingers ease it out of the jacket, and put it on his stereo, and remained standing listening to the words of Malcolm X's speech, *The Ballot or the Bullet*. He was asleep, standing, before the introduction of Malcolm X had finished. And he was stirred from his reverie by the opening of the door, and walked out into the dark cold parking lot, to his car now buried and made invisible by the falling snow. Marco was somewhere else: in another cell, held until *his* parents could come down from North York, to sign him out. Two men walked beside him. They were not in uniform. He recognized his car, for the snow had not touched the letters, BLUE, on the license plate. And he made the gesture to go to it, even though he did not have the keys. And he was corrected. "We're going for a little drive . . ." And he was put into the back of the cruiser. Left alone, to himself, behind the plastic protector thick as brick, strong as steel, and with his two hands free. The blue unmarked cruiser drove off in white pouring quiet.

From the top of the street, near Bathurst, she could see the red lights. They were whirring. They scared her each time so much just to see them, that they gave her the impression they were making great noise, and that the red lights were silencers of that noise. She could see the four police cruisers parked in the middle of the road, and one at the side. She could see the large red, ugly vehicle of the fire department. She could see a smaller, but equally ugly white-painted ambulance. And from the distance she was, turning into the smaller street where she lived, she could see the road filled with people. People were leaving doors open and running and passing her as she walked, heading in the direction of the spinning red lights on top of the police cruisers and the fire department truck and the ambulance. She had never witnessed a fire of this bigness in this city before, and so, she walked as fast as she could, in the deep sliding snow, to reach the sight.

The road became more crowded when another police vehicle, a small panel-type truck marked Tactical Squad, forced itself into the road, from the other end of the street. She was sure now that someone was holding someone hostage. She had watched many of these scenes every day on the soap opera shows in the mansion down in the Ravine where she worked. And tickled by the transformation of a movie into a slice of her real life, she tried to hasten her stride, but without success, for the snow was too deep. She felt the excitement the spinning red lights gave off, the curiosity of staring at these kinds of lights on a highway ahead of you, and she passed each house from one end to the next now as long as a block, her blood quickening, and not once through her mind passed the thought of "Who's sick?"; and she did not once consider her neighbors nor the landlord in this absent thought of compassion. It was the excitement she was heading to. People, she could see them now, people were being kept back behind a ribbon of yellow plastic, and one policeman stood guarding the yellow plastic ribbon, which measured the area round one house, and disappeared out of sight, perhaps down a lane, or the thin unwalkable space between two houses, and this ribbon reminded her of birthday parties back home, and on Christmas morning, and once when she was no longer a child, taken by her mother to an opening of something where they had a long ribbon like this before the entrance. On that occasion, the vicar of her church cut the ribbon with scissors. Her excitement was now in her blood, and with her blood hot, she was no longer recognizing things, and landmarks and the shape of the uneven concrete steps the landlord had incorrectly built to save money, and that caused her to slip even in the summer. She was forcing herself against these strangers to reach the entrance. And she could see the splotches and the drying small pools, the spots, taking some time to be registered in her excitement as blood. She could see the blood on the steps and blood along the narrow lane, and the lane became difficult to see, as it went beside the house on the left. A dog walked out as if it was drunk. And when it vomited, what came out was like grape juice.

She could see policemen inside the room, collecting things, some of which they were already bringing out. And she could see the attendants from the ambulance arranging something heavy on to a stretcher. She could see the clothes being brought out. She could see the stereo equipment, speakers, CD player, amplifier. And the books. And the small Bible. She wondered who lived here. She could see the books. Books always interested him. And then she realized she was thinking of her son. He always had his head inside a book. And one book she saw was the Holy Qur'an. She wondered if this was the wrong address.

She could see the policemen inside the room, at the back near the door to her kitchen, walking round the small space, nervous and silent. The street outside was silent too. No one was talking. But she could hear their anger and their resentment and their hatred. She was beginning to learn how to listen to this kind of silence.

And then, there was a sound. A sound very similar to surprise, or to shock, or even to the satisfaction that what you are about to see is the shock, but that you are not prepared for it.

They were bringing a body out. Two ambulance attendants carried the stretcher which had wheels like a bier of a coffin, but which had to be lifted part of the journey, the short journey from the back of the house down the two short cement steps which the landlord had not got around to fixing properly, a little way to the right of the rear door, and to the ambulance after going through the thin lane, down two more steps and up the three steps of the basement apartment front door. As they lifted it up the steps, the wind which was cold and strong blew the cloth off the body of the corpse. A cry went through the people. It was a young man. A boy, still with his mother's features. No more than sixteen or seventeen or eighteen. A black youth, with a close-trimmed haircut, with Zeds for patterns and an X for style, dressed in a black woolen jersey, black slacks, white socks and black shoes that could, if he was alive, help him to jump against gravity, like a basketball star. Or Michael Jordan. And when the wind had taken the blanket on its short wild curtsey to the wind and to the night, the people made that sound again, like a gigantic taking in of wind.

She could see it too. And she saw the head, and it was out of shape from something that had hit it. Disfigured. And the blood was covering the face. And the stretcher was covered in thick blood. And the black clothes the youth was dressed in, were red now, more than black. The blood seemed to have its own unkind and disfiguring disposition, and it seemed to drip and mark the journey from the room at the back of the basement apartment through the room itself, through the small backyard, through the lane and out into the cold wind. It looked as if a cannon had struck the head, and the head had exploded and had been cut into pieces, like a watermelon that had slipped out of the hand. To her, it seemed as if the brains of the young man were coming through his mouth, as if his eyes were lost against the impact of the bullet. To her, it looked like a watermelon that was smashed by the wheels of a car.

It was too much. It was too cold. It was too brutal. It was too cruel. And there was too much blood. Worse than the American soap opera she had watched earlier the afternoon of this Friday night, down in the Ravine.

"BJ! BJ! Fuck!"

It was somebody screaming. She did not know the voice. She looked around, in this crowd of people only one of whom she knew, her landlord, and then she saw the owner of the voice. It was a young man. There were tears in the young man's eyes. He was dressed in a black jogging suit, black Adidas, and white athletic socks, and he seemed to have something wrong with his right hand or his right side, for he was doing something with his body which made it shake, as if he had a nervous habit, like a tick, hitting his right hand against his right thigh. He looked Portuguese to her. She did not know him. "BJ! BJ! Fuck!"

The Wedding Ring

•

Mavis Gallant

On my windowsill is a pack of cards, a bell, a dog's brush, a book about a girl named Jewel who is a Christian Scientist and won't let anyone take her temperature, and a white jug holding field flowers. The water in the jug has evaporated; the sand-and-amber flowers seem made of paper. The weather bulletin for the day can be one of several: No sun. A high arched yellow sky. Or, creamy clouds, stillness. Long motionless grass. The earth soaks up the sun. Or, the sky is higher than it ever will seem again, and the sun far away and small.

From the window, a field full of goldenrod, then woods; to the left as you stand at the front door of the cottage, the mountains of Vermont. The screen door slams and shakes my bed. That was my cousin. The couch with the India print spread in the next room has been made up for him. He is the only boy cousin I have, and the only American relation my age. We expected him to be homesick for Boston. When he disappeared the first day, we thought we would find him crying with his head in the wild cucumber vine; but all he was doing was making the outhouse tidy, dragging out of it last year's magazines. He discovers a towel abandoned under his bed by another guest, and shows it to each of us. He has unpacked a trumpet, a hatchet, a pistol, and a water bottle. He is ready for anything except my mother, who scares him to death.

My mother is a vixen. Everyone who sees her that summer will remember, later, the gold of her eyes and the lovely movement of her head. Her hair is true russet. She has the bloom women have sometimes when they are pregnant or when they have fallen in love. She can be wild, bitter, complaining, and ugly as a witch, but that summer is her peak. She has fallen in love.

My father is—I suppose—in Montreal. The guest who seems to have replaced him except in authority over me (he is still careful, still courts my favor) drives us to a movie. It is a musical full of monstrously large people. My cousin sits intent, bites his nails, chews a slingshot during the love scenes. He suddenly dives down in the dark to look for lost, mysterious objects. He has seen so many movies that this one is nearly over before he can be certain he has seen it before. He always knows what is going to happen and what they are going to say next. At night we hear the radio—disembodied voices in a competition, identifying tunes. My mother, in the living room, seen from my bed, plays solitaire and says from time to time, "That's an old song I like," and "When you play solitaire, do you turn out two cards or three?" My cousin is not asleep either; he stirs on his couch. He shares his room with the guest. Years later we will be astonished to realize how young the guest must have been—twenty-three, perhaps twenty-four. My cousin, in his memories, shared a room with a middle-aged man. My mother and I, for the first and last time, ever, sleep in the same bed. I see her turning out the cards, smoking, drinking cold coffee from a breakfast cup. The single light on the table throws the room against the black window. My cousin and I each have an extra blanket. We forget how the evening sun blinded us at suppertime—how we gasped for breath.

My mother remarks on my hair, my height, my teeth, my French, and what I like to eat, as if she had never seen me before. Together, we wash our hair in the stream. The stones at the bottom are the color of trout. There is a smell of fish and wildness as I kneel on a rock, as she does, and plunge my head in the water. Bubbles of soap dance in place, as if rooted, then the roots stretch and break. In a delirium of happiness I memorize ferns, moss, grass, seedpods. We sunbathe on camp cots dragged out in the long grass. The strands of wet hair on my neck are like melting icicles. Her "Never look straight at the sun" seems extravagantly concerned with my welfare. Through eyelashes I peep at the milky-blue sky. The sounds of this blissful moment are the radio from the house; my cousin opening a ginger-ale bottle; the stream, persistent as machinery. My mother, still taking extraordinary notice of me, says that while the sun bleaches her hair and makes it light and fine, dark hair (mine) turns ugly—"like a rusty old stove lid"—and should be covered up. I dart into the cottage and find a hat: a wide straw hat, belonging to an unknown summer. It is so large I have to hold it with a hand flat upon the crown. I may look funny with this hat on, but at least I shall never be like a rusty old stove lid. The cots are empty; my mother has gone. By mistake, she is walking away through the goldenrod with the guest, turned up from God knows where. They are walking as if they wish they were invisible, of course, but to me it is only a mistake, and I call and run and push my way between them. He would like to take my hand, or pretends he would like to, but I need my hand for the hat.

My mother is developing one of her favorite themes—her lack of roots. To give the story greater power, or because she really believes what she is saying at that moment, she gets rid of an extra parent: "I never felt I had any stake anywhere until my parents died and I had their graves. The graves were my only property. I felt I belonged somewhere." *Graves?* What does she mean? My grandmother is still alive.

"That's so sad," he says.

"Don't you ever feel that way?"

He tries to match her tone. "Oh, I wouldn't care. I think everything was meant to be given away. Even a grave would be a tie. I'd pretend not to know where it was."

"My father and mother didn't get along, and that prevented me feeling close to any country," says my mother. This may be new to him, but, like my cousin at a musical comedy, I know it by heart, or something near it. "I was divorced from the landscape, as they were from each other. I was too taken up wondering what was going to happen next. The first country I loved was somewhere in the north of Germany. I went there with my mother. My father was dead and my mother was less tense and I was free of their troubles. That is the truth," she says, with some astonishment.

The sun drops, the surface of the leaves turns deep blue. My father lets a parcel fall on the kitchen table, for at the end of one of her long, shattering, analytical letters she has put "P.S. Please bring a four-pound roast and some sausages." Did the guest depart? He must have dissolved; he is no longer visible. To show that she is loyal, has no secrets, she will repeat every word that was said. But my father, now endlessly insomniac and vigilant, looks as if it were he who had secrets, who is keeping something back.

The children—hostages released—are no longer required. In any case, their beds are needed for Labor Day weekend. I am to spend six days with my cousin in Boston— a stay that will, in fact, be prolonged many months. My mother stands at the door of the cottage in nightgown and sweater, brown-faced, smiling. The tall field grass is grey with cold dew. The windows of the car are frosted with it.

My father will put us on a train, in care of a conductor. Both my cousin and I are used to this.

"He and Jane are like sister and brother," she says— this of my cousin and me, who do not care for each other.

Uncut grass. I saw the ring fall into it, but I am told I did not—I was already in Boston. The weekend party, her chosen audience, watched her rise, without warning, from the wicker chair on the porch. An admirer of Russian novels, she would love to make an immediate, Russian gesture, but cannot. The porch is screened, so, to throw her wedding ring away, she must have walked a few steps to the door and *then* made her speech, and flung the ring into the twilight, in a great spinning arc. The others looked for it next day, discreetly, but it had disappeared. First it slipped under one of those sharp bluish stones, then a beetle moved it. It left its print on a cushion of moss after the first winter. No one else could have worn it. My mother's hands were small, like mine.

Horse Meat

·

Joe Rosenblatt

A horse is loyal, but when the creature can't haul his weight he's shuffled off to the glue factory. Loyalty zips out through Death's round door. Connoisseurs who've taken their brood to the circus to watch the fine-lined creatures prance, their tails tied in a bun and heads held high, say the servant's meat—all the specialty cuts from equine carnage laid out in specially licensed shops—tastes sweet. The poor horse, a purely herbivorous creature, also serves in death, but in life a pony loves a fresh carrot with blackened soil on its tapered carotene body, and the stallion loves a sugar cube and neighs its vital thanks, a love purer than man's as he drags a junk wagon or a cart heaped with voluptuous vegetables around a corner.

I remember the old peddlers in the forties leading their four-legged companions down our street. During the heat of a summer's day, kids offered the nag a sugar cube or an apple, and the long yellow nicotine-colored teeth chomped on our tidbits, our offerings. Then, the peddler shooed us away, complaining we had molested his precious and boon companion. The peddlers have disappeared;

chrome-plated horseless machines have taken over, but I remember when an old bearded peddler lifted me up on his nag's back and I cried when I stared down at the ground and kicked the creature in the flanks with my baby shoes. I'm sure the old horse smiled. They always seemed to smile in their garage-style barns, the dirt floors strewn with hay. How they survived the winters I'll never know. I don't recall wood burning stoves, although there were plenty of horse blankets and an old man's affection. A deep bond existed between horse and peddler, a miserable pair broken by a deadening vocation, existing on the small change of life, making the street rounds searching for broken shoes, a soiled jacket, a tie, an ironing board, a frayed lamp shade. It was a cycle: the poor feeding on the poor. Horse and master, a visible minority verbally abused by street toughs. Shunned, both horse and peddler were considered—by those riding the wheels of social mobility—fossilized ghetto figures.

So, horse and wagon have disappeared, along with trails of steaming golden apples glittering in the afternoon sun. They were scooped up for fertilizer by street folk to increase the voltage of plants in a front garden. I stared at the supernatural glow in the faces of sunflowers and marvelled at how that magical dung sustained those wild blooms. Today, the only horse balls are those dropped by the stallions of city cossacks down at city hall square, and no sunflowers loom up in the minds of cops.

There was a happier time when a horse had his or her favorite watering hole. I remember a coppery fountain on the southwest corner of Spadina and College, the fountain's green skin of floral patterns fringing its surface. The artisan who designed the fountain had a sense of humor: there was a cherubic figure who greeted the snouts of horses with a jet of cold water and a small nude comedian peed in an arc and many a kid leaped under it, frolicking in the maw of the fountain during a July heat wave until, nudged by a horse, he retreated, with the peddler shouting that the sanctity of the fountain had been profaned by a pint-sized hooligan. To make his point, the man waved his horse whip above his head.

To this day, I can't stand the thought of using glue. I instantly associate it with horses who've been sold out. What would Roy say about glue and horses. He'd never have put Trigger on a conveyor belt. To hell with mucilage made from horses . . . the viscous stuff sickens me. I smell horse in the glue bottle, and suspect horse glue on a postage stamp. How would you like to lick old Dobbin goodbye? They've made ashtrays out of the knuckles of elephants and shoes from grinning alligators, and the testicles of tigers are dried and ground to powder for septuagenarians hoping to get it up one last time in the Far East. Nothing is sacred, not even human skin, which provides a delicate pinkish hue for lampshades, so rosy a light for concentrated romance. Pain and leather conjoin. An old prole of a drayhorse is offered a few sugary rocks, or a carrot (the animal's pacifist heart clouds its judgment) and other sweetened tidbits, so he ambles through a maze of stalls wiped clean of blood and there's muzak in the air: a smart marching tune calms the creature into thinking he (or she) is at a horse fair out in the country, or back home. Even the air has the tang of the freshest alfalfa and sweet grass, a special brand, or type, reserved for the thoroughbred winner.

The cynical engineer has contrived an intricate plan. The animal moves through stalls of friendly colors, and neighs: a few have been painted symbologically—a pleasing bovinish landscape . . . a peaceable kingdom that would have delighted Rousseau . . . bovine figures lurking in high grass, a brown squirrel cleverly pawing a chestnut . . . a cobalt-hued bird on a branch and a lamb asleep at the foot of a shepherd wearing a candy striped robe . . . loud bulbous blooms . . . stamens licking exaggerated bumblebees . .

. and a spring peeper on the face of a leaf on a branch . . .

An innocent intellect gestates in the retired dray-horse. His herbivorian heart swells. Grunting, he has discovered paradise, lulled into the maw of a delicately crafted Bucolics; in short, he is a primitive Virgil absorbed in an elegiac atmosphere, and he deliberates on tonalities intermingling in the paintings. Already anaesthetized through wave lengths of color, the horse heads toward a stall in which a hole has been cut to fit an equine head. The beast views a carrot tree awaiting him through the hole. It is the piece d'ocassion. The retired prole pushes his head and neck through the hole, deducing through some inverted logic that it has been especially cut by his master to accommodate him. He not only views hyped-up carrot trees but an apple tree with its low boughs burgeoning with lusty apples. Of course, it's too damned good to be true, and there's something out of place with the carrot tree; by now, the animal has remembered that carrots don't grow on trees. Locked in the feed hole, he will be spared the mental arithmetic used exclusively by horses—that carrot tree and apple fixation don't amount to heaven—they are only a clever joke as the cynic's heavenly moment arrives. He releases the trigger of his hammer gun. There's a sickening thud as a steel rod slices through the horse's skull, shooting the brains out at the other end, and sometimes a puzzled seed of a brown eye. Another workman moves with a precise mechanical rhythm, ax in hand. He neatly cleaves off the head at the neck. The creature's magnificent head flies into a basket (entitled The Last Sure Bet by the boys in the slaughterhouse). Not to be outdone by this clean single rhythm, he is joined by another burly workman draped in a plastic yellow jacket and in boots like chestwaders any angler would be pleased to wear at a trout stream. The man slashes open the horse's belly (the hole in the stall has mechanically enlarged itself and another workman has shoved the decapitated beast back, receiving a splash of blood pumped from the still active heart) and the guts slide out onto the floor . . . the material oozes on the phony green carpet that simulated a mossy grass to the passing horse on its way to the round hole, the Grim Reaper's entrance to his condominium.

The belly-ripper is joined by a clean-up man who shoves a long gloved hand into the interior of the belly, pulling out any stubborn organs and entrails; in fact, he has become a specialist, a poetic mortis of gastro-intestinal delicacies and this belly brigade works fast and furiously. They hose out the innards, wash down the horse, clean up the blood on the phony grass floor with a high pressure hose . . . and then, falling on their knees, they scrub the blood out with tungsten brushes, oblivious to a huge hook and chain lifting the horse's carcass up and along a track toward a steamy vat where the cadaver is dumped. It is the final cooking pot, and the boys love to jazz a kid new on the job by plucking an eyeball from the horse's quiet socket. "Go on, make a man out of you . . . come on punk, suck on this eyeball . . ." The testicles and the immense member of the horse which has released a streak of violence—wag by: "Boy, if the old lady could see that one. Jeeze, I wish I wuz that well hung . . . Hey kid . . . don't you wish you had a stick like that . . . what a porker . . ."

The kid throws up his breakfast. He'll learn it's best to eat after the work shift. Still, the idea of a horse fills your belly with bile and creeps up into your throat at two in the morning and then slides back into your lungs until you think you are going to choke to death. It's a hard life. But your friends say you're suffering overactive guilt anxiety and you keep on trucking because you're not a quitter and there are good benefits . . . health plans . . . free dental care . . . a pension and other fringe benefits that make up cradle-to-the-grave security. You may even advance to overseer of the big glue pot, the soup where bits and pieces of horse flesh fall apart from the bones . . . the soup having the consistency of good black beans, but the odd joker will point to an eyeball floating and quip that the dark vision consumes in consomme.

The soup gives off a sickening smell, sweet, and sometimes acidy, with traces of sulphur and shit (legend has it, depending on who lips the narrative, that a few lads fell into the pot while stoned on super-grass, and the morning crew found them floating, cooked inside and out, the flesh shedding, the human bones joining the horse frames at the bottom: the more poetic amongst the staff thought that the soup might serve as a sacrificial well . . . maybe bring in a hooker off the street . . . maybe a show before the soup is served, a little mooning before the moon goddess is placated). The kid backs away like a maggot who has just smelled clean meat, squeezing his hand over his mouth trying to keep from wretching on the cleaned green . . . and somewhere arrows are singing out in space . . . but the punk hasn't heard of the Battle of Hastings, about dry ice evaporating: what does the punk know about Harold and the arrowhead in his eyeball . . . Only the last chilling cry reaches him just before the thud of the rod crushes the skull of another animal. The triggerman doesn't like anybody crowding his job, infringing on his relationship with the horse. Nobody joins the triggerman for a beer after work. And the triggerman doesn't care; like the hangman, he feels he has a mission as Keeper Of The Glue. Sometimes the triggerman complains about the music; he doesn't know tone from a bone. He hates sound, any sweet sound. He loves only the spit and rattle of his gun, the way it vibrates in his hand. He loves the closed expression of the dead horse. The triggerman loves horses. He has a collection of horse paintings on velvet; the masterpiece was painted by a woman who had no hands, claiming she painted it with a brush clamped between her teeth . . .

The muzak continues. A red light flares. The trigger-man is ever alert for the approach of a horse. All the time he is thinking about hyper space; he knows there's a trigger-man or woman for everybody, and if he gets it, will he feel pain? Do any of us feel pain after we die? His clammy finger squeezes the trigger. He doesn't hear the *bpop* of the rod singing in the horse's skull. Meat. And more meat. The trig-german laughs, and he can't stop laughing. Laughter has taken possession of him. It's finally come to that. Frost has formed around his mouth. He could be dead, but his mind goes on humming and laughter becomes his cosmic wisdom. His mouth is open as though with each squeeze of the trig-ger he lost his cherry . . . he is virgin death, alive on black velvet. A horse neighs among the painted crocuses. Those floating eyes, the pollen of what we know, what's been seen. This Way To The Crocuses Ladies And Gentlemen.

Is there freezer burn out in space?

Marylou Had Her Teeth Out

•

Patrick Lane

Marylou had her teeth out. No one ever seemed to notice Marylou. She wasn't exactly ugly or anything. It wasn't that. If she'd been real ugly then I guess people would've noticed her. People notice ugly people just like they notice beautiful people. They stand out. Marylou didn't stand out. She was just there. You know, ordinary.

No. More than that. Sort of like a post in a fence. Once the wire is hung the post is just there. That's what she was like ever since she'd been born. Of course, it was a big family. I'd say there must have been at least fourteen or fifteen of them. I never counted. No one did. I wonder now if even her folks counted them. When you get past six or seven they kind of all blend together I think.

Marylou's teeth had always been a problem. When they grew in, they grew in wrong, all pointing every which way. Some kids are like that. People say it's what they eat but I don't know. Some kids have just got bad teeth I think. She never complained at all. None of the kids in that family complained. What was the good of that? And who'd you complain to if you wanted?

That family never had much money to speak of. Marylou's old man was born to be poor. It was like he'd aimed his whole life at having nothing and it'd worked. He had nothing. They had a house if you could call it that, and a few other things, but not much. How Jack Trackle even got a house I'll never know. They'd been living there for years. I think that old farm had just been deserted and Trackle moved his whole brood onto it. There's still lots of old places around here from before the war.

Jack Trackle had a clubfoot and he was a little guy. Always complained about that foot. Said there was no way he could work it hurt so bad though you'd see him at a dance on Saturday night at the Oddfellows Hall and he'd be kicking that foot six feet up a wall. That never seemed to bother him.

Dancing was one thing Trackle could do. Saturday night he'd lock that house of his so the kids would stay put, and he'd bring his wife to the hall. Just her, not Marylou or anyone else. The wife would hang like a fly by the sandwich table and never move while Jack would dance with anyone he'd a mind to. Most would. You didn't say no to Jack.

Anyway, Marylou had them out. The whole mouthful. Had them pulled out down in Kamloops one day when she and her mother went out. I think that's all they went out for, Marylou's teeth. They were welfare people. Jack Trackle didn't work like I said and I guess she had her hands full looking after all those kids *and* Jack. There was no way she could work. Trackle wouldn't have let her anyway. He was way too proud for that. I don't even know her name come to think of it. No one talked to Jack Trackle's wife. Anyway, out they went on the CN Mainliner and Marylou came back with all her teeth out. Came back the same day. Down in the morning and back by six o'clock. That's when the eastbound comes back through.

I still think it had a lot to do with that young first-aid-man they had down at the mill. Not that he interfered with people all that much. People sort of interfered with him. The mill reopening after all those years really changed things in Little River. There were a lot more people in town, that's for sure. The bunkhouses were filled. They'd been empty for years.

The first-aid-man was one of the biggest things to happen to Little River besides the mill starting up. We all knew he couldn't do things like a real doctor but it was a lot better than the health nurse who used to come up twice a year. Now she used to interfere a lot I'll tell you. But it was him, I think, who arranged the teeth thing for Marylou. So out she went and came back with no teeth.

I guess I should say something more about Marylou seeing as how what happened. She was about fifteen or so. Around there. I said she was ordinary. They were all ordinary. She had long black hair and a kind of straight-forward face. You couldn't say she was good-looking at all. Oh, she had a body on her in a way. I never paid attention. That kind of thing was never too important to me at all. It might've been once a long time ago but not really. I guess I just missed out on all that. I'm glad now I did.

So that was her. There's not a lot more you could say. Fifteen about. Black hair. Ordinary. What else can you say? The whole family was that.

I talked to her a few times. She used to come in to get things once in a while. Her teeth were terrible. I only saw them the once. She was scared this one day by the Dutchman's dog and she opened her mouth real wide. I was standing right there and you couldn't miss them. That was the only time. The rest of the time she talked, when she talked at all I mean, she kept her mouth kind of closed so the words came out muffled. Or she'd say something to you and keep her hand in front of her mouth so you had to figure out what she said by what was happening. If she was coming it was hello. If she was going it was goodbye. That's almost all I ever heard her say.

I guess those teeth really embarrassed her I don't know. When they're young like that things like teeth can seem real important. Kind of a lonely girl now that I think of it. But there was a big family. How can you be lonely when you've got that many brothers and sisters?

So it was that young first-aid-man who started it all. At least that's what I figure. Anyway there she was, back. I saw her come in on the train with her mother. I meet the train regular. I don't nose into other people's business. Don't get me wrong. I like to see who's coming and going that's all. I saw her that day. Her cheeks were all sunken in like one of those old people with only gums. Jack Trackle was there to meet them and he was mad.

I don't know what it is with little guys. They're always trying too hard. I never saw a fight yet that wasn't started by a little guy. Seems like they're always looking for trouble. He was there, Jack Trackle, waiting. When they got off he grabbed his wife. He twisted her arm so hard I thought he was trying to take it right off. She didn't yell or anything, just stood there and let him do it. Marylou just stood there too with her hand covering her mouth. It looked sore. Jack Trackle was yelling at his wife real bad and just twisting that arm. I felt like maybe going over and stopping him but what good would that've been? He'd a real reputation for that stuff and if you got in the way it just made things worse.

The first-aid-man was there too. He'd been picking up some stuff off the Express Car when Trackle started yelling. He was saying things like "Don't you never go anywhere unless I say so!" Things like that. He was swearing at her too. I thought for sure he was going to kick her with that heavy boot he had on that clubfoot. I saw him once kick a guy right in the head at a dance after the guy had danced or maybe just tried to dance with his wife. Kicked him with that boot. That guy never came back to Little River. They shipped him out on a fast freight to Kamloops and the Hospital there. He was a real bad one was Jack Trackle. Nobody had anything to do with him or his family for that matter. They just let them alone. It wasn't worth it, him being the kind of man he was.

I'd have told the first-aid-man if he'd asked me. I'd have told him to let her alone and to stay out of Jack Trackle's way. It was asking for trouble. But he didn't. I'm not saying he was the interfering kind but in this case he troubled himself a little too much. I guess he heard Trackle yelling and he ran down the cinders by the track there and grabbed him and pulled him off the wife. I could've sworn I heard her arm pop when Trackle let go. That young guy was mad as hell. He wasn't from Little River that's for sure. Somewhere back east I think.

Well, I don't think anyone had ever right out and grabbed that man in his whole life. Nobody in Little River. Jack Trackle just stood there and looked at the first-aid-man. He was totally surprised. That's when the wife ran over and put her arms around Trackle. Real thin arms she had. Pipestems with a bit of gristle attached. She yelled at the first-aid-man and told him to leave them alone.

Marylou didn't say anything. She was still standing there with her hand over her mouth watching it all. I could tell by her look she was seeing it all in slow-motion. People when they're doing that have a certain kind of stunned look about them. The same as a steer does when it's hit between the eyes with a ball-peen hammer. Still-like as if the whole world just slowed right down.

That first-aid-man backed off then but he didn't go. No way. He went over to Marylou and said something to her. She gave him a piece of paper and then Trackle grabbed his wife and her. Not with his hand or anything. Just with a look. It was like they were attached to him by his eyes.

They headed up the road from the station there, Trackle's boot kicking up the dust with every step and his wife behind him walking with her head down and Marylou behind her still with her hand over her mouth. I watched them go. I wouldn't have wanted to be those two when he got them home. You'd think they'd have known better, knowing what he was like and all.

The first-aid-man stood there watching them and then he read the piece of paper. After he finished he threw it away. He took off then. Grabbed a box from the cinders by the Express Car, walked down to the head of the train, and went around the engine to the mill on the river side. There were people on the train looking out watching but when I looked back at them they all turned away. It was the dining car. You'd think they were watching some kind of movie. Those eastern people, all dressed up and going to wherever it is they go, Montreal or Toronto. Places like that.

The first-aid-man was just a young guy. He was walking real stiff-like in jerks, like he was mad, and I guess he was. His hard hat was pulled right down to his eyes. That's when I picked up the paper and read it. I know it wasn't any of my business. It didn't say much. It had a printed name at the top. The dentist who'd pulled all of Marylou's teeth I guess. I don't remember it now, some kind of foreign name like the Pakies up on the hill. Underneath it said: Stitches to be removed in three weeks. That was all. I guess when you've had all your teeth pulled they stitch up the gums. That's what Karl Arnverg's wife says. She says they pack the gums full of cotton stuff and stitch them over so they won't bleed. Helps them to heal she says and it keeps them right for when you get your false ones. What you do, Arnverg's wife said, after the gums are healed, is to cut the stitches and pull them real gentle through the gums so they don't tear or anything. Sounds simple enough to me.

It made sense. The paper I mean. What you had to do was take those stitches out. I figured Marylou and her mother would be heading back down to Kamloops in three weeks for that. Well, that's not what happened. Talking like this, I remembr it all.

I was pretty busy around then. Oh, I still found time to sit down at the Dutchman's store and meet the trains but I was pretty busy all the same. I'd shot a moose up on Mad River and I'd had to cut that all up and freeze it. Then I had to bring in the cordwood I'd stacked up above town. Good wood. Nice seasoned fir. I'd knocked a tree down that spring and let her dry real well all summer. Full of sap. Still, it was a lot to do.

Thinking back on it now I never saw Marylou or her mother in Little River during those weeks. I saw Trackle once but I didn't say anything to him. He looked the way he usually did. He'd walked into Little River from that house of his six miles up the road, picked up a box or two of stuff and walked right back out. Never said anything to anyone as far as I could tell.

No, that's not right. I almost forgot. He didn't come in alone. He had one of his kids with him pulling that wagon he'd made. It's true. I wonder why I forgot that? Strange how things get to be so ordinary you get used to them. That kid, one of the boys it was, about thirteen or so, was hitched up to the wagon just like he was a horse or something. I mean, he didn't have a bridle on or reins but he did have on a leather belt with loops attached to it. The loops were there to hold the two-by-fours sticking out from the wagon-box. Two bicycle wheels. That's all. Just like a damned horse. Can you beat that?

Well, Trackle filled the wagon with the stuff from the Dutchman's and that kid of his hauled it back. Trackle never paid for any of that stuff. It was all welfare food. The Dutchman made good money from welfare, I'll tell you.

Down the road they went, Trackle walking on ahead and coming along behind was the boy leaning into it and pulling the wagon. I never laughed when I saw that. It looked funny in a way but he wasn't one to take too kindly to people laughing at anything he did. Or his family did either.

I minded my own business especially when it came to him. I think if I took pictures, though, I'd have taken a picture of that. Can you imagine hitching one of your kids to a cart just like a horse? I'm glad I never had kids. Glad all that sort of thing passed me by. It's enough looking after yourself. You look after yourself and let others do the same. That's what I say.

Anyway, things went on for awhile. It was a few weeks later and I was sitting on the steps of the store when I saw Jack Trackle coming into Little River. He had Marylou this time pulling the wagon and his wife was with him too. There she was, Marylou I mean. Same clothes, same black hair, bare feet, same look about her. In they came. They stopped in the dirt outside the Dutchman's and he left them both there and went in to do whatever business it was he had.

I never said a thing, just minded my own business. You live a long time if you do that. There they stood, right in the hot sun. Marylou's feet in the dust like brown frogs run over by a truck, the wagon hanging from her belt and looking straight down at the dirt between her feet as if she could see something there so important she couldn't take her eyes off it. She had her hand as usual over her mouth, but I could tell just by looking at her there was something wrong. Her face was all swollen. Even from where I was sitting I could smell her. There was something terrible wrong in her mouth, that was for sure.

Trackle's wife stood in front of her and just stared straight ahead, right through the wall of the store and past it to the poplars down by the river and over the river and right

into the side of Green Mountain. That kind of look. Not
stunned. Not like Marylou's look down at the station that
time when they first came back from Kamloops. It was different. She was looking right through everything. It was like
her eyes would've burned you if she's looked right at you.

I just sat there.

That was when the first-aid-man drove up in the
company truck. He always came right at that time to pick up
the mail. Everybody knew that. As soon as he saw Marylou
and Trackle's wife he started walking fast. He went right
over and stood in front of the wife. She was standing in
front of Marylou. There wasn't much room to get around. I
remember the conversation real well. It's not like there was a
lot said.

"Move away," he said to her. "I'm supposed to take
those stitches out." Trackle's wife didn't say a word. She just
looked right through that young guy like he wasn't even
there. If he doesn't have two holes burned right through his
chest to this day I don't know. He asked her again and she
didn't move.

It was Marylou who spoke. She said, "I'm okay, mister. You leave us alone." She didn't say it scared-like at all,
and she didn't look up either and for sure she didn't take her
hand away from her mouth. Just said it muffled and flat.
You'd think a rock had talked to you to hear her. That's it
exactly. Just like a rock talked to you.

The first-aid-man stepped back like someone had hit
him. That's when Trackle came out of the store. There was
Marylou looking straight down at the dirt, and the wife
burning holes through the first-aid-man's body, and him
standing there looking at what he could see of Marylou.

Trackle came down those steps solid. That clubfoot
of his banged every second step like a hammer hitting iron,
and the iron wasn't winning I can tell you. I never moved
an inch, just felt the whole porch trembling. He walked

down with a step bang step bang step bang step thump into the dirt and threw a big box of groceries into the wagon. The two-by-fours jumped and lifted Marylou six inches in the air he threw that box in so hard. I thought, well, this's it now.

The first-aid-man stood there stiff, those two eyes of the wife burning him, and Trackle about one foot away from both of them. "Wha d'you want?" Trackle asked. I never heard anyone say anything like that in just that way. I saw a snake once strike at a stick in a circus when I was a boy. A rattler it was. The man who ran the snakepit used to make them strike so the people who were watching would get their money's worth. If he didn't they'd get mad. I mean, a snake will just lie there still as a stone forever unless you make him mad deliberately. That's what the man would do. I went there every day for the three days the circus was in town just to see him make that snake strike at a stick. That's what Trackle sounded like. A snake someone's poked a stick at "What d'you want?" Just like that. A snake jumping so fast and so cold you could damn near die hearing it.

The young guy just looked at him. I give him credit. He didn't back away or anything. He stood his ground, what there was of it. "If it's Marylou you want, then you can just forget it."

That's when the first-aid-man spoke. "I'm supposed to take those stitches out," he said. He was trembling from holding himself so stiff, and Trackle standing there a good head and a half shorter.

"That's looked after."

I swear everything stood still for awhile. Everything just got still. Trackle on that clubfoot, the first-aid-man, the wife staring right through everything and everyone at God knows what, and Marylou looking down with her hand over her mouth. I could smell her right inside my own mouth it was that bad.

The first-aid-man said it again, but this time it wasn't quite the same. It was like he didn't understand something suddenly. He was young and he wasn't from around here. Like I said, from back east probably. "But I have to take them out," he said again.

Trackle moved then. He held out his hand in a tight little fist and opened it right under the first-aid-man's nose. "Here," he said. "You want them stitches so bad you can have them."

The first-aid-man didn't move.

Trackle reached out with his other hand and took the young guy's hand and emptied into it what he had. "Here," he said. Then he kind of cut his hand at Marylou and the wife and said, "These here ones are mine." That's all. He turned then and walked up the road, him in the lead just like always, the wife right behind him still staring, and then Marylou pulling the wagon. I can see it now like a picture inside my eye. Their backs all in single file and the wagon behind with the bicycle wheels. They didn't have tires on them. You could hear them grind every time they hit a bit of gravel. We both watched them until they rounded the turn by the poplars up at the corner above the store.

I went over to him then. I felt kind of sorry for him. He was an important man in Little River even if he was so young. He was looking down at those stitches in his hand. There were about thirty of them like little black spiders on his fingers. "Jesus," he said. "They aren't even cut."

I brushed them out of his open hand so they fell on the ground. I didn't say anything. What was there to say? He looked at them lying there in the dust between his boots. "He didn't even cut them," he said. He wasn't talking to me, just talking to himself.

I left him there. It was almost five o'clock. The CN Mainliner was due in an hour and there were still a few things I had to do. I just left him standing there looking down into the dust.

The Inside Killer

·

Anne Dandurand

Sunday, November 15

It's already snowing. Real suicide weather. My torture has lasted eight years now, day after day. From Monday to Friday, every day, my boss strokes my bottom.

I've talked to him. I've raged at him. I've cried. Nothing works. I'm a prisoner. My boss, Robert Lalancette, continues to deny everything and increases my pay. My salary is now beyond my abilities; unemployment is rampant; I can't give it up; I'd never find anything as good.

Today I'm taking up the journal again that I abandoned eight years ago.

To inscribe my life before I explode.

And so I write: I am a prisoner of my boss, his money and my shame.

November 16

He won't even admit that he touches me. He protests his innocence in virginal tones. I am tired of fighting emptiness.

I don't understand; I am no beauty and with the

years I have even forced myself to become nondescript: I only wear brown or black clothes that are too big. Nothing ever changes.

This evening when I got in, it was odd—the radio was off.

November 17

Tonight again the radio was silent when I got home. But it is working. And I'm sure I set it at a rock station before I left this morning. Generally light classical music welcomes me back, but I thought that rock might get rid of my uneasiness.

At five thirty though, nothing. I check the locks on the doors and windows right away. Nothing out of the ordinary.

I am a little worried.

November 18, seven o'clock

In spite of my fears I slept heavily and didn't dream. A fresh blow this morning, though. During my sleep, someone turned out the fluorescent lights in my bookcase. That's where I keep my doll collection lit up all night. If I wake up, they reassure me with their fixed smiles. Now I am panic-stricken. It has snowed, snowed. No footprints. In a frenzy, I searched the remotest corners of the house before I left. I called the police—they laughed at me.

Actually, a radio that goes off by itself and a collection of dolls whose light goes out is something grotesque.

November 18, eleven o'clock

This evening I came home very apprehensive. What a relief to hear Vivaldi on Radio-Canada. But that was only a reprieve. On the floor of my bedroom next to the bed, I found a pair of black silk stockings attached to garters. They were laid out like the open legs of a woman.

A cousin had given me them as a joke years ago. I never wore them— it's not my style. I didn't even know I had kept them.

Now it looks like an obscene grimace. A stench of cigarette butts and sweat rises from them. They have been worn: the heels are dirty, the knees baggy.

I tried to think but my head was whirling. Suffering from a violent migraine, I took refuge in a hotel.

the 19th, in the morning

The hotel is no better. The clothes I carefully folded yesterday evening are soiled with a sticky kind of grease. The sleeves are knotted and there are rips in the underclothes.

I no longer know what to think. I stayed motionless for a long while, my heart bursting out of my chest, a taste of rust in my mouth. I finally called the hotel management, who assured me of the hotel's security. When you lock your room from the inside, no one can get in. And this morning the bolt was in place.

November 20

I returned home. I am frightened. Who is following me? I live all alone, without any friends. All my money goes on my valued collection.

Why me?

Everything seems quiet, but I no longer trust anything.

November 23, in the morning

The whole weekend, I sat in the middle of the house, waiting. For what? I don't know. Every evening I slide into the heavy sleep which is beginning to puzzle me. But when I try to think about this abnormal torpor, I get tangled up and can't concentrate. I vaguely see a door in the mist. As in a dream, every effort to reach it, draws me further away . . .

At least nothing has happened.

the 23rd, around noon

This morning at the office, the police were waiting for me. My boss, Robert Lalancette, was strangled with a black silk stocking last night. I thought I'd faint. I answered the inspectors' questions: yes, his business was flourishing; no, I was not really aware that he had any enemies, then I went straight home.

Obviously I only have one black stocking left.

November 24

I have a week off. Madame Lalancette told me she would take the business in hand after she had looked after the funeral formalities. It seemed to me that she hadn't particularly liked the deceased either. She was so calm, even hiding a smile. She had been visiting her sister in Boston the night of the murder. She told me she didn't really understand the motive for the murder. It wasn't theft, since nothing had been taken.

Madame Lalancette was talking to me, but all of a sudden I had difficulty hearing her. I was fascinated by her strange face and her long neck. She batted her eyelids very slowly like one of those cruel carnivorous plants, Venus flytraps.

When she had gone, I stayed I don't know how long breathing in her perfume that hung like a scarf in the dusty office. And all the noise of the jungle deafened me.

November 25

Nothing strange last evening or last night. Here I am figuring normal and abnormal days. I cleaned everything today, washed everything, removed anything useless clinging to me. I would have sprinkled the walls with holy water, but I haven't believed in anything for a long time.

I'm finished. It smells of wax, ammonia, and vine-gar.

Caught under one of the floorboards I found a small photo of Jean-Pierre.

I look at it. It tears me apart inside. And I've been hardening myself for eight years now. I didn't even think about him anymore. I even forgot to tell myself that I had forgotten him.

My mouth tastes of sand. Why did he leave my life so suddenly; why did he just vanish as though he had only ever existed in my head?

He went out for milk and disappeared. I looked for him. I cried. I never found out whether he died. I decided to close myself off. I took the monotonous job with Lalancette. I concentrated on becoming a shadow of myself, a skinny lit-tle old maid, with no desire, and a manic passion for porce-lain dolls.

Lalancette with his roaming hands and stupid tricks supplied me with a convenient enemy, so petty next to my pain.

I look at the photo and see a sign. What if it's Jean-Pierre? He used to like frightening me.

I never changed the locks and he left with my key, eight years ago.

November 26

I woke up very late even though I had gone to sleep very early. "He" came again last night. My dolls were moved. My three "Bye-Los" were strung up by their feet. My little "Bru", so cute in her flowered hat, was floating in the toilet. The "Frozen Charlottes" were lined up like bacon slices in the frying pan. The eighteen "Pierrots" were drowning in the garbage can among greasy paper and carrot scrapings. Desecrated.

I spent the day cleaning, starching and ironing tiny

clothes.

Everything was back to normal, but the fear won't leave me.

If it is Jean-Pierre what is he trying to tell me? And if it isn't him, who is it?

November 27

A normal night, except for this strange dreamless sleep.

Around five o'clock I went to see my neighbor at the back. I don't like her very much. She teaches nursery school. I run into her occasionally, mornings or evenings. She's always exhausted, as though her crew of brats engaged her in merciless combat, or some secret vice occupied her nights.

I got tired of having coffee with her—I had the feeling that I was listening to a worn record. She hates her sisters, her colleagues, her friends. After a few hours she would even have bad things to say about Jean-Pierre whom she'd known at university.

But I went to see her to find out if she had noticed anything strange at my place. After the usual complaints, I discovered that she had actually seen a man go into the house by the back door around four in the morning on the 26th. He'd had a key, and she hadn't seen him leave. Now at least I know I'm not crazy.

November 28

I walked the streets today. It reminded me of the time when Jean-Pierre disappeared. The clear sky hurt my eyes; I walked on the shady side of the street all day.

I systematically crisscrossed the centre of town, like I had eight years ago. After Jean-Pierre left I went to the morgue day after day, for six months, to see the unidentified corpses. The rest of the time I spent looking for him. I would stare at every man I met. I told myself that Jean-Pierre had lost his memory and must surely be wandering around in the depths of the city. It was time wasted.

At the corner of St. Laurent and Ste. Catherine, an outrageous young transvestite stepped into my path. He remarked, "Heh Réal, how come you're dressed up like a woman today, damn it?" After kissing me on the mouth, he took off, laughing.

Does he have some connection with my puzzle? Réal who?

November 29

I went to buy a doll. My favorite dealer, a dwarf, muttered behind my back, "Tu hueles à la muerte, mi bella! " It sent chills down my spine.

On the way home I pressed the doll to me as a talisman. In the bus I found a *Journal de Montreal* wedged between my seat and the wall. I haven't read the papers for a long time. Why did I glance at that one? What obscure desire pushed me to my ruin?

I recognized his picture easily on page two. In the night my transvestite of yesterday had been strangled.

November 30, in the evening

This morning around five o'clock he tried to burn down the neighbor's house behind mine.

She wasn't sleeping. She saw the same man as on the 26th, wearing a cape and a black hat. In the darkness she couldn't see his face. He tossed some old papers on the doorstep, sprinkled them with what appeared to be lighter fluid, and then, deliberately lit a cigarette which he threw onto the pile. Then he quickly entered my house, using his key.

When he'd gone my neighbor was able to put out the fire but her oak door will stay charred.

The police came to ask me questions; I couldn't tell

them anything, I'd been sleeping like a corpse. In spite of the fresh snow, there were no footprints, neither on my pink carpet nor on the pine floors.

The police searched the house with no results.

They've gone now, leaving me in terror.

I don't understand a thing.

Jean-Pierre and I loved each other when he left.

So why would he be angry with me?

On the other hand, if he's gone crazy, or if it's not him, I'll have to find some way of getting away from him alone.

December first

It's raining. It smells of poverty and weariness outside.

I went to the hardware store to buy an electrical cable, a large iron tub, a set of big insulated "alligator" clips, a four-foot square piece of carpet and a long copper pipe that I had bent into a circle five feet in diameter.

I worked the rest of the day setting up my trap.

For the first time in two weeks I fell asleep with a calm heart.

JOURNAL DE MONTRÉAL
DECEMBER 6 EDITION PAGE 3
MURDER OR MYSTERIOUS SUICIDE?

Called by a neighbor who noticed a strange smell, officers of the Quebec Police Force made a macabre discovery.

In the cellar of 9797 Visitation, they found the remains of Blanche Bellemare, 34, a resident at that address, in a state of decomposition.

The circumstances of her death remain unclear.

Lieutenant Réjean Rainville has reconstructed what

may have happened. When the victim entered her home, she fell into the cellar through a trap door hidden by a small rug. Just below this door was a large tub of salt water which she dropped into. In an attempt to regain her balance, she caught hold of a copper hoop, suspended horizontally midway between the floor and the cellar ceiling.

As this copper hoop was soldered to an electrical cable that was plugged into a distribution box, Blanche Bellemare was electrocuted by a charge of 220 volts.

The mystery thickens when we try to understand the motives for the murder, or the reasons for the suicide. A notebook with burnt pages was discovered at the site.

Moreover the police are puzzled by the men's clothing the dead woman was wearing, in particular, a cape and a black hat, and by the collection of dolls, lined up as though for a show on the smooth dirt floor of the cellar.

Translated by Luise von Flotow-Evans

The Forest Path to Malcolm's

•

Bill Gaston

> The cougar was waiting for me part way up a maple
> tree in which it was uncomfortably balanced . . .
> —Malcolm Lowry.
> "The Forest Path to the Spring"

Unlike the above epigraph, this is not a fiction. I have a distrust, a fear, a hatred of fiction, and I have my reasons. You will find these reasons colourful. I'll give one example now, and it alone should suffice: my middle name is Lava, this name the pathetic result of having had an eccentric and literary lush for a mother.

I have things to say on other subjects, but this has primarily to do with Malcolm Lowry. Deep Cove's most famous man. You'll find I can speak with authority here, my credentials being that I grew up not more than one hundred yards from Cates Park. For those who don't know, Cates Park is the new name for Dollarton Beach, the very place Lowry had his shack, wrote *Under the Volcano*, lived with M—, drank himself cat-eyed, and all the rest. As concerning all famous people, one hears contradictory "facts." What I will supply are the facts indeed.

The first so-called "fact" is this. It is said that Lowry's first shack, containing his only complete draft of *Volcano,* all his possessions, etc., was accidentally consumed by fire. And it is said he was consequently overcome with despair but proceeded, using his vast reserves of memory and imagination, to write an improved draft. None of this is correct.

The true facts are that, one, in a drunken rage, his feet bandaged, Lowry burned his shack on purpose, having cut his feet too many times on the broken glass which glittered all around it. He was in the habit of disposing of his empty gin bottles out a window with but a careless flick of the wrist, and, you see, it was time to relocate. (If you want proof, the cost of car fare to Deep Cove will give you proof. The glass is still there, and children still cut their feet.) And, fact two: while a draft of *Volcano* was destroyed, it was a draft that embarrassed him. The three other drafts were scattered around the parlours of Deep Cove's sparse literati. My mother had one.

I will push on with my account now, confident that I need supply no further proof. But I should add that not only do I abstain from alcohol as resolutely as I eschew spinning fictions, I hold no tolerance for those who indulge in either. It amazes me that men like Malcolm Lowry are ever believed, let alone admired, at all. When, head in hands, he announced that morning to the various fishermen, neighbours, and squatters "My god, my home is gone! My book is burned! But at least M—and I are alive," he no doubt looked wretched and despairing. To be fair, how could his audience have known the truth? It was easy for Lowry to look wretched and despairing when he was in fact hungover and ashamed. But I have to ask why anyone would ever believe one whose profession was to weave pained yarns on paper? One who tried to lie and lie well? One whose voice all day was but a dry run for grander lies spawned with purple ink later that night in the name of art? Add to that his drinking. Lowry was incapable of telling the truth. Perhaps I should feel sorry for him. I don't.

While living in Deep Cove, Lowry wrote a story called, "The Forest Path to the Spring." It was published posthumously, by M—. The story is a rather long, rambling affair, and while some of it is a lie, much of it is not, and so I recommend it to those who must read. In fact, it is perhaps the closest Lowry came to not Lying, for the mistruths found in it are not so much lies *per se* as they are drunken inaccuracies. I'd like to tell you about them.

The story involves his life in Deep Cove, his life on the beach with the inlet fronting him and the dripping coastal forest pressing on his back. I find it a very nostalgic experience each time I read it, and I have read it many times. (Again, I have my reasons.) Lowry describes the unfurling of sword ferns, the wonderful damp rot of a forest at sunrise. The soft tides of Indian Arm, the greedy, fish-rank croaks of gulls and herons, the smell of shattered cedar, the sacred light in a dewdrop reflecting the sun, the mysterious light in a dewdrop reflecting the moon. He describes creeks and trails I myself know well. He dived off rocks that I and my friends once used for the same purpose. And, more, he mentions in passing the elementary school I attended as a child (where no one knew my middle name); he describes the tiny cafe where I used to buy greasy lunchtime french fries for a dime after having thrown away one of my mother's inedible eccentric sandwiches.

Again, it is a rambling story, its focus hard to find. Love, perhaps. He tells of his love for midnight walks through the forest, his love for fetching crystal mountain water from the spring, his love of dawn plunges off his porch, his love of M—, his love of life. We know that last one is a bald lie. He hated life, which is why he drank, and why he created a lying life on paper. In any case, the story's climax of sorts occurs one fateful day in the woods when a cougar leaps out of a tree across his path. He is startled, awestruck, petrified. And in what amounts to a none other than cosmic revelation he learns that his Eden, his forest-haven-of-a-life has on its outer edges forces of amorality and destruction. He discovers, it seems for the first time, that a rose has thorns. Critics cluck like sympathetic hens and suggest that what we have here is a classic hidden theme, one which reveals no less than a genius admitting to a suicidal battle with the bottle.

The cougar! What a bitter laugh! All of it!

Before I explain why I am laughing, I want to discuss my mom. Rather, memories of my late mother. Her name was Lucy, and she was unmarried. If there are two kinds of eccentric—one who doesn't try to be eccentric, and one who does—my mother was the latter. People tend to dislike her kind, withdrawing from their reek of fakery. And since my mother's kind choose their eccentricities, their choices tend to be exaggerations of qualities they admire. Mom, for instance, wanted to be a mad poet. At the start, she was neither, and by the end she was only mad.

In Deep Cove in the Forties it was most unattractive to dress up in flour sacks, mauve scarves, bangles, and canary-yellow hats. To spout bad poetry in public was abhorrent. This was Mom's choice. Deep Cove was at the time a tight collection of sulking fishermen and poor squatters, and though my mother had a captive audience she had few fans. Perhaps they could smell her self-consciousness; perhaps they noticed her eyes lacked that electrified blankness which marks the true eccentric. And while you may think what you want of her, she was but the tactless extrovert, a wider extension, if you will, of the loud housewife in the turquoise kaftan, and harmless. The harm set in when she began drinking. I see the cause of her drinking to be identical to that of the man who lived one hundred yards down the beach from her: an over-active imagination and no appreciative fans. For Lowry was at that time in no way famous.

I gather these facts from years of researching my personal history. My sources are the aforementioned fishermen and squatters. When they speak of my mother they speak kindly but apologetically. They hadn't much liked her, and I can see in their faces their embarrassment. I keep mum, but am tempted to ease their pain and tell them I not only didn't like her much either, I detested her. And loved her, painfully, in the intense and secret way reserved for only sons. To illustrate: not long after she died I tried to read her poetry, and while I read for only ten minutes, I threw up for twenty. It was dreadful poetry, revealing an embarrassing mind. But only I who loved her so much have the right to hate her so much.

I don't know if Lowry liked my mother or not. In any case I have gathered that it was she who took to him first, if he took to her at all. She must have seen him there on Dollarton Beach, looking slyly Slavic-eyed, yet burping and twitching like a lunatic in the hot noon sun. He would have been as naked as legally possible, for (in the early days) he was proud of his build. Mother would have known he was a struggling writer. She must have thought: At last! Another eccentric, another sparkling mind! I believe she first tried to attract his attention in the local bar, where it's reported she attempted (successfully) to buy him drinks. I don't know what M—, secure in her childlike love for him, must have made of that. And it's said she would sometimes flag him down in the streets, the trails, on the beach. Perhaps she'd borrow a canoe and arrange to accidentally bump bows out on the inlet. I can picture her trying to impress him. My spine creeps as I envision her passing a lime-green scarf seductively over her unblinking Mata Hari gaze. Having caught his eye, my mother now goes for his mind, and, with that flaccid flare of spontaneity-rehearsed-for-days, she points to the sun and cries laughing, "The moon! The moon! " (I believe my mother was capable of little more than cheap paradox. I also believe she was the last person of this century who held alliteration to be somehow profound. Not long before she died she said to me, in that awesome hoarse whisper of hers, "Meeting Malcolm melted my mind.")

I would suspect that by now you share my embarrassment. But I would also hope that you are coming to understand my loathing for imagination, and writers, and fiction, and drink. If not, keep an open mind. My sole purpose here is to convince with the facts; to free the steel blade of truth about Lowry from the pastejewelled scabbard of fable that now hides it. I can assure you I'm not denigrating Mom here for pleasure.

So I doubt that Lowry liked my mother much, unless he was a bigger fool than I imagine. His writing demands that I at least admit he, unlike my mother, possessed subtlety. Perhaps fleeting genius; clarity in bursts (burps). Whatever the case, how my mother got hold of his manuscript is unclear. It could be that, like an adult relenting at last and giving candy to a brat, Lowry handed over a copy so she would go away. He likely thought it would take a woman like Lucy a full year to sift through such a book as *Volcano*, but he was wrong. No, in Mom's words, she "communed with his mind for twenty-three hours straight," and finished it. And her "communion" with him proved to be the beginning of her end. For my mother, whose mind's sole ambition was to snap colourfully, Lowry's fiction, his obsessive flowery painpacket verbiage, was the necessary nudge. It was on the day following Mom's twenty-three hour binge that the Event—and my reason for writing this—took place.

The Event has to do with the story, "The Forest Path to the Spring"; specifically with the cougar Lowry saw. As I mentioned, he was out collecting water from the spring, looked up, and there was the cougar. He describes the encounter this way:

> The cougar was waiting for me part way up a maple tree in which it was uncomfortably balanced. . . crouched on a branch really too small for him, caught off guard or off balance, and having perhaps already missed his spring, (it) jumped down clumsily, and then, overwhelmed, cat-like, with the indignity of this ungraceful launching, and sobered and humiliated by my calm voice—as I liked to think afterwards—slunk away guiltily into the bushes, disappeared so silently and swiftly that an instant later it was impossible to believe he'd ever been there at all.

There is more, much more. Page upon page about the cougar, Lowry's fear of it, his thoughts about his fear, his thoughts about these thoughts, his clinging passionately to M— all through the ensuing night, shaking and having tremulous sex together in the knowledge that Danger Lurks.

That cougar made quite an impression on him. However, I'd like to draw your attention to the last eleven words of the quotation I've supplied. Having done so, I'll simply come out with it, here and now. That was not a cougar. That was my mom.

I wonder just how drunk a man can get. I often think about that as I try year by year to understand this man Malcolm Lowry.

Wandering Cates Park again this week, along the path which is now proclaimed by sign to be Malcolm Lowry Walk, I took a good steady look. A sober look. I studied hard this plot of land and sea so described by Lowry to be "everywhere an intimation of Paradise." He found "delicate light and greenness everywhere, the beauty of light on the feminine leaves of vine-leaved maples and the young leaves of the alders shining in sunlight like stars." Oh, he goes on and on and on. Unadulterated opulence, with four adjectives per noun. But here is the one I can't help smiling grimly at: "The wonderful cold clean fresh salt smell of the dawn air, and then the pure gold blare of light from behind the mountain pines, and the two morning herons, then the two blazing eyes of the sun over the foothills." Did you get that? two suns? The words *blaring* and *blazing* to describe light? This is a description not of nature but of a raging dawn hangover. I have lived here on the beach all my life and I have never seen herons travel in pairs. While walking the identical path I saw beauty too, certainly, but not Lowry's bombastic brand. I too saw rustling dainty foliage of one hundred shades of green. I saw sturdy stoic trees, and mountains with their awesome noble mysterious elan. (It's easy to be Lowry.) Boats on the oh so wonderful water, King Neptune's refreshing riplets tickle-slapping the angel-white hulls, etcetera.

But what else did I see? I saw slugs in mid-path, dry pine needles stuck to their dragging guts, their bellies torn open by the sensible shoes of strolling old ladies. I saw dull clouds muffling mountains logged off and scarred forever; clouds muffling the high notes of birds; clouds reflected better in the oil slicks than in the odd patch of clear water. I saw rotten stumps, diseased leaves, at least as much death as life. In short, I saw reality. I had no need of hiding from the truth of the visible. I didn't have the need of a man ashamed, the need of a vision hungover and in constant pain. Lowry donned his rose-coloured glasses and raised the shuffling grey world to the level of an Eden in order to stay sane. Art was his excuse and his tool. He probably believed what he wrote.

But on to my mother, and the Event. I should add

that I heard all of this straight from Mom's mouth, and the disturbing mix of anguish and ecstasy in her eyes as she spoke makes me doubt not one word of it. She told me many times, and the story never varied. Her words:

"I just finished reading *Volcano*. In twenty-three hours. Oh, I was in rapture. I was under a spell. He had called out to me, to me alone, and I wanted to answer. I had to answer in a worthy way. I decided to go to him dressed as someone celebrating the Day of the Dead. In the book this was the first thing mentioned—the Day of the Dead, the costumes, the skulls, and all of those things that so horrified poor Geoffrey Firmin. And in the end Death is the last thing Firmin sees. It is the book's heart: Death. It was important that Malcolm knew I understood, as he knew I would. So I made the skeleton costume. The material should have been black, of course, but I had no time, and all I had was a brown one, a rabbit costume left from a Halloween dance. I cut off the ears, and painted on the bones. It wasn't a good job I'm afraid. My word, I had just read *Volcano* and naturally my hands were shaking." I recall as a boy being scared as my mother told me this part, because each time she told me, even though the Event was years past, even though Lowry was years dead and Mother was in her hospital room not really knowing I was there, her hands would begin to shake as she spoke.

"But the idea itself was enough. My first plan was to show up at his door, because I knew M—was back east for three months. She hadn't taken to me, you see. Can't say as I blame her, of course. Malcolm would act positively fidgety around me, a torn man. But anyway I had a better plan. I knew it was important that he *look up* to see me, to see Death, just as Firmin did at the end. So I climbed a tree and waited. I knew he'd be along soon. I spied on poor Malc and I knew his habits. Englishmen, especially Englishmen who drink, have very strict habits." Here Mother would always stare coyly down at her feet, pretending naughtiness, and laugh like a little girl. The final time I heard this story Mom looked very old, her fingers were ochre with tobacco, she was dressed as insanely as always (the staff let her keep her stash of scarves, beads, and hats under her bed), and yet she could still giggle as pure and free as a little girl. I felt like crying. I felt like looking up and shouting: You may be dead, Mr. Lowry, but look what you've done.

"So I found a nice tree and waited. And my lord don't you know I fell asleep. All that reading, and no sleep. Also, I confess to having sipped some." That is, had a lot to drink. But I admit I love to picture her up that tree, and love even more Lowry's version, that of a "lion uncomfortably balanced." What a nobly optimistic euphemism for a snoring drooling drunk crazy lady hanging there like a noodle on a chopstick. "But I knew Malcolm would understand. When he gave me the book he said, in that marvelous Oxonian of his, 'This is a tome best read drunk, for so the best bits were thunk.' Ah, Malc, a lad so boyish. A boyish genius." Here Mom would drift off. If I felt like hearing more I'd prod her.

"So there I was asleep, eight feet up. The next thing I knew, I heard a scream. Yes, a scream. My lord don't you know I thought it was a woman? I must have started, for I fell. And considering I could have met Death myself right then and there, I wasn't hurt much. A broken rib and a cut on my back—thank the lord for having sipped some. And when I looked up, there was Malcolm running with his empty water pails back in the way of his cabin. He was making the most curious noises in his throat. I was concerned. I think he'd been sipping rather heavily that week, what with you-know-who gone."

My mother's story would go on one segment longer. She would gaze off, as if through the walls of years, then seeing what she wanted to see her eyes would close and she'd say, "And I followed Malcolm Lowry home. In I walked, dressed as Death, bleeding from my back, and told him I loved him. He rose slowly from his bed with great big wide eyes and told me he loved me too." Once, and once only, she added: "We . . . communed." But, perhaps realizing for the first time that her audience was a thirteen-year-old boy, Mom went instantly shy and changed the subject. My mother may have been an extrovert, and insane, but she was exceedingly conservative when it came to certain subjects . . . .

I saw Malcolm Lowry only twice that I remember. I was about ten, and it was just before he returned to England for good. The first time, my mother had sent me to his cabin with a letter, sealed in a black envelope and smelling—good god—of an awful perfume. Lowry bellowed "Come!" at my knock, and there he was, sitting at his writing table. He had erect posture and a barrel chest, but a big and flabby stomach. A very proud bearing. His eyes looked vaguely Oriental. He just sat there, quite sober I think, and he seemed to know who I was. He didn't look pleased to see me. I gather from my probing that he'd during those years been spending considerable energy avoiding my mother, and it seems likely he'd seen us together and knew whose son I was. I gave him the letter and fled.

The second time, two weeks later, I was again a messenger boy. I knocked at the same door, and hearing only the oddest whoops and titters but no invitation to enter, I peered in at a window. There sat the same man, but hardly. This time he was naked. (I have heard he sometimes wrote that way.) He looked dark and somehow Mexican, like a greasy feline-eyed peasant. His table was littered with papers and books, and crumpled balls of foolscap covered his cabin floor like a layer of giant's popcorn. He was hunched over, and rolls of pale fat lay on his lap. He began to make noises again, noises that are unforgettable but now hard to describe: a high-pitched kind of squealing, but with a deep bass undertone at the same time. As he squealed he swung his head back and forth in great arcs, and while his mouth was clamped open in a toothy grin his scrunched eyes looked on the verge of painful tears. Swinging his head faster and faster, he finally stopped and took several desperate gollups from a bottle he had beneath him on the floor. I recognized the brand: the same English gin my mother drank. I stared, fascinated. My gut reeled with the avid hollowness it gets at car accidents, when there are cars upside down and bodies strewn about, and a cop with a flashlight stands beside a pool of someone's blood. What made me run in the end was this: Lowry finally managed to get a pipe lit after missing the bowl with several matches. He took a long draw and then settled back and sighed as if in satisfaction. But he looked anything but satisfied. Instead he grew dizzy from the smoke. He began to sway in his chair. And suddenly he shot up, threw back his head and howled. At the same instant of howling—I swear this is true—he accidentally shit himself. I *think* it was an accident. In any case it was more like an explosion of diarrhea, expelled in a one second burst. Much of it sprayed his buttocks and legs and, screaming now, Lowry began to twirl and slap at the wetness, stumbling as he did so. I ran then.

I realize I am more or less trampling on the reputation of a man a good many readers respect and admire. And I don't mean to rub it in further—no, I only mean to establish thoroughly my reasons for writing this—when I tell you it was that same afternoon I first heard Malcolm Lowry was a famous man. Handing me that latest note, Mother told me, "Be careful with this, dear, you are taking it to a very special person. He is a writer, and his book is in all the bookstores of the world." Well, I had just seen my first writer, my first famous man, and now fame and fiction had a face.

You may already have guessed a number of things. First, the reason for my bitterness—namely, that Lowry and my mother had sex after she fell out of the tree. My feelings stem not so much from the act itself but rather because what meant so much to my mother meant so little to Lowry. I believe it was his utter rejection of her after the Event that launched her down insanity's slide.

Mother never told me about it herself. This I admit. But the evidence pointing to their carnal union is over- whelming, and I don't for a moment doubt it took place. The clues are these. One, she told me she followed him back. Two, M—was away. Three, as she told me but once, they "communed." And my research has given me these clues as well: There was a two week period during M—'s absence when Lowry was purportedly most upset. "Crazy," my sources put it. On a non-stop gin binge, he was raving to all who'd listen that he'd met Death in the flesh, that he'd met Death and defeated it. More than one barfly heard him distinctly say, "I rogered Death all night, from behind like a dog." (I don't like to picture this.) During that period of time he would laugh and rave, rave and cry. What ended his raving was news of a cougar sighting in the area. Hearing this news seemed to cheer him up. He took to saying he too had seen the cat, and so his run-in with Death suddenly went the way of bad dreams.

It takes no detective to sort out the self-serving machinations of this drunken man's mind. For sanity's sake, for relief from devils, he made himself believe he'd seen a cougar, not my mother, not Death.

I hate but can't help picturing the scene. Lowry, drunk and whimpering, finds that Death has not only leapt at him from a tree but has followed him to his door. My mother, ludicrous in a rabbit's costume with a skeleton etched on it, with a broken rib and bleeding freely from the back, tells him she loves him. She embraces him, and, scared, Lowry can't deny Death its desire. My mother insti-gates the unthinkable act. And so two hideously incongru-ous dream worlds unite there in a shack on Dollarton Beach: My mother believing she has won over her aloof trea-sure, her boyish genius, at last. Lowry believing he is copu-lating with Death.

In Lowry's behalf, I like to assume that at some point in his passion he reached that minimal level of sobri-ety where he realized it was in fact a mortal woman in his bed. It appears he at least realized that *something* had hap-pened with *someone*. Someone who was not M—. Though in "The Forest Path to the Spring" he writes that after his brush with the cougar he and M—embraced "all the night long," I should restate that during this time M—was gone for three months, and I doubt whether even a gin-riddled Lowry would be unaware of that. So did he know it was my mother? Or did he make himself believe it was M—? What shaped pretzel of tortured logic did he finally construct in order to stay sane? Lowry was by all accounts a loving and monogamous husband, and so perhaps it was his horror at this odd adultery that made him go mad for a while. We'll never know.

For years, my mother assumed he'd known it was her. But when she first learned of his death—she did not read newspapers, and it was me who told her—she said, "But I thought he'd send word. Something." Then she laughed, and lapsed instantly back into what was now her world, a very advanced state of waking dream. And when "The Forest Path to the Spring" came out in 1960, and after Mother read certain parts over and over, she closed the book at last and whispered plaintively, "Oh, I thought he *knew.*"

I could go on and on about Lowry's life, Lowry's lies to himself. Indeed, I could water my prose with imagination and assault the man with a decadently flowery language he would have well recognized. It is tempting. For I see now how the taking up of a pen and the posture of writing itself seem to abet some kind of exaggeration. That is, imagination, dream, lie. I can only hope that by now you understand my loathing for fiction is so resolute, it has allowed me during this account to tell you nothing but the accurate truth. But I must admit how much I am tempted to sink into venom, attach the leash of speculation to Lowry's name and drag it through any number of scandalous cesspools. But I won't.

Nor will I go on to describe his final fall, for to do so would be to ennoble it. His tawdry death. Myth be damned: his death was nothing but tawdry, as tawdry as my mother's. I'll draw no cheap conclusion from this, but the equation is there for all to see: two people, lashed by self-doubt, forced by life's incessant grinning skull to turn to dreams and poetry and imagination, poisoned yet further by alcohol—two people die a tawdry death. My point is made. I give it to you and leave it; I ask only that you restrain from embellishing either their lives or their deaths with yet more poetry. I have the right to ask this.

I'll likely never discover whether Lowry knew he was my father. He may have known; he may only have guessed, as you might have. Perhaps Mom told him. Perhaps she pestered. But, not being the kind to ask for money or seek a scandal, my mother would have preferred cherishing me in secret, me her precious relic of a single sacred meeting. I'll never know, and not knowing has been hard on me. Harder, in fact, than having had no taste of fatherhood, save for a singular image of a naked man squealing, stumbling, slapping at glistening legs. But it's been hardest of all to admit to myself that, in the cloudy, booze-blurred moment of my conception, not only was I not planned, not sought for but was in fact the result of a man's lust for a woman other than my mother. To be blunt, Lowry's sperm was meant for M— (or perhaps for Death!), and was waylaid, like a manuscript, by a lonely woman in a pathetic bid for a bit of attention. Such was the flavour of my beginning, and such remains the flavour of my little life.

Proof that I'm his son? It took no wizardry to ascertain the year and month of the cougar Event, add to it nine months, and, lo and behold, arrive at my birthday. My mother had no boyfriends and was not known to have affairs. Lucy was a remarkable woman in many ways, not the least of which being that she knew a man's nakedness but once in her life, and this while wearing a rabbit costume.

As I mentioned when I began, my middle name is Lava. Throughout "The Forest Path to the Spring," Lowry called Deep Cove "Eridanus." Why did he rename it? No doubt for poetry's lying sake: no doubt Eridanus is someplace mythologically significant. I've never looked it up. My mother's inspiration for "Lava" was equally metaphoric. In this case, though, I know the meaning. In her way of speaking to me as though I weren't there, staring up into space and so talking over my head both literally and figuratively, Mother more than once intoned grandly, "Lava. You are my Lava. My little dear man. You are the emission of a volcano."

She doubtless imagined I'd be as fiery as my father. But, much as I've come to detest poetry, I'll travel that road as far as I can stomach and just this once extend her metaphor for her: hot lava is shot blindly out into the world, soon grows cold, and resents having been spewed there. Lava is nothing like the fiery bowels of its father. If lava could feel, it would feel like sloppy effluent, carelessly ejaculated, cold and abandoned—I cannot resist—under the volcano.

As I've been writing this history, I've often stopped and asked myself: whose voice is this? Is it solely the voice of bitterness? Malc and Lucy's bitter bastard boy? If not, why do I smear both a mother and a father? I seek neither notoriety nor a noble name, neither a paternity suit nor a share of his estate, if he left one. So why do I expose? Whose voice is this?

I like to think it is Malcolm Lowry's voice, his voice had he lived, his voice had he learned to stop staring into the roaring guts of himself, had he learned to stop lying, had he learned to lift his head high and breathe for good and all the pure cold energetic air of objectivity. If children inherit one thing from their parents it is the fear, the claustrophobic fear, of their parents' faults. So I can thank mine for helping me, through revulsion, toward clarity. My mind's best food has been the flesh of their faulty, tawdry lives.

I've been drunk but once in my life. I was seventeen. My mother had just died, and I knew who my father was. That it happened to be my high school graduation party didn't matter to me—unlike my friends, this wasn't a celebration but an exorcism. We drank under the stars in—where else?—Cates Park. Dollarton Beach. Eridanus. Paradise. A body had been found there in a burned-out car earlier that week, a suspected murder, so added to the evening was an air of danger lurking. And I drank gin, my parents' brand. I slept with neither cougar, ghost, nor woman, but still I had a wondrous time. I cried about my mother and raged about my father, pounding a driftwood club into the beachfire, sending showers of glowing amber skyward. None of the other kids noticed me really, for many were on a first-drunk as well, and flailing about in their own style and for their own reasons.

The Day I Sat with Jesus
on the Sun Deck and a Wind Came Up and Blew My Kimono Open and He Saw My Breasts

•

Gloria Sawai

When an extraordinary event takes place in your life, you're apt to remember with unnatural clarity the details surrounding it. You remember shapes and sounds that weren't directly related to the occurrence but hovered there in the periphery of the experience. This can even happen when you read a great book for the first time—one that unsettles you and startles you into thought. You remember where you read it, what room, who was nearby.

I can remember, for instance, where I read *Of Human Bondage*. I was lying on a top bunk in our high school dormitory, wrapped in a blue bedspread. I lived in a dormitory then because of my father. He was a religious man and wanted me to get a spiritual kind of education: to hear the Word and know the Lord, as he put it. So he sent me to St. John's Lutheran Academy in Regina for two years. He was confident, I guess, that's where I'd hear the Word.

Anyway, I can still hear Mrs. Sverdren, our housemother, knocking on the door at midnight and whispering in her Norwegian accent, "Now, Gloria, it iss 12 o'clock. Time to turn off the lights. Right now." Then scuffing down the corridor in her bedroom slippers. What's interesting here is that I don't remember anything about the book itself except that someone in it had a club foot. But it must have moved me deeply when I was sixteen, which is some time ago now.

You can imagine then how distinctly I remember the day Jesus of Nazareth, in person, climbed the hill in our back yard to our house, then up the outside stairs to the sundeck where I was sitting. And how he stayed with me for a while. You can surely understand how clear those details rest in my memory.

The event occurred on Monday morning, September 11, 1972 in Moose Jaw, Saskatchewan. These facts in themselves are more unusual than they may appear to be at first glance. September's my favourite month, Monday my favourite day, morning my favourite time. And although Moose Jaw may not be the most magnificent place in the world, even so, if you happen to be there on a Monday morning in September it has its beauty.

It's not hard to figure out why these are my favourites, by the way. I have five children and a husband. Things get hectic, especially on weekends and holidays. Kids hanging around the house, eating, arguing, asking me every hour what there is to do in Moose Jaw. And television. The programs are always the same; only the names change! Roughriders, Stampeders, Blue Bombers, Whatever. So when school starts in September I bask in freedom, especially on Monday. No quarrels. No TV. The morning, crisp and lovely. A new day. A fresh start.

On the morning of September 11, I got up at 7, the usual time, cooked Cream of Wheat for the kids, fried a bit of sausage for Fred, waved them all out of the house, drank a second cup of coffee in peace, and decided to get at last week's ironing. I wasn't dressed yet but still in the pink kimono I'd bought years ago on my trip to Japan—my one and only overseas trip, a $300 quick tour of Tokyo and other cities. I'd saved for this while working as a library technician in Regina, and I'm glad I did. Since then I've hardly been out of Saskatchewan. Once in a while a trip to Winnipeg, and a few times down to Medicine Lake, Montana, to visit my sister.

I set up the ironing-board and hauled out the basket of week-old sprinkled clothes. When I unrolled the first shirt it was completely dry and smelled stale. The second was covered with little grey blots of mould. So was the third. Fred teaches junior-high science here in Moose Jaw. He uses a lot of shirts. I decided I'd have to unwrap the whole basketful and air everything out. This I did, spreading the pungent garments about the living-room. While they were airing I would go outside and sit on the deck for a while since it was such a clear and sunny day.

If you know Moose Jaw at all, you'll know about the new subdivision at the southeast end called Hillhurst. That's where we live, right on the edge of the city. In fact, our deck looks out on flat land as far as the eye can see, except for the backyard itself, which is a fairly steep hill leading down to a stone quarry. But from the quarry the land straightens out into the Saskatchewan prairie. One clump of poplars stands beyond the quarry to the right, and high weeds have grown up among the rocks. Other than that it's plain—just earth and sky. But when the sun rises new in the morning, weeds and rocks take on an orange and rusty glow that is pleasing. To me at least. I unplugged the iron and returned to the kitchen. I'd take a cup of coffee out there, or maybe some orange juice. To reach the juice at the back of the fridge my hand passed right next to a bottle of dry red Calona. Now here was a better idea. A little wine on Monday morning, a little relaxation after a rowdy weekend. I held the familiar bottle comfortably in my hand and poured, anticipating a pleasant day. I slid open the glass door leading to the deck. I pulled an old canvas folding-chair into the sun, and sat. Sat and sipped. Beauty and tranquillity floated toward me on Monday morning, September 11, around 9:40.

First he was a little bump on the far, far-off prairie. Then he was a mole way beyond the quarry. Then a larger animal, a dog perhaps, moving out there through the grass. Nearing the quarry, he became a person. No doubt about that. A woman perhaps, still in her bathrobe. But edging out from the rocks, through the weeds, toward the hill he was clear to me. I knew then who he was. I knew it just as I knew the sun was shining.

The reason I knew is that he looked exactly the way I'd seen him 5000 times in pictures, in books and Sunday School pamphlets. If there was ever a person I'd seen and heard about, over and over, this was the one. Even in grade school those terrible questions. Do you love the Lord? Are you saved by grace alone through faith? Are you awaiting eagerly the glorious day of his Second Coming? And will you be ready on that Great Day? I'd sometimes hidden under the bed when I was a child, wondering if I really had been saved by grace alone, or, without realizing it, I'd been trying some other method, like the Catholics, who were saved by their good works and would land in hell. Except for a few who knew in their hearts it was really grace, but they didn't want to leave the church because of their relatives. And was this it? Would the trumpet sound tonight and the sky split in two? Would the great Lord and King, Alpha and Omega, holding aloft the seven candlesticks, accompanied by a heavenly host that no man could number, descend from heaven with a mighty shout? And was I ready? Rev. Hanson in his high pulpit in Swift Current, Saskatchewan, roared in my ears and clashed against my eardrums.

And there he was. Coming. Climbing the hill in our backyard, his body bent against the climb, his robes ruffling in the wind. He was coming. And I was not ready. All those mouldy clothes scattered about the living-room, and me in this faded old thing, made in Japan, and drinking—in the middle of the morning. He had reached the steps now. His hand touched the railing. His right hand was on my railing. Jesus' fingers were curled around my railing. He was coming up. He was ascending. He was coming up to me here on the sundeck.

He stood on the top step and looked at me. I looked at him. He looked exactly right, exactly the same as all the pictures: white robe, purple stole, bronze hair, creamy skin. How had all those queer artists, illustrators of Sunday School papers, how had they gotten him exactly right like that?

He stood at the top of the stairs. I sat there holding my glass. What do you say to Jesus when he comes? How do you address him? Do you call him *Jesus?* I supposed that was his first name. Or *Christ? I* remembered the woman at the well, the one living in adultery who'd called him *Sir.* Perhaps I could try that. Or maybe I should pretend not to recognize him. Maybe, for some reason, he didn't mean for me to recognize him. Then he spoke.

"Good morning," he said. "My name is Jesus."

"How do you do," I said. "My name is Gloria Johnson."

My name is Gloria Johnson. That's what I said, all right. As if he didn't know.

He smiled, standing there at the top of the stairs. I thought of what I should do next. Then I got up and unfolded another canvas chair.

"You have a nice view here," he said, leaning back against the canvas and pressing his sandaled feet against the iron bars of the railing.

"Thank you," I said. "We like it."

Nice view. Those were his very words. Everyone who comes to our house and stands on the deck says that. Everyone.

"I wasn't expecting company today." I straightened the folds of my pink kimono and tightened the cloth more securely over my knees. I picked up the glass from the floor where I'd laid it.

"I was passing through on my way to Winnipeg. I thought I'd drop by."

"I've heard a lot about you," I said. "You look quite a bit like your pictures." I raised the glass to my mouth and saw that his hands were empty. I should offer him something to drink. Tea? Milk? How should I ask him what he'd like to drink? What words should I use?

"It gets pretty dusty out there," I finally said. "Would you care for something to drink?" He looked at the glass in my hand. "I could make you some tea," I added.

"Thanks," he said. "What are you drinking?"

"Well, on Mondays I like to relax a bit after the busy weekend with the family all home. I have five children you know. So sometimes after breakfast I have a little wine."

"That would be fine," he said.

By luck I found a clean tumbler in the cupboard. I stood by the sink pouring the wine. And then, like a bolt of lightning, I realized my situation. Oh, Johann Sebastian Bach. Glory. Honour. Wisdom. Power. George Frederick Handel. King of Kings and Lord of Lords. He's on my sundeck. Today he's sitting on my sundeck. I can ask him any question under the sun, anything at all, he'll know the answer. Hallelujah. Well now, wasn't this something for a Monday morning in Moose Jaw.

I opened the fridge door to replace the bottle. And I saw my father. It was New Year's morning. My father was sitting at the kitchen table. Mother sat across from him. She'd covered thc oatmeal pot to let it simmer on the stove. I could hear the lid bumping against the rim, quietly. Sigrid and Freda sat on one side of the table, Raymond and I on the other. We were holding hymn books, little black books turned to page one. It was dark outside. On New Year's morning we got up before sunrise. Daddy was looking at us with his chin pointed out. It meant be still and sit straight. Raymond sat as straight and stiff as a soldier, waiting for Daddy to notice how nice and stiff he sat. We began singing. Page one. Hymn for the New Year. Philipp Nicolai. 1599. We didn't really need the books. We'd sung the same song every New Year's since the time of our conception. Daddy always sang the loudest.

> *The Morning Star upon us gleams:*
> *How full of grace and truth His beams,*
> *How passing fair His splendour.*
> *Good Shepherd, David's proper heir,*
> *My King in heav 'n Thou dost me bear*
> *Upon Thy bosom tender.*
> *Near–est. Dear–est. High–est. Bright–est,*
> *Thou delight–est Still to love me.*
> *Thou so high enthroned a–bove me.*

I didn't mind, actually, singing hymns on New Year's, as long as I was sure no-one else would find out. I'd have been rather embarrassed if any of my friends ever found out how we spent New Year's. It's easy at a certain age to be embarrassed about your family. I remember Alice Olson, how embarrassed she was about her father, Elmer Olson. He was an alcoholic and couldn't control his urine. Her mother always had to clean up after him. Even so, the house smelled. I suppose she couldn't get it all. Anyway, I know Alice was embarrassed when we saw Elmer all tousled and sick-looking, with urine stains on his trousers. Actually, I don't know what would be harder on a kid—having a father who's a drunk, or one who's sober on New Year's and sings *The Morning Star*. I walked across the deck and handed Jesus the wine. I sat down, resting my glass on the flap of my kimono. Jesus was looking out over the prairie. He seemed to be noticing everything out there. He was obviously in no hurry to leave, but he didn't have much to say. I thought of what to say next.

"I suppose you're more used to the sea than to the prairie."

"Yes," he answered. "I've lived most of my life near water. But I like the prairie too. There's something nice about the prairie." He turned his face to the wind, stronger now, coming toward us from the east.

Nice again. If I'd ever used that word to describe the prairie, in an English theme at St. John's, for example, it would have had three red circles around it. At least three. I raised my glass to the wind. Good old St. John's. Good old Pastor Solberg, standing in front of the wooden altar, holding the gospel aloft in his hand.

> *In the beginning wass the Word*
> *And the Word wass with God*
> *And the Word wass God*
> *All things were made by him;*
> *And without him wass not anything made*
> *That wass made.*

I was sitting on a bench by Paul Thorson. We were sharing a hymnal. Our thumbs touched at the centre of the book. It was winter. The chapel was cold—an army barracks left over from World War II. We wore parkas and sat close together. Paul fooled around with his thumb, pushing my thumb to my own side of the book, then pulling it back to his side. The wind howled outside. We watched our breath as we sang the hymn.

> *In thine arms I rest me, Foes who would molest me*
> *Cannot reach me here; Tho the earth be shak–ing,*
> *Ev–ry heart be quak–ing, Jesus calms my fear;*
> *Fires may flash and thunder crash,*
> *Yea, and sin and hell as–sail me,*
> *Jesus will not fai–l me . . . .*

And here he was. Alpha and Omega. The Word. Sitting on my canvas chair, telling me the prairie's nice. What could I say to that?

"I like it too," I said.

Jesus was watching a magpie circling above the poplars just beyond the quarry. He seemed very nice actually, but he wasn't like my father. My father was perfect, mind you, but you know about perfect people—busy, busy. He wasn't as busy as Elsie though. Elsie was the busy one. You could never visit there without her having to do something else at the same time. Wash the leaves of her plants with milk or fold socks in the basement while you sat on a bench by the washing-machine. I wouldn't mind sitting on a bench in the basement if that was all she had, but her living-room was full of big soft chairs that no-one ever sat in. Now Christ here didn't seem to have any work to do at all.

The wind had risen now. His robes puffed about his legs. His hair swirled around his face. I set my glass down and held my kimono together at my knees. The wind was coming stronger now out of the east. My kimono flapped about my ankles. I bent down to secure the bottom, pressing the moving cloth close against my legs. A Saskatchewan wind comes up in a hurry, let me tell you. Then it happened. A gust of wind hit me straight on, seeping into the folds of my kimono, reaching down into the bodice, billowing the cloth out, until above the sash, the robe was fully open. I knew without looking. The wind was suddenly blowing on my breasts. I felt it cool on both my breasts. Then as quickly as it came, it left, and we sat in the small breeze of before.

I looked at Jesus. He was looking at me. And at my breasts. Looking right at them. Jesus was sitting there on the sundeck, looking at my breasts.

What should I do? Say excuse me and push them back into my kimono? Make a little joke of it? Look what the wind blew in, or something? Or should I say nothing? Just tuck them in as inconspicuously as possible? What do you say when a wind comes up and blows your kimono open and he sees your breasts?

Now, there are ways and there are ways of exposing your breasts. I know a few things. I read books. And I've learned a lot from my cousin Millie. Millie's the black sheep in the family. She left the Academy without graduating to become an artist's model in Winnipeg. A dancer too. Anyway, Millie's told me a few things about body exposure. She says, for instance, that when an artist wants to draw his model he has her either completely nude and stretching and bending in various positions so he can sketch her from different angles. Or he drapes her with cloth, satin usually. He covers one portion of the body with the material and leaves the rest exposed. But he does so in a graceful manner, draping the cloth over her stomach or ankle. Never over the breasts. So I realized that my appearance right then wasn't actually pleasing, either aesthetically or erotically—from Millie's point of view. My breasts were just sticking out from the top of my old kimono. And for some reason that I certainly can't explain, even to this day, I did nothing about it. I just sat there.

Jesus must have recognized my confusion, because right then he said, quite sincerely I thought, "You have nice breasts."

"Thanks," I said. I didn't know what else to say, so I asked him if he'd like more wine.

"Yes, I would," he said, and I left to refill the glass. When I returned he was watching the magpie swishing about in the tall weeds of the quarry. I sat down and watched with him.

Then I got a very, very peculiar sensation. I know it was just an illusion, but it was so strong it scared me. It's hard to explain because nothing like it had ever happened to me before. The magpie began to float toward Jesus. I saw it fluttering toward him in the air as if some vacuum were sucking it in. When it reached him, it flapped about on his chest, which was bare now because the top of his robe had slipped down. It nibbled at his little brown nipples and squawked and disappeared. For all the world, it seemed to disappear right into his pores. Then the same thing happened with a rock. A rock floating up from the quarry and landing on the breast of Jesus, melting into his skin. It was very strange, let me tell you, Jesus and I sitting there together with that happening. It made me dizzy, so I closed my eyes.

I saw the women in a public bath in Tokyo. Black-haired women and children. Some were squatting by faucets that lined a wall. They were running hot water into their basins, washing themselves with white cloths, rubbing each other's backs with the soapy washcloths, then emptying their basins and filling them again, pouring clean water over their bodies for the rinse. Water and suds swirled about on the tiled floor. Others were sitting in the hot pool on the far side, soaking themselves in the steamy water as they jabbered away to one another. Then I saw her. The woman without the breasts. She was squatting by a faucet near the door. The oldest woman I've ever seen. The thinnest woman I've ever witnessed. Skin and bones. Literally. Just skin and bones. She bowed and smiled at everyone who entered. She had three teeth. When she hunched over her basin, I saw the little creases of skin where her breasts had been. When she stood up the wrinkles disappeared. In their place were two shallow caves. Even the nipples seemed to have disappeared into the small brown caves of her breasts.

I opened my eyes and looked at Jesus. Fortunately, everything had stopped floating.

"Have you ever been to Japan?" I asked.

"Yes," he said, "a few times."

I paid no attention to his answer but went on telling him about Japan as if he'd never been there. I couldn't seem to stop talking about that old woman and her breasts.

"You should have seen her," I said. "She wasn't flat-chested like some women even here in Moose Jaw. It wasn't like that at all. Her breasts weren't just flat. They were caved in, as if the flesh had sunk right there. Have you ever seen breasts like that before?"

Jesus' eyes were getting darker. He seemed to have sunk farther down into his chair.

"Japanese women have smaller breasts to begin with, usually," he said.

But he'd misunderstood me. It wasn't just her breasts that held me. It was her jaws, teeth, neck, ankles, heels. Not just her breasts. I said nothing for a while. Jesus, too, was not talking.

Finally I asked, "Well, what do you think of breasts like that?"

I knew immediately that I'd asked the wrong question. If you want personal and specific answers, you ask personal and specific questions. It's as simple as that. I should have asked him, for instance, what he thought of them from a sexual point of view. If he were a lover, let's say, would he like to hold such breasts in his hand and play on them with his teeth and fingers? Would he now? The woman, brown and shiny, was bending over her basin. Tiny bubbles of soap drifted from the creases of her chest down to her navel. Hold them. Ha.

Or I could have asked for some kind of aesthetic opinion. If he were an artist, a sculptor, let's say, would he travel to Italy and spend weeks excavating the best marble from the hills near Florence, and then would he stay up night and day in his studio, without eating or bathing, and with matted hair and glazed eyes, chisel out those little creases from his great stone slab?

Or if he were a curator in a large museum in Paris, would he place these wrinkles on a silver pedestal in the centre of the foyer?

Or if he were a patron of the arts, would he attend the opening of this grand exhibition and stand in front of these white caves in his purple turtleneck, sipping champagne and nibbling on the little cracker with the shrimp in the middle, and would he turn to the one beside him, the one in the sleek black pants, and would he say to her, "Look, darling. Did you see this marvellous piece? Do you see how the artist has captured the very essence of the female form?"

These are some of the things I could have said if I'd had my wits about me. But my wits certainly left me that day. All I did say, and I didn't mean to—it just came out—was, "It's not nice and I don't like it."

I lifted my face, threw my head back, and let the wind blow on my neck and breasts. It was blowing harder again. I felt small grains of sand scrape against my skin.

Jesus lover of my soul, let me to thy bosom fly.
While the nearer waters roll, while the tempest
still is nigh . . . .

When I looked at him again, his eyes were blacker still and his body had shrunk considerably. He looked almost like Jimmy that time in Prince Albert. Jimmy's an old neighbour from Regina. On his twenty-seventh birthday he joined a motorcycle gang, The Grim Reapers to be exact, and got into a lot of trouble. He ended up in maximum security in PA. One summer on a camping trip up north we stopped to see him—Fred and the kids and I. It wasn't a good visit, by the way. If you're going to visit inmates you should do it regularly. I realize this now. Anyway, that's when his eyes looked black like that. But maybe he'd been smoking. It's probably not the same thing. Jimmy Lebrun. He never did think it was funny when I'd call him a Midnight Raider instead of a Grim Reaper. People are sensitive about their names.

Then Jesus finally answered. Everything seemed to take him a long time, even answering simple questions.

But I'm not sure what he said because something so strange happened that whatever he did say was swept away. Right then the wind blew against my face, pulling my hair back. My kimono swirled about every which way, and I was swinging my arms in the air, like swimming. And there right below my eyes was the roof of our house. I was looking down on the top of the roof. I saw the row of shingles ripped loose from the August hail storm. And I remember thinking—Fred hasn't fixed those shingles yet. I'll have to remind him when he gets home from work. If it rains again the back bedroom will get soaked. Before I knew it I was circling over the sundeck, looking down on the top of Jesus' head. Only I wasn't. I was sitting in the canvas chair watching myself hover over his shoulders. Only it wasn't me hovering. It was the old woman in Tokyo. I saw her grey hair twisting in the wind and her shiny little bum raised in the air, like a baby's. Water was dripping from her chin and toes. And soap bubbles trailed from her elbows like tinsel. She was floating down toward his chest. Only it wasn't her. It was me. I could taste bits of suds sticking to the corners of my mouth and feel the wind on my wet back and in the hollow caves of my breasts. I was smiling and bowing, and the wind was blowing in narrow wisps against my toothless gums. Then quickly, so quickly, like a flock of waxwings diving through snow into the branches of the poplar, I was splitting up into millions and millions of pieces and sinking into the tiny, tiny holes in his chest. It was like the magpie and the rock, like I had come apart into atoms or molecules, or whatever it is we really are.

After that I was dizzy. I began to feel nauseated, there on my canvas chair. Jesus looked sick too. Sad and sick and lonesome. Oh, Christ, I thought, why are we sitting here on such a fine day pouring our sorrows into each other? I had to get up and walk around. I'd go into the kitchen and make some tea. I put the kettle on to boil. What on earth had gotten into me? Why had I spent this perfectly good morning talking about breasts? My one chance in a lifetime and I'd let it go. Why didn't I have better control? Why was I always letting things get out of hand? *Breasts.* And why was my name Gloria? Such a pious name for one who can't think of anything else to talk about but breasts. Why wasn't it Lucille? Or Millie? You could talk about breasts all day if your name was Millie. But Gloria. Gloria. Glo-o-o-o-o-o-o-oria. I knew then why so many Glorias hang around bars, talking too loud, laughing shrilly at stupid jokes, making sure everyone hears them laugh at the dirty jokes. They're just trying to live down their name, that's all. I brought out the cups and poured the tea. Everything was back to normal when I returned except that Jesus still looked desolate sitting there in my canvas chair. I handed him the tea and sat down beside him.

Oh, Daddy. And Phillip Nicolai. Oh, Bernard of Clairvoux. Oh, Sacred Head Now Wounded. Go away for a little while and let us sit together quietly, here in this small space under the sun.

I sipped the tea and watched his face. He looked so sorrowful I reached out and put my hand on his wrist. I sat there a long while, rubbing the little hairs on his wrist with my fingers. I couldn't help it. After that he put his arm on my shoulder and his hand on the back of my neck, stroking the muscles there. It felt good. Whenever anything exciting or unusual happens to me, my neck is the first to feel it. It gets stiff and knotted up. Then I usually get a headache, and frequently I become nauseous. So it felt very good having my neck rubbed.

I've never been able to handle sensation very well. I remember when I was in grade three and my folks took us to the Saskatoon Exhibition. We went to see the grandstand show—the battle of Wolfe and Montcalm on the Plains of Abraham. The stage was filled with Indians and pioneers and ladies in red, white and blue dresses, singing "In Days of Yore From Britain's Shore." It was very spectacular but too much for me. My stomach was upset and my neck ached. I had to keep my head on my mother's lap the whole time, just opening my eyes once in a while so I wouldn't miss everything.

So it felt really good having my neck stroked like that. I could almost feel the knots untying and my body becoming warmer and more restful. Jesus too seemed to be feeling better. His body was back to normal. His eyes looked natural again.

Then, all of a sudden, he started to laugh. He held his hand on my neck and laughed out loud. I don't know to this day what he was laughing about. There was nothing funny there at all. But hearing him made me laugh too. I couldn't stop. He was laughing so hard he spilled the tea over his purple stole. When I saw that I laughed even harder. I'd never thought of Jesus spilling his tea before. And when Jesus saw me laugh so hard and when he looked at my breasts shaking, he laughed harder still, till he wiped tears from his eyes.

After that we just sat there. I don't know how long. I know we watched the magpie carve black waves in the air above the rocks. And the rocks stiff and lovely among the swaying weeds. We watched the poplars twist and bend and rise again beyond the quarry. And then he had to leave.

"Goodbye, Gloria Johnson," he said, rising from his chair. "Thanks for the hospitality."

He leaned over and kissed me on my mouth. Then he flicked my nipple with his finger, and off he went. Down the hill, through the quarry, and into the prairie. I stood on the sundeck and watched. I watched until I could see him no longer, until he was only some dim and ancient star on the far horizon.

I went inside the house. Well, now, wasn't that a nice visit. Wasn't that something. I examined the clothes, dry and sour in the living-room. I'd have to put them back in the wash, that's all. I couldn't stand the smell. I tucked my breasts back into my kimono and lugged the basket downstairs.

That's what happened to me in Moose Jaw in 1972. It was the main thing that happened to me that year.

Meneseteung

•

Alice Munro

I

Columbine, bloodroot,
And wild bergamot,
Gathering armfuls,
Giddily we go.

Offerings the book is called. Gold lettering on a dull-blue cover. The author's full name underneath: Almeda Joynt Roth. The local paper, the *Vidette*, referred to her as "our poetess." There seems to be a mixture of respect and contempt, both for her calling and for her sex—or for their predictable conjuncture. In the front of the book is a photograph, with the photographer's name in one corner, and the date: 1865. The book was published later, in 1873.

The poetess has a long face; a rather long nose; full, sombre dark eyes, which seem ready to roll down her cheeks like giant tears; a lot of dark hair gathered around her face in droopy rolls and curtains. A streak of gray hair plain to see, although she is, in this picture, only twenty-five. Not a pret-

ty girl but the sort of woman who may age well, who probably won't get fat. She wears a tucked and braid-trimmed dark
dress or jacket, with a lacy, floppy arrangement of white
material—frills or a bow—filling the deep V at the neck. She
also wears a hat, which might be made of velvet, in a dark
color to match the dress. It's the untrimmed, shapeless hat,
something like a soft beret, that makes me see artistic intentions, or at least a shy and stubborn eccentricity, in this
young woman, whose long neck and forward-inclining head
indicate as well that she is tall and slender and somewhat
awkward. From the waist up, she looks like a young noble-
man of another century. But perhaps it was the fashion.

"In 1854," she writes in the preface to her book, "my
father brought us—my mother, my sister Catherine, my
brother William, and me—to the wilds of Canada West (as it
then was). My father was a harness-maker by trade, but a cul-
tivated man who could quote by heart from the Bible,
Shakespeare, and the writings of Edmund Burke. He pros-
pered in this newly opened land and was able to set up a
harness and leather-goods store, and after a year to build the
comfortable house in which I live (alone) today. I was fourteen years old, the eldest of the children, when we came into
this country from Kingston, a town whose handsome
streets I have not seen again but often remember. My sister
was eleven and my brother nine. The third summer that we
lived here, my brother and sister were taken ill of a prevalent
fever and died within a few days of each other. My dear
mother did not regain her spirits after this blow to our family. Her health declined, and after another three years she
died. I then became housekeeper to my father and was
happy to make his home for twelve years, until he died suddenly one morning at his shop.

"From my earliest years I have delighted in verse and
I have occupied myself—and sometimes allayed my griefs,
which have been no more, I know, than any sojourner on

earth must encounter—with many floundering efforts at its composition. My fingers, indeed, were always too clumsy for crochetwork, and those dazzling productions of embroidery which one sees often today—the overflowing fruit and flower baskets, the little Dutch boys, the bonneted maidens with their watering cans—have like-wise proved to be beyond my skill. So I offer instead, as the product of my leisure hours, these rude posies, these ballads couplets, reflections."

Titles of some of the poems: "Children at Their Games," "The Gypsy Fair," "A Visit to My Family," "Angels in the Snow," "Champlain at the Mouth of the Meneseteung," "The Passing of the Old Forest," and "A Garden Medley." There are other, shorter poems, about birds and wildflowers and snowstorms. There is some comically intentioned doggerel about what people are thinking about as they listen to the sermon in church.

"Children at Their Games": The writer, a child, is playing with her brother and sister—one of those games in which children on different sides try to entice and catch each other. She plays on in the deepening twilight, until she realizes that she is alone, and much older. Still she hears the (ghostly) voices of her brother and sister calling. *Come over, come over, let Meda come over.* (Perhaps Almeda was called Meda in the family, or perhaps she shortened her name to fit the poem.)

"The Gypsy Fair": The Gypsies have an encampment near the town, a "fair," where they sell cloth and trinkets, and the writer as a child is afraid that she may be stolen by them, taken away from her family. Instead, her family has been taken away from her, stolen by Gypsies she can't locate or bargain with.

"A Visit to My Family": A visit to the cemetery, a one-sided conversation.

"Angels in the Snow": The writer once taught her

brother and sister to make "angels" by lying down in the snow and moving their arms to create wing shapes. Her brother always jumped up carelessly, leaving an angel with a crippled wing. Will this be made perfect in Heaven, or will he be flying with his own makeshift, in circles?

"Champlain at the Mouth of the Meneseteung": This poem celebrates the popular, untrue belief that the explorer sailed down the eastern shore of Lake Huron and landed at the mouth of the major river.

"The Passing of the Old Forest": A list of the trees—their names, appearance, and uses—that were cut down in the original forest, with a general description of the bears, wolves, eagles, deer, waterfowl.

"A Garden Medley": Perhaps planned as a companion to the forest poem. Catalogue of plants brought from European countries, with bits of history and legend attached, and final Canadianness resulting from this mixture.

The poems are written in quatrains or couplets. There are a couple of attempts at sonnets, but mostly the rhyme scheme is simple—*a b a b* or *a b c b*. The rhyme used is what was once called "masculine" ("shore"/"before"), though once in a while it is "feminine" ("quiver"/"river"). Are those terms familiar anymore? No poem is unrhymed.

II

> White roses cold as snow
> Bloom where those "'angels'" lie.
> Do they but rest below
> Or, in God's wonder, fly?

In 1879, Almeda Roth was still living in the house at the corner of Pearl and Dufferin streets, the house her father had built for his family. The house is there today; the manager of the liquor store lives in it. It's covered with aluminum siding; a closed-in porch has replaced the veranda. The woodshed, the fence, the gates, the privy, the barn—all these are gone. A photograph taken in the eighteen-eighties shows them all in place. The house and fence look a little shabby, in need of paint, but perhaps that is just because of the bleached-out look of the brownish photograph. The lace-curtained windows look like white eyes. No big shade tree is in sight, and, in fact, the tall elms that overshadowed the town until the nineteen-fifties, as well as the maples that shade it now, are skinny young trees with rough fences around them to protect them from the cows. Without the shelter of those trees, there is a great exposure—back yards, clotheslines, woodpiles, patchy sheds and barns and privies—all bare, exposed, provisional-looking. Few houses would have anything like a lawn, just a patch of plantains and anthills and raked dirt. Perhaps petunias growing on top of a stump, in a round box. Only the main street is gravelled; the other streets are dirt roads, muddy or dusty according to season. Yards must be fenced to keep animals out. Cows are tethered in vacant lots or pastured in back yards, but sometimes they get loose. Pigs get loose, too, and dogs roam free or nap in a lordly way on the boardwalks. The town has taken root, it's not going to vanish, yet it still has some of the look of an encampment. And, like an encampment, it's busy all the time—full of people, who, within the town, usually walk wherever they're going; full of animals, which leave horse buns, cow pats, dog turds that ladies have to hitch up their skirts for; full of the noise of building and of drivers shouting at their horses and of the trains that come in several times a day.

I read about that life in the *Vidette*.

The population is younger than it is now, than it will ever be again. People past fifty usually don't come to a raw, new place. There are quite a few people in the cemetery already, but most of them died young, in accidents or child-birth or epidemics. It's youth that's in evidence in town. Children—boys—rove through the streets in gangs. School is compulsory for only four months a year, and there are lots of occasional jobs that even a child of eight or nine can do—pulling flax, holding horses, delivering groceries, sweeping the boardwalk in front of stores. A good deal of time they spend looking for adventures. One day they follow an old woman, a drunk nicknamed Queen Aggie. They get her into a wheelbarrow and trundle her all over town, then dump her into a ditch to sober her up. They also spend a lot of time around the railway station. They jump on shunting cars and dart between them and dare each other to take chances, which once in a while result in their getting maimed or killed. And they keep an eye out for any strangers coming into town. They follow them, offer to carry their bags. and direct them (for a five-cent piece) to a hotel. Strangers who don't look so prosperous are taunted and tormented. Speculation surrounds all of them—it's like a cloud of flies. Are they coming to town to start up a new business, to per-suade people to invest in some scheme, to sell cures or gim-micks, to preach on the street corners? All these things are possible any day of the week. Be on your guard, the *Vidette* tells people. These are times of opportunity and danger. Tramps, confidence men, hucksters, shysters, plain thieves are travelling the roads, and particularly the railroads. Thefts are announced: money invested and never seen again, a pair of trousers taken from the clothesline, wood from the woodpile, eggs from the henhouse. Such incidents increase in the hot weather.

Hot weather brings accidents, too. More horses run wild then, upsetting buggies. Hands caught in the wringer while doing the washing, a man lopped in two at the sawmill, a leaping boy killed in a fall of lumber at the lum-beryard. Nobody sleeps well. Babies wither with summer complaint, and fat people can't catch their breath. Bodies must be buried in a hurry. One day a man goes through the streets ringing a cowbell and calling, "Repent! Repent!" It's not a stranger this time, it's a young man who works at the butcher shop. Take him home, wrap him in cold wet cloths, give him some nerve medicine, keep him in bed, pray for his wits. If he doesn't recover, he must go to the asylum.

Almeda Roth's house faces on Dufferin Street, which is a street of considerable respectability. On this street, merchants, a mill owner, an operator of salt wells have their houses. But Pearl Street, which her back windows overlook and her back gate opens onto, is another story. Workmen's houses are adjacent to hers. Small but decent row houses—that is all right. Things deteriorate toward the end of the block, and the next, last one becomes dismal. Nobody but the poorest people, the unrespectable and undeserving poor, would live there at the edge of a boghole (drained since then), called the Pearl Street Swamp. Bushy and luxuriant weeds grow there, makeshift shacks have been put up, there are piles of refuse and debris and crowds of runty children, slops are flung from doorways. The town tries to compel these people to build privies, but they would just as soon go in the bushes. If a gang of boys goes down there in search of adventure, it's likely they'll get more than they bargained for. It is said that even the town constable won't go down Pearl Street on a Saturday night. Almeda Roth has never walked past the row housing. In one of those houses lives the young girl Annie, who helps her with her housecleaning. That young girl herself, being a decent girl, has never walked down to the last block or the swamp. No decent woman ever would.

But that same swamp, lying to the east of Almeda Roth's house, presents a fine sight at dawn. Almeda sleeps at the back of the house. She keeps to the same bedroom she once shared with her sister Catherine she would not think of moving to the large front bedroom, where her mother used to lie in bed all day, and which was later the solitary domain of her father. From her window she can see the sun rising, the swamp mist filling with light, the bulky, nearest trees floating against that mist and the trees behind turning transparent. Swamp oaks, soft maples, tamarack, bitternut.

III

Here where the river meets the inland sea,
Spreading her blue skirts from the solemn wood,
I think of birds and beasts and vanished men,
Whose pointed dwellings on these pale sands stood.

One of the strangers who arrived at the railway station a few years ago was Jarvis Poulter, who now occupies the next house to Almeda Roth's—separated from hers by a vacant lot, which he has bought, on Dufferin Street. The house is plainer than the Roth house and has no fruit trees or flowers planted around it. It is understood that this is a natural result of Jarvis Poulter's being a widower and living alone. A man may keep his house decent, but he will never—if he is a proper man—do much to decorate it. Marriage forces him to live with more ornament as well as sentiment, and it protects him, also, from the extremities of his own nature—from a frigid parsimony or a luxuriant sloth, from squalor, and from excessive sleeping or reading, drinking, smoking, or freethinking.

In the interests of economy, it is believed, a certain estimable gentleman of our town persists in fetching water from the public tap and supplementing his fuel supply by picking up the loose coal along the railway track. Does he think to repay the town or the railway company with a supply of free salt?

This is the *Vidette,* full of shy jokes, innuendo, plain accusation that no newspaper would get away with today. It's Jarvis Poulter they're talking about—though in other passages he is spoken of with great respect, as a civil magistrate, an employer, a churchman. He is close, that's all. An eccentric, to a degree. All of which may be a result of his single condition, his widower's life. Even carrying his water from the town tap and filling his coal pail along the railway track. This is a decent citizen, prosperous: a tall—slightly paunchy?—man in a dark suit with polished boots. A beard? Black hair streaked with gray. A severe and self-possessed air, and a large pale wart among the bushy hairs of one eyebrow? People talk about a young, pretty, beloved wife, dead in childbirth or some horrible accident, like a house fire or a railway disaster. There is no ground for this, but it adds interest. All he has told them is that his wife is dead.

He came to this part of the country looking for oil. The first oil well in the world was sunk in Lambton County, south of here, in the eighteen-fifties. Drilling for oil, Jarvis Poulter discovered salt. He set to work to make the most of that. When he walks home from church with Almeda Roth, he tells her about his salt wells. They are twelve hundred feet deep. Heated water is pumped down into them, and that dissolves the salt. Then the brine is pumped to the surface. It is poured into great evaporator pans over slow, steady fires, so that the water is steamed off and the pure, excellent salt remains. A commodity for which the demand will never fail.

"The salt of the earth," Almeda says.

"Yes," he says, frowning. He may think this disrespectful. She did not intend it so. He speaks of competitors in other towns who are following his lead and trying to hog the market. Fortunately, their wells are not drilled so deep, or their evaporating is not done so efficiently. There is salt everywhere under this land, but it is not so easy to come by as some people think.

Does this not mean, Almeda says, that there was once a great sea?

Very likely, Jarvis Poulter says. Very likely. He goes on to tell her about other enterprises of his—a brickyard, a limekiln. And he explains to her how this operates, and where the good clay is found. He also owns two farms, whose woodlots supply the fuel for his operations.

Among the couples strolling home from church on a recent, sunny Sabbath morning we noted a certain salty gentleman and literary lady, not perhaps in their first youth but by no means blighted by the frosts of age. May we surmise?

This kind of thing pops up in the *Vidette* all the time.

May they surmise, and is this courting? Almeda Roth has a bit of money, which her father left her, and she has her house. She is not too old to have a couple of children. She is a good enough housekeeper, with the tendency toward fancy iced cakes and decorated tarts that is seen fairly often in old maids. (Honorable mention at the Fall Fair.) There is nothing wrong with her looks, and naturally she is in better shape than most married women of her age, not having been loaded down with work and children. But why was she passed over in her earlier, more marriageable years, in a place that needs women to be partnered and fruitful? She was a rather gloomy girl—that may have been the trouble. The deaths of her brother and sister, and then of her mother, who lost her reason, in fact, a year before she died, and lay in her bed talking nonsense—those weighed on her, so she was not lively company. And all that reading and poetry—it seemed more of a drawback, a barrier, an obsession, in the young girl than in the middle-aged woman, who needed something, after all, to fill her time. Anyway, it's five years since her book was published, so perhaps she has got over that. Perhaps it was the proud, bookish father encouraging her?

Everyone takes it for granted that Almeda Roth is thinking of Jarvis Poulter as a husband and would say yes if he asked her. And she is thinking of him. She doesn't want to get her hopes up too much, she doesn't want to make a fool of herself. She would like a signal. If he attended church on Sunday evenings, there would be a chance, during some months of the year, to walk home after dark. He would carry a lantern. (There is as yet no street lighting in town.) He would swing the lantern to light the way in front of the lady's feet and observe their narrow and delicate shape. He might catch her arm as they step off the board-walk. But he does not go to church at night.

Nor does he call for her, and walk with her to church on Sunday mornings. That would be a declaration. He walks her home, past his gate as far as hers; he lifts his hat then and leaves her. She does not invite him to come in—a woman living alone could never do such a thing. As soon as a man and woman of almost any age are alone together within four walls, it is assumed that anything may happen. Spontaneous combustion, instant fornication, an attack of passion. Brute instinct, triumph of the senses. What possibilities men and women must see in each other to infer such dangers. Or, believing in the dangers, how often they must think about the possibilities.

When they walk side by side, she can smell his shaving soap, the barber's oil, his pipe tobacco, the wool and linen and leather smell of his manly clothes. The correct, orderly, heavy clothes are like those she used to brush and starch and iron for her father. She misses that job—her father's appreciation, his dark, kind authority. Jarvis Poulter's garments, his smell, his movements all cause the skin on the side of her body next to him to tingle hopeful-

ly, and a meek shiver raises the hairs on her arms. Is this to
be taken as a sign of love? She thinks of him coming into
her—*their*—bedroom in his long underwear and his hat. She
knows this outfit is ridiculous, but in her mind he does not
look so; he has the solemn effrontery of a figure in a
dream. He comes into the room and lies down on the bed
beside her, preparing to take her in his arms. Surely he
removes his hat? She doesn't know, for at this point a fit of
welcome and submission overtakes her, a buried gasp. He
would be her husband.

One thing she has noticed about married women,
and that is how many of them have to go about creating
their husbands. They have to start ascribing preferences,
opinions, dictatorial ways. Oh, yes, they say, my husband is
very particular. He won't touch turnips. He won't eat fried
meat. (Or he will only eat fried meat.) He likes me to wear
blue (brown) all the time. He can't stand organ music. He
hates to see a woman go out bareheaded. He would kill me
if I took one puff of tobacco. This way, bewildered, side-
long-looking men are made over, made into husbands,
heads of households. Almeda Roth cannot imagine herself
doing that. She wants a man who doesn't have to be made,
who is firm already and determined and mysterious to her.
She does not look for companionship. Men except for her
father—seem to her deprived in some way, incurious. No
doubt that is necessary, so that they will do what they have
to do. Would she herself, knowing that there was salt in the
earth, discover how to get it out and sell it? Not likely. She
would be thinking about the ancient sea. That kind of speculation is what Jarvis Poulter has, quite properly, no time
for.

Instead of calling for her and walking her to church,
Jarvis Poulter might make another, more venturesome declaration. He could hire a horse and take her for a drive out to
the country. If he did this, she would be both glad and

sorry. Glad to be beside him, driven by him, receiving this attention from him in front of the world. And sorry to have the countryside removed for her— filmed over, in a way, by his talk and preoccupations. The countryside that she has written about in her poems actually takes diligence and determination to see. Some things must be disregarded. Manure piles, of course, and boggy fields full of high, charred stumps, and great heaps of brush waiting for a good day for burning. The meandering creeks have been straightened, turned into ditches with high, muddy banks. Some of the crop fields and pasture fields are fenced with big, clumsy uprooted stumps; others are held in a crude stitchery of rail fences. The trees have all been cleared back to the woodlots. And the woodlots are all second growth. No trees along the roads or lanes or around the farmhouses, except a few that are newly planted, young and weedy-looking. Clusters of log barns—the grand barns that are to dominate the countryside for the next hundred years are just beginning to be built—and mean-looking log houses, and every four or five miles a ragged little settlement with a church and school and store and a blacksmith shop. A raw countryside just wrenched from the forest, but swarming with people. Every hundred acres is a farm, every farm has a family, most families have ten or twelve children. (This is the country that will send out wave after wave of settlers— it's already starting to send them—to northern Ontario and the West.) It's true that you can gather wildflowers in spring in the woodlots, but you'd have to walk through herds of horned cows to get to them.

IV

The Gypsies have departed.
Their camping-ground is bare.
Oh, boldly would I bargain now

At the Gypsy Fair.

Almeda suffers a good deal from sleeplessness, and the doctor has given her bromides and nerve medicine. She takes the bromides, but the drops gave her dreams that were too vivid and disturbing, so she has put the bottle by for an emergency. She told the doctor her eyeballs felt dry, like hot glass, and her joints ached. Don't read so much, he said, don't study; get yourself good and tired out with housework, take exercise. He believes that her troubles would clear up if she got married. He believes this in spite of the fact that most of his nerve medicine is prescribed for married women.

So Almeda cleans house and helps clean the church, she lends a hand to friends who are wallpapering or getting ready for a wedding, she bakes one of her famous cakes for the Sunday-school picnic. On a hot Saturday in August, she decides to make some grape jelly. Little jars of grape jelly will make fine Christmas presents, or offerings to the sick. But she started late in the day and the jelly is not made by nightfall. In fact, the hot pulp has just been dumped into the cheesecloth bag to strain out the juice. Almeda drinks some tea and eats a slice of cake with butter (a childish indulgence of hers), and that's all she wants for supper. She washes her hair at the sink and sponges off her body to be clean for Sunday. She doesn't light a lamp. She lies down on the bed with the window wide open and a sheet just up to her waist, and she does feel wonderfully tired. She can even feel a little breeze.

When she wakes up, the night seems fiery hot and full of threats. She lies sweating on her bed, and she has the impression that the noises she hears are knives and saws and axes—all angry implements chopping and jabbing and boring within her head: But it isn't true. As she comes further awake, she recognizes the sounds that she has heard sometimes before the fracas of a summer Saturday night on Pearl Street. Usually the noise centers on a fight. People are drunk, there is a lot of protest and encouragement concerning the fight, somebody will scream, "Murder!" Once, there was a murder. But it didn't happen in a fight. An old man was stabbed to death in his shack, perhaps for a few dollars he kept in the mattress.

She gets out of bed and goes to the window. The night sky is clear, with no moon and with bright stars. Pegasus hangs straight ahead, over the swamp. Her father taught her that constellation—automatically, she counts its stars. Now she can make out distinct voices, individual contributions to the row. Some people, like herself, have evidently been wakened from sleep. "Shut up!" they are yelling. "Shut up that caterwauling or I'm going to come down and tan the arse off yez!"

But nobody shuts up. It's as if there were a ball of fire rolling up Pearl Street, shooting off sparks—only the fire is noise; it's yells and laughter and shrieks and curses, and the sparks are voices that shoot off alone. Two voices gradually distinguish themselves—a rising and falling howling cry and a steady throbbing, low-pitched stream of abuse that contains all those words which Almeda associates with danger and depravity and foul smells and disgusting sights. Someone—the person crying out, "Kill me! Kill me now!"—is being beaten. A woman is being beaten. She keeps crying, "Kill me! Kill me!" and sometimes her mouth seems choked with blood. Yet there is something taunting and triumphant about her cry. There is something theatrical about it. And the people around are calling out, "Stop it! Stop that!" or "Kill her! Kill her!" in a frenzy, as if at the theatre or a sporting match or a prizefight. Yes, thinks Almeda, she has noticed that before it is always partly a charade with these people; there is a clumsy sort of parody, an exaggeration, a missed connection. As if anything they did—even a murder—

might be something they didn't quite believe but were powerless to stop.

Now there is the sound of something thrown—a chair, a plank?—and of a woodpile or part of a fence giving way. A lot of newly surprised cries, the sound of running, people getting out of the way, and the commotion has come much closer. Almeda can see a figure in a light dress, bent over and running. That will be the woman. She has got hold of something like a stick of wood or a shingle, and she turns and flings it at the darker figure running after her.

"Ah, go get her!" the voices cry. "Go baste her one!"

Many fall back now; just the two figures come on and grapple, and break loose again, and finally fall down against Almeda's fence. The sound they make becomes very confused—gagging, vomiting, grunting, pounding. Then a long, vibrating, choking sound of pain and self-abasement, self-abandonment, which could come from either or both of them.

Almeda has backed away from the window and sat down on the bed. Is that the sound of murder she has heard? What is to be done, what is she to do? She must light a lantern, she must go downstairs and light a lantern—she must go out into the yard, she must go downstairs. Into the yard. The lantern. She falls over on her bed and pulls the pillow to her face. In a minute. The stairs, the lantern. She sees herself already down there, in the back hall, drawing the bolt of the back door. She falls asleep.

She wakes, startled, in the early light. She thinks there is a big crow sitting on her windowsill, talking in a disapproving but unsurprised way about the events of the night before. "Wake up and move the wheelbarrow!" it says to her, scolding, and she understands that it means something else by "wheelbarrow"— something foul and sorrowful. Then she is awake and sees that there is no such bird. She gets up at once and looks out the window.

Down against her fence there is a pale lump pressed—a body.

Wheelbarrow.

She puts a wrapper over her nightdress and goes downstairs. The front rooms are still shadowy, the blinds down in the kitchen. Something goes *plop, plup,* in a leisurely, censorious way, reminding her of the conversation of the crow. It's just the grape juice, straining overnight. She pulls the bolt and goes out the back door. Spiders have draped their webs over the doorway in the night, and the hollyhocks are drooping, heavy with dew. By the fence, she parts the sticky hollyhocks and looks down and she can see.

A woman's body heaped up there, turned on her side with her face squashed down into the earth. Almeda can't see her face. But there is a bare breast let loose, brown nipple pulled long like a cow's teat, and a bare haunch and leg, the haunch showing a bruise as big as a sunflower. The unbruised skin is grayish, like a plucked, raw drumstick. Some kind of nightgown or all-purpose dress she has on. Smelling of vomit. Urine, drink, vomit.

Barefoot, in her nightgown and flimsy wrapper, Almeda runs away. She runs around the side of her house between the apple trees and the veranda; she opens the front gate and flees down Dufferin Street to Jarvis Poulter's house, which is the nearest to hers. She slaps the flat of her hand many times against the door.

"There is the body of a woman," she says when Jarvis Poulter appears at last. He is in his dark trousers, held up with braces, and his shirt is half unbuttoned, his face unshaven, his hair standing up on his head. "Mr. Poulter, excuse me. A body of a woman. At my back gate."

He looks at her fiercely. "Is she dead?"

His breath is dank, his face creased, his eyes bloodshot.

"Yes. I think murdered," says Almeda. She can see a

little of his cheerless front hall. His hat on a chair. "In the night I woke up. I heard a racket down on Pearl Street," she says, struggling to keep her voice low and sensible. "I could hear this—pair. I could hear a man and a woman fighting."

He picks up his hat and puts it on his head. He closes and locks the front door, and puts the key in his pocket. They walk along the boardwalk and she sees that she is in her bare feet. She holds back what she feels a need to say next—that she is responsible, she could have run out with a lantern, she could have screamed (but who needed more screams?), she could have beat the man off. She could have run for help then, not now.

They turn down Pearl Street, instead of entering the Roth yard. Of course the body is still there. Hunched up, half bare, the same as before. Jarvis Poulter doesn't hurry or halt. He walks straight over to the body and looks down at it, nudges the leg with the toe of his boot, just as you'd nudge a dog or a sow.

"You," he says, not too loudly but firmly, and nudges again.

Almeda tastes bile at the back of her throat.

"Alive," says Jarvis Poulter, and the woman confirms this. She stirs, she grunts weakly.

Almeda says, "I will get the doctor." If she had touched the woman, if she had forced herself to touch her, she would not have made such a mistake.

"Wait," says Jarvis Poulter. "Wait. Let's see if she can get up."

"Get up, now," he says to the woman. "Come on. Up, now. Up."

Now a startling thing happens. The body heaves itself onto all fours, the head is lifted—the hair all matted with blood and vomit—and the woman begins to bang this head, hard and rhythmically, against Almeda Roth's picket fence. As she bangs her head, she finds her voice and lets out an openmouthed yowl, full of strength and what sounds like an anguished pleasure.

"Far from dead," says Jarvis Poulter. "And I wouldn't bother the doctor."

"There's blood," says Almeda as the woman turns her smeared face.

"From her nose," he says. "Not fresh." He bends down and catches the horrid hair close to the scalp to stop the head-banging.

"You stop that, now," he says. "Stop it. Gwan home, now. Gwan home, where you belong." The sound coming out of the woman's mouth has stopped. He shakes her head slightly, warning her, before he lets go of her hair. "Gwan home!"

Released, the woman lunges forward, pulls herself to her feet. She can walk. She weaves and stumbles down the street, making intermittent, cautious noises of protest. Jarvis Poulter watches her for a moment to make sure that she's on her way. Then he finds a large burdock leaf, on which he wipes his hand. He says, "There goes your dead body!"

The back gate being locked, they walk around to the front. The front gate stands open. Almeda still feels sick. Her abdomen is bloated; she is hot and dizzy.

"The front door is locked," she says faintly. "I came out by the kitchen." If only he would leave her, she could go straight to the privy. But he follows. He follows her as far as the back door and into the back hall. He speaks to her in a tone of harsh joviality that she has never before heard from him. "No need for alarm," he says. "It's only the consequences of drink. A lady oughtn't to be living alone so close to a bad neighborhood." He takes hold of her arm just above the elbow. She can't open her mouth to speak to him, to say thank you. If she opened her mouth, she would retch.

What Jarvis Poulter feels for Almeda Roth at this moment is just what he has not felt during all those circumspect walks and all his own solitary calculations of her probable worth, undoubted respectability, adequate comeliness. He has not been able to imagine her as a wife. Now that is possible. He is sufficiently stirred by her loosened hair—prematurely gray but thick and soft—her flushed face, her light clothing, which nobody but a husband should see. And by her indiscretion, her agitation, her foolishness, her need?

"I will call on you later," he says to her. "I will walk with you to church."

At the corner of Pearl and Dufferin streets last Sunday morning there was discovered, by a lady resident there, the body of a certain woman of Pearl Street, thought to be dead but only, as it turned out, dead drunk. She was roused from her heavenly—or otherwise—stupor by the firm persuasion of Mr. Poulter, a neighbour and a Civil Magistrate, who had been summoned by the lady resident. Incidents of this sort, unseemly, troublesome, and disgraceful to our town, have of late become all too common.

V

I sit at the bottom of sleep,
As on the floor of the sea.
And fanciful Citizens of the Deep
Are graciously greeting me.

As soon as Jarvis Poulter has gone and she has heard her front gate close, Almeda rushes to the privy. Her relief is not complete, however, and she realizes that the pain and fullness in her lower body come from an accumulation of menstrual blood that has not yet started to flow. She closes and locks the back door. Then, remembering Jarvis Poulter's words about church, she writes on a piece of paper, "I am not well, and wish to rest today." She sticks this firmly into

the outside frame of the little window in the front door. She
locks that door, too. She is trembling, as if from a great
shock or danger. But she builds a fire, so that she can make
tea. She boils water, measures the tea leaves, makes a large
pot of tea, whose steam and smell sicken her further. She
pours out a cup while the tea is still quite weak and adds to
it several dark drops of nerve medicine. She sits to drink it
without raising the kitchen blind. There, in the middle of
the floor, is the cheesecloth bag hanging on its broom handle between the two chairbacks. The grape pulp and juice
has stained the swollen cloth a dark purple. *Plop, plop,* into
the basin beneath. She can't sit and look at such a thing.
She takes her cup, the teapot, and the bottle of medicine
into the dining room. She is still sitting there when the
horses start to go by on the way to church, stirring up clouds
of dust. The roads will be getting hot as ashes. She is there
when the gate is opened and a man's confident steps sound
on her veranda. Her hearing is so sharp she seems to hear
the paper taken out of the frame and unfolded—she can
almost hear him reading *it,* hear the words in his mind.
Then the footsteps go the other way, down the steps. The
gate closes. An image comes to her of tombstones—it makes
her laugh. Tombstones are marching down the street on
their little booted feet, their long bodies inclined forward,
their expressions preoccupied and severe. The church bells
are ringing.

Then the clock in the hall strikes twelve and an
hour has passed.

The house is getting hot. She drinks more tea and
adds more medicine. She knows that the medicine is affect-
ing her. It is responsible for her extraordinary languor, her
perfect immobility, her unresisting surrender to her surroundings. That is all right. It seems necessary.

Her surroundings—some of her surroundings—in the
dining room are these: walls covered with dark-green gar-

landed wallpaper, lace curtains and mulberry velvet curtains on the windows, a table with a crocheted cloth and a bowl of wax fruit, a pinkish-gray carpet with nosegays of blue and pink roses, a sideboard spread with embroidered runners and holding various patterned plates and jugs and the silver tea things. A lot of things to watch. For every one of these patterns, decorations seems charged with life, ready to move and flow and alter. Or possibly to explode. Almeda Roth's occupation throughout the day is to keep an eye on them. Not to prevent their alteration so much as to catch them at it—to understand it, to be a part of it. So much is going on in this room that there is no need to leave it. There is not even the thought of leaving it.

Of course, Almeda in her observations cannot escape words. She may think she can, but she can't. Soon this glowing and swelling begins to suggest words—not specific words but a flow of words somewhere, just about ready to make themselves known to her. Poems, even. Yes, again, poems. Or one poem. Isn't that the idea—one very great poem that will contain everything and, oh, that will make all the other poems, the poems she has written, inconsequential, mere trial and error, mere rag? Stars and flowers and birds and trees and angels in the snow and dead children at twilight—that is not the half of it. You have to get in the obscene racket on Pearl Street and the polished toe of Jarvis Poulter's boot and the plucked-chicken haunch with its blue-black flower. Almeda is a long way now from human sympathies or fears or cozy household considerations. She doesn't think about what could be done for that woman or about keeping Jarvis Poulter's dinner warm and hanging his long underwear on the line. The basin of grape juice has overflowed and is running over her kitchen floor, staining the boards of the floor, and the stain will never come out.

She has to think of so many things at once—Champlain and the naked Indians and the salt deep in the earth, but as well as the salt the money, the money-making intent brewing in heads like Jarvis Poulter's. Also the brutal storms of winter and the clumsy and benighted deeds on Pearl Street. The changes of climate are often violent, and if you think about it there is no peace even in the stars. All this can be borne only if it is channelled into a poem, and the word "channelled" is appropriate, because the name of the poem will be—it *is*—"The Meneseteung." The name of the poem is the name of the river. No, in fact it is the river, the Meneseteung, that is the poem—with its deep hole and rapids and blissful pools under the summer trees and its grinding blocks of ice thrown up at the end of winter and its desolating spring floods. Almeda looks deep, deep into the river of her mind and into the tablecloth, and she sees the crocheted roses floating. They look bunchy and foolish, her mother's crocheted roses—they don't look much like real flowers. But their effort, their floating independence, their pleasure in themselves do seem to her so admirable. A hopeful sign. *Meneseteung.*

She doesn't leave the room until dusk, when she goes out to the privy again and discovers that she is bleeding, her flow has started. She will have to get a towel, strap it on, bandage herself up. Never before, in health, has she passed a whole day in her nightdress. She doesn't feel any particular anxiety about this. On her way through the kitchen, she walks through the pool of grape juice. She knows that she will have to mop it up, but not yet, and she walks upstairs leaving purple footprints and smelling her escaping blood and the sweat of her body that has sat all day in the closed hot room.

No need for alarm.

For she hasn't thought that crocheted roses could float away or that tombstones could hurry down the street. She doesn't mistake that for reality, and neither does she mistake anything else for reality, and that is how she knows that she is sane.

VI

I dream of you by night,
I visit you by day.
Father, Mother,
Sister, Brother,
Have you no word to say?

April 22, 1903. At her residence, on Tuesday last, between three and four o'clock in the afternoon, there passed away a lady of talent and refinement whose pen, in days gone by, enriched our local literature with a volume of sensitive, eloquent verse. It is a sad misfortune that in later years the mind of this fine person had become somewhat clouded and her behaviour, in consequence, somewhat rash and unusual. Her attention to decorum and to the care and adornment of her person had suffered, to the degree that she had become, in the eyes of those unmindful of her former pride and daintiness, a familiar eccentric, or even, sadly, a figure of fun. But now all such lapses pass from memory and what is recalled is her excellent published verse, her labours in former days in the Sunday school, her dutiful care of her parents, her noble womanly nature, charitable concerns, and unfailing religious faith. Her last illness was of mercifully short duration. She caught cold, after having become thoroughly wet from a ramble in the Pearl Street bog. (It has been said that some urchins chased her into the water, and such is the boldness and cruelty of some of our youth, and their observed persecution of this lady, that the tale cannot be entirely discounted.) The cold developed into pneumonia, and she died, attended at the last by a former neighbour, Mrs. Bert (Annie) Friels, who witnessed her calm and faithful end.

January, 1904. One of the founders of our community,

*an early maker and shaker of this town, was abruptly removed
from our midst on Monday morning last, whilst attending to his
correspondence in the office of his company. Mr. Jarvis Poulter
possessed a keen and lively commercial spirit, which was instru-
mental in the creation of not one but several local enterprises,
bringing the benefits of industry, productivity, and employment to
our town.*

So the *Vidette* runs on, copious and assured. Hardly
a death goes undescribed, or a life unevaluated.

I looked for Almeda Roth in the graveyard. I found
the family stone. There was just one name on it—Roth.
Then I noticed two flat stones in the ground, a distance of
a few feet—six feet?— from the upright stone. One of these
said "Papa," the other "Mama." Farther out from these I
found two other flat stones, with the names William and
Catherine on them. I had to clear away some overgrowing
grass and dirt to see the full name of Catherine. No birth
or death dates for anybody, nothing about being dearly
beloved. It was a private sort of memorializing, not for the
world. There were no roses, either—no sign of a rosebush.
But perhaps it was taken out. The grounds keeper doesn't
like such things; they are a nuisance to the lawnmower, and
if there is nobody left to object he will pull them out.

I thought that Almeda must have been buried somewhere else When this plot was bought—at the time of the
two children's deaths—she would still have been expected
to marry, and to lie finally beside her husband. They might
not have left room for her here. Then I saw that the stones
in the ground fanned out from the upright stone. First the
two for the parents, then the two for the children, but
these were placed in such a way that there was room for a
third, to complete the fan. I paced out from "Catherine"
the same number of steps that it took to get from

"Catherine" to "William," and at this spot I began pulling grass and scrabbling in the dirt with my bare hands. Soon I felt the stone and knew that I was right. I worked away and got the whole stone clear and I read the name "Meda." There it was with the others, staring at the sky. I made sure I had got to the edge of the stone. That was all the name there was—Meda. So it was true that she was called by that name in the family. Not just in the poem. Or perhaps she chose her name from the poem, to be written on her stone.

I thought that there wasn't anybody alive in the world but me who would know this, who would make the connection. And I would be the last person to do so. But perhaps this isn't so. People are curious. A few people are. They will be driven to find things out, even trivial things. They will put things together. You see them going around with notebooks, scraping the dirt off gravestones, reading microfilm, just in the hope of seeing this trickle in time, making a connection, rescuing one thing from the rubbish.

And they may get it wrong, after all. I may have got it wrong. I don't know if she ever took laudanum. Many ladies did. I don't know if she ever made grape jelly.

Biographical Notes

ALEXANDRE AMPRIMOZ was born in Rome in 1948. He teaches Romance studies at Brock University. He has published two collections of stories, *Hard Confessions* (1987) and *Too Many Popes* (1990), as well as five collections of poetry.

MARGARET ATWOOD was born in Ottawa in 1939 and grew up in Toronto and in the bush. She has received two Governor General's Awards, the first in 1967 for her collection of poetry, *The Circle Game,* and the second in 1985 for her novel, *The Handmaid's Tale.* She is also well-known as a critic (*Surfacing*) and has edited Oxford anthologies of Canadian poetry and short stories. Her collections of short fiction include *Dancing Girls* (1977), *Murder in the Dark* (1983), *Bluebeard's Egg* (1983), *Wilderness Tips* (1990), and *Good Bones* (1992).

HUBERT AQUIN was born in Montreal in 1929. He worked for Radio Canada and as a stockbroker. He was founder/editor of *Liberte.* His published works include *Prochaine episode* (1965), *Trou de memoire* (1968), *L'Antiphonain* (1969), and *Neige noir* (1974). He committed suicide in 1977.

MARIE-CLAIRE BLAIS was born in Quebec City in 1939. She published her first novel, *La Belle Bête* in 1959. She won her first Governor General's Award and the Prix France-Canada in 1965 for *Une saison dans la vie d'Emmanuel*. She won her second Governor General's Award for *Deaf to the City*. She lives in Montreal.

VICTOR-LÉVY BEAULIEU, born in 1945, lives in Quebec where he is a novelist, critic, and publisher. He has had over forty books published, including *Jos Connaissant* (1970) and *Un rêve québécois* (1972). *Don Quichotte de la démande* (1974) won the Governor General's Award in 1975.

BRIAN BRETT was born in Vancouver in 1950 and presently lives in White Rock, British Columbia. Co-founder of Blackfish Press, he is a poet and short fiction writer. He has had three books of his poetry published, as well as two collections of stories, *The Fungus Garden* (1988) and *Tanganyika* (1991).

BARRY CALLAGHAN was born in Toronto in 1937. He is editor/publisher of *Exile* magazine and Exile Editions. He has published two novels, *The Way the Angel Spreads Her Wings* (1982) and *When Things Get Worst* (1993). His short stories are collected in *The Black Queen Stories* (1982) and *A Kiss is Still a Kiss*, forthcoming in 1994.

MORLEY CALLAGHAN, born in 1903, is, according to Edmund Wilson, "Perhaps the most unjustly neglected novelist in the English speaking world." Canada's first modernist, he was the author of twenty novels and over one hundred short stories, most of which are collected in *Stories* (1959) and *The Lost and Found Stories* (1986). He died in 1990.

AUSTIN CLARKE was born in Barbados in 1932 and emigrated to Canada in 1956 to study economics. He has published three collections of short stories, *When He Was Young and Free and Used to Wear Silks* (1971), *Nine Men Laughing* (1986), and *In This City* (1992), as well as several novels. A fourth collection of stories, *There Are No Elders*, will be published in the fall of 1993.

ANNE DANDURAND, born in 1953, is an actress and writer who lives in Quebec. She and her twin sister, Claire De, published a collection of short stories, *La louve-garou*, in 1982. Her other published work includes *Voila c'est rien jangoisse* (1987), *L'assassin de 'interieur* (1988), and *Un coeuir qui craque* (1992).

JACQUES FERRON was born on the Gaspe Peninsula of Quebec in 1921. A physician, he was a founder of the Rhinoceros Party and an author of plays, novels, and scholarly medical papers. *Contes du pays uncertain* (1962) won the Governor General's Award in 1964. His other work includes *Contes anglais et autres* (1964), *Contes* (1968), and *Selected Tales* (1984). He died in 1985.

MAVIS GALLANT was born in Montreal in 1922 and has lived in Paris since 1950. Her short stories have appeared in numerous publications, including *The New Yorker*. She won the Governor General's Award in 1981 for *Home Truths*. Her other works include *The Other Paris (1956), My Heart is Broken (1964), The Pegnitz Junction (1973), The End of the World (1974), From the 15th District (1979), Overhead in a Balloon (1985), and In Transit (1988).*

BILL GASTON, born in 1953, has been a professional hockey player, lumberjack, and fishing guide, and has taught at various universities. Educated at the University of British

Columbia, he now lives in Nova Scotia. He has published two novels, *Tall Lives* and *The Cameraman*, and two collections of stories, *Deep Cove Stories* and *North of Jesus' Beans*.

DIANE KEATING was born in Saskatchewan and now lives in Toronto. A poet and fiction writer, she has published three books of poetry. She is working on a novel, *The Crying Out*. Two sections of it, "The Crying Out" and "Salem Letters," were included in the *Journey Prize Collection*.

PATRICK LANE was born in Nelson, British Columbia in 1939. He won the Governor General's Award in 1979 for his first *Selected Poems*, the revised volume of which appeared in 1987. "Marylou Had Her Teeth Out" first appeared in *Canadian Fiction* (1989) and later in *How Do You Spell Beautiful?* (1992).

ALISTAIR MacLEOD was born in Saskatchewan in 1936. He grew up in Alberta and Nova Scotia and presently teaches at the University of Windsor. He has published two collections of stories, *The Lost Salt Gift of Blood* (1976) and *As Birds Bring Forth the Sun* (1986).

ERIC McCORMACK was born in Scotland in 1938 and emigrated to Canada in 1966. He teaches at St. Jerome's College in Waterloo, Ontario. His published collections include *Inspecting the Vaults* (1987), *Paradise Motel* (1988), and *The Mysterium* (1992).

ALICE MUNRO was born in Ontario in 1931. After living in Victoria for a number of years, she returned to Clinton, Ontario. She has published one novel, *Lives of Girls and Women* (1971). She won the Governor General's Award in 1968 for her collection of stories, *Dance of the Happy Shades*.

Her other collections of short fiction include *Something I've Been Meaning to Tell You* (1974), *The Beggar Maid* (1978), which was published in Canada as *Who Do You Think You Are?*, *The Moons of Jupiter* (1983), *The Progress of Love* (1986), and *Friends of my Youth* (1990).

LEON ROOKE was born in North Carolina in 1934 and has lived in Canada since 1969. Winner of the Governor General's Award in 1983 for *Shakespeare's Dog*, he has published eight other collections: *Sing Me No Songs I'll Say You No Prayers* (1974), *The Love Parlour* (1977), *The Broad Back of the Angel* (1977), *Cry Evil* (1980), *Death Suite* (1981), *The Birth Control King of the Upper Volta* (1982), and *The Bolt of White Cloth* (1984).

JOE ROSENBLATT was born in Toronto in 1933. A poet and artist, he now lives in Vancouver. He won the Governor General's Award in 1976 for *Top Soil*. He has published fourteen books of poetry, including *Sleeping Lady* (1980) and *Brides of the Stream* (1983), as well as one prose memoir, *Escape from the Glue Factory* (1985).

GLORIA OSTREM SAWAI was born in Minneapolis, Minnesota in 1932 and raised in Saskatchewan. She presently lives in Edmonton, Alberta. She writes short fiction and plays. Her stories have appeared in *3 X 5*, *Best Canadian Stories of 1982*, *The Oxford Anthology of Canadian Short Stories*, and several other anthologies. Her plays have been produced in Calgary and in Alberta. She is presently working on a novella.

CAROLE SHIELDS was born in Oak Park, Ilinois in 1935 and became a Canadian citizen in 1971. She teaches at the University of Manitoba. She has published several novels, as well as the short story collections *Small Ceremonies* (1976),

Various Miracles (1985), and *The Orange Fish* (1990).

MICHEL TREMBLAY was born in Montreal in 1942. A dramatist and fiction writer, his published works include *Contes Pour Buveurs Attardes* (1966), *Les Belles Soeurs* (1972), *Bonjour, là, Bonjour* (1974), and *La grosse femme d'a côté est enceinte* (1978).

GUY VANDERHAEGHE was born in Saskatchewan in 1951 and now lives in Saskatoon. His first collection of short stories, *Man Descending* (1982) won the Governor General's Award. His other collections include *The Trouble with Heroes* (1983), *My Present Age* (1984), *Homesick* (1989), and *Things as They Are* (1992).

SEÁN VIRGO was born in Malta in 1940. He emigrated to Canada in 1966. He has published three books of poetry and a novel, *Selankhi* (1987). His collections of short stories include *White Lies* (1980), *Through the Eyes of a Cat* (1983), *Wormwood* (1989), and *Waking in Eden* (1990).